ISBN 978-1-331-60531-7
PIBN 10211884

English
Français
Deutsche
Italiano
Español
Português

www.forgottenbooks.com

Mythology Photography **Fiction**
Fishing Christianity **Art** Cooking
Essays Buddhism Freemasonry
Medicine **Biology** Music **Ancient**
Egypt Evolution Carpentry Physics
Dance Geology **Mathematics** Fitness
Shakespeare **Folklore** Yoga Marketing
Confidence Immortality Biographies
Poetry **Psychology** Witchcraft
Electronics Chemistry History **Law**
Accounting **Philosophy** Anthropology
Alchemy Drama Quantum Mechanics
Atheism Sexual Health **Ancient History**
Entrepreneurship Languages Sport
Paleontology Needlework Islam
Metaphysics Investment Archaeology
Parenting Statistics Criminology
Motivational

IGEL BROWNING

BY

AGNES GIBERNE

AUTHOR OF

"SUN, MOON, AND STARS," "THE OCEAN OF AIR," "MISS CON,"
ETC.

'What He would have in us is purity of intention, an ever-ready yielding of
our will."—FÉNÉLON.

LONDON:
LONGMANS, GREEN, AND CO.
AND NEW YORK: 15 EAST 16th STREET.

1890.

To the Memory.

OF

MY DEARLY-LOVED MOTHER

. . . . " A loss for ever new,
A void where heart on heart reposed ;
And where warm hands have prest and closed,
Silence, till I be silent too."

CONTENTS

NIGEL BROWNING

CHAPTER I.

FROM ROUND THE WORLD.

"But, soft ! what light through yonder window breaks !
    *   *   *   *   *   *   *
It is my lady : O, it is my love :
O, that she knew she were !"—*Romeo and Juliet.*

"HERE, I want this luggage taken— Hallo, Pollard ! you're the man for me !"

"Mr. Nigel Browning !" ejaculated the porter addressed, a huge individual over six feet three in height, and massive in frame, with a large face, resplendently good-humoured. He had been heaving great trunks and packing-cases out of the van, tossing one upon another, as a girl might heap together a pile of bandboxes. Now the train passed on, groaning dismally after the fashion of these modern behemoths; and the platform crowd began to disperse.

It was past nine o'clock, on a chilly autumn evening:

not the kind of evening which might tempt anybody to linger under the flaring gaslights, dimmed by
fogginess.

Pollard, in full career across the platform, brought
up his truck with a jerk on hearing his own name,
then plucked at his cap with an air of delight.

"Mr. Nigel Browning!" he exclaimed.

"To be sure. Whom else would you take me for?
Shake hands, Pollard. I've been round the world since
I saw you last."

The man's hard palm closed with a grip round the
gentlemanly fingers held out to him.

"And you ain't changed, Mr. Nigel! No need for
to ask that, though! If you was, you wouldn't be a-
shaking hands with me here, like to old days. And
the niggers ain't got hold of you, nor none of they
cannibals neither."

"Why, no—I've not been enjoying very largely the
society of cannibals!"

"Well, sir, you've come back anyway a deal stouter
and stronger than you was—not as you're stout yet, so
to speak, but you was thin and no mistake when you
went away. And I do see a difference. I don't know
as you ain't taller too."

"Taller after twenty! That would be against all
rule. However, I certainly did depart a scarecrow, so
perhaps it's admissible to turn up a Hercules. All
well at home, Pollard?—wife and chicks, eh?"

"Yes, sir, thank you. Nought but the old woman's

rheumatiz for to grumble at—and she do say it takes a deal o' patience to carry that about with a body."

"I don't doubt it,—poor thing! And all right at the Grange?"

"Yes, sir—so as I've heard. Save and except Mr. Browning's the same as usual, sir. Which in course you knows."

"Ah—yes!" the two syllables being divided by a thoughtful break. Manner and voice had till this moment been marked by a frank joyousness, boy-like yet manly, but now there came a touch of gravity, almost of sadness, into Nigel's face. He stood for three seconds gazing across the rails into a misty distance, lost in cogitation; then roused himself.

"You will have the trunks up soon. I must be off."

"All right, sir."

Leaving his ticket with the collector Nigel passed into the street. He went onwards in a swift steadfast manner; vigour and decision being apparent in every motion of the alert well-proportioned figure, and in every glance of the dark eyes.

It did not surprise Nigel that nobody was at the station to meet him after his year of absence, wherein he had travelled literally "round the world." He had not expected to arrive till next morning, but finding an earlier train than he had hoped for "within catch," the temptation to surprise his home-folks had proved irresistible.

Newton Bury had been his home through life, and

every wall and window in this busy High Street was familiar to him. Shops were shut, and people from within were airing themselves on the pavements after a hard day's work. Nigel saw many a well-known face as he went by; but he had no wish to be delayed, and it was easy to avoid recognition in the broken light of gas-lamps placed by no means too near together.

Leaving High Street and Broad Street, he hesitated one moment at the foot of some stone steps leading upward. This was the short-cut between station and home; for Newton Bury was a town built partly upon hills, and the Grange stood high. But a certain attraction drew him along the main thoroughfare.

"After all, it's not ten minutes' difference; and I *should* like one glimpse," he said to himself.

"Hallo! What next? Have a care, young fellow!"

Nigel certainly was going at express speed, when on turning a sharp corner he barely escaped collision with a short and round-shouldered individual of advanced age, wearing a fur-bordered great-coat almost down to the heels, and a Glengarry cap, from beneath which flowed thick locks of snow-white hair. Two black eyes, bright as beads, flashed a glance of indignant remonstrance, and the high-pitched voice, petulant in tone, was unmistakable.

"Mr. Carden-Cox! I beg your pardon. How do you do?" Nigel put out his hand in greeting.

The other stared haughtily. "Eh! who are you?"

"Don't you know me?"

" No, sir. I have not that pleasure ! "—with an aggrieved sound.

" I'm Nigel—just come home."

" Young Browning ! Humph ! "

It was windy and damp, the fogginess having deepened—and this no doubt was partly the reason why Nigel had so nearly run the old gentleman down, added to that old gentleman's perverse habit of walking on the wrong side of the pavement. But Mr. Carden-Cox had plainly no intention of allowing his movements to be influenced by weather. He pulled off one of his gloves, fished laboriously for a double eye-glass, adjusted the same carefully on the bridge of his nose, and retreated to the neighbourhood of the nearest lamp, beckoning Nigel to follow.

" Here—let me see ! Nigel Browning ! I declare I shouldn't have known the lad."

" Am I so altered ? "

" Altered ! There's not an inch of you the same." This was absurd, and Nigel smiled.

" What are you after here—eh ? "

" Going home. Just arrived. They don't expect me till to-morrow, so it's to be a surprise."

" Why on earth didn't you take the steps ? Missed them in the dark ? That's not like you. Some folks do go mooning about with their eyes in the stars ; but I thought you were practical."

" I didn't miss the steps. I came this way by choice."

" What for ? "

Nigel laughed, and his sunburnt cheek gained an extra tinge of colour, not lost upon the keen-eyed old gentleman.

" Hey ?   What for ? "

" A fancy of mine.   I must be off, or my luggage will arrive first."

" Not if you keep up the pace you were going just now."   Mr. Carden-Cox paused to survey Nigel all over, from head to foot, as if gauging his value.   "Yes —you've filled out—expanded—developed—twice the man you were !   But there's something about you which I don't quite understand, Nigel Browning.   Good-bye. We shall meet again soon."

Nigel did not fail to keep up his former pace, even to accelerate it.   If he wished to arrive before his luggage he really had no time to lose, for Pollard would not be guilty of delay ; and instead of following the bend to the right which Pollard would follow, Nigel soon shot away to the left, through a dark lane, with high walls on both sides, and a fringe of tall trees from enclosed gardens peeping over the wall-tops.

This lane led direct into a large square, chiefly composed of old-fashioned red-brick houses, each varying in shape and size from its neighbours.   At the entrance to the square, where three short posts barred the way to vehicles, Nigel paused to look.

That was what he had come for : to indulge himself in a look.

The square was rightly named "Church Square," for

its centre was occupied by a venerable edifice, parts of which, including the square solid tower, were at least seven hundred years old. Generation after generation of English Churchmen, through century after century, had met for worship within those aged walls. They had outlived countless historical tides and storms, and still stood there, rock-like and calm, always the same, in themselves a silent yet speaking history of ages past. Where Nigel stood he could distinguish two flying buttresses, and two nearer side-windows, pointed yet somewhat broad. What he could not see he could imagine; for every inch of the structure was familiar and dear to him.

At one corner of the square, that to Nigel's left, a red-brick house stood alone, not placed in line like the rest, but occupying a small garden, wherein flourished an abundance of shrubs, but few flowers; for the Rev. Lancelot Elvey, Vicar of Newton Bury, with a cure of six thousand souls, and a stipend of two hundred and eighty pounds a year, had little money to spare for luxuries. What he *could* spare from absolute home necessaries went to the Parish.

Nigel had not meant to advance one step farther than this entrance to the square, where the three posts stood side by side. He cast one glance towards the central building; then his eyes went to the Vicarage.

It was very near; within a stone's throw. He could distinctly see the two small windows of the little drawing-room, a queer-shaped room, as he knew, all corners

and crevices, with furniture old enough to be pictur-
esque, and old enough also to be shabby. Lights were
lighted within, and blinds were drawn. As Nigel
gazed, the shadow of a girlish figure was thrown with
clear outline upon one of the blinds. Ethel—of course!

He had not intended to go a step nearer, but the
pull was strong. That soft shade upon the blind had
set all his pulses throbbing. The year's absence had
made no difference at all—unless the difference that
Ethel was dearer to him than ever—and the longing
for one glimpse of her face became overwhelming. His
luggage might arrive first; his home-folks might be
perplexed, worried, perhaps hurt that he could put
them second to anybody,—yes, he knew all this, but
for three seconds nothing seemed of the smallest
importance, except the glimpse for which he craved.

Nigel left the posts and went quickly towards the
Vicarage; a few steps bringing him within the garden
gate. At the same moment somebody drew up one of
the blinds, and opened wide the window.

Ethel herself! He could see in strong relief against
the light within, her slim prettily-rounded figure, could
hear the soft happy tones which had always seemed to
him to have a ripple of music running through them.

"Mother, we'll let in a breath of air—just for a
minute. It is so mild to-night. Lance, is that somebody in the garden?"

Nigel almost uttered the word—"Ethel!" Almost,
but not quite. It was leaving his lips, when he caught

it back. Once within that room, how could he tear himself away ?

There were reasons why it might be better not. With an effort Nigel turned and walked out of the gate ; and as he went he found himself face to face with somebody coming in—a large loosely-built man in a great-coat, walking with the tired stoop in head and shoulders often born of a hard day's work. The light of the nearest lamp fell upon a rugged face, full of the beauty of goodness.

"Anything wanted ? " asked the Vicar.

Mr. Elvey never by any chance passed a human being who might "want" something of him.

"No—thanks," Nigel answered, dutifully hoping but not wishing to pass on.

"I know that voice !" said the Vicar.

CHAPTER II.

THE DAUGHTERS OF THE HOUSE.

"There are briars besetting every path,
  Which call for patient care."—A. L. WARING.

"FULVIE—"

"Anice, my dear, allow me to remark that the way to get work done is *not* to sit in a brown study for exactly half an hour."

"Half an hour! O Fulvie!"

"A metaphorical one, of course. How many stitches have you put into that leaf since dinner?"

"I don't know—but—I can't imagine why Nigel didn't settle to come home to-night."

"No train, he says."

"But there is a train."

"He thought there was not."

"Daisy found one directly she looked—just at the right time."

"Daisy's a clever young woman. Daisy isn't Nigel, however."

"No—" and a pause, Anice leaning back dreamily.

"No. But I have been wondering—what if Nigel did know of the train, only perhaps he wanted a night in London."

"Why shouldn't he have said so then? You little wretch, to suspect him of deceit."

"O no—only perhaps he might have been glad of the excuse. I mean, he might have made the mistake first, and then not have cared to change. He might have been afraid that we should mind his not hurrying home, if he did stay."

Fulvia stamped her foot. "Anice, you put me out of patience. But you are all alike! You none of you understand Nigel. Never did and never will, I suppose. You needn't stare at me so reproachfully, for it is true. Now do get on with that unfortunate leaf. What shade do you mean to use next?"

Three girls—Mr. Browning's two daughters, Anice and Daisy, and his ward, Fulvia Rolfe—sat alone in the Grange drawing-room. Lamps and candles dotted about the large room gave a pleasant light; curtains were drawn, and a fire blazed.

Daisy, the younger girl, huddled into a sofa-corner, with a book which absorbed all her attention, was round-faced and plump, with a clever full brow and innocent lips. Though close upon sixteen, she was childish still, alike in manner and in the almost infantile simplicity of her thick white frock. Anice, nearly three years older, wore a white dress likewise, but of thinner texture and more elaborate make, and

while undoubtedly a pretty girl, with delicate features
and changeful colouring, her face not only lacked force
but had a look of marked self-occupation, sufficient to
spoil the fairest outline. Daisy's contented brown eyes
contained better promise for the future; and people
were apt to grow early tired of Anice.

Fulvia Rolfe presented a contrast to the sisters.
Some two years the senior of Anice, she was not so
tall as the latter, nor so stout as Daisy; and the first
idea commonly received about her was of a sturdy
vigour of body and mind. Though by no means beautiful, since her face was rather flat, with a retroussé nose,
and eyes which had an odd Eastern slant in the manner
of their setting, she yet possessed a certain power of
attraction. Those same light-gray eyes were full of
sparkle; the lips were expressive; the abundant red-
brown hair was skilfully arranged; the figure, though
not slight, was particularly good; and · the hands, if
neither small nor especially white, were well-formed
and soft.

"Which shade?" Anice repeated vacantly. "I don't
know. One of these four, I suppose."

"If a table-cloth is worth making at all, it is worth
making not hideous. Let me see the greens. Impossible to choose in this light. You will have to leave it
till to-morrow. Where is the madre all this time?"
For Fulvia Rolfe, left early an orphan, and unable to
recollect her own parents, had fallen into a mode of
calling Mrs. and Mr. Browning by the titles of "madre"

and "padre." The mode was copied, not seldom, by their own children.

"She went to the study. Padre wanted her, I believe. It is one of his bad days, and I suppose he couldn't stand all of us."

Fulvia's lips took a naughty set. "And so, because he is a little bad, we are all to be very sad."

"Father isn't well!" Anice looked reproachful.

"He's not bound to be utterly doleful too, my dear."

"Madre said he was so depressed."

"Of course. Exactly what I mean. I never can quite see why one is to act as a wet-blanket to all one's friends, merely because one feels poorly or out of spirits. I'm not talking about padre in particular. The sort of thing is common enough. But I wonder when one *is* to exercise self-control, if not when it goes against the grain. There's no merit in cheerfulness when one feels lively."

"I don't know what you mean, but you ought not to speak so of father."

"I'm laying down a broad axiom—not applying it. No, of course you don't understand. Nobody understands anybody in this house. If one expects to be understood, one is disappointed. Hark!—is that the study door opening? . . . Yes, I thought so. Here comes the madre — doesn't she look sweet? And actually!—absolutely!—the padre too!"

The lady, entering first, was slender in figure, and graceful in movement, with regular features, and the softest dark eyes imaginable, full of wistful tenderness. She wore an evening dress of black velvet, trimmed with old lace, and her little hands hung carelessly, like snowflakes, against the sombre background. Though forty-five in age, no streaks of gray showed yet in the brown hair, upon which a light lace cap rested; and pretty as Anice unquestionably was, the daughter's prettiness paled before the mother's rare beauty.

Behind Mrs. Browning came her husband. There was nothing of the invalid about him apparent at first sight. A dignified middle-aged man; solid, but not corpulent in build; with gray hair, fast thinning, agreeable manners, and a face which did not lack its modicum of good looks—this was Mr. Browning. A keen observer would have noted a tried look about the brow—a good brow like Daisy's—and a restless dissatisfaction almost amounting to apprehension in the eyes; but Fulvia was the only keen observer present, and people in general were apt to pass over these little signs. Mr. Browning was a favourite in society. " A delightful man—so clever, and polite, and genial, and all that, you know ! "—was the verdict passed on him by a considerable circle of Newton Bury ladies.

The entrance of these two caused a general stir. Daisy sat in a less huddled position, and Fulvia drew forward an easy-chair for Mrs. Browning, while Anice changed her own seat to one nearer her father, as he took possession of the unused sofa-corner beside Daisy, and heaved a sigh.

"We thought you meant to forsake us altogether this evening," Fulvia remarked to Mrs. Browning.

"No, dear. Padre is so unwell to-day—he has that pain again, and it depresses him," was the under-toned answer. "But he promised to come in for a little while. It is better for him I am sure—less dull."

"Better for you too."

"I don't think that matters. I wish anything could be done to touch this sad depression," as again, in response to some words of Anice, sounded the heavy sigh. "We have been talking about a little trip abroad. Perhaps it might do him good."

"When? Not before Christmas?"

"Yes, I think so. He seems to wish it."

Others were listening besides Fulvia, and a chorus of exclamations sounded. "*Now*, mother!" "Go abroad before Christmas!" "How about Nigel?" this was Fulvia's voice. "Mother, you don't really mean it?" from Anice. "Why, mother!" Daisy's rounded eyes suiting the tone of her second utterance. "You must have forgotten about Fulvia's birthday—Fulvia's coming of age."

"Hush, hush!" Mrs. Browning said nervously. She did not in the least know why her husband disliked any allusion to Fulvia's twenty-first birthday, but she knew that he did dislike it. His sudden movement was not lost upon her.

Daisy was of a persistent nature, not easily silenced. "But, mother, you *know* the twenty-first of December is Fulvia's birthday; and we meant to have all sorts of fun. If once we go abroad, we shall never get back in time. I know we sha'n't."

"Madre said nothing about our going, Daisy."

"Well, then, that will be worse still. Horridly dull to keep your twenty-first birthday without father and mother."

"Daisy, do hold your tongue. You are worrying madre," whispered Fulvia.

"Why?" in a return whisper of astonishment.

"I haven't a notion! The fact is patent enough. Do let things go."

Daisy subsided, and for two minutes nobody spoke. Then a peal sounded at the front door.

Anice's lips parted, and her cheeks flushed. She almost said, "Nigel!"

"Nonsense!" Fulvia replied to the motion of her lips. "Not to-night."

But Simms came in. Simms was one of those unexceptionable modern men-servants, who always have their wits about them, and who never can be startled. Simms prided himself on a perfect command of feature and of manner. Whatever happened, he seemed to have known it beforehand, to have been at that moment expecting it. In his usual style of composed confidence he entered, and as calmly as if announcing dinner, he said—

"Pollard from the station, sir, with Mr. Nigel's luggage!"

" Mr. Nigel come ! " cried Daisy, springing up.

" No, Miss."

" Not come ! " echoed other voices.

" No, ma'am. Pollard saw Mr. Nigel at the station, and expected him to be here first. But Mr. Nigel has not arrived."

" Strange—" Mr. Browning said.

" Buying himself a new neck-tie by the way," suggested Fulvia, and Daisy's laugh sounded; but Mrs. Browning and Anice exchanged looks, their faces falling.

CHAPTER III.

ETHEL.

"There is none like her, none."—TENNYSON.

"I KNOW that voice! Why—it's—"

Mr. Elvey did not finish the sentence. He caught Nigel's hand within two muscular palms, and nearly wrung it off.

"I didn't expect to be found out. Yes, I'm back. But you mustn't keep me, Mr. Elvey. How are you all? How is—Ethel?"

"Ethel's all right. The best girl that ever lived, if an old father has a right to say so. Come and see for yourself. There she is at the open window. My wife and all of them inside. How is *she?* Oh, much the same as always—very ailing, poor dear! Never knows what it is to be really well. But come, come along! Not keep you indeed! Rubbish and non-sense!" cried the Rector joyously, forgetting all about his own fatigue, and allowing Nigel no loophole for explanation. "Why, we were talking of you only an

hour ago, wondering if the year of travel would alter
you much. Has it? I can't see here. Come along—
come!"

"I really ought not, I am afraid," protested Nigel,
feeling as if the silken pull of Ethel's near presence,
together with the Rector's grasp of his arm, were
overcoming all his powers of resolution. "My baggage
has gone home, and they will be expecting me!"

"Well, well—we won't keep you three minutes.
One shake-hands all round. Why, what brought you
here, if it wasn't for that? Ethel, Ethel!—Gilbert—
Ralph—Lance—My dear!"—this meant his wife—"I've
found an old friend in the garden, and he's trying to
elope. Guess who! Open the door—somebody!"

They were almost under the window by this time,
and Mr. Elvey did not need to raise his tones; indeed,
the full impressive voice was used enough to making
itself heard, and no barrier of glass intervened.

"What does father mean?" they heard Ethel ask
merrily; and in another moment she stood at the open
hall door, scanning the outside darkness.

She was plainly visible herself, under the hall light.
Nigel knew in a moment that the face which he
had carried with him through his wanderings was
unchanged—only a little developed, a little ripened,
"prettier than ever," he told himself. Yet people in
general did not count Ethel pretty. She had to be
known intimately, to be admired; and after all "pretty"
was not the right word. It suited Anice well; but for

Ethel it was too commonplace, since Ethel was not commonplace at all.

Though a mere girl of nineteen or twenty, there were signs about her already of character, of force, of "dependableness"—signs that she would belong to the number of those upon whom others lean, not to the weaker company of those who never in life learn to stand alone. And this does not mean that Ethel was not womanly, or that she could not crave for sympathy. Rather, because she was so womanly others turned the more readily to her for help, and she the more readily gave it. Weakness is not womanly, though many a woman is weak.

She wore an old black dress, much older than anybody would have guessed from its appearance, since Ethel's fingers were gifted in the art of renovation. The shape of her face was that "short oval" which novelists are now so careful to distinguish from the unlovely "long oval." Brown hair was massed on the top of her head, straying over the brow, and brown fringes subdued the sparkling sunny eyes. The features could hardly be called good, and it was commonly a pale face, with none of Anice's quick changes of hue. But for the blue of the eyes, and the red of the lips, it might have been said—and indeed by some it was said—to lack colour. Nigel, however, could never think that anything was wanting in that direction. He would not have had a line or a tint altered.

He had not spoken of his love to any human being.

With all Nigel's frankness and transparency, there were reserve-depths below. He could not readily talk of the things which he felt most intensely. Some people no doubt can; but Nigel could not.

Whether others had guessed his secret before he left home he had no means of knowing. Sometimes he thought his mother had; and sometimes also he felt sure that his trip round the world had been arranged for him, not only on account of his health, but in reference to this. He had often a strong impression that Mr. Browning had desired for him the test of a year's separation from Ethel. But these ideas he kept to himself. The year's separation had been lived through, and had made no difference. Ethel was dearer to him than ever.

"Father, did you say somebody was come? Who is it? Oh!—Nigel!!"

The lighting up of her whole face was worth seeing; and the little gasp of joy between those two words was worth hearing. Nobody thought anything of her delight; for had not she and Nigel been close friends from childhood? and was it not natural? But to Nigel this moment made up for all the long months of absence. He held her hand tightly for three seconds, how tightly he did not know; and the touch of those little fingers scattered to the winds all his previous resolutions. He stepped into the house.

"Nigel himself! Yes, I found him outside the garden gate. Actually protesting that he had come for a look, and didn't mean to be seen. Here, Lance, my boy — help me off with this coat. That's it. Come, Nigel—come and be inspected. My dear, I've brought an old friend, but you'll hardly recognize him. Eh?"

Mrs. Elvey, knitting slowly in an easy-chair, was a contrast to her sunny-tempered husband and daughter. Her face offered as good a specimen of the bony "long oval," as Ethel's of the shorter and more rounded type; and there was about it a somewhat unhappy look of self-pity and of discontented invalidism. No doubt she was not strong, and often did suffer much. But no doubt also many in Mrs. Elvey's place would have been brighter, braver, less of a weight upon others' spirits, more ready to respond to others' interests.

She welcomed Nigel kindly, but with the limp and listless air of one who really had so many trials of her own, that she could not be expected to care much whom she did or did not see.

"Hardly up to the mark to-day, you see—tired out, poor dear!" explained the Rector, himself a hard-worked and often weary man; but he was counted strong, and few gave him a word of sympathy on that score. He looked solicitously at his wife, and then turned to the young man. "Come; I must see what has been the effect upon you of it all—Japan, Timbuctoo, and the rest! Eh, Ethel? Is he the better or the worse?"

"Pollard thinks it a matter for congratulation that I have not become food for cannibals," laughed Nigel.

He was standing on the rug—a fine young fellow, of good height and muscular make, a wonderful development from the overgrown reedy youth who had gone away more than twelve months earlier. The sickly white complexion of those days had given place to a healthy tan; and the face was strong, bright, good-looking: with a straight nose, neither too long nor too short; a broad forehead; eyes which could be either black or gray in varying moods, but were generally dark; hair and budding moustache of brown, some shades deeper in tint than Ethel's. The eyes showed penetration and thought; the mouth spoke of firmness; the nose had that indefinable line, seen in side-face, which almost invariably denotes a sweet temper.

"He'll do!" thought Mr. Elvey, after a moment's survey. "Successful experiment!"

"But you didn't go to the South Sea Islands," Ethel said, in answer to Nigel's last remark, while the three boys, varying in ages from sixteen to thirteen, stood admiringly round the returned traveller.

"No, we had not time. I should have liked it. But I didn't want to be more than a year away."

"And now—college?" asked Mr. Elvey.

"I hope so. After Christmas."

"And then— ? "

"If my father is willing—the Bar."

"He knows your wish."

"Has known it for years. I never could understand the reasons for his hesitation."

Mr. Elvey might have answered—"Nor anybody else!"—but did not.

"Well, you have both had time for consideration—and you have time still, for the matter of that. No need to decide yet."

"I would rather work through college with a definite aim."

A movement of assent answered him. "You know, of course, that Malcolm is ordained to the Curacy of St. Peter's."

"Yes. Capital for you all having him within reach."

Nigel could hardly take his eyes off Ethel. He knew that it was time for him to say good-bye; yet he lingered, craving a few words with her first. Mr. Elvey soon turned to speak to his wife, and Nigel seized the opportunity, moving to Ethel's side.

"I must not stay—they will be expecting me at home, and wondering why I don't come," he said. "It's desperately hard to go so soon, but if I don't—"

"Yes. O don't wait," she said at once; "we shall see you again very soon."

Nigel's face changed. He had not expected this. Was she so indifferent?

"I'm afraid I must," he repeated; yet he did not stir. Ethel's presence was like a fascination, holding him to the spot against his will, or rather enchaining his very will, so that for the time nothing else seemed to have weight. "I can't tell you what it is to me to come back again—here," he said softly. "It is like—"

"Like old days, isn't it?" she responded gaily. "You always were just one of our boys, you know,—in and out when you liked. We shall expect the same again."

"Will you? Don't you think I might come too often?"

Poor Nigel! He was in such desperate earnest; while Ethel, through her very delight at the return of her old friend, was brimming over with fun.

"I won't venture to say that! Anybody *might* come too often, perhaps. I'm a desperately busy person, and never have a moment to spare. But of course you'll pay us a polite call now and then."

"Yes," Nigel answered seriously.

"And if I'm out, you can leave your card."

"Yes—"

"A month or six weeks later somebody is sure to find time to return your call."

"Yes—" was all Nigel could say. He knew that it was utterly absurd to take this bantering for anything beyond banter; but how could he help it?

Then a moment's pause, and Ethel looked at the clock.

"Nigel, I don't want to seem unkind," she said, lifting her straightforward blue eyes; "but, do you know, I really almost think you ought not to stay any longer—if you haven't seen your home-people yet."

This finished Nigel off! Ethel wished him to go! Ethel thought him wrong to have come! His face did not fall into a vexed or doleful set, but it grew exceedingly grave, and all sparkle was gone. He did not question her judgment. Of course she was right, entirely right; and all along he had known himself to be acting with no great wisdom. Still he did feel acutely that if the meeting with him had been to Ethel what the meeting with Ethel was to him, she could not so cheerfully have proposed to shorten the interview.

Could she not? That was the question!

Nigel had no doubt at all about the impossibility. A gray cloud had swept over his sky, blotting out his hopes. Yet he acted at once upon her suggestion, for if Ethel wished him to go, nothing else could keep him.

"Yes, certainly—good-bye," he said, holding out his hand.

"You don't mind my saying it? I'm only thinking of your mother."

O no; he did not mind, if "minding" meant being angry. He could honestly reply with a "No." Ethel was "only thinking" of his mother, and he had been "only thinking" of Ethel. That made the difference.

"No, you are right; I ought not to have forgotten," he said vaguely, though he had not quite forgotten; and in another minute he was walking swiftly homewards through the streets.

But how different everything looked! The shadow which had fallen upon himself seemed to envelope the whole town.

It was late when Nigel reached the Grange door. He stood outside for a moment, lost in thought; his hand upon the bell, but not pulling it. The deep tones of St. Stephen's clock were booming out ten strokes in slow succession, and the bass notes of the Grange hall clock seemed trying to overtake church time.

Nigel heard both without heeding. "What would they say at home?" pressed now as a question of importance, though it had not seemed important when he was with Ethel. Then he had no need to ring, for Daisy flung the door open, and, as the French would say, "precipitated herself" upon him.

"Nigel! O Nigel, I knew it was you! You dearest of old fellows! It's delicious to have you back! But why didn't you come straight from the station? What have you been doing all this time? Father has gone to bed, and mother and Anice are in such a way!" The last few words were whispered.

"Did they mind?" asked Nigel. "Why, Daisy, you are a young lady!"—as he kissed the fresh round cheek.

"Don't! I hate to be called a 'young lady'! I don't mean ever to be a young lady, if I can help it. I only want to be just 'Daisy' until I'm middle-aged. Nigel, come in—do! What makes you stand and dream? You dear old fellow! It's awfully jolly to see you again. O come along—make haste! Fancy waiting to take off your coat, after a whole long year away! I was watching at the staircase window, and I saw you in the garden; but nobody else knows."

She pulled him across the hall and into the drawing-

room, bursting open the door with a crash of sound
which would have seriously disturbed Mr. Browning,
had he been present.

"Daisy! Daisy!" expostulated Fulvia.

"It's Nigel!" cried Daisy.

"At last!" murmured Anice.

Nigel's first move was to his mother's side. She had
risen with a startled look on his entrance, her large
eyes wide open; but the response to his greeting was
scarcely what might have been expected. His arms
were round her, while her arms hung limply against
the velvet dress, and the cheek which she offered to
him was cold and white. "Mother, you are not well!"
he exclaimed when—the short round of brotherly kisses
over—he came to her again. Fulvia took stand as a
sister in the household. She had wondered a little,
privately, whether after this long break he would greet
her precisely as in their boy and girl days; but it
seemed that the idea of a change had never occurred
to him.

"I am sure you are not well," repeated Nigel.

"Mother has been so worried, waiting for you."

It was Anice who said this. Nobody but tactless
Anice, not even the impulsive Daisy, would have said
the words. Indignant fire shot from Fulvia's eyes;
and Nigel stood looking down upon his mother's face,
beautiful even when fixed and colourless, with an air
grieved, and yet absent. He could not shake off the
cloud which he had carried away from the Rectory.

"I am sorry to have worried you," he said. "Pollard was quick; and I have been longer than I meant."

"You found the train after all," Fulvia observed.

"Yes, at the last moment."

"How about meals? Have you had anything to eat?"

"Yes, thanks; as much as I want."

"You are sure?" his mother said in her low voice. She had scarcely spoken hitherto.

"Quite."

He drew a chair near to Mrs. Browning and sat down, holding still the hand which he had taken a second time. She was dearly beloved by all her children, and by none more than by Nigel; so dearly that they could scarcely see a fault in her. The exacting nature of her love for them, above all for her only son, did imply a fault somewhere, only they could not see it. If Nigel saw, he would not acknowledge the fact to others; and if Fulvia saw, she would not acknowledge it even to herself. At least, she had not done so hitherto.

"It was mother!" they all said, and "mother" had ever been in that household the embodiment of all that was lovely and lovable. If something of delusion existed, the very delusion was beautiful. And if Mrs. Browning had her faults—as who has not?—she was the best of wives, the most devoted of mothers, the fairest and sweetest of women. Nobody could see her and not admire; nobody could know her and not love.

There was a curious constraint upon them all this
evening; not least upon Nigel, and this perplexed
Fulvia. Mrs. Browning's look she understood well;
too well! Had any one except Nigel been in question,
Fulvia would have been the first to spring up in
defence of the "madre's" sensitiveness. The grieved
curve of those gentle lips made her very heart ache;
and in her heart Fulvia counted that Nigel had done
wrongly, for it was a household axiom, without an
allowed exception, that nobody might ever do or say
aught which should distress the beloved "madre."
But how could she blame him—just returned from a
long year of absence?

She could not make out Nigel's look. He did not
appear to be touched, as she would have expected, by
Mrs. Browning's manner. He hardly seemed to be
aware that he had caused displeasure; if displeasure is
the right word. The dark eyes had, indeed, trouble
in them, but also they told of thoughts far away. She
and Daisy made conversation, Nigel responding with
forced attention; and presently that too faded. Fulvia
could almost have believed that he had forgotten his
present position, so still was the manner, so absorbed
the downcast gaze. Mrs. Browning drew her hand
away, and the movement was not noticed.

"What *are* you dreaming about?" Daisy burst out
at length, bringing Nigel back, with something of a
start, to the consciousness of his immediate surroundings.
"What are you thinking of?"

"Perhaps your first word was the more correct—dreaming, not thinking. Don't things seem rather like a dream to you this evening?"

"No, they don't. It's all sober reality. And you are your substantial self; not half so much of a wraith as when you went away. Is he, Fulvia? There!"—with a mischievous pinch of his arm—"that's the proper test. It's genuine, you see! If you can make yourself wince, you may be quite sure you're not dreaming. I've tried to pinch myself in a dream, and it doesn't hurt. Do you know, you're most wonderfully altered, Nigel—bigger and broader, and as brown as a berry. And actually growing a moustache! And *I* think you are going to be handsome."

"Daisy, if you take to personalities, I shall have to give you a lesson."

"Do, please! I like lessons!"

Nigel laughed, but he did not seem inclined to carry out his threat by active measures. "How has my father been lately?" he asked next. "Not well to-day?"

"Very far from it," Mrs. Browning murmured.

"Nothing definitely wrong?"

"Yes; weakness and depression; and the old pain about the heart, worse than it used to be. He will not have advice; says it is only neuralgia and nothing can be done. But he ought to consult a London physician One never can be sure. I have tried in vain to persuade him."

"Perhaps he will listen to me. And you too—you are not just as you ought to be," Nigel said affectionately.

"I! O that is nothing. I never expect to feel strong."

Then Anice's voice was heard again. "But, Nigel, what can have made you so late? Why didn't you come straight from the station?"

"Anice is a self-appointed Inquisitress-General," interposed Fulvia. "Did you meet anybody by the way?"

"I nearly ran down Mr. Carden-Cox."

"He wouldn't forgive anybody else; but you are a privileged person—you may do what you like. Was he much delighted?" asked Fulvia, while Anice could be heard complaining—"I don't see why you should call me that! I don't see why Nigel shouldn't tell us."

"If he was, he showed it in characteristic style," said Nigel.

"Where did you see him?"

"In George Street."

"George Street! But what could have taken you there?" exclaimed Anice. "Didn't you come up the steps?"

"Inquisitress—" whispered Fulvia, simultaneously with Nigel's—

"No."

"But why?"

"Really, Anice, if he had a fancy to go round I don't see that it is our business."

"No—only—after a whole year away, I should have thought he *would* have chosen the quickest way home."

"Would, could, might, and ought are often mistaken," asserted Fulvia.

"Fulvia is right. I had a fancy to go round," said Nigel, and for a moment he was strongly tempted to say no more. But an explanation was expected; his call at the Rectory was sure to become known; he disliked needless mysteries, and his habitual openness won the day. With scarcely a break he went on—"A fancy to look at old haunts by gaslight. I walked some distance."

"Which way?" asked the persistent Anice.

"By Church Square."

"To the Elveys'?" Mrs. Browning bit her lip nervously.

"Not intending to see them, mother. It was as I say—a fancy to take a look. I fully meant to be here as soon as Pollard; but I met Mr. Elvey, and he persuaded me to go in for five minutes."

Fulvia's brows were knitted, yet she laughed. "I don't see why you should not. The Elveys always were great cronies of yours."

"No—only—one would have thought—" murmured Anice. "Yes, of course they are old friends. Only—to put them before us—"

"You goose!" exclaimed Fulvia angrily. "As if

D

there were any putting before or behind in the
question! I don't see ·for my part how Nigel could
well help going in, when Mr. Elvey met him. How
can you be so absurd!"

Anice's eyes filled with ready tears, and she gazed
dolorously on the carpet; yet distressed as she might
be at Fulvia's blame, her distress did not prevent
a renewed faint mutter of—"Before his mother and
sisters!"

Nigel took the matter into his own hands. He looked
straight at Anice, speaking with a readiness and decision
which impressed them all. They knew from that
moment that the brother who had gone away a boy had
come back a man.

"You are unjust, Anice. I have told you that I had
no idea of calling at the Rectory. Surely that is enough.
Why must you make a mountain of a mole-hill?"

Anice sighed plaintively, as if to declare that she was
silenced but not convinced; and Mrs. Browning said
nothing.

"Do you think my father would like to see me now?"
Nigel asked.

CHAPTER IV.

FULVIA'S RESOLVE.

" Heart, be still !
In the darkness of thy woe,
Bow thee silently and low ;
Come to thee, whate'er God will ;—
    Be thou still !

" Be thou still !
Vainly all thy words are spoken!
Till the word of God hath broken
Life's dark mysteries—good or ill—
    Be thou still ! "—*Shadow of the Rock.*

THIS caused a move. Nigel vanished, not to return for some time, and when he did, Fulvia thought he looked anxious; but nothing was said, and nobody asked what he thought of Mr. Browning. Prayers over, the younger girls retired, and Mrs. Browning prepared to follow. Something in the constrained tone of her " Good-night," drew from Nigel an apologetic—" You didn't really mind so much, mother ? "

The muscles of her white throat worked visibly, voice failing when she tried to speak. Fulvia brought forward a glass of water.

"Take some of this," she said, adding in a whisper, "Don't give way, madre; it will worry him."

The words had less effect than Fulvia intended. Mrs. Browning turned from her, and broke into one grieved utterance—"Nigel, my own boy! don't leave off loving me!"

"My dear mother! As if that were possible!"

Young men are not perhaps as a rule peculiarly tolerant of needless hysterics; but Nigel was very patient, holding her in his strong arms, and trying to soothe the real though unfounded sorrow. Fulvia admired the self-restraint and quietness of his manner, noting therein a development from the impetuosity of olden days. She could not help wondering how this sort of thing would strike him now. A young man sees matters differently from a boy; and he knew more of life than twelve months earlier. The year of travel had been equal to two years of ordinary existence. His very gentleness seemed to Fulvia to spring from a manly pity for Mrs. Browning's weakness.

Fulvia would not let the little scene continue. "It was too bad;" she murmured, "just after his coming home!" and then she blamed herself for blaming the sweet madre; but none the less she separated the two, insisted on water being taken, laughed, joked, and saw Mrs. Browning off to her room. "I'll be back directly," she said to Nigel; and in five minutes or less she returned. As she expected, he was in the drawing-room still, standing on the rug, with folded arms and eyes intent.

" Are you very tired ? " she asked abruptly, beginning to fold some of the work which lay about. "Tidying up" was a task which somehow always devolved on Fulvia Rolfe. One marked Browning characteristic was disorderliness in small matters; while Fulvia could never endure to see anything left out of its rightful place.

"No, I believe not. It is late," he said, rousing himself again with a manifest effort.

" You have not heard any bad news to-day ? "

" Is there bad news to be heard ? "

"Not that I'm aware of. You look as if you had something on your mind. That made me ask. But the botherations this evening are enough to account for it—nearly! If only people had a little common-sense, and wouldn't manufacture troubles to order. However, you will not think that nobody is glad to see you back."

Nigel laughed.

" Of course—you know what it is all worth. How did the padre's condition strike you ? Was he in bed ? "

" No. I can't judge so soon. It seems to me that he ought to have advice."

" If only for the sake of his own peace of mind, not to speak of the madre's. He doesn't *look* ill, at all events. You thought he did! Odd! I should have said he was the picture of health. Then perhaps you will encourage his going abroad."

Nigel had not heard of the scheme, and she enlightened him.

"Of course there is no real difficulty; except the expense. Somehow, padre is always and for ever talking now about expenses—why, I can't imagine. And except also for family traditions connected with twenty-first birthdays. We made such a fuss about yours before you left,· that the girls have had it in their heads ever since to make a fuss about mine."

"Heiresses usually expect something of a stir on those occasions."

"Do they? I am not sure that I care. Yes; perhaps I should like it. I should like to give a big dinner to the poor, and to have all our friends here as well. We have talked it over many a time. But whether padre would stand the excitement—! Well, December is nearly a month away still. Nigel, do you know at all the amount that is to come to me? I have never been told definitely. Padre hates business-talk."

"About forty thousand, I believe."

"So much! I thought it was twenty or thirty thousand."

"It was to be as much as forty by this time, certainly, —by the time you are of age."

"I believe I heard—part was to accumulate at compound interest. But padre was to use some of the interest."

"Yes; through your minority. That was the arrangement made by your father."

"Then my coming of age will be a loss to him. Is that why he dislikes any mention of it ?"

"I hope not !"

"Why ? People don't like losing part of the income they are accustomed to. But of course I shall let him have any amount still that he wants, only keeping enough for my own clothes. What do I want with more ? "

"When you set up a separate establishment—"

"Nonsense ! As if—"

"At all events don't pledge yourself. Promise nothing till you see your way."

She had again the sense of his new manliness, of the change from boy to man. He was only a year older than herself; and twelve months earlier the difference had seemed to be on the other side. Now he had outstripped her; and with a sense of pleasure she knew that she might begin to look up to him, to appeal to his judgment. But nobody could have guessed these thoughts to be passing through Fulvia's mind, as she stood near the fire, winding a ball of worsted, while the light fell on her reddish fluffy hair and plain though piquant face.

"You to advise that !"

"Why not ? "

"I thought——well, you might yourselves be the losers. Why should I not hand it all over to padre as it comes in ? I don't know what on earth to do with such a lot of money."

"You can't hand over the responsibility."

His earnest look struck her.

"No, perhaps not," she said, half seriously. "I wish one could transfer responsibilities sometimes; but I don't see after all why one should not—in a sense. I mean, that might be the right use for the money; and then the question of spending would come upon padre."

She swept up some remnants of patchwork, Daisy's leavings, from a side-table, put straight a few books, closed the open piano, and came back to the rug. Nigel's face had fallen again into a thoughtful set; eyes and brow so grave as to be even sad. Fulvia gave him a good look unobserved, for he was gazing into the fire.

"I see you haven't lost your old trick of day-dreams. Has anything teased you at the Rectory? Ethel—did you see Ethel?"

Fulvia could not in the least have told what made her ask the question. She had never thought of Ethel in connection with Nigel. Malcolm Elvey was Nigel's particular friend, and it followed as a matter of course that Nigel should see much of all the Elvey family. But Ethel—why, Ethel was merely a bright useful girl, on frank and easy terms with Nigel. The very intimacy between the two had always been so simple and natural, so little talked about by either, as almost to exclude from the minds of lookers-on a thought of anything beyond. Fulvia was not, and never had been, greatly

in love with the Elveys as a family. She liked Mr.
Elvey, but not Mrs. Elvey; and she did not fully understand Ethel. Her first utterance of the name on this
occasion was involuntary, with no particular intention
underlying. Something in Nigel's face struck her, however; she could not have said what, and he could not
control it. She at once asked, "Did you see Ethel?"

"Yes."

"Was she glad to have you back?"

"I did not ask her."

"She might have shown it without being asked."

Fulvia's gray eyes could equally well look soft and
kind, or hard and cold. The latter expression came
into them now.

"I had a pleasant welcome, of course."

"From Ethel?"

"Yes, from Ethel."

"But not all that you expected?"

"Yes—"

"Then what *did* Ethel say or do?"

Nigel had reached his utmost limit of endurance for
one evening.

"Somebody else seems taking up with the inquisi-
torial line now," he said, not so lightly as he wished.
"Are you going to bed?"

She gave him a searching glance, then held out her
hand, keeping her head well back.

"Good-night," came abruptly. "So Ethel does stand
first, as Anice said,—before mother and sisters!"

"If you wish to make mischief—" began Nigel.
Sweet-tempered though he was, he could be roused.

"I'm not going to make mischief. Don't you know
me better? Such things have to be, of course; and I
always find them out before anybody else. You are
getting to the correct age for the epidemic; but you
may trust me not to speak. I'm not anxious to break
the madre's heart sooner than need be. I don't mean
that she would object to Ethel more than to anybody else—particularly—so you need not look at me
like that. It's the fact of *anybcdy* that will be the
rub; and of course you can't be expected to live a life
of celibacy on her account. Ethel is a nice enough
girl—at least I suppose so. I never feel that I know
her; but that may be my own fault. However, it is
time we should both be in bed, so good-night."

She allowed no opportunity for another brotherly
salutation, but retreated with a mocking smile. "Go
and dream of Ethel; only don't look doleful," she said.
Then she mounted deliberately the shallow oak stairs,
warbling a ditty by the way till her room was reached,
and the door was locked. Warbling ceased when she
found herself alone.

Fulvia turned on the gas-jet over the dressing-table
and pulled out a supply of hairpins, letting down her
splendid hair. It rippled over her shoulders reaching
her waist, and sparkling where the light touched it.
Fulvia stood gazing at her own reflection with folded
arms, bare below the elbows.

"No; I am not beautiful—not even pretty," she murmured. "But is Ethel?"

Another pause, during which she gazed steadily.

"So that is to be it—after all! After all these years! I would have done anything—given anything—for him. Forty thousand!—that is nothing where one loves. He did not know why I was glad to hear it was so much— for his sake, not mine. Little thinking then—and only a minute later— But Ethel has nothing to give him. She can mend his gloves—laugh at him, perhaps, as I have heard her do. *I* could not laugh at Nigel—" forgetting that she had just done so. "At anybody else— not Nigel. How he has changed—so manly and strong, yet the same! And this—this the end of it all! Will Ethel understand him? Does anybody fully—except—? O I think I could have made him happy, if—"

Then the consciousness swept over her of what she was saying, of what she was allowing to herself, and with it came a rush of angry blood, suffusing her whole face. She turned sharply away, and walked to and fro, her hands locked together.

"Shame! Nonsense! Rubbish! That *I* should be the first to think— I!—and he of course has never given a thought to me! Why should he? Why should I expect it? Nigel will never marry for money! Should I like him if he could? . . . And if I have not seen, I might have seen. He and Ethel! Why, it has been so for years! He would do for her years ago what he would not do for me. I never could think why, but I

know now. If I had not been infatuated, I should have
seen it all along. Does the madre see? Is that why
she minded so much? . . . No, I don't love Ethel.
I don't care for her. I don't half like her. She rubs
me up the wrong way, somehow. Has it been this?
. . . Poor madre! every one will pity her, and nobody
will pity me! Hush—I will *not* have that come up!
Unwomanly!—contemptible!—to give one's love where
it is not wanted." Fulvia stamped her foot with fierce
resolution. "Nobody shall ever guess my folly! Anything rather than betray myself! Nigel—how Nigel
would despise me, if he knew! And how I despise
myself!"

She stood again before the glass, noting the flush
which remained.

"No wonder; I may well be ashamed. It is too
weak—too foolish! But I will hide it! stamp it down!
hold up my head!" and she flung back her abundant
hair with a proud gesture. "If love can die, mine shall
be killed. Nobody shall see! Nobody shall know! I
see how!—I'll laugh at Nigel—tease him—make myself
as disagreeable as I can! . . . No, no, that might be
read. And why must I pain him? He will have
worries enough among them all. No, no, I'll follow a
nobler line—more womanly. That at least remains.
If *I* cannot be happy, he may be. I'll give him sympathy, and help it forward. I'll smooth things down for
him, as I know I can—more than any other human
being. I shall not be misunderstood then—shall not

be understood, I mean! What nonsense I am talking.
. . . Yes, that will do! He shall think I am glad—
delighted. He shall owe some of his happiness to me.
And she—I will try to love Ethel—will try to make
her see better what Nigel is. And if he is happy—
really happy—should I not be happy too, knowing it?
But, oh—"

One moment Fulvia stood upright, smiling triumph-
antly at her own reflection. The next, an irresistible
stab of pain came, and tears burst forth in a deluge.
She dropped to the ground, rather than threw herself
down, hid her face upon those same folded arms now
laid against a chair, and shook with smothered weeping,
all the more intense because smothered.

Fulvia had never cried easily. From earliest childhood it had taken a great deal to bring tears—unlike
Anice, who had a supply always ready to hand for the
slightest call. But with Fulvia, when once the flow
began, it was as difficult to check as it had been difficult
to start. She could weep on to an almost indefinite
extent; until indeed bodily exhaustion should put an
end to the paroxysm.

Fulvia was strong, however, and bodily exhaustion
was long in coming. Again and again she strove to
master herself, almost with success; again and again a
return wave of violent distress completely mastered her.
From the moment that she collapsed, something not far
from two hours passed before she could lift her head.
When she again stood before the glass she had grown

sick and dizzy with agitation. Her face was blistered and burnt; and the eyes had almost vanished beneath their swollen lids.

"This must be the last time," she said aloud, resolutely. "I will not give way again."

But what if she were overcome by some sudden strain? A new dread of her own weakness assailed Fulvia, who had never felt herself weak before.

"It shall not be!" she muttered through clenched teeth, with clenched hands. "I will not give way! I will not! Any woman can be strong who chooses. I *will* be strong! I will *not* betray myself—whatever happens."

She began at length to make ready for going to bed, in a mechanical fashion, plaiting loosely her long hair to keep it out of her eyes, noting the lateness of the hour. Not far from two o'clock!

"What would the madre think of me? But they shall not know. I must look like myself to-morrow. If only I can sleep!"

Late though it was, she read a few verses from her Bible; a perfunctory matter commonly; and not less so now than usual. She could not have told five minutes afterwards what she had read.

Then she knelt down, leaning against the back of a chair, with a feeling of utter weariness. What did it matter whether she prayed or not? What did anything matter? Fulvia had prayed sometimes—really prayed; still, hitherto she had not accomplished great things in the line of practical prayer. Not that she did not believe in its power; but she had been conscious of no marked needs. There had been no especial connection between her morning and evening "saying" of prayers, and the every-day life lived between.

Now a change had come. Fulvia was aware of a definite and sore need; though the bearing which prayer might have upon this need did not even occur to her as a possibility. She only murmured a few unmeaning phrases about nothing in particular; and when she rose no help had come, for she had not sought it. In her trouble she turned to self only, resting on her own strength of will. Fulvia was a girl of steady principle and of noble impulses; but as yet she had never given over the guidance of her barque to the hand of the Master-Pilot. There was danger of its being swept to and fro out of the right course, by wind and wave, against her will.

"Yes, that will do," she said, before putting out her light. "Nigel shall be happy, at all events. I always have said that if one really cares for another, one can wish nothing so much as his happiness. Well, I have to prove it now. Nobody shall ever guess! That has to be crushed down—crushed!" and again she clenched her teeth. "I will be mistress of myself. And if I have any power to smooth things for him and Ethel, I will do it."

The resolution was praiseworthy; but would she have strength to carry it out?

CHAPTER V.

" Rather, steel thy melting heart
 To act the martyr's sternest part,
 To watch with firm unshrinking eye
 Thy darling visions as they die,
 Till all bright hopes and hues of day
 Have faded into twilight gray."—*Christian Year.*

" WHAT is Nigel going to do with himself to-day ? " asked Daisy, next morning.

Breakfast—supposed to begin at nine, seldom in reality before half-past—was nearly over. People had dropped in at intervals, till all were present except Mr. Browning. Fulvia, for a marvel, had been one of the last instead of the first to appear, and she had to endure some banter from Daisy, replying thereto with spirit. It had seemed to Fulvia before coming down-stairs that her pale cheeks, and the dark shades under her eyes, must surely be remarked upon. But nobody seemed to see anything unusual. Fulvia had always been strong, and was almost always well. Nobody expected her to be otherwise, and people in general are not observant. Mrs. Browning was absorbed in thought about her husband, and the girls were absorbed in attentions to Nigel, while Nigel laughed and joked with them, and Fulvia knew that his mind was away at the Rectory. She could see "Ethel" written on every line of his face; and she knew that he was not noticing her at all.

In one sense it might be a relief that none should observe more keenly, for the part she had to act became easier thereby.

Yet human nature is curiously "mixed" in its ways, always wanting what it does not possess. Fulvia missed the very solicitude which she most desired to avoid. It seemed hard that nobody should offer a word of kindness; that not a human being should care to hear how she had lain awake the whole night. For what? That none might learn; and if inquiries had come, Fulvia must have repelled them; but since they did not come, she craved a sympathizing word. The sick sense of weariness was on her still; long hours of tossing to and fro had not meant rest; and breakfast was a mere sham. She could eat nothing; but nobody saw. Fulvia might do as she liked, so long as other people's needs were attended to.

So she told herself bitterly, while pouring out unlimited cups of tea, behind the silver urn. Breakfast was always a lengthy meal at the Grange. Everybody waited for everybody else, since all were expected to be present at family prayers afterwards. Fulvia had wandered away into a little dreamland of her own, when she was recalled by Daisy's question—

E

" What is Nigel going to do with himself to-day ? "

" Varieties," Nigel answered.

" Mother wants you to go and see Mr. Carden-Cox."

This was Anice's remark. If Anice desired a thing herself, she was sure to quote Mrs. Browning.

" I shall have to see Mr. Carden-Cox soon, of course."

" Nigel, if you go this morning, I wish you'd take me," cried Daisy. " His study is so delicious, and he always gives one something nice."

" To eat ? "

" No—nonsense. A book, or a picture, or something."

" He is said to spoil children."

" Well—and I'm a child—not a young lady ! Do take me."

" Nonsense, Daisy. Nigel can't be saddled with a pair of sisters all day long,·' interposed Fulvia, foreseeing a like request from Anice.

" You don't call me a ' pair,' do you ? Besides, what's the harm ? Nigel has been more than a year away, and we do want to see something of him. You don't care, of course. He isn't your brother," pursued Daisy, unconscious of giving pain. " Nigel has nothing to do except amuse himself. Nobody will expect to see him. The Elveys won't, because he has been there ; and other people don't matter, except Mr. Carden-Cox."

" Nigel has not seen Malcolm yet."

Nigel looked up at Fulvia in gratitude ; and he did not at once look away. His eyes studied her gravely for two or three seconds ; and Fulvia knew at once that she might have, but must not allow, the word of sympathy for which she had been craving.

"Malcolm—no. But—" Daisy began.

"You know that he is curate at St. Peter's now, of course," Fulvia said cheerfully, smiling at Nigel. His eyes were on her still, in a kind gaze—exactly the frank concerned gaze which a brother might bestow on a sister, and, as she knew, not at all the kind of gaze that he would have bestowed upon Ethel under like circumstances. But the kindness was marked; and Fulvia found herself tingling with a rush of feeling. She saw that he was about to speak. This would never do! She was lifting a full breakfast-cup to pass across the table, and the next moment it had dropped from her hand, causing a crash of broken china, and deluging the white table-cloth. So neatly was the thing done, that even Nigel did not at once suspect its non-accidental nature.

"How stupid of me! I must be demented," exclaimed Fulvia, starting up. "And I have always prided myself on never letting anything fall. I shall begin to think my fingers are growing buttery at last." She rang the bell, and came back to stand over the swamped table, laughing. "What a horrible mess! I hope nobody wants any more tea, for the tea-pot is pretty well emptied. O, we were just speaking about Malcolm. You know that he is going to live at home for a time, don't you?"

Nigel seemed to be lost in a brown study. "Yes—

the last letters from home told me," he said, when a pause drew his attention to the question. "I don't see why he should not. St. Peter's is near to St. Stephen's."

But his eyes went again to Fulvia inquiringly.

"The best thing in the world for them all, I should say," she remarked in a light tone. "Ethel seemed delighted with the plan. There was talk of lodgings for him at first, I believe, but that is given up—naturally. By the bye, I wonder if you thought Ethel improved in looks. Mr. Carden-Cox declares she has grown quite pretty. I never do think her that, but she has pretty manners—and after all it is a matter of opinion. Almost everybody is thought handsome by somebody. However, you could hardly tell in a few minutes. Of course you will be going there again to-day, to see Malcolm."

Mrs. Browning did not like this, neither did Anice; and Daisy's brown eyes were round as saucers. Fulvia could see the faces of all three, without looking at any of them; her senses being doubly acute this morning. The last words had been hard to utter smilingly, and again she was aware of Nigel's attention. It was almost more than she could bear, meaning to her so much, yet in itself so little. The tingling sensation came back, and with it a choking in her throat. She had just power to say—

"Well, if you all like to sit round an ocean of spilt tea, pray do! It is too damp an outlook for my taste.

Simms doesn't seem inclined to appear, so perhaps—
And there is tea all down my dress! What a bother!
it will be ruined, if I am not quick. I must see to
it at once."

Then she was gone, passing swiftly up-stairs to her
own room.

The maids were not there, as she had expected;
but Fulvia dared not let feeling again have the mastery.
She attended first to the wet dress, and then for half
a minute, not longer, stood at the open window, full
in the fresh breeze.

"O—it is hard—hard!" she whispered. "But I
must—I must—I must conquer! I will not give way.
They shall not, *shall not* see!"

Nigel meantime was asking, as the door closed—
"What is the matter with Fulvia?"

"Fulvia! Why, Nigel—what should be the matter?
Nothing is, of course. Nothing is ever the matter with
Fulvia," declared Daisy. "Why should you think
anything was? She has only made a fine mess."

"She seems to be not quite herself."

"I don't think anything is wrong," said Anice.

Nigel made no answer, but he resolved to use his
own eyesight. Mrs. Browning could think of nobody
except her husband; and Daisy was a mere child;
and Anice, like many quasi-invalids, objected to others
besides herself being counted deserving of attention
on the score of health. Her father's condition she
had to put up with; but Fulvia and Daisy were always

to be strong, and she was always to be the one cared for. In fact, Anice liked a monopoly of delicate health.

"Fulvia is not as she used to be," Nigel said to himself; and though she came to prayers in a few minutes, wearing an extra cheerful air, he did not alter his opinion. If she were not unwell, she was in trouble. He could not resolve which it might be.

Mr. Carden-Cox sat in his study, late that afternoon, before a blazing fire, lost in cogitation.

It was a comfortable room, containing everything that might be desired by a bachelor of moderate means. Nobody counted Mr. Carden-Cox wealthy, but everybody knew that he had enough to "get on upon."

In his mode of living he was neither lavish nor stingy. He gave away a good deal; but always after his own fashion—which means, that he refused everybody's requests for money, yet did a good many unknown kindnesses. He was an eccentric man; something of an enigma to people generally. Nobody could ever guess beforehand, with certainty, what Mr. Carden-Cox would do, or how he would do it.

He had never been married. This fact everybody knew, while few could tell the wherefore. Perhaps two or three, among his acquaintances, looking back nearly a quarter of a century, might speak of the time when Arthur Carden-Cox, then close upon forty in age, had showed signs of being "touched" by the rare charms of that wonderfully fair young creature, Clemence Duncan. But few had thought much of it. All men who came within her range were fascinated, without effort on her part. The question was not, whether she would marry Albert Browning or Arthur Carden-Cox, but upon which among a dozen ardent suitors her choice would fall. Arthur Carden-Cox had not seemed by any means the most ardent; and when Clemence Duncan became Mrs. Browning others were more pitied.

However, those others had comforted themselves, sooner or later recovering; and all of them, now living, were middle-aged men, married and with families. Arthur Carden-Cox alone had made no further effort to find a wife. He had been long and late falling in love; and once in he could not easily fall out again.

Perhaps Mrs. Browning guessed what the true cause might be of his lonely life. But she never spoke of it. If he had proposed to her, she told the fact to no one. Other people counted him only " an odd old bachelor; " and this explained everything.

It was inevitable that he should be intimate at the Grange, since, though not related to the Brownings themselves, he was uncle to Mr. Browning's ward, Fulvia Rolfe.

Fulvia's mother had been half-sister to Arthur Carden-Cox; and Fulvia's father, John Rolfe, had been an old and intimate friend of Mr. Browning. John Rolfe and Arthur Carden-Cox had not been on

very happy terms, owing to a quarrel over the marriage
settlements of John's wife; but John Rolfe had reposed
the most unbounded confidence in Albert Browning.
When Rolfe died, shortly after the death of his wife,
he was found to have appointed Albert Browning his
sole executor, sole guardian of his infant child, sole
trustee of the fortune which was to be hers.

A strange thing to do, many said; and Mr. Carden-
Cox doubtless felt himself slighted. Albert Browning
at first seemed to shrink from the responsibility, even
though it meant advantage to himself, since by the
terms of the will he was expressly allowed to use a
certain share of the interest, until Fulvia should be
of age. He accepted the charge, however; and he
and his young wife adopted the little Fulvia as their
own. Thenceforth she grew up like one of the Browning
family, taking her stand as Nigel's companion, and as
the eldest of his sisters. She could recall no other
home.

Mr. Carden-Cox' position at the Grange was curious,
like himself. Sometimes he was in and out every
day; sometimes he would not go near the house for
weeks together. To a certain extent he was a privileged
being there, able to do and say what he chose; yet
he never seemed entirely at his ease; and he and Mr.
Browning were by no means on affectionate terms.
Each civilly slighted the other, though they never
quarrelled. Towards Mrs. Browning Mr. Carden-Cox
was ceremoniously polite. He could not to this day

quite forgive her for having preferred somebody else to himself; nevertheless they were good friends.

With the three girls he was not unlike a fairy godfather, treating them to divers gifts and pleasures, making no great distinctions between the three, though Fulvia was his niece, and would doubtless inherit whatever he possessed. If he had a special pet, that pet seemed to be Daisy.

The girls were, however, secondary in his estimation. Nigel was the real delight of the old man's heart.

For at sixty-three Mr. Carden-Cox was already an old man; older in divers respects than many a vigorous contemporary of seventy-five.

His cogitations that afternoon were about Nigel. As he sat, nursing one leg over the other, his hands clasped round the upper knee, his small figure bent forward, his features wrapped in gravity, he thought only of Nigel. Much of the love which Mr. Carden-Cox had once lavished upon Nigel's mother was lavished now upon Nigel; but Nigel did not guess this, or suppose himself to be more than "rather a favourite." As few had divined the strength of Arthur Carden-Cox' devotion in past days, so few divined it now. He was not at all in the habit of wearing his heart upon his sleeve, for anybody to peck at. There were plenty of daws in Newton Bury, ready to perform that office, if he would have allowed them.

It was a disappointment that Nigel had not yet come. All day Mr. Carden-Cox had stayed in for the chance—

or, as he viewed it, for the certainty—of a call. "What could the boy be about?" he asked repeatedly, as the hours went by; and two ruts deepened in his forehead.

Somebody tapped, and the door opened, Mr. Carden-Cox looking up sharply, secure of Nigel; but "Dr. Duncan" was announced instead.

Dr. James Duncan, first cousin to Mrs. Browning, and leading medical man of Newton Bury, knew himself to be at the moment unwelcome; and he bore the knowledge cheerfully. He understood Mr. Carden-Cox too well, besides being too thorough a gentleman and large-hearted a man to take offence lightly. That sort of thing—"that sort of nonsense," he would have called it—he left to smaller natures.

Though younger than Clemence Duncan, James Duncan had once upon a time been in the ranks of her admirers. Like Arthur Carden-Cox, he had found Albert Browning preferred to himself. Unlike Arthur Carden-Cox, he had wisely consoled himself in later years with somebody else.

Mr. Carden-Cox, disgusted with Nigel's non-appearance, would not rise, and Dr. Duncan did not sit down. He stood upon the rug, hat in hand, opposite the small man in the easy-chair; himself of good medium height, and well-made, though disposed to thinness. He had a frank English face of the best type, not critically handsome, but very like that of Nigel. Placed side by side, the two might have passed for father and son.

"Well?" growled Mr. Carden-Cox.

"Have I interrupted anything of importance?" asked Dr. Duncan, in a voice which matched his face—frank, quiet, well-modulated.

"No, no. It doesn't matter. I'm only on the look-out for that young fellow. By the bye, have you seen him yet?" and Mr. Carden-Cox grew lively. "Don't know who I mean! eh? Haven't you heard he is come? Why, your former patient, of course—Nigel. You won't have much to say to him now in that capacity. He's transmogrified. Looks ten times the man I ever expected."

"I'm glad to hear it—very glad. I had hopes."

"Yes; you were right after all. I didn't half believe in the scheme before he went, but you were right. And you've not seen him?"

"No. Clemence told me he was expected soon—which day I had forgotten. I have been rather overwhelmed this week."

"Seen nobody but a lot of sick folk, I suppose. That's the way with you doctors. Horribly dull life. But I say, Duncan, there's some mistake. I didn't send for you. It's a blunder. I'm all right—never felt better—don't need any physic—haven't an ache or a pain."

The other smiled. He had a pleasant smile, like Nigel's, hardly so brilliant, but also not so evanescent. The play of it lingered longer round his lips.

"No; I came for a word with you about somebody's health. Not your own."

"Nigel to wit?"

" I have not seen Nigel. You say he is all right."

" Looked so, when I saw him in the dark—by lamp-light, I mean. Well, what's wrong? Some old woman wanting a red cloak to cure ' rheumatiz ' ? "

" Not at this moment."

" An old man then ? "

" Browning is not exactly old."

" Browning ! Hey ! Why, what's wrong there ? "

" I can say nothing in my medical capacity. Put that out of sight, if you please."

" Can't, man, unless you put yourself out of sight."

" I am speaking simply as their relative — as Clemence's cousin."

" Ay ? Well, what about him—speaking as an ordinary individual, not as a doctor ? "

" He ought to consult a London physician."

" Why not consult you ? "

" We have put that possibility aside. He has not asked my advice, and I cannot thrust it upon him." " Rubbish ! " muttered Mr. Carden-Cox ; Dr. Duncan continuing, unchecked—" But advice he ought to have. If he would rather not come to me, let him go to London by all means."

" Why should he not go to you ? "

" Can't say ! The fact is patent."

" And you don't think him in good health ? Why, I should have said— Why, he came in here last week, looking positively robust. Fads and fancies enough, I dare say, but as for being ill—"

" Looks are deceptive sometimes."

"Except to the initiated, I suppose. You don't mean that anything is seriously wrong ? "

" I can't speak with authority. I have not examined the case. All I say is—as anybody might say—that he ought not to go on without advice."

" And if he does ? "

Dr. Duncan was silent.

" But I say, now—look here ! What do you expect me to do ? Why don't you speak to Mrs. Browning ? "

"Because, if she could not persuade him, I should have alarmed her to no purpose. You have influence with them."

" Perhaps—yes."

"Your opinion will not frighten her as mine would—even while they may act upon it."

" I told Browning last week that he seemed in splendid condition. Am I to eat my own words so soon ? "—ruefully.

" What did he say ? "

" Oh, sighed, and declared he 'suffered' a good deal, couldn't sleep, and so forth ! All a case of masculine nerves, I thought. What ! going already ? "

" I must ! I'll leave the matter with you."

" But I say—stop !—what about this notion of going abroad ? I believe the girls don't know it yet. Browning broached it to me. Why, he has always hated travelling."

" He should consult a physician before deciding."

" What do you suppose to be the matter with him ? "

Dr. Duncan buttoned his glove.

" Eh ! what's wrong with the man ? "

" I can say nothing definite.   He is not as he should be.   Good-bye."

" But, hallo—I say ! " and Mr. Carden-Cox sprang up. " Am I to quote you ? "

Dr. Duncan looked down from his superior height, smiling again.   " No," he said, and vanished.

" Knew he meant that," growled Mr. Carden-Cox, dropping back into the easy-chair.   " Extraordinary ! Browning ill !   Browning !   I should have said he was as jolly and well-to-do a man as any alive.   But Duncan doesn't speak without reason.   Well, I must obey orders, I suppose. What next ?   Hey ?   Yes—come in !   Nigel this time ? "

The two shook hands quietly, and fell into a talk. Nobody would have guessed, looking on, how long they had been apart, nor how much the reunion meant to the elder man.

Nigel's brightness of manner was a little forced.   He had been again to the Rectory, and both Malcolm and Ethel were out.   Only Mrs. Elvey had received him; and Mrs. Elvey was not a reviving person.

CHAPTER VI.

DRAGGING HOURS.

> " Come what come may,
> Time and the hour runs through the roughest day."
>
> SHAKSPEARE.

"WHAT has become of Nigel?"

It seemed to Fulvia that the world never would stop tormenting her with this question. First, Daisy popped in to put it; then Mr. Browning, with heavy step and dejected mien, did the same; afterward, Anice appeared, loitered about, and discussed its bearings; lastly, Mrs. Browning glided through the doorway, and desired information. When Fulvia counted the catechizing at an end, Daisy began over again.

Fulvia was always the person asked; for people had a way of appealing to her, rather than to anybody else. She was practical and clear-headed, apt to remember little details which others were apt to forget, and as a rule she did not mind trouble. But this afternoon she did mind. While Anice and Daisy were on the move, unable to settle down in the excitement of Nigel's return, Fulvia never stirred from the easy-chair where after lunch she had taken refuge. Restlessness had had its swing with her through the night-hours, and had been finished off by a long walk in the morning. Now the weather had grown dismal and drizzling, and she sat persistently over her crewel-work.

Usually Fulvia was a rapid and beautiful worker, yet advance to-day seemed slow. While anybody was present, her needle went in and out like clockwork. "How you *can!*" Daisy exclaimed, "and Nigel only just come back!" Fulvia smiled, and worked on. But when alone, she dropped the work on her knee, holding it in readiness for another start so soon as the door-handle should turn, and laid her head against the chair-back, for indulgence in a dream. Violent weeping always left Fulvia in a state of reactionary inertia. She had not cried for—how many years was it? She could recall the last time, and the long stupid exhaustion following. That had been a case of childish naughtiness; but Mrs. Browning had petted and cared for her. Nobody thought of petting being needed now.

The afternoon was wearing away. Fulvia had never before known so long a stretch of night and day. It seemed more like twenty-four weeks than twenty-four hours, since yesterday's light chatting between herself and the other girls, about Nigel's return.

Was the whole of life to be dragged through in the same fashion? Fulvia asked this wearily, forgetting that the sharpest pain does in time lose something of its acuteness. She had known little hitherto of any pain; and endurance is not easy. Fulvia felt like a tired-out child; as if it would have been the greatest comfort to lay her head on somebody's knee, and have another good cry.

Nobody knew, of course, how tears were threatening the whole day. That had been the way with Fulvia from her cradle. She might pass through a year or any number of years, without the smallest break-down, always bright and even-spirited; but if once the sluices were forced open, she had to battle for days to regain her usual standing, and a word might overcome her. "Fulvia Rolfe does not often cry, but when she does, she goes in for a regular rainy season," an old gentleman had once said. The last "rainy season" lay so far back, however, that the possibility of its recurrence was forgotten.

Such a "rainy season" was on her now, only nobody supposed the fact. Nobody saw anything unusual. The girls could only think of Nigel; and Nigel at lunch would only talk and laugh with Daisy, not seeming to notice Fulvia at all. Soon after two he had gone out; and now, at nearly six, he was still absent.

"What has become of Nigel?"

Daisy asked this again, bouncing the door open, banging it to in her childish fashion, and dancing across the room. Daisy's dancing was not sylph-like; and the room vibrated to her steps. Fulvia could

F

have cried out sharply, "Oh, don't!" but she did not, because Daisy would at once have inquired—"Why?" The fire was blazing, and she took up her work.

"Why don't you have lights? You'll hurt your eyes."

"Simms came, but I sent him away. This looked pleasanter."

"I can't imagine what makes Nigel stay out such a time. Can you? Mother is getting into a worry. He couldn't be the whole afternoon with Mr. Carden-Cox, you know, or at the Rectory either. Fulvie, what did make you say that at breakfast-time about his going again to the Rectory?"

"I made myself."

"Well, but why? When you know mother can't bear him to go!"

Fulvia was silent, and Daisy's childish eyes scanned her. They were clever eyes, only undeveloped.

"Fulvie, why does mother dislike the Elveys? I think they are so nice."

"She doesn't."

"Yes, she does."

"No, it is not dislike. You are talking nonsense."

"Well then, she doesn't like Nigel to like them so much."

"Go and get something to do."

"I've done lots—heaps. I don't want to be busy now. Why does mother mind? Is it only because she wants him all to herself? Mother never does like

any of us to be too fond of anybody—outside people,
I mean. You may just as well answer me, because I
can't possibly help seeing things; and I am not a baby."

"I think you are; a creature in long clothes. Daisy,
get along, and leave me in peace."

"Why? You're not really working. You are just
making believe. I believe you like to sit and think
about Nigel's being at home again." The words stung
—how sharply innocent Daisy little dreamed. "And
I believe Nigel's at the Rectory, and you know it."

"No, I don't."

"I don't see why he shouldn't—except for madre.
Poor darling madre! I'll never like anybody out of the
house, I'm quite determined, except just a moderate
little amount. But I suppose Nigel must have friends.
Anyhow, he's the dearest old fellow alive—isn't he?"

Fulvia was silent.

"He's grown so jolly and handsome! I do like a big
strong brother. Don't you?"

Silence still. Fulvia was pricking her work dreamily
with the needle.

"Fulvie, you always used to praise Nigel more than
anybody. Why don't you answer?"

"It is unnecessary now. He is able-bodied, and can
look to himself."

"How funny you are! Well, Nigel praises *you*. He
told Anice and me before lunch—after we came in and
you went up-stairs—he told us we didn't make half
enough of you. And he said—"

Daisy paused to examine the fringe nailed round a small table. Fulvia's heart beat fast.

"How funny! here's a spot of candle grease. I wonder how it came."

"He said—what?"

"Oh, about you—what was I telling? I forget now. It is too bad of him to stay away such a time."

"What do you mean by 'not making enough' of me?" demanded Fulvia. She could not resist putting the question.

"Nigel said it, not I. He said a lot more. Oh, he only meant—what was it?—let me see—he only meant you were such a dear jolly old thing, always doing something for somebody, and he said we let you do too much. Do we? Anice was put out—didn't you see at lunch? That was why she wouldn't eat, and why Nigel and I talked so, for fear mother should notice. Nigel gave us a regular lecture, I can tell you. Anice said you were so strong it didn't matter; and Nigel said he wasn't so sure about that, only you were unselfish, and never thought of your own wishes, and he said it did matter, because you were not our own sister, and we had no business to make a Cinderella of you. Anice was quite cross. And then Nigel said— No, I wasn't to repeat that. I'm forgetting. He told me not."

"Not to repeat what?"

"Only about what he said—it was about you, so I mustn't. But I really didn't know before how much Nigel cared for you. Somehow I always thought he

liked Ethel best, after mother and Anice and me. I
expect Anice was jealous. Well, there's no harm in
repeating one thing Nigel said, and that was that he
had never seen anybody like you anywhere."

Fulvia could not speak for the moment. A wild hope
sprang up, and her heart beat faster, faster, in thick
throbs, so hard and loud that she thought Daisy must
surely hear. How foolish! how absurd! She who
prided herself on being always equable and composed—
she to be palpitating like this at the words of a mere child,
which might mean absolutely nothing. And yet—yet
—what if she had misunderstood matters the evening
before? Could it be possible? Had she made too much
of a word, a look? Had Nigel no such feeling for Ethel
as she had taken for granted? After all, how little had
passed between them! how easily Nigel might have misunderstood her thought, and she might have misread his!

"Anice hates being lectured, you know," Daisy went
on. "But I don't mind it—at least not from some
people. Not from dear old Nigel. Well, I don't mean
to tell you one scrap more, because he said I mustn't.
But really and truly I never meant to let you do too
much. It always seemed natural that you should do
things. Why didn't you ever tell me?"

Daisy ran away, not waiting for an answer; and
Fulvia sat in a dream, hardly thinking, only letting herself listen to a whisper of hope. What if—after all—?
She was trembling still with the sudden joy, unnerved,
and scarcely able to restrain a burst of tears.

Till suddenly Nigel entered the room ; and then in one moment Fulvia was calm.

"Fulvie going in for blind man's holiday ! That is something new."

"Daisy has been here, chattering—making me waste my time. Quite in despair at your absence."

"I didn't intend to be so long. One can't always help it. Everybody expects to hear everything "— apologetically. "And then—"

"Yes ?" Fulvia said, looking up. She noted something of trouble, and asked, "Did you see Ethel and Malcolm ?"

"No ; only Mrs. Elvey."

"Disappointing for you."

"Yes. Fulvia—"

Now it was coming. Would he confess to her his love for Ethel ? ask her help ? He glanced round at the door to see if anybody might be there to hear. He had something confidential to say, evidently. The pause he made occupied a mere fraction of a second, but Fulvia had time for distinct thought and conjecture, and her heart sank.

"Fulvia—have you thought my father ill lately ?"

Then the troubled look was not for Ethel. He was only anxious about Mr. Browning, and in his anxiety he turned to Fulvia. The previous throbbing came back, all over her from head to foot ; yet it was in her most natural voice that she answered—

"Padre ill ! No. He is nervous about himself, and I fancy he has worries."

" Mr. Carden-Cox spoke to me. He seems to have a notion that things are not right."

" Mr. Carden-Cox ! Why, he is always telling padre how well he looks."

" That was not his style to-day. He wanted me to insist on Dr. Duncan, or a London opinion."

" Odd ! Mr. Carden-Cox isn't generally a weather-cock."

" Hush—don't say any more now. Another time ! Here comes Daisy."

CHAPTER VII.

TO GO, OR NOT TO GO?

"God counts as nothing that which is most brilliant in the eyes of men. What He would have in us is purity of intention, an ever-ready yielding of our will; and these are more safely, and at the same time more truly, proved in common than in extraordinary matters. Sometimes we care more for a trifle than for some object of importance; and there may be more difficulty in giving up an amusement, than in bestowing a large sum in charity."—FÉNÉLON.

THROUGH the lower part of Newton Bury ran a river, much used by the inhabitants. Newton Bury was to some extent a manufacturing town, and manufacturing people are apt to congregate about a stream —not to the increase of its loveliness. But higher up, before coming within sight of wharves or mills, the river was exceedingly pretty, with varied banks, wooded heights at a short distance, and abundant willow growths, diversified by clay strata. Here gentlemen who lived in the neighbourhood did a good deal of boating; and young fellows like Nigel were especially addicted to the amusement. As a dreamy boy, Nigel had counted no recreation equal to that of rowing up or down the stream on a summer day, with or without a companion.

Some said he preferred the "without" to the "with";
though Nigel himself, while agreeing generally, always
made a mental reservation in favour of Ethel.

He was not now especially given to dreaming; but
the old taste for boating survived.

Mr. Carden-Cox owned a trim rowing-boat, which
it was tacitly understood that Nigel might always use.
His garden, a long and narrow slip, "ugly but useful"
the owner said, sloped down a steep hillside to the very
water's edge, and ended in a small boat-house beside
some steps. A good many gentlemen's houses followed
this plan with their gardens, thereabouts; but the
Grange stood on the next hill, with part of the town
between it and the river-side.

A small steam-launch existed in Newton Bury, for
hiring purposes; and Mr. Carden-Cox in his delight
at his favourite's return thought of the steam-launch.
The second day after Nigel's arrival proved mild and
sunny, almost like an April day; certainly not like
November. Newton Bury boasted a clear atmosphere,
despite its tall chimneys, and a Londoner would scarcely
have recognized this as a November day at all, unless
by the mistiness of far-off hollows. Even the Newton
Bury people said they had seldom seen the like.

"In honour of Nigel!" Mr. Carden-Cox averred,
looking out of the window before breakfast; and he
immediately determined to "set going something"
which might please "the boy." Why not an excursion
up the river in the steam-launch?

"Capital! Nothing could be better!" Mr. Carden-Cox rubbed his hands jubilantly; and breakfast had to wait, growing cold, while he dispatched a messenger to secure the launch. That settled, he gave sundry orders as to provisions, and wrote a note to the Grange, commanding the presence of "Nigel and all three girls" at an appointed hour. If Mr. and Mrs. Browning would honour him with their company, so much the better. Meanwhile he desired to see Nigel.

"Hurrah!" Daisy cried when the note was read aloud; the Grange breakfast being still in process of consumption. Mr. Carden-Cox was on principle an early man.

Nigel started off at once for Mr. Carden-Cox' house, and found that gentleman in a fluster of nervous excitement.

"You see, there was no time to lose," he said, button-holing the young man with agitated fingers. "Another such day is not to be expected. It's an effort to one of my years; but I dare say I shall not be the worse. I shall put off all responsibility on you. Of course you and the girls will come—eh?—yes, I thought so. Mr. and Mrs. Browning, if they can—well, you'll see nearer the time. We don't start till a quarter to twelve. Must allow some time for preparations. I thought we would take our lunch soon after twelve, before getting to the prettiest part of the river; and then have early afternoon tea, coming down again. Mind everybody takes wraps. It's warm—marvellous for

November; but the river air is apt to be chilly. Of course we shall be in before dark. How is your father to-day? Seen Duncan yet? No, I supposed not. He never hurries himself. I'm asking Duncan, by the bye, but of course he'll not come. And the Elveys."

Nigel's face lighted up.

"Yes, I knew you'd like that. Great chums of yours. I don't dislike young Elvey; and Ethel is a sensible sort of girl. I sent a note early, and promised to send for an answer. You wouldn't mind being my messenger, perhaps?"

Mind it! Nigel was delighted. He went at railway speed down the hill towards Church Square, now and then exchanging a nod and smile with some old acquaintance, rich or poor. Passing the short posts which admitted foot-passengers into the square, he encountered a young man, half a head shorter than himself, slim and compact, clerical in attire, with a soft wide-awake crushed low over the forehead, a thin hatchet face, and sharp features. Fast as Nigel walked, the other walked faster still.

"Hallo, Nigel!"

"Hallo, Malcolm!"

That was their British greeting after a year's separation. They were great friends, none the less; though not from similarity.

"Coming?" asked Nigel.

"Where?"

"Steam-launch?"

"Haven't heard a word of it."

"Mr. Carden-Cox. Excursion up the river for lunch and fun. All of you invited. You *must* come, old fellow." Malcolm Elvey was a business-like individual, and his friends learnt brevity in dealing with him.

"What time?"

"Start at a quarter to twelve, and back before dark."

"I don't mind if I do. Yes, I think I can. I've had a racking headache for two days, and that might rid me of it."

"And the rest of you?"

"I wish you may get my father—no hope, I'm afraid. Ethel, yes—you must insist upon that. She has so little pleasure. Most likely the note is there, not opened. I can't go back with you, but you'll find Ethel."

"Mind you're at the bottom of Mr. Carden-Cox' garden—11.40 sharp!"

"All right. I'll come: if nothing prevents."

Nigel went on to the Rectory, and after a moment's hesitation entered by the front door without ringing, as of old. Why not?

Nobody was in the hall; so he went to the dining-room, and found nobody there either. Ethel's work-basket stood open on the table, and a pair of socks with big holes lay beside it, while the little silver thimble had dropped to the floor. Nigel lifted and placed it on the table, then he walked to the rug, and saw upon the mantelpiece a note, addressed to "Miss Elvey," in Mr. Carden-Cox' handwriting. But the note had not been opened.

"What a shame! It ought to have been given to her." Nigel did not realize that the two young Rectory maids, having all the work of the house on their hands, were glad to spare themselves needless runs up and down stairs; indeed, they had instructions so to do. At the Grange maids were plentiful, with scarcely enough work to keep them out of mischief.

Ethel had been up-stairs when the note came, so the cook laid it on the mantelpiece, which was right; but she forgot to tell Ethel that it was urgent, and that an answer would be called for, which was not right.

"I wonder if she will come!" thought Nigel.

He went to the bookcase and stood there, gazing. A good many aged volumes of sermons, bound in venerable calf, helped to fill the shelves. No doubt their continued existence was owing mainly to their calf attire; since nobody ever read them. Also many modern specimens of boys' books could be seen, in coats of faded red or blue. Nigel knew these well. He had been a book-devourer in boyhood, and had borrowed every readable volume from his friends.

Ethel did not appear, and he pulled out one or two, smiling at the tremendous boyish adventures depicted in the illustrations, and handling them kindly as old friends.

Then a plain black volume, pushed half in among the rest, fell to the ground; and a sheet of paper fluttered out. Ethel's handwriting! The heading was "Extracts," and Nigel read what followed without compunction.

I.

"There is something more awful in happiness than in sorrow, the latter being earthly and finite, the former composed of the substance and texture of Eternity, so that spirits still embodied may well tremble at it." [1]

II.

"The great cure to be wrought in us is the cure of self-will, that we may learn self-resignation; and all God's various dealings with us have this one end in view." [2]

III.

"Unloving words are meant to make us gentle, and delays teach patience, and care teaches faith, and press of business makes us look out for minutes to give to God, and disappointment is a special messenger to summon our thoughts to heaven." [3]

IV.

"To strive each day to do the wonted service more perfectly; to infuse and maintain in every detail a purer motive; to master each impulse, and bring each thought under a holier discipline; to be blameless in

[1] N. Hawthorne.   [2] R. Suckling.   [3] E. M. Sewell.

word; to sacrifice self, as an habitual law, in each sudden call to action; to take more and more secretly the lowest place; to move amid constant distractions, and above them, undisturbedly; to be content to do nothing that attracts notice, but to do it always for the greater glory of God." [1]

v.

"Go forth then with boldness to suffer, as your Lord has suffered before you; endeavour to embrace with calmness, and even with joyfulness, the pain or the sorrow which He brings you, and which is but doubled by the lingering will, the timid withdrawal." [2]

This was all; but at the close was written in small letters: "Ethel: November: Sunday evening."

"Why, Nigel, how do you do? I wasn't told that you were here."

Nigel woke up from abstraction, and shook hands. "This is yours," he said. "I found it, and—read the sentences. Do you mind?"

Ethel coloured faintly. "Oh, I could not think where it was gone. I was reading *Voices of Comfort* to mother, and I had a fancy afterwards to copy out those few pieces. How stupid of me to leave it about!"

She held out her hand, and Nigel said, "I suppose I mustn't ask to keep the paper."

"Why—you don't want it?"

[1] T. T. Carter.   [2] Skeffington.

" Yes."

" I don't mind, of course—only—"

" Then I may ? I'll make another copy for you."

" I don't really need it—only—it was just a fancy, you know."

" Yes. Were you feeling particularly cheerful on Sunday evening ? "

Ethel looked up, smiling.   " Now, why must you ask that ? "

" I should like to know. I don't trace the connection between all the extracts."

" Perhaps I'll tell you some day. Not this morning. I have not time."

" And I am taking up your time. But I don't seem to have seen anything of you yet."

" No. And I didn't mean—only it would be a long talk to go into those extracts. And I have everything to see to. But I don't mind saying—no, I wasn't *very* cheerful on Sunday evening. I wanted to go to church, and I couldn't be spared. Mother was poorly, and everything seemed awry, and I found myself on the edge of grumbles. So I looked out something to do me good."

" Perhaps it will do me good too. Ethel, your mother will spare you to-day."

" What for ? "

He handed her Mr. Carden-Cox' note. Ethel read it, with a flash of delight. " O that would be nice ! that would be delightful ! " Then a shade of doubt crept over the blue eyes. " But I am afraid I can't."

"But you must—you must indeed," urged Nigel, almost in despair. "We shall not have another day like this all the winter. Mrs. Elvey will say you must."

"No; she will say I may if I like. That makes all the difference."

"Your father—"

"He is gone out, and he. won't be back till one o'clock. It doesn't matter. Even if he said I might, I don't think I could feel I ought."

"But if things could be arranged somehow—if it is only possible! Do just try—for my sake, won't you? Tell Mrs. Elvey that I want it, and remind her how long I have been away. Do see if it can't be done."

"I'll speak to my mother," Ethel said, and vanished. Nigel waited with the best patience he could muster, till she came quickly in, her step so light and her face so sunny, that he said joyfully, "That's right! I knew you could."

"No, I can't," Ethel answered, smiling. "It won't do."

"But—!" Nigel would have found it hard to say which dismayed him most, the fact that she could not go, or the fact that she should care so little.

"Mother can't spare me. It is one of her bad days, and if I am not here everything is sure to go wrong. You see, it isn't as if there were anybody else. The boys are no good, and I must be at hand."

"It is too bad! I did hope—Malcolm is coming, and he told me you could. Don't you think you might? Malcolm said you must."

G

" Malcolm doesn't understand. I would really, if I could," she said, with so ultra-cheerful an air that Nigel ought to have seen through it. If she had not resolutely kept her back to the light, he must have noticed a suspicious reddening of her eyes, bright though they were. " I would if I could, but I don't see how. Mother would let me go, of course, if I pressed for it; but how can I, when I know I can't be spared ? My father will be out almost all day; and there is a cousin coming down for the night from London—you don't know him, I think. It's the Australian cousin Tom. He's such a nice fellow, and he will be here before lunch. We were with him in the summer, down in Devonshire, staying at my uncle's house, when he was there too. He would feel neglected, I am afraid, with my father out, and all of us away, and my mother poorly. It would not be right. Don't say anything to Malcolm, please; or he will wish he had stayed at home. And he ought not; he ought to go. He works so hard; and a few hours on the river will do him no end of good. And I am quite well, and don't need it."

Nigel had grown silent, as she talked gaily on. " Then I must tell Mr. Carden-Cox only to expect Malcolm," he said at length.

" I'm afraid so. It is tiresome "—(" Only tiresome ! Is that all ? " thought Nigel)—" very tiresome that I can't go; but things *will* sometimes decline to fit in. They seem to 'go perwerse,' as old nurse used to say. I hope you will all enjoy yourselves immensely. You

must tell me about it afterwards." Ethel spoke fast,
smiling all the while.

"I hope you will too—at home," Nigel said with a
great effort. He did not hope anything of the kind,
really. This "Australian cousin Tom," who was "such
a nice fellow," weighed upon him like an incubus.

"I'm sure to do that. One always can enjoy oneself,
one way or another," said Ethel merrily. "And as I
shall not have the refreshment of the river, I shall have
the refreshment of Tom's talk. He's full of ideas, and
he has some fun in him too. I wish you and he could
meet, but he only stays one night. By and by I hope
he will pay us a long visit. Must you go? Well, please
don't say a word to Malcolm to spoil his day. He
doesn't know about Tom arriving before lunch. Mother
only told me just now that she had heard it. We didn't
expect Tom till late; but you see that makes a difference. I couldn't possibly be away—could I?"

"No; I see," assented Nigel.

"You'll come in again some day soon, I dare say, for
a proper reasonable call. You know how glad we all
are to see you always."

Nigel did not care about "we all." He wanted Ethel
individually to be glad. But he only said "good-bye"
seriously, and went.

Ethel watched him through the window, till he was
out of sight, smiling still. Then she turned to the
table and took up her work, but had to put it down
again, for three or four large tears *would* have their

way at last, and everything was deluged in a watery mist.

"How silly! O I wish I could go! But I know I am right. It would have been such a delight—the river and Nigel and all! There, I mustn't let myself think. Mother mustn't guess how I mind. I'm so glad Nigel didn't see. It would have spoilt his day, if he had thought me much disappointed, and now they will all be as merry as kittens."

She made another attempt at the sock, and tried to break into a song; but the sound which came was more like a sob, and two more big tears welled up.

"This won't do. I don't mean to be a goose."

She stood up, and pressed both hands hard over her face, as if determined to squeeze back the obtruders. "O how I wish I didn't so desperately love my own way. There's nothing in the world I should like so much—such a lovely day, and all of them there, and— And only poor good-natured old Tom at home, instead! Yes, of course he has some fun in him, but such slow fun! Did Nigel mind very much? I hope not—I don't want his pleasure to be spoilt—and yet I shouldn't like him not to care at all. But I suppose he did, a little. He seemed to want me to go; and when he looks so preternaturally grave it always means that he is vexed or worried. I'm glad he has turned out like this—so manly and strong. One used to feel half sorry for him, even while one liked him so much; but now there is nothing of that sort. I think he will be a man to be leant upon. O if I could have been with them to-day!

"There now—I'm going in for discontent again. If it had been right for me, I should have seen it all clear about going. And as it isn't, I have to be happy without. I suppose this is part of 'the great cure'—'the cure of self-will'—and perhaps this particular disappointment is a 'special messenger.' I wonder if it is. After all, no disappointment can be too small to come from God; and it doesn't feel small to me. And He knows that, because He is my Father. But I don't mean to be dull now, and mopish. There's no need. I wonder what made Nigel want those extracts to keep. So curious of him; but I couldn't well say no. I think I'll go out and feed the chickens the first thing. It's easier to manage oneself out in the open air. And then I have any amount to get through before Tom comes, with his endless talk about Australia. The sock shall wait," concluded Ethel cheerily. If her eyes were still moist, she left the room singing.

CHAPTER VIII.

FIRE AND WATER.

"Willows whiten, aspens quiver,
   Little breezes dusk and shiver
   Thro' the wave that runs for ever
   By the island and the river."—TENNYSON.

"Wherein I spake of most disastrous chances,
   Of moving accidents by flood and field,
   Of hair-breadth 'scapes."—SHAKSPEARE.

"You don't mean to say you are going in a washing summer-dress! Fulvie! And this—November!" exclaimed Daisy, with rounded eyes.

"It is the prettiest dress I have." Fulvia spoke composedly, looking at herself in the pier-glass. The colour of her costume, dark navy-blue, with portions of a light shade, was suitable for any season; and the material, though really a washing fabric, did not look like it. Fulvia knew this to be a becoming dress. It had been made in particularly graceful style by a London dressmaker, and fitted beautifully, showing her figure to the best advantage; while the colour harmonized well with her reddish hair. Several people had assured her that in this dress she looked "quite handsome."

Some impulse came over her to don it, when making ready for the boat-trip; she could hardly have told why. Of course the real wish was a desire to look well in Nigel's eyes, and of course this was the last admission she would have made even to herself. But she obeyed the impulse. Then Daisy came in, and remonstrated.

" Nobody would take it for a summer dress, and I like the coolness. It is so warm this morning—quite oppressive. I feel as if I could hardly breathe. Besides, I don't mind if this gets splashed. My nice serge might be spoilt."

" Why don't you put on your old brown thing ? Mr. Carden-Cox wouldn't care."

" I detest myself in that brown. It makes me hideous."

" Well, what matter ? Nobody would mind. There'll be nobody to see, who signifies. Only Nigel and us, and a few others."

" I should mind. I like to look respectable."

" You'll take cold."

" As if I ever did ! Besides, I have plenty underneath the dress to keep me warm."

" Then you'll wear your fur cloak, I suppose."

" No ; I shall take the cloak, but I couldn't endure the weight of it all day. I mean to wear this," as she lifted a "half season" jacket of thin cloth, which was tailor-made and fitted like a glove.

"I think you are crazy," declared Daisy. "Why, Anice and I are going in serge dresses, and our thickest winter jackets."

"Quite right to be prudent. Anice can't take too many warm wraps."

She had to undergo another ordeal of criticism downstairs on her lack of wisdom, but it was too late then to change, even had she been willing, and they were speedily off.

Fulvia was the prominent person in the boat that day. Mr. Carden-Cox being host, his niece fell naturally into the position more or less of hostess. Mr. Carden-Cox might make a favourite of Daisy, but he paid due honour to the eldest girl, and he never failed to acknowledge the family tie between himself and her. She was indeed almost the sole relative left to him.

Mr. and Mrs. Browning were not present. Mr. Browning proved unpersuadable; and as a matter of course Mrs. Browning stayed at home with him. Dr. Duncan failed to accompany his genial wife, and his pretty fifteen-years-old daughter, Annibel, Daisy's great chum. The particular friend of Anice, Rose Bramble, and Rose's brother, Baldwyn, were of the party. Fulvia had no great chums, or particular friends. She always said she could not find anybody who suited her.

Malcolm Elvey appeared at the last moment, racing

at headlong speed down the garden, just when all hope
of him was given up, and Mr. Carden-Cox had actually
given the word of command to cast off. Of course
they held on a few instants longer. The garden ended
in a steep wall, which was level with the path on one
side, went sheer down into deep water on the other
side, and was broken by the flight of steps and small
boat-house. A narrow space divided the steam-launch
from the wall, and Malcolm sprang lightly across. He
had been an agile school-boy not long ago.

"Just in time!" Nigel said.

"I couldn't get here sooner. Impossible," panted
Malcolm.

Some of the party were in high spirits; not all.
Baldwyn Bramble, an odd plain young man, who went
in for being witty, made jokes without end, for the
benefit of the girls. He rather admired Anice, counting
her "awfully pretty, you know!" but found Daisy's
retorts sometimes too sharp to be agreeable. Malcolm
threw off the cares of Parish work, and entered with
zest into all that went on, while never uttering a
word which might jar on the most sensitive ears, as
inconsistent with his position. Before luncheon, through
luncheon, and after luncheon, as they still steamed up
the river, silence had no chance of reigning for the
shortest space, and the pretty banks rang with bursts
of laughter.

Nigel could not get into the full swing of fun.
Though joining sufficiently to prevent remark, he was

unable to shake off the recollection of Ethel at home gaily talking to the "Australian cousin Tom," and pleased to be there rather than on the river. If only he had seen her a little grieved and disappointed, he could have borne her absence better. As it was, he felt sadly that he was not making way with Ethel. Things were different from what they once had been. The old frankness and freedom, the complete trust and understanding between them, seemed to be lacking. He loved Ethel more than ever, but he could not at all tell how much she cared for him.

She did care for him, of course, in a measure. "We all," as she had told him, were always ready to give him a welcome; but Nigel craved far more than this.

Ethel had grown older now, and so had he. Perhaps she wished him to feel that things were and must be a little different, that the boy-and-girl friendship had to be transposed into something more calm and distant. He wanted it transposed himself, but by no means into something more distant.

And here was Tom—a nice fellow, full of fun and full of talk! Ethel had plainly seen a good deal of him; and who could tell what manner of impression he had made upon her? How bright she had looked at the very thought of seeing Tom a few hours earlier than had been expected! and how little she had cared about losing the boat excursion, with himself!

Nigel had seldom felt less full of fun and talk than this afternoon. He had great difficulty in keeping up

to the mark at all. Ethel was never out of his mind.
He managed pretty well at lunch, and for a while after;
but presently he left other folks alone, standing to gaze
at the wooded heights, in apparent admiration of their
beauty, while he was really looking in imagination at
the Rectory drawing-room, hearing Tom's amusing conversation, and seeing Ethel's bright eyes smiling a ready
response. If somebody had asked him suddenly whether
his eyes were fixed upon turf or trees, he could not have
told without fresh observation; but of course nobody
thought of asking.

Fulvia alone saw all this, noted every turn of expression, and was aware of his struggle against what Ethel
would have called " preternatural gravity." Fulvia was
not fully herself to-day. She had not yet recovered
from that tearful night-watch, and the "rainy season"
lasted still, fitfully; though no traces of tears were
visible, beyond a general softening of the face. Hope
aided in the softening. She saw Nigel's gravity, but
she did not ascribe it to Ethel. He had taken Ethel's
absence so quietly, hardly uttering a word of regret.
No; it was not Ethel. He was only anxious about his
father; good affectionate son that he always had been;
and he could not shake off the weight.

Nigel was undoubtedly a good son, an affectionate
son; and he did feel disturbed about his father's
possible condition. Mr. Carden-Cox' warning had been
strong enough to cause uneasiness. But the load upon
him to-day arose from another cause; the real pain

unable to shake off the recollection of Ethel at home gaily talking to the "Australian cousin Tom," and pleased to be there rather than on the river. If only he had seen her a little grieved and disappointed, he could have borne her absence better. As it was, he felt sadly that he was not making way with Ethel. Things were different from what they once had been. The old frankness and freedom, the complete trust and understanding between them, seemed to be lacking. He loved Ethel more than ever, but he could not at all tell how much she cared for him.

She did care for him, of course, in a measure. "We all," as she had told him, were always ready to give him a welcome; but Nigel craved far more than this.

Ethel had grown older now, and so had he. Perhaps she wished him to feel that things were and must be a little different, that the boy-and-girl friendship had to be transposed into something more calm and distant. He wanted it transposed himself, but by no means into something more distant.

And here was Tom—a nice fellow, full of fun and full of talk! Ethel had plainly seen a good deal of him; and who could tell what manner of impression he had made upon her? How bright she had looked at the very thought of seeing Tom a few hours earlier than had been expected! and how little she had cared about losing the boat excursion, with himself!

Nigel had seldom felt less full of fun and talk than this afternoon. He had great difficulty in keeping up

to the mark at all. Ethel was never out of his mind. He managed pretty well at lunch, and for a while after; but presently he left other folks alone, standing to gaze at the wooded heights, in apparent admiration of their beauty, while he was really looking in imagination at the Rectory drawing-room, hearing Tom's amusing conversation, and seeing Ethel's bright eyes smiling a ready response. If somebody had asked him suddenly whether his eyes were fixed upon turf or trees, he could not have told without fresh observation; but of course nobody thought of asking.

Fulvia alone saw all this, noted every turn of expression, and was aware of his struggle against what Ethel would have called " preternatural gravity." Fulvia was not fully herself to-day. She had not yet recovered from that tearful night-watch, and the "rainy season" lasted still, fitfully; though no traces of tears were visible, beyond a general softening of the face. Hope aided in the softening. She saw Nigel's gravity, but she did not ascribe it to Ethel. He had taken Ethel's absence so quietly, hardly uttering a word of regret. No; it was not Ethel. He was only anxious about his father; good affectionate son that he always had been; and he could not shake off the weight.

Nigel was undoubtedly a good son, an affectionate son; and he did feel disturbed about his father's possible condition. Mr. Carden-Cox' warning had been strong enough to cause uneasiness. But the load upon him to-day arose from another cause; the real pain

unable to shake off the recollection of Ethel at home gaily talking to the "Australian cousin Tom," and pleased to be there rather than on the river. If only he had seen her a little grieved and disappointed, he could have borne her absence better. As it was, he felt sadly that he was not making way with Ethel. Things were different from what they once had been. The old frankness and freedom, the complete trust and understanding between them, seemed to be lacking. He loved Ethel more than ever, but he could not at all tell how much she cared for him.

She did care for him, of course, in a measure. "We all," as she had told him, were always ready to give him a welcome; but Nigel craved far more than this.

Ethel had grown older now, and so had he. Perhaps she wished him to feel that things were and must be a little different, that the boy-and-girl friendship had to be transposed into something more calm and distant. He wanted it transposed himself, but by no means into something more distant.

And here was Tom—a nice fellow, full of fun and full of talk! Ethel had plainly seen a good deal of him; and who could tell what manner of impression he had made upon her? How bright she had looked at the very thought of seeing Tom a few hours earlier than had been expected! and how little she had cared about losing the boat excursion, with himself!

Nigel had seldom felt less full of fun and talk than this afternoon. He had great difficulty in keeping up

to the mark at all. Ethel was never out of his mind. He managed pretty well at lunch, and for a while after; but presently he left other folks alone, standing to gaze at the wooded heights, in apparent admiration of their beauty, while he was really looking in imagination at the Rectory drawing-room, hearing Tom's amusing conversation, and seeing Ethel's bright eyes smiling a ready response. If somebody had asked him suddenly whether his eyes were fixed upon turf or trees, he could not have told without fresh observation; but of course nobody thought of asking.

Fulvia alone saw all this, noted every turn of expression, and was aware of his struggle against what Ethel would have called " preternatural gravity." Fulvia was not fully herself to-day. She had not yet recovered from that tearful night-watch, and the "rainy season" lasted still, fitfully; though no traces of tears were visible, beyond a general softening of the face. Hope aided in the softening. She saw Nigel's gravity, but she did not ascribe it to Ethel. He had taken Ethel's absence so quietly, hardly uttering a word of regret. No; it was not Ethel. He was only anxious about his father; good affectionate son that he always had been; and he could not shake off the weight.

Nigel was undoubtedly a good son, an affectionate son; and he did feel disturbed about his father's possible condition. Mr. Carden-Cox' warning had been strong enough to cause uneasiness. But the load upon him to-day arose from another cause; the real pain

much and so little. A few more words would have
made all the difference. She might have told how
Ethel, while talking truly "a good deal" about this
cousin, had laughed at his slowness, at his ponderous
jokes, at his love of bestowing information upon everybody. Not unkindly; for Ethel never laughed unkindly
at any one; but it was in a way which effectually
prevented any notion of a possible attachment between
the two. Fulvia could distinctly recall how the Elvey
boys had voted Tom "a bore"; and how Ethel had
said, "Poor fellow! don't be too hard on him. He
does his best to be agreeable."

But Fulvia said no more. Even while she despised
herself for it, she was silent; trying to believe that
her silence couid make no real difference. She was
at liberty to jest, if she liked. Nigel might find out
when he chose exactly how matters really stood.
Besides, who could tell what might happen? Many
a girl ends by marrying the man whom at first she
criticized. If Nigel cared, he had but to ask.

Nigel's next remark was in a different tone. "I
must try to bring about that interview between my
father and Jamie in a day or two." Dr. Duncan
was commonly known at the Grange as "Jamie" or
"Cousin Jamie."

"Have you said anything to padre yet?"

"Yes; a little. I fancy he will give way."

"You don't suppose him to be really ill, do you?
Not seriously?"

"One can't tell. Don't mention this again, but I saw Duncan yesterday afternoon, and pressed for an opinion. He confessed he had seen for some time that my father was very much out of health, and he thought the matter ought not to be left. He would not say anything more definite."

"And that is why you are so grave to-day?" Fulvia asked gently, even wistfully.

The answer was evasive. "One can't help being uneasy. Jamie is not a man to look on the dismal side without some reason. Things may be better than he expects; but I don't understand my father's state, mental or bodily. He seems to take depressed views all round. Did you know that he objected to Oxford for me?"

"No!"

"Doesn't like the expense."

"But, Nigel—why, what absurdity! As if that had not been settled years ago!"

"He says he cannot afford it. Don't tell the girls."

"No"—with a glow of pleasure at his confidence. "But what can padre mean?"

"That is all he says—too much expense—and the Bar too uncertain. He talks of an appointment at the Bank."

"Newton Bury Bank! Nonsense! A clerk on a three-legged stool, under Mr. Bramble!"

"He says it might lead to partnership and wealth."

"Wealth! What does that matter? You will have

H

enough of your own. Besides, the Bar would lead to
wealth too, if you were successful; and you would be
successful. I know you would."

"Not so soon."

"But that is the very thing that does not matter,
when you have plenty to live upon meantime. You
can afford to wait. Padre has not to provide for a
dozen boys. You, the only son, surely ought to be
free to choose. It must be a fit of the dumps. Don't
let him decide on anything in a hurry. Cannot you
talk matters over with uncle Arthur? Anyhow, do
keep padre from acting till he gets over this mood.
Too much expense! I never heard anything so absurd
in my life. Did he explain what he meant?"

"He spoke of 'embarrassments.'"

"To be sure, he always is talking now of expenses,
but still— Nigel!" as a thought struck her, "is it
because I am coming of age? That will make no
difference. Of course he will go on having just the
same, so long as I live at the Grange. Not right!
Yes, it is right. Any other plan would not be right.
I can assure you I will only stay on those terms. I
should have told him long ago, only I have never liked
to assume that it would not be so as a matter of course.
But I'll take care to tell him now."

Nigel muttered something about "Generous!"

"It is not generosity. It is the merest common
justice. Do you think he has been worrying about
that? You could not give up college—it would be

too terrible a disappointment, when your mind has been
set on it all these years. And the Bar! Why, uncle
Arthur always declares you are just made for a special
pleader. You don't fritter yourself away in energetic talk
about nothing, but when anything *does* stir you, there's
no mistake about it. Fancy coming down from that
to a country bank! Perhaps padre will be brighter
after seeing Dr. Duncan. We must wait a few days;
and I'll manage to have a talk with him."

It was positive gladness to Fulvia to learn this
fresh cause for his depression. Anything, rather than
Ethel!

Nigel presently strolled away again, and she saw him
laughing with Malcolm, more heartily than since they
had started. The joke, whatever it was, seemed in-
fectious; and the merriment became general. Fulvia
rose and moved to a seat nearer, where she could hear
what went on.

Baldwin Bramble had been smoking a cigar, and had
tossed away the still lighted end—overboard he believed,
but it had fallen short, dropping on the deck almost
under the chair which Fulvia now took. Nobody saw
it fall there except Daisy, and Daisy forgot the fact in
half a second. The red end smouldered still, and when
Fulvia sat down, her dress rested upon it. Had she
worn a woollen fabric no harm might have resulted;
but a washing summer fabric is a different matter.

Fulvia noted the strong scent, and rather wished
that Mr. Bramble could have existed without his

favourite solace for a few hours; but she was unconscious of her peril.

Mr. Bramble presently walked to the further end of
the launch, and Malcolm disappeared behind the funnel.
Nigel was talking to Mrs. Duncan, Annibel and Daisy,
beyond hearing. Only Anice and Rose remained near
where Fulvia sat. Fulvia had lost the joke after all.

"What were you laughing at just now?" she asked.

"Oh, just something Mr. Elvey said," Rose answered.
"What was it, Anice? I couldn't quite understand,
only everybody laughed, and so—"

"And so you did too!" Fulvia spoke with a touch
of disdain. She counted Rose an inane specimen of
giggling young ladyhood.

"Well, of course, I couldn't keep out of it," explained
Rose. "It looks so stupid to sit with a solemn face
when other people are laughing."

"Why didn't you ask?"

"Oh!—ask for a joke to be explained! That is
more stupid still. Baldwin always says a joke never
bears being repeated. Besides, one looks so silly, not
to understand at once."

"I wonder whether 'to be' or 'to look' is the worst,"
murmured Fulvia.

Rose's density was proof against this, or she might
have been offended. "Anice can tell you," she said.

No, Anice could not. Anice, like Rose, had laughed
because others laughed, not because she divined the
joke. Fulvia shrugged her shoulders, and was mute.

Some seconds, or some two or three minutes might have passed—Fulvia could not afterward recall which, —when she became conscious of a peculiar odour, not only the scent of the cigar but a distinct smell of burning. Then she was vaguely aware of a blue smoke. She had gone back in thought to Nigel's future, and was cogitating deeply, so deeply that though physical consciousness was awake, her mind did not at once respond.

An impulse to escape from the girls' chatter came over her, and she stood up, moving a few steps away from her sheltered seat, into the breeze; the very worst thing she could have done, had she only known it.

Strange, this idea of Mr. Browning's about Nigel! Could his affairs really be under serious embarrassment? If it were so— Well, in any case Fulvia would have ample means of her own. A sense of joy shot through her, at the thought of becoming a family benefactor. Would Nigel be willing? Yes, surely—if he still viewed her as sister! What more natural? Besides, he need not know. She would find out from "padre" the real state of affairs, and would insist upon putting everything straight. She had, or at least in a few weeks she would have, both the power and the right. Nobody then might say her nay, if she chose to give away any part of her possessions. Nothing should or must stand in the way of Nigel's going to college. She knew how he was bent upon it. Of course—that was why he looked so sad. Not Ethel; only this. So what she had said about Ethel did not matter. This was the real trouble; and how delightful to think that her hand might remove it!

"Fulvie! Fulvie!! O Fulvie!—your dress is on fire!! Oh!!"

Anice's shriek reached slowly her absorbed mind, at first bringing bewilderment. Then she was aware of smoke, smell, heat, and she sprang forward to get some woollen wrap; but the movement brought her yet more fully into the fresh breeze. In the tenth of a second the fanned flame ran greedily up her skirt, and was swept round her, licking with fierce touch the bare skin of her hand, and rising to scorch her face.

Fulvia's scream was agonizing. She had been always known as a girl of much presence of mind, by no means given to crying out; but she was taken by surprise, and utterly unnerved. Anice and Rose fled at once, in fear for themselves, calling to others to help. Fulvia never forgot that moment, the brief yet prolonged horror, the anguish of isolation. It was as if everybody had forsaken her; none would dare to approach; and she was left face to face with awful peril, face to face with death.

"Nigel!" was the one word which broke from her in hoarse appeal. She could not think, could not recall what ought to be done. She could only rush forward, throwing out her hands in agony. And then, instantly, she saw Nigel's face close at hand, so calm and strong that it brought hope.

Shouts and cries were sounding. " A shawl ! a rug !
I say—throw her down ! Have her flat !" Malcolm
was flying along the deck. But Nigel had reached her
before the first hoarse shriek of his name came to an
end ; and he did not hesitate. As he sprang forward,
he grasped Fulvia firmly, dragged her to the side of the
vessel, and with one clear leap went over, Fulvia in his
arms. There was a flash of red flame, followed by a
heavy splash, and the two sank out of sight.

CHAPTER IX.

WHISPERINGS.

"For ebbing resolution ne'er returns,
But falls still further from its former shore."—HORNE.

"STOP! Stop! Put her about! Stop, I say!" roared Mr. Carden-Cox, in a state of desperation which rendered him almost incapable of speech. He strode wildly about, while Anice and Rose continued to shriek, Daisy seemed turned to stone, and Malcolm flung off his coat.

But the two heads almost instantly rose, and Nigel shouted, "All right."

"I'm coming," cried Malcolm.

"No, no—only a rope!"

"A rope—a rope—hoy!—hey!—a rope, I say!—put her about—stop—a rope!" spluttered Mr. Carden-Cox, seizing Malcolm's arm, and holding on like a vice, not in the least aware of what he did.

"I say! do let me go," expostulated Malcolm, "she'll be too much for him." In response to which Mr. Carden-Cox tightened his grasp, reiterating—

"A rope! a rope!—hoy!—a rope, I say! Put her about! Stop!"

The engines had been at once reversed, but the boat was going up stream, and some seconds had to elapse before actual movement in the opposite direction could begin. The current was pretty strong, carrying Nigel and his charge downward, despite his best efforts. Nigel was not a little impeded by his clothes. He had not waited even to throw off his coat; and Fulvia hung as a dead weight, seeming to be stunned by the double shock.

Then sense returned, and in a moment she was clinging to him with a convulsive grasp which threatened to sink them both.

"Let go, Fulvia!" He spoke in a sharp clear voice. "Don't hold me! I'll take care of you."

Fulvia gasped for breath. They were almost under water; and though for an instant she obeyed, her hands clutched at him wildly again.

"Fulvie dear, you *must not!* Let go! You will drown us both. Keep still, and trust me."

He had done the business now. She clenched her hands together, and left herself to him like a log. That "Fulvie dear" settled the matter; yet the words meant nothing. Nigel hardly even knew what he had said. It was merely the instinctive recurrence at a critical moment to the old childish terms. Fulvia had always been his sister, "every inch as much as Anice or Daisy," he would have said. Nigel had never thought of her in any other light. But Fulvia could not realize this; for she did not think of Nigel as of a brother.

Nigel could keep himself afloat now, and hold up Fulvia, till the boat steamed near, and a rope was flung. The open loop fell upon them, and in another minute both were hauled in, and helped upward.

Fulvia, again scarcely conscious, was laid flat on the deck, streaming with water, her face white, her hair loose in heavy dripping masses. It had been much singed, and part of her skirt was reduced almost to tinder, yet her skin had escaped marvellously. One hand and arm only were scorched to any painful degree. Her first words were a murmured, "It smarts so!" but the next moment she added, "Never mind. I'm not really hurt."

"Thanks to this dear brave boy," Mr. Carden-Cox said huskily. "I declare, I never saw anything finer."

"It was the natural thing to do," Nigel asserted.

A hurried consultation took place. They were more than two hours distant by boat from Newton Bury; the steamer contained no change of clothes; and the minute cabin afforded no facilities for drying. Five minutes lower down the river lay a village, large enough to own a good landing-place and a respectable inn; and Mrs. Duncan counselled a stoppage there. Two or three hours in wet clothes on a November afternoon were not to be thought of.

The suggestion was speedily carried out. Anice,

crying helplessly still, was left on board with the Brambles and Annibel; but Mrs. Duncan and Mr. Carden-Cox, Daisy and Malcolm, accompanied the soaked pair. Fulvia had by this time so far rallied that she insisted on walking from the river-bank to the inn, a matter of two hundred yards; and she even achieved two or three hysterical laughs by the way at her own deplorable appearance. Nigel looked rather white round the lips, as if chilled by his bath; but he seemed to have sprung suddenly into a fit of high spirits, saying the most ridiculous things he could think of, and sending Daisy into convulsions of laughter.

The inn reached, rooms were secured, big fires were ordered, and the sympathies of the portly landlady, Mrs. Brice, were enlisted. The good woman could only hold up her plump hands at first, with dismayed utterances of—"My!" and "I never did!" but orders for hot water and big fires received speedy attention. Mrs. Brice's own clothes would, as Daisy said, have "folded twice round Fulvia, with something to spare." She had, however, a daughter, and a neat brown dress belonging to the latter was speedily produced, not more than three inches too large at the waist. Nigel fared equally well at the hands of the landlady's son; and while these changes of apparel were taking place, Mr. Carden-Cox found consolation in ordering a solid afternoon tea, inclusive of eggs and meat.

"For they'll need to be warmed up after their ducking," he said, as Daisy bounced in. "Everybody will be the better for something hot. Well, child, how is Fulvie?"

"She is getting on—only feels shivery and queer; but I should think a cup of coffee would put her right. Isn't it strange?—a lot of Fulvie's hair is all frizzled up with the fire, and yet her face isn't touched; not even the eyelashes burnt."

"Can't think how on earth the thing happened."

"O it was Mr. Bramble, I know. I saw his cigar-end drop there, when he threw it away; and then I forgot all about it, we were having such a lot of fun. I wish I hadn't!"

Mr. Carden-Cox shook his head mutely. If any one but his favourite Daisy had been speaking, he would have read her a homily on thoughtlessness.

"Yes, I know—it was dreadfully stupid," Daisy said, her eyes filling. "I can't think how I could. But when Mr. Bramble tried to make out that it was a spark from the engine, I had to bite my lips not to speak. Wasn't it horrid of him not to help, but only to stand staring and saying—'Aw!' Of course everybody couldn't jump into the river—needn't, at least—but he might have *wanted* to help. Malcolm was only one second behind Nigel; and he would have been in too, if you hadn't kept him back."

"I keep him back! Tut, tut, child! He didn't go in because it was not necessary."

Daisy's brown eyes opened to their widest extent. "O I say, how unfair! Poor Malcolm! When you tugged at him with all your might and main, and wouldn't let go."

A dim recollection of facts came across Mr. Carden-Cox. "Well, well—it doesn't matter now," he said. "Malcolm would have acted if Nigel had not."

"And Anice and Rose ran away. I think that was so cowardly," said Daisy, with the stern condemnation of sixteen. "If *I* had been near, I would have made Fulvie lie down, and have tried to put out the fire. But the first thing I knew was the screaming, and then I saw the blaze, and Nigel going across with such a leap. And I felt so odd—as if somehow I couldn't stir for just a moment—and then it was all done. Shall I tell Fulvie to come before the tea gets cold?"

Mr. Carden-Cox offered no objection; and outside the door Daisy was met by a subdued—"I say!"

"Nigel, how comical you do look!"

"Narrow as to the shoulders, and baggy as to the waist. Not quite a perfect fit—but I'm glad to be dry again. I say, Daisy—"

"Fulvia's better, and we're all going to have lots of tea, and to be jolly."

"So I hear. We ought to be back on the boat soon. It will get awfully cold on the river for Anice. I say, Daisy—just listen one moment. I want you to do something for me."

"O, what?"

"If I am asked to cut bread or carve meat, will you act the energetic younger sister and do it instead—

before I can rouse myself to the effort? Mr. Carden-
Cox means us to go in for substantials, I hear."

"Yes, of course. But why? What do you mean?
Are you tired?"

"No—only I managed to scorch my hands a little.
Nothing of consequence—I'll see to them by-and-by,
but I don't want a fuss now. It would upset Fulvie—
don't you see?

"O—do show me!"

"No, nonsense—hands off, Daisy!" as she pulled in
vain at his coat-sleeve. "Don't!" and he spoke with
unwonted sharpness, actually catching his breath. Daisy
stared.

"Did I hurt? Was it that?"

"Never mind—it is nothing to signify. I won't have
a word said; only I just want your help, like a good
child, about the cutting and carving. Malcolm knows;
and you and he between you can keep it from Fulvie."

"I'll be sure," Daisy answered, a sound like a gulp
accompanying the words.

"That's right. You've been as plucky as possible,
not giving in. Yes, I saw, of course—didn't you think
I should? It's so much more sensible to take things
cheerfully. What earthly good would it do, if we all
sat down and howled?"

Daisy gave his arm a great squeeze of assent,
delighted to find her efforts appreciated. She did not
know what the squeeze meant to him, and he forbore
even to wince.

Somewhat later, Fulvia sat dreamily in an arm-chair, close to the parlour fender. She could not get warm, despite a roaring fire and a thick shawl. Icy chills chased one another persistently through her frame, even to the extent of chattering teeth; and she was overpowered by weakness. She could not for a moment shake off the remembrance of that terrible tongue of flame wrapping itself round her, followed by the plunge into cold water, the struggle for breath, the deadly fright; then Nigel's face, as it had first come to her in the moment of hopeless horror, and Nigel's voice as it had spoken a minute later—"Fulvie dear!—Fulvie dear!" Memory refused to carry her beyond those two words.

Fulvia made an effort to lift her weighted eyelids, that she might glance towards Nigel. How sunshiny he looked, seated between Daisy and Malcolm, merrily avowing himself "lazy," and letting Daisy cut supplies of bread-and-butter for everybody, himself included! Was he so bright because he had saved *her* life? Anybody might rejoice to save any fellow-creature from a terrible death; but was she no more than "any fellow-creature" to him? He was rather pale still, as if bodily or mentally overwrought; but the eyes sparkled in their gayest style, as he responded to Daisy's chatter. And Ethel was not present. He had not seen Ethel for hours. That look could not mean "Ethel!"

What had made him speak so in the water? "Fulvie

dear " was not his usual style.   As a little boy he had
been addicted to the mode of address, so much as to
be laughed at; but for years she had not heard the
expression.   Could it be that the sudden peril to her
had drawn his deeper feeling to the surface ?

Fulvia hardly shaped these questions into words.
She felt them, rather than said them even to herself,
as she sat by the fire, apart from the rest, silent and
unable to enter into all that went on.   The shock of
that moment's horror was on her still; and her faculties
were benumbed.   She drank some hot tea, but could
not eat; and she was unaware how anxiously others
watched.

Drowsiness presently had her in its grasp; not growing into actual sleep, at least for a while, but slowly
enchaining her as with weights of lead.   The sound of
voices lessened, till she could only hear an occasional
whisper.   There was, as it were, a barricade like a stone
wall between her and the outer world.   Thought went
on dimly within, uncontrollable by any effort of her
own ; and more dimly still she was aware of movements
and utterances on the other side of the wall.   Now
and again a few words were clear.

" I told you so !   It is exhaustion.   She must have
her sleep out, poor girl ! "

Fulvia knew Mrs. Duncan's tones, and could have
smiled to think that she was not asleep, had not the
exertion of a smile been too great.   She was capable
only of passive endurance.

"Ethel—Nigel—my resolution." A voice within the enclosing walls said this.

"O no—no—no!" sighed Fulvia; but the very sigh was internal. Outwardly she seemed to be in a profound sleep; and soon the seeming became reality.

*   *   *   *   *

"Plucky! yes." The words stole in upon Fulvia with a subtle power; and she divined at once of whom they were spoken. "Never should have guessed anything was wrong."

"But Daisy had found it out."

"No, he asked her to cut the loaf at tea—didn't want Fulvia to know. Thoughtful of the lad! She was upset enough already, poor thing. I say, Mrs. Duncan"—Mr. Carden-Cox lowered his voice to almost a whisper—"I say, Mrs. Duncan, what do you think? Anything likely in that quarter?" Fulvia heard a little snap of his fingers. Strange to say, the idea that she ought not to listen never occurred to her. She was hardly out of dreamland yet; and body and mind were so stupefied that movement seemed impossible.

"Nigel and Fulvia! No!"

"Why not?—eh?" with a sound of disappointment.

"Why should they?"

"Why should they like one another? Nothing more natural. Always together from childhood."

"That's the very thing! Intimacy doesn't end as a rule in a real attachment. People get to know each other too well. Half the marriages that take place

I

never would take place, if the husband and wife were better acquainted beforehand. A hazy uncertainty is more favourable to love-making."

" Nonsense ! "

" It's sense, I am afraid. Intimacy is apt to do away with the poetical glamour."

" Poetical rubbish !" in a whisper of high disdain. "I beg your pardon, but really—! The fact is, his father wants this, and I want it. First time Browning and I have ever wished the same thing. Couldn't be anything more suitable, from every point of view."

" Unless from Nigel's own. He will choose for himself, you may be sure! If you had said 'Nigel and Ethel !'"

" Ethel Elvey ! no, no. That won't do. Good girl, and immense favourite of mine, but not a penny will come to her. No—no, that won't do at all."

" Nigel will hardly marry for money."

" Nobody ever does. He may chance to fall in love with the girl who has money."

" I doubt it."

" Well, all I have to say is that Nigel will not marry Ethel Elvey !"

" Nobody can tell yet."

" He will not, my good lady !" Mr. Carden-Cox was always strengthened in his opinion by opposition. " You mark my words ! He may or may not marry Fulvia. He will not marry Ethel."

Fulvia was wide awake now ; stupefied no longer ; her

head burning, her blood coursing wildly. She knew she
ought to speak, but how could she?—how betray that
she had heard so much?

"However," pursued Mr. Carden-Cox, as if dismissing
the subject, "however, I was telling you about Nigel's
hurts."

"Much burnt, you say?"

"Right palm a mass of blisters, chafed by the rope.
Couldn't think what made him sit through tea-time,
doing nothing! Not like Nigel! Daisy wouldn't have
told—little monkey—but he betrayed himself getting
on board. Stumbled and grasped at something, and I
saw his face. I should never have guessed, otherwise.
Anice' wailed, of course; and Daisy was most womanful,
—actually had had the sense to take with her some
rag and linseed oil. She did up the hand as nattily as
could be. There's some stuff in that girl, I do believe.
Hallo!"

For Fulvia sat up, asking, "Is Nigel hurt?"

"My dear, are you just awake?" said Mrs. Duncan,
coming near. "Better for the rest, I hope. You need
not worry yourself about Nigel. He scorched his
hand; that is all. They have gone home in the boat,
and we are to follow in a fly, as soon as you can start.
Would you like to get ready now?"

"The sooner the better! How lazy I have been!"
said Fulvia.

CHAPTER X.

"The languages, especially the dead,
    The sciences, and most of all the abstruse,
    The arts, at least all such as could be said
        To be the most remote from common use."—BYRON.

"VERY pretty," said Ethel, gaping furtively behind one hand, as she gazed upon the open page of Tom Elvey's beloved companion, a neat herbarium of dried flowers and leaves. The cover of the volume was dark brown, the pages were light brown, and most of the gummed-down specimens were of a more or less dirty brown. Tom handled his treasure affectionately, and Ethel viewed each new page with outward politeness and inward wonder. That anybody should care for dead brown leaves, when living green ones were to be had, was a mystery to her.

"Yes, very pretty," she repeated, smothering a second yawn, as Tom waited for appreciation. What would Nigel be doing just then? Ah, coming homeward, of course, for the afternoon was growing old. "At least, I mean that it must have been pretty once," continued truthful Ethel. "What is that on the next page? Edelweiss—is it really? I like the edelweiss. Yes, that does bear drying. How nice!"

"It is a first-rate specimen," said Tom.

"Did you gather it yourself?"

"On the Matterhorn—no, I mean on the Jungfrau. I never put any specimen into this herbarium which I have not procured with my own hands."

"I see—so it becomes a sort of record of your wanderings," said Ethel. "And you really are a mountain-climber."

"Not to any perilous extent. I went for this specimen."

"And turned back as soon as you had got it!"

Tom's "yes" was innocent. He did not understand Ethel's tone.

"Of course I could have bought a specimen; but that would not have been the same thing."

"Like bagging partridges," suggested Ethel, wanting a flash of some sort to relieve the dead level of talk. But though Tom could sometimes originate slow fun, he never could respond to anybody else's fun; and his look of blank inquiry made it needful for her to explain. "I mean, you would only count the partridges which you had shot yourself; not what— But perhaps you don't shoot."

"I have been after kangaroos—once," said Tom.

Ethel gave a private glance towards the clock, taking care that Tom should not see. She was bent upon making this a pleasant visit to him, not letting him see how very much she would have preferred to be somewhere else. Ethel had been trained in habits of true Christian courtesy. She knew how uncomfortable it is to find oneself not welcome anywhere, knew how she would dislike the consciousness for herself; and therefore she would not inflict it on poor Tom. After all, it was not Tom's fault that she could not go in the steam-launch. He had not known that his coming would deprive her of the enjoyment; and even if he had not come, there might still have been insuperable difficulties.

Some girls would have been glum and flat under the circumstances; but Ethel was not. She had a happy way of taking such every-day deprivations as parts of the life planned for her; as opportunities for patience, not as occasions for ill-temper or dolefulness. She did not try to make out to herself that loss was not loss; but she did resolutely insist that the loss should be borne in a cheery spirit. Some people's idea of Resignation is a beautiful woman in sombre clothing, with upturned mournful eyes and streaming tears. But resignation is just as much needed in lesser as in greater troubles; for all come equally from above. I am by no means sure that blue-eyed Ethel Elvey, smiling over the dull herbarium, with a sore pull of disappointment at her heart, would not make a truer picture of Resignation, than the lady with sorrowful looks and streaming tears, popularly accepted as such.

At all events Ethel appeared neither glum nor doleful. She exerted herself to be bright, made Tom tell her all about the one kangaroo hunt which had been a leading event in his existence, and when he came back to the inevitable herbarium she submitted without a sigh to be lectured upon "the Australian flora."

, Tom was quite a botanist in a small way; and he dearly liked to air his knowledge before a good listener. Ethel loved flowers intensely, yet she was no botanist. She made friends of her plants, studied their ways, and was delighted to know how they grew, how they bore flowers, what manner of soil suited them, whether they preferred heat or cold, sunshine or shade. But she detested classifications and Latin names, and would have nought to do with what Lance irreverently termed "Tom's genuses and specieses." She cared not one rap whether a blossom had stamens which adhered to the corolla or sprang from the calyx; whether the anthers opened inwards or outwards; whether the petals were in multiples of twos or of threes. The Elveys were not as a family scientifically inclined, and Ethel's tastes had never been cultivated in that direction. Tom on the other hand delighted in rolling off his tongue this or that lengthy Linnean "—andria," or Natural History "—aceæ"; and Ethel submitted with the utmost sweetness.

Tom was charmed. He thought Ethel one of the most agreeable girls he had ever seen. The ripple of her brown hair, and the sparkle of her blue eyes, fascinated him. No doubt there was a suspicion of fun in that same sparkle; but honest Tom, full of a lumbering self-confidence, never dreamt that anybody could be so insane as to laugh at *him;* and Ethel's fun was never unkind, so it did no harm.

She was immensely improved, Tom thought—"really quite intelligent, and capable of growing into a well-informed young woman, with proper supervision." Who so fitted to give the needed supervision as Tom himself? He began to think that a long visit at the Rectory would be no bad plan. Something had been said about it. Yes, he would accept the invitation; and then he could take Ethel's higher education in hand. Mr. Elvey was a very able man, no doubt, a man indeed of considerable attainments, but "classical—merely classical!" Tom decided pityingly. Ethel would never gain any scientific bias from her father.

So it was full time that Tom should step forward and bestir himself, with perhaps a view to future possibilities. Who could tell what might come of it? Tom was young still, under thirty, and not bad-looking, though of awkward make. He would be a well-to-do man out in Australia one of these days. Even now he could afford to enjoy life, and to indulge himself in an occasional bout of sight-seeing—more correctly, of specimen-hunting.

In due time he would require a wife to look after him, to sew on his buttons, to pour out his tea, to attend generally to his needs. Tom had come to England with the vague idea of finding a wife before he

went back. He began to wonder whether Ethel might
not do. Those dainty little fingers of hers would be
invaluable for arranging dried flowers upon the pages of
his herbariums. Tom's own fingers being thick, and by
no means dainty in action, there was the more need that
he should choose a wife to supply his own deficiencies.

Thus a new thought grew into existence as the
afternoon waned—a short afternoon to Tom, though a
long one to Ethel. But Tom's mental processes were
always slow; and he gave no sign of what was brewing.

Mrs. Elvey made her appearance down-stairs for a
space, and Tom regaled her with sumptuous descriptions
of the eucalyptus. Mrs. Elvey sighed, and said "How
nice!" to everything. By-and-by she vanished, and
again Ethel found it inconveniently difficult to hide
her recurring yawns. Mr. Elvey had a succession of
engagements all day, therefore he could not give any
help; and the boys always fled from Tom, in dread of
Tom's perpetual outpour of "information."

So Ethel had nothing in the way of assistance from
others, and talk began to flag irresistibly. They had
gone through the herbarium from end to end. They
had done any amount of Australian kangaroos and plants.
Ethel had shown Tom everything in the house worth
seeing. She had taken him round the garden for a
stroll, and had proposed "a good ramble," which Tom
to her disappointment had declined. His bodily action
was like his mental action, somewhat slow; and though
he could walk any amount with an object—in search

of a "specimen," for instance—he scorned exercise for the sake of exercise. Ethel loved it, and she thought it would be so much easier to get on out-of-doors than indoors; if only Tom would have consented. Would the afternoon never end? Was Malcolm ever coming back?

A step at last! Ethel sprang up, with a word of excuse, and flew to the front door.

No, not Malcolm, but her father! Mr. Elvey looked down with a stirred expression, and said, "Well—" a long breath following. "Have you heard?"

"No, what? O father—not an accident!"

"Nothing serious, though it might have been. Why, Ethel—child—I did not mean to frighten you. They are all right—safe at home—and Malcolm will be here presently. Fulvia's dress caught fire, and she would have been badly burnt, but for Nigel. Yes, Nigel! He was splendidly prompt—caught Fulvia in his arms, and went straight over into the river. Mr. Carden-Cox says it was the finest thing he ever saw. Just like Nigel, eh? Capital fellow, isn't he?"

The light of pride and joy shining through Ethel's eyes, even while they brimmed with tears, was a pleasant sight. "Not hurt?" she managed to say.

"Fulvia hardly at all, only shaken and scorched. Nigel's right hand has suffered a good deal. Duncan says he will have to wear a sling for some days. Nobody knew a word about it for ever so long: he didn't want to distress Fulvia. I'm not sure that he did not show greater pluck there than in saving her. Difference of doing a thing when one is under excitement, and when one is cool, you know. But he's a hero both ways—brave boy! We shall have to make much of him after this. Why, child!—"

Ethel's face dropped against the shoulder of his greatcoat, and there was the sound of a sob.

"Father—if he had been—"

"Had been badly hurt? But he was not, nor she either—thank God! Come, cheer up."

He patted her arm, and Ethel clung to him more closely. Somebody was passing through the garden, and Mr. Elvey smiled but said nothing till the somebody came close; then only, "It is about you! Never mind. She'll be herself in half a minute."

"I thought I would call, for fear of any exaggerated story getting round," said Nigel, his voice brighter than usual, as he stood with his arm in a sling, looking at Ethel. She lifted a pair of wet cheeks and glazed eyes.

"I'm going in to see Tom. You can reassure her yourself," cheerily observed Mr. Elvey, who, being the most innocent of men, never suspected anybody of growing up or wishing to marry. Ethel and Nigel were "the children" to him still. But as he turned away his grasp fell upon the young man's shoulder, and "God bless you!" went with it.

"I'm not the worse, really. It is nothing—not worth your caring about," Nigel said to Ethel, though the fact

of her so caring was worth a great deal to him. "Come
here for a minute—won't you?" and he opened the
dining-room door. "It was a shock, I dare say, to
hear about Fulvia. Things might have been serious,
if we had not had the river so near; but I don't think
she will suffer, after a good night's rest."

"Yes—Fulvia. O yes," murmured Ethel, trying to
recover herself. "Yes—but it must have been such
danger—"

"Would have been, without the river—for Fulvia, I
mean. Not for me. In the water—no. I am a good
swimmer. Even if she had pulled me under, there
were plenty at hand to help. Malcolm was wild for
a bath."

"I wish I had been there."

"It's a good thing you were not. That was the first
moment I could be glad we had left you at home. I
shouldn't have liked you to be looking on. You might
not have been so discreet as Anice and her friend."

"Why, what did they do?"

"The better part of valour! Most wise, others being
at hand to help. I'm not sure that you would have
been sensible enough to run away."

"Nobody can tell till the moment comes; I think I
should have seen that you were hurt."

"Yes—you always see everything. But one didn't
want Fulvia to be more upset than she was. How
have you got on at home—with—"

"O, very well. We've done lots of botany."

Ethel's face lighted up with fun, and Nigel thought it was with a recollection of enjoyment. He suddenly remembered Tom Elvey, and Fulvia's words about Tom.

Then, before the two could arrive at an understanding Lance dashed in, shouting a string of inquiries about the day's adventure; and the little *tête-à-tête* was over.

CHAPTER XI.

" THE WORLD FORGETTING."

" 'Tis pleasant, through the loopholes of retreat,
 To peep at such a world ; to see the stir
 Of the great Babel, and not feel the crowd ;
 To hear the roar she sends through all her gates,
 At a safe distance, where the dying sound
 Falls, a soft murmur, on the uninjured ear.
 Thus sitting, and surveying thus at ease
 The globe and its concerns, I seem advanced
 To some secure and more than mortal height,
 That liberates and exempts me from them all. "
          COWPER.

AT the mouth of the river upon which Newton Bury
was built, and an hour or more distant by train from
Newton Bury, was a certain small town, Burrside by
name, the pet watering-place of the Newton Bury
people. In summer, Burrside was gay with brass bands,
and well-dressed promenaders; in summer therefore it
was contemptuously eschewed by Mr. Carden-Cox. But
in winter, when nobody went to Burrside, when it was
transformed into an Arabia Deserta of empty lodgings
and unfrequented streets, then Mr. Carden-Cox was
given to betaking himself thither for a week or a fort-

night of blissful quiet—"the world forgetting, by the world forgot."

It is not at all disagreeable to be forgotten by the world for a few days, just when one happens to be in the right mood. Not that Mr. Carden-Cox ever did forget the world of human beings to which he belonged, or ever really believed that the said world forgot him; but he thought he did, which came to much the same thing.

On such occasions he found it agreeable to hug his solitude, to muse over the peculiarities of his own nature, to admire his own individuality of taste in thus fleeing the world, and to picture what friends might be saying about his absence. A curious mode of "forgetting the world;" but few people carry out their theories consistently.

One or two weeks ended, Mr. Carden-Cox' gregarious side was wont to come uppermost. By that time he had usually had enough of solitude, and was glad to return to his circle of acquaintances, finding a new pleasure in relating to them his Burrside experiences. Some of the said acquaintances privately called this return " coming out of his sulks," and nothing could persuade those unreasonable people that he had not fled in a huff. But nobody ever ventured to hint to himself that such an interpretation of his lofty communing with Nature was a possibility.

Just before the steam-boat excursion, and indeed before the day of Nigel's arrival was known, Mr. Carden-Cox had decided on a trip to Burrside. He and one of the churchwardens had had a "tiff" on the subject of certain Church-funds, and Mr. Carden-Cox had come off worst in the encounter. The said Churchwarden was a good man, albeit somewhat blunt; and Mr. Carden-Cox was not always in the right; but as an immediate result of the affair he grew tired of the Newton Bury world, and settled to flee.

Nigel's arrival altered the complexion of things, and slew his desire for solitude. However, Mr. Carden-Cox disliked to change his plans; it looked "unsettled" to do so, and he counted "unsettledness" tantamount to weakness. So he merely deferred the trip for a few days, and then vanished. Nobody saw him later than the morning after the steam-yacht excursion.

Once at Burrside he liked the change, as usual, after a fashion. Banishment from the conventional round of commonplaces was in theory agreeable to him; and the Burrside natives, if commonplace, were not conventional. Mr. Carden-Cox found their simplicity delightful. He never grew weary of the old sailor on the shore, who knew Nigel, and could talk of Nigel by the hour together; and his landlady from the same cause was a perpetual pleasure. The landlady, a highly respectable woman, looked upon him with a touch of compassionate interest, as "not quite all right *there!*" but this he could not guess, and she did her best for his comfort.

Mr. Carden-Cox was a man greatly addicted to letter-writing. He had not much to do besides, except to take care of himself, and to sit in judgment upon others,

—an employment in which he was a proficient. Idleness was abhorrent to him, and enforced work hardly less so, while letter-writing exactly suited his nervous nature and dilettante tastes. He could begin and leave off when he liked, could write as much or as little on any one subject as he chose, could be secure against interruption and opposition, at least till he had said his say, could expatiate to any extent on his own feelings, and above all could indulge in a comfortable belief in the over-crowded state of his time. Let him write as many letters as he would, there were always more which might be written; and until Mr. Carden-Cox should achieve the impossible horizon-chase of " no further demands " in the correspondence line, he was enough pressed with business to be able to grumble. What true Englishman could want more ?

"My letters are legion—legion !" he groaned complacently, surveying the pile beside his breakfast-plate, three mornings after his arrival at Burrside.

"Legion !" he repeated, looking at his landlady for sympathy, as she placed a covered dish upon the table ; for even in the enjoyment of solitude somebody to be appealed to is necessary, and he had nobody else. Mrs. Simmons was commonplace enough, being of no particular age, and having no particular features; but she was not, for all that, without her own individuality.

"Legion !" reiterated Mr. Carden-Cox. " How would *you* like to have all these to answer ? " He lifted the pile as he spoke, weighing it in both hands, with a

K

deprecating and mournful smile. He would by no means have liked not " to have all these to answer ; " but none the less he pitied himself.

Mrs. Simmons smoothed down a corner of the table-cloth, which had " got rucked up," as she expressed it. " I'm sure I don't know how ever I should get through 'em, sir, what with the dusting and cooking," she said.

" Cooking ! ah !—" Mr. Carden-Cox answered with mild benignity. He knew enough about cooking to believe that a joint would " do" itself, if left before the fire, and that a pudding could be tossed together in five minutes. It seemed absurd to think that dusting or cooking could hinder correspondence, though he would not hurt Mrs. Simmons' feelings by suggesting that she over-estimated her vocation. " Ah !—" he repeated. " Yes. No doubt. But the Penny Post is a great burden, a great burden. You and I can hardly be thankful enough that in our young days no Penny Post existed. We were spared that trouble."

Mrs. Simmons might be of no particular age, but she was not so old as Mr. Carden-Cox; and naturally she resented being placed on his level.

" Indeed, sir, I don't pretend to be able to go back to *them* days," she said with emphasis. " And I don't say but what the Penny Post has got its good points ; not but what it's got its bad points too. As my father was used to say ; for he did live in the times when there wasn't none."

" Everything in life has its advantages and its disadvantages," Mr. Carden-Cox said, looking at her with his bright eyes, as he weighed the postal delivery still. "The question in any particular case is—which over-balances the other? Do the advantages more than compensate for the disadvantages, or *vice versa?* You ·perceive? Sometimes there seems to be a complete balance of forces—an equilibrium—the scale will not incline either way."

"No, sir," assented Mrs. Simmons, anxious to escape before she should find herself in a mental quagmire.

"Nothing then remains but to hold one's opinion in abeyance, till one side or the other sinks. You under-stand?"

"To be sure, sir!" Mrs. Simmons answered, with a heartiness which might almost have meant comprehen-sion. "Poor gentleman!" she was saying to herself. "No, he isn't quite all right there; but I've got to humour him."

"You are a sensible woman; a very sensible woman, Mrs. Simmons," Mr. Carden-Cox stated approvingly. "It is a relief to find one of your sex who can listen to logic, without argumentative opposition."

Mrs Simmons liked this. "My mother was a sen-sible woman, sir," she averred, delaying her flight.

"Probably. Like mother, like daughter. But about the Penny Post—that would be a case in point." Mrs. Simmons backed. "The advantages and disadvantages being about equal, one could neither wish to have it done away, nor—" Mr. Carden-Cox paused to examine the handwriting of the uppermost envelope, " nor—I was about to say—"

Mrs. Simmons was gone, and Mr. Carden-Cox never finished his sentence.

He sighed, sat down, enjoyed a cutlet and a cup of coffee, then applied himself slowly to the day's business. As a rule he delved from top to bottom of the pile with exemplary orderliness; but this morning his weighing process had shaken out a thick envelope, addressed in Daisy's childish handwriting, which proved irresistible. Mr. Carden-Cox drew out the sheet, propped it against the toast-rack, and began to read his favourite's effusion.

" My dear Mr. Carden-Cox,

" Fulvie wants me to answer your note, and to tell you all about everybody, as she isn't well enough, She's not ill, I suppose, but she is awfully seedy somehow—hasn't been out of her room since the boat day. Cousin Jamie says it is the chill and the shock. And mother is worried, and father is depressed, and Nigel's hand doesn't get on; so we are in a sort of hospital state.

" Fulvia and Nigel want padre very much to consult cousin Jamie about himself, and he won't. At least he says ' some day, perhaps,' and he keeps putting it off. He is talking again about going abroad, and I can't think what for. It is such a stupid time of the year for going abroad—nothing to see or do. We think he wants to escape Fulvie's birthday, but why should he? Of course we must give up making a fuss, if he isn't well and doesn't like it. At least Fulvie says so.

"I slept in Fulvie's room last night, because she seemed to need somebody, and she did nothing but talk and ramble about all sorts of nonsense, and call out to Nigel to help her. I suppose she fancied she was burning or drowning, by the things she said.

"I believe she thinks herself worse than she really is; for last night she seized hold of me, and said, 'Daisy, if I die, tell Nigel—' and then she went off into a mutter. I said, 'You're not going to die; nonsense, Fulvie, it is just a cold!' But she did not hear me, and began again, 'Tell Nigel, he and Ethel—he and Ethel—' and then she burst out crying, and she did cry so! I asked her what she meant about Nigel and Ethel, and Fulvie said, 'O, when he marries Ethel—and when I'm dead!' I couldn't get her to say anything more that was rational, except, 'Nobody knows—nobody must know,' and she sobbed herself off into a sort of stupid state, not like sleep.

"This morning I told her what she had said, and she wouldn't believe me. She was angry, and she asked how I could be so ridiculous. Then she said I had been dreaming, and she made me promise not to tell madre, or Nigel, or cousin Jamie. Of course we don't tell anything to padre, and Anice is no good; but I'm sure somebody ought to know the sort of state she is in, and so I thought I would tell you, because we always tell you nearly everything in our house. Only please don't let out that I have said so much.

"I wonder if Nigel ever *will* marry Ethel. Don't you? I like Ethel very much. He is always going there, and trying to see her; but Ethel has so much to do that I don't believe he very often succeeds, and then he looks melancholy. And mother is so unhappy whenever he goes. I do wish mother didn't mind everything so much. *I* mean to give up minding things, and to take everything just as it comes. And I don't mean ever to worry mother by caring too much for anybody. But I don't think Nigel notices how she feels, exactly as he used to do.

"I meant to tell you lots more, but there is no time, and I must stop. Mother wants me for something.

"Ever yours affectionately,

"DAISY BROWNING."

Mr. Carden-Cox sat for ten minutes in a brown study. Then he rang for the removal of the breakfast-things, and turned over the pile of letters remaining. Among them he found a short note from Nigel, plainly written with the left hand, and a few lines from Ethel.

"DEAR MR. CARDEN-COX,

"Can you give me the name of that law-book which you mentioned on the boat? I want to read it. Excuse this scrawl.

"Fulvia seems poorly still—cannot leave her room.

"Ever yours,

"N. B."

" DEAR MR. CARDEN-COX,

"Could you possibly let my father have your magic-lantern next week ? It is asking a great deal at short notice, but he wants to get up the Infants' Treat earlier than was intended, and we have so little time to arrange anything.

"We are very sorry Fulvia is so ill. Of course you hear all about everything, or else I would tell you more. Nigel seems rather anxious about her, but I do not know that anybody else is. His hand is bad still.

"Believe me,

"Yours sincerely,

"ETHEL ELVEY."

In answer to these Mr. Carden-Cox wrote, with great deliberation, three letters, and also a fourth to Fulvia. By inserting a good deal of chit-chat he managed to fill up exactly one sheet to each, signing his name at the bottom of the fourth page.

Then he fell into a state of flurry, and scribbled four postscripts on four additional half-sheets. His state of mind was shown by the fact that, instead of writing P.S. at the top of each half-sheet, he comically wrote N.B., not discovering his own blunder. After all, the one was as good as the other, though unusual. He thrust the postscripts into the four stamped and addressed envelopes, paying small heed to the addresses, and hurried to the post-box round a near corner. Not unnaturally, each postscript went to a wrong destination.

CHAPTER XII.

NOTA BENE!

"It is sometimes a very trifle from whence great temptations proceed. And whilst I think myself somewhat safe, when I least expect it, I find myself sometimes overcome with a small blast."— THOMAS À KEMPIS.

THESE were the postscripts, indited by Mr. Carden-Cox upon four half-sheets, in his state of mental flurry, and thrust into the wrong envelopes.

To Nigel: sent by mistake to Fulvia.

"N.B.—One line more. My dear fellow, you do not really mean to go in for law before Christmas!—just home from your world-tour. Most exemplary, of course; but is it necessary? I do not wish to act the part of an old hinderer in suggesting delay, still—nobody has seen you yet, and everybody wants to hear everything that you have done. After Christmas you will be going, no doubt, to Oxford; and later on will come the crucial question as to your career—the Bar or no! I say yes; but your father says no; and after all the decision must rest with him. Happily there is time enough. Meanwhile we have to think of Fulvia's twenty-first birthday. I want to make something of that affair, if your father will let us. He seems strangely averse.

"Are you sure that your mind is free at this moment for law-studies? Well, well, I must not inquire too closely. But I can tell you, if *that* comes about, the dearest hopes of your father and of myself will be fulfilled. I have set my heart upon it, ever since you and the little Fulvia trotted about hand-in-hand, in your frocks and knickerbockers. You two always suited each other. And not to speak of Fulvia's money, which is a consideration, for undoubtedly your father's embarrassments have increased—not to speak of that, for you are not one to marry for money, Fulvia will be a good wife, true and unselfish. I shall not soon forget your leap into the river, with Fulvia in your arms. It seemed to me a happy augury for the future. Was it not so to you? One knows well enough how you feel—how you must feel—for the good girl whom you rescued—but not all young fellows have such an opportunity of putting their feelings into action. She *is* a good girl, and you are a good boy; and I wish you both happiness, with all my heart—you and her together."

To Daisy : sent by mistake to Ethel.

"N.B.—One word more. As for what you say about Nigel, that is all nonsense. Don't trouble your little head; what do you know of such matters? He will marry no doubt some day, but not in *that* direction. So Fulvia is very poorly, and rambles at night. Yes, I dare say; it was a shock to her, of course. Mind, Nigel must not know how she calls for him. Won't do to hinder matters by pressing them on. Young men like to be let alone, and not interfered with. But you are a sensible and womanly girl, and I don't mind saying to you that *that* is what his father and I most want for him. I have the greatest esteem for the other good girl; and she *is* an uncommonly good girl; but all the same it wouldn't do. Wouldn't do for a moment. Nigel will never marry *her*, unless in direct opposition to his father; and he is not that sort, you know. Nor does he really wish it, though there may once have been a passing fancy. Fulvia is made for him. Mind —all this in strict confidence. Not a word to any one; least of all to E. E. You are a good little Daisy, and I trust you."

To Ethel: sent by mistake to Daisy.

" N.B.—I am sorry, by the bye, to hear such poor accounts of Fulvia. But I hope she will soon pick up again. She must feel gratified by the manner of her rescue. Devotion could scarcely have been more plainly shown. She and that boy have always been much one to another. I have often hoped that the 'much' would grow into more. In fact, his father and I quite agree on that point—about the only point, between ourselves, on which Browning and I ever did agree. This in confidence. You are enough of a friend to Nigel to be able to rejoice in the prospect of his happy future. Tell Mr. Elvey I am delighted that he should use my magic-lantern as often as he likes."

To Fulvia: sent by mistake to Nigel.

"N.B.—One word more to my dear Fulvia. I am sorry to hear that your faithful knight has not yet regained the use of his hand. But never mind! He will count it worth his while. What brave knight ever yet shrank from fire or water for the sake of his faire ladye? Well, I must not joke you; but it is easy to guess how *he* feels—good boy!"

The four letters with their ill-fitting postscripts reached Newton Bury that same evening, being faithfully delivered according to their several addresses; three at the Grange, one at the Rectory.

"A perfect cartload from Mr. Carden-Cox," Nigel remarked. He read his own sheet quickly through, wondering how any sensible and intellectual man could manage to say so little, in so many words. If it had been a woman, or even a brainless man—but Mr. Carden-Cox was not a woman, nor was he brainless. Nigel then turned to the postscript, with a preliminary laugh at the N.B., and a final pause at the sixth word.

"Hallo! this is not for me! Here, Daisy," folding the half-sheet and tossing it towards her, "it is Fulvia's, not mine!"

Daisy was screwing up her big childish forehead in perplexity. "How funny!" she commented aloud, over her half-sheet. "He doesn't write like that to me generally. Why, I declare—if it isn't to Ethel!"

"What?"

"Mr. Carden-Cox has sent me a wrong piece. It's to Ethel, not to me. A sort of postscript. How stupid! —and I never guessed till I got to the end. Yes, I read it, of course. How could I tell? It might have been all in answer to my letter, only it's not exactly how he always writes. Speaking of padre as 'Browning,' and—"

"Stop! you've no business to repeat a word. It was not meant for your eyes."

"No; to be sure," responded Daisy. "Well, we must send it on to Ethel, I suppose."

"Put it up in an envelope. I'll take it at once, and explain."

Daisy obeyed with promptitude. Nobody else was present to remonstrate. Mr. and Mrs. Browning were in the study, and Anice was with Fulvia. Dinner would not be until eight o'clock; and it was now only a few minutes after seven.

"That is Fulvia's. You had better carry it up-stairs. Don't forget," Nigel said, indicating the folded half-sheet, as Daisy handed to him a closed envelope, addressed "Miss Elvey."

"Yes, I will—I mean, I won't forget. Tell Ethel I'm very sorry I read hers. How odd of Mr. Carden-

Cox! Why didn't he take more care? Perhaps there's a half-sheet to you, sent to Fulvia by mistake."

"No; Anice would have brought it down by this time."

Nigel was pulling on his great-coat, when the study-door opened, and Mrs. Browning glided out. "It is raining fast. Where are you going?" she asked.

"To rectify a blunder."

"Mother—Mr. Carden-Cox has made such a mistake," exclaimed Daisy, hanging over the balusters. "He has sent part of a letter to me which ought to have gone to Ethel, and another part to Nigel which is meant for Fulvia. Isn't it queer? Just as if he had got all the letters mixed up in a jumble. I'm taking Fulvia hers, and Nigel is taking Ethel's."

A shadow fell upon Mrs. Browning's face. "Always the Rectory!" her calm voice said.

"I shall not be long, mother."

She retreated into the study, and Nigel went off—something of the shadow falling on him; he could hardly have defined how or why.

Fulvia's letter had gone straight to her, on its first arrival. She was seated in her bedroom, by the fire, wearing a pale blue dressing-gown. The reddish hair, knotted lightly behind, fell low in masses. Though not ill enough to stay in bed all day, she was by no means well enough to be about the house. She looked thin and flushed. Anice was leaving the room to get a book, at the moment of the maid's entry with the letter, and Fulvia said, "Don't hurry, I am all right."

"I don't mean to be long," Anice replied.

But Fulvia was alone when she opened the envelope. Out of it dropped the sheet and also the half-sheet, both closely covered by Mr. Carden-Cox' minute and precise handwriting.

Some impulse made Fulvia turn first to the half-sheet; and in a moment she saw that it was not intended for herself. She glanced at the sheet—yes, that began all right, "My dear Fulvia;" but this had "My dear fellow."

Fulvia read on, notwithstanding. A kind of fascination seemed to hold her eyes to the page. It was a fascination which might have been and ought to have been resisted. Conscience cried loudly, yet she did not resist. She read steadily on, straight and fast, to the end.

A gleam came to her eyes, and a brilliant glow to her cheeks. For half a minute she had only one distinct sense—that of an overwhelming joy. Nothing else in life could matter now—now—if Nigel and she were to be one! The wish of his father!—the wish of Mr. Carden-Cox!—the desire of Nigel himself!—what then could hinder?

But upon this came a rush of yet more overwhelming shame, an agony of contempt at her own action, seen in imagination with Nigel's eyes. The shame and contempt actually bowed her forward, till her face

rested upon her knees, and the flush of joy deepened
into a fixed burning of brow and cheeks, surely enough
to betray her. What had she done? What had she
been about? Nigel's letter!—but she could not let
Nigel have it! He must never know that her eyes
had read those words—O, never! Cold chills shot
through her at the very thought.

Anice was coming back. Fulvia heard the approaching steps, and dire need brought composure. She
thrust the half-sheet deep into a pocket of her dressing-
gown, pushed away the candle that her face might be
in shade, and began quietly to read her own letter.

"From Mr. Carden-Cox?" asked Anice, recognizing
the cramped hand. "Anything particular?"

"Nothing much. Just chit-chat! He seems getting
tired of Burrside already."

"He always does in a day or two."

"Or a week or two."

Unobservant Anice noticed nothing unusual in
Fulvia's shaking hands or crimsoned face; but the next
moment Daisy rushed in.

"O, did I make a noise? I'm sorry. I quite forgot.
Why, Fulvie—what a colour you are! As red as beet-
root! Cousin Jamie would say you were feverish, I'm
sure."

"Nonsense. What have you there?"

"Only a postscript from Mr. Carden-Cox for you. It
went to Nigel by mistake. I can't imagine what Mr.
Carden-Cox has been about. He sent another to me

instead of to Ethel. You haven't one too, I suppose, meant for somebody else? Only that sheet—" as Fulvia pointed to the one lying on her knee. " Fulvie! I say! I'm sure you are not so well this evening. What is the matter? Anything Mr. Carden-Cox has said? I shall have to call madre. Why, your hands are like fire, and beating as if they were alive. I can feel them."

Fulvia snatched the said hands petulantly away.

" Nonsense! don't! I wish you would not tease. I will not have a word said to madre, and I only want to be quiet. There is such an amount of talk and bustle, and my head is wild."

Daisy grew gentle. "I'm sorry. We won't talk any more," she said in a penitent voice. "Fulvie, if you will just get into bed, I'll only help you and not say a word. Please do."

Fulvia leant back, and shut her eyes. " I can't yet. I have to finish my letter—and I want a little peace. Go and dress for dinner first—both of you."

" And then—" Daisy said.

" Yes, then perhaps. I'll see. Only go now, and don't say a word to worry madre."

The girls took her at her word, retiring softly, and Fulvia found herself alone; safe for awhile, she knew, since neither Anice nor Daisy could ever dress in less than half-an-hour, the one from innate slowness, the other from lack of method.

Fulvie's hands beating! She could have told Daisy

that she was beating all over; the clang of a hard
pulsation echoing through every nerve and fibre of her
body. "Am I going to be very ill? I feel like it,"
she asked of herself; and then aloud, with a laugh—
" Nonsense! There are nerves enough in the family
already. · I'll not sport them!"

Then she glanced through Mr. Carden-Cox' chit-chat
sheet, only to find nothing in it worth attention, and
read her own postscript. Thereupon came again the
thrill of intense joy, followed by the withering shame.

"What would Nigel think? How could I—how
could I? Such a disgraceful thing to do! Tell him!—
oh, I can never, never confess! He must never know.
Nigel, the very soul of honour—and I all the time
knowing it was not meant for me. *I!* why I have
always prided myself on never stooping to anything
mean—and now, this! What could have come over
me that moment? I must have been demented. How
I *could!* Yes, it was temptation of course—but why
did I give way?"

Yet she drew the half-sheet from her pocket, and
her eyes fell upon it anew. "No harm now! I have
read the whole—I can't help having read it," she
murmured. Then, with a renewed rush of most bitter
self-contempt, she caught her glance away, crumpled
up the piece of paper, and actually flung it upon the
fire. Yet at the last instant she recoiled, and as the
little crushed ball of paper ·fell upon a surface of
unburnt black coal, her fingers snatched it away.

L

Impossible yet to destroy those words, so full of light and hope for her. Oh, not yet! She would not read them again, but she would keep them; just for a few days.

Fulvia crossed the room with trembling steps, smoothing the crumpled half-sheet as she went. She unlocked her dressing-box, slipped the paper behind the little looking-glass which had its nest within the lid, and relocked the box.

Once more in her easy-chair, she could only lean back and think, with a strange mixture of intense joy and something like despair. As minutes went on, the latter predominated.

If Nigel should ever know—should ever guess what she had done! Fulvia felt that she would sink into the very earth with shame. She could picture so well his look, could foretell what he would think and say. Suppose Mr. Carden-Cox were to recall that he had sent the postscript to Fulvia? Suppose she should be questioned? What could she say, and how might she shield herself?

"I will *not* speak untruths, and I will *not* tell!" she resolved aloud, clasping her hands. But the two resolves might prove incompatible—only she would not face that possibility.

Why had she not, when Anice was returning, dropped the half-sheet on the floor, then picked it up as a discovery and sent it straight to Nigel by Anice? This suggestion came up; and shame dyed Fulvia's brow anew, at the idea of such deception. Yet—she almost regretted that she had not thought of it in time !

By the half-hour's end, when Daisy returned, it was as much as Fulvia could do to creep into bed. No wonder that the night following was one of feverish unrest. Daisy had little sleep, though not easily kept awake; for Fulvia rambled incessantly, in a half-awake, half-unconscious style.

Strange to say she kept sealed lips throughout as to the crumpled half-sheet locked up in her dressing-case. Once there was a passionate cry, "O Nigel, forgive me !" and Daisy sat up in bed, staring with round eyes of astonishment; but no more followed, and Fulvia seemed to be asleep, so Daisy lay down again.

"I'm glad I told Mr. Carden-Cox, though," commented Daisy. "Somebody ought to know how she goes on, most certainly !"

CHAPTER XIII.

"WILL NEVER MARRY *HER!*"

"He jests at scars that never felt a wound."—SHAKSPEARE.

"ETHEL, just look at that blind. It hangs all crookedly."

"Yes, mother."

"Now you have pulled it too much the other way. You do things in such a hurry."

Ethel gave a slow pull this time, cheerily, though her mother's tone was depressing. Mrs. Elvey could not be called ill-tempered, but she was given to complaining moods, and such moods were trying to those about her.

"Something must be wrong with the oil we are using now. The lamp has a most disagreeable smell."

"Father noticed it yesterday evening. I'll go to the shop and speak about it to-morrow."

"Yes, do; it is enough to make one positively ill."

"Shall I take away the lamp and light candles?"

"O no, that would be extravagant; I must just bear it. What has become of everybody this evening? the house seems so dull."

"Father is writing in the study, and the boys are at their prep. still. Lance wants me to help him presently."

"Then, pray, go; don't mind about me. Lance must not lose his place in his classes on any account. Do go at once, Ethel."

Mrs. Elvey spoke in an injured tone, as if it were cruel of Ethel to leave her; but this was so usual a state of things that Ethel hardly noticed the manner. She folded up her work, and sped into the hall, just as the postman dropped a letter into the box.

"For me," Ethel said, taking it out. "From Mr. Carden-Cox. About the magic-lantern, of course. I am glad he has answered quickly. Well, Lance," as the boy ran past, "do you want me?"

"Not for five minutes," Lance answered.

The boys did their "prep." in the little old school-room. Ethel turned into the dining-room to read her letter, standing under the gas, which had been left alight. The remains of the evening meal, a dinner-tea, were on the table still. Post arrived at the Rectory somewhat later than at the Grange, Church Square coming at the end of a certain "beat."

She went through the sheet first, amused at the amount of talk about nothing, then came to the post-script, with a little laugh at the "N.B." Puzzlement followed quickly. "What did I say about Nigel? I can't remember. What does he mean? 'Not to trouble my head'—well, but I don't. 'Such matters!' —I can't understand. 'Nigel to marry some day'— yes, very likely; anybody might suppose that." A pink spot found its way to Ethel's pale cheek. Did Mr. Carden-Cox imagine that she was running after Nigel, and wish to administer a friendly warning? Impossible, surely!—and yet— "He is so odd! he might mean it," faltered Ethel, glad that nobody was present to remark her looks. "But I should not have expected it from him."

She read on slowly, bewildered still. "Fulvia calling for Nigel at night"—quite natural after the shock she had had; but could Mr. Carden-Cox really suppose that she, Ethel, would tell Nigel, even if she had known the fact? *What* was it that Mr. Browning and Mr. Carden-Cox wanted for Nigel?—and who was this "other good girl?" "Fulvia, no doubt," thought Ethel. "'It wouldn't do!' What wouldn't do? 'Nigel marry in opposition to his father!'—no, indeed, nothing less likely." But what had made Mr. Carden-Cox write all this to Ethel? Was he demented?

Suddenly, at the end, understanding came in a flood. One moment she was smiling under the gas-burner in amused perplexity, the next instant she saw the whole, as with a flash of lightning.

This postscript was to Daisy Browning, not to herself. She, Ethel Elvey, and not Fulvia Rolfe, was "the other girl," whom Nigel might never marry, whom indeed he had no wish to marry.

Ethel did not give the sheet another glance. There was no need, for she knew it all by heart. More especially those words, " Nigel will never marry *her!*" were stamped upon her memory, never to fade away. They seemed to settle the matter finally.

She stood quietly, again pale, the pink spot gone from her cheek. Her eyes were fixed on the opposite wall, but she could not see or think steadily. No tears came, only a numb chilled sensation, reaching down to her finger-tips; and indeed those little fingers were all at once strangely cold.

"I say, Ethel—Eth-el!" called Lance imperiously.

"Coming!" cried Ethel, not without a husky sound.

She folded the half-sheet, and thrust it into her pocket, absolutely forgetting at the moment that it was not her own. "O Nigel, Nigel!" a voice within her heart was wailing sadly; and as she crossed the hall towards the school-room he entered by the front door.

"Ethel, I'm just come to bring—"

He paused a moment to pull off his glove, and grasp her hand. Ethel's fingers lay cold and limp in his, not returning the pressure. He looked so bright, so pleased to be there. For one moment she could have believed it all a bad dream. But those words were with her still, —he would never marry *her!* He did not really wish it! Not really! No, why should he? He was only her old kind affectionate playfellow; and she had to be the same to him, expecting nothing beyond, and taking care that nobody should think she could expect anything beyond. That last item was the difficulty: how to guard her own position, and yet not to give him pain. At the present moment such a line of conduct was not even possible. She had to give him pain; and at the very moment that her fingers touched his, the grave shadow which she so well knew, and which she never could see without a heartache, crept over his eyes.

"I'm come to bring part of your letter from Mr. Carden-Cox, posted to Daisy. He seems to have been in a state of confusion. There was a postscript for Fulvia sent to me, and Daisy received this, which she says is yours. Daisy read it before she discovered the blunder, and she wants me to apologize."

"Thanks," Ethel replied, taking the envelope. She did not look straight at him, after her wont, but leant against the wall, pale, and even a little breathless, as if she had been running up-hill. It flashed across her mind that, if she followed Daisy's example, she would send to Daisy by Nigel the postscript which she had herself received. "But I cannot—cannot!" she cried to herself. "Impossible! I will send it back to Mr. Carden-Cox."

Nigel stood gazing at Ethel, with a face of grieved surprise. He could not make her out.

"You don't mind, I hope. Daisy did not find that it was meant for you till the end. Of course she will tell nobody what she has read."

"Mind! O no! Mr. Carden-Cox' letters are not so very important—commonly."

"It is not half-past seven yet. May I come in for a few minutes? We don't dine till eight," said Nigel, sorely chilled by her manner, yet hoping against hope that it might mean nothing.

"Yes, of course. Mother is in the drawing-room."

"And you will come too?"

"I can't. Lance wants me; and I have to write a note for the post."

"Just for a minute! The post doesn't go till eight."

"Our pillar is emptied a quarter before; and Lance—"

"Can't Lance wait?"

"No; I have to help with his lessons."

Dead silence for a moment.

"Is anything wrong?" Nigel asked.

Ethel lifted her blue eyes, giving him a calm return-glance. She would not for the world have betrayed herself.

"I ought to go to Lance," she said.

"And that is all?"

Ethel could not answer in the affirmative, for she was true always. Silence was her response.

"Good-night," Nigel said seriously, holding out his left hand. "No, I think I will not come in this evening. There isn't really much time—only, if I could have seen a little of you— But some other day must do instead. I suppose I may tell Daisy that you do not mind very much."

"About the postscript? O no!"

Then Nigel was gone, and Ethel still leant against the wall, with downcast eyes, feeling as if all the sunshine of her life had gone with him.

The school-room door opened, and Lance's head popped out.

"I say, Eth— Hallo, there you are!" lowering his voice from a shout.

"I'll come in a minute, Lance. I must write just one line to catch the post."

"That's what girls are always doing," retorted Lance. "I suppose 'just one line' means just ten pages. Well, mind you're quick, for I'm at a standstill, and you promised to come ages ago."

Lance retreated, and Ethel went quickly to the dining-room side-table, where she first opened and read the postscript sent on by Daisy. Had it come alone it would not have meant very much to Ethel; she could have afforded then to smile at it; but following close upon the other, it brought a renewed pang. Ethel sat for a few minutes thinking, and then she dashed off, with small hesitation—

"DEAR MR. CARDEN-COX,

"The enclosed half-sheet came to me by mistake. I am very sorry that I stupidly read it through before finding out that it was meant for somebody else. I send it to you instead of to Daisy, because I would rather no one should know that I have seen it.

"Thanks for your letter to me, and for giving leave about the magic-lantern.

"Fulvia is very nice; and I am glad you think he is going to be so happy.

"In haste,

"Yours sincerely,

"ETHEL ELVEY."

The last paragraph was not written without a struggle, but pride insisted. Something had to be said or done to put her into a right position—to convince Mr. Carden-Cox that, at all events, she was not seeking Nigel.

In another minute the letter was ready. Ethel caught up a shawl, threw it over her head, and ran out of the front door, through the garden, across the road, to the red pillar-box, careless of pattering rain.

Then the envelope was beyond recall; and Ethel came slowly back, wondering if she had done wisely.

"If one could only be always sure!" she murmured within the door, shaking off a little shower of rain-drops. "And, O, if only I need not hurt *him!*"

With an effort she braced herself up, tossed aside the shawl, and entered the school-room.

"You've kept me waiting a jolly time, and no mistake," averred Lance. "Just see, Ethel, how in the world am I to make out all this French gibberish?"

Ethel sat down for an hour of patient work, going steadily into such explanations as Lance needed, and making herself very clear. But all the while she never ceased to see a pair of dark eyes, full of pain at the touch of her cold fingers.

Did he care? Yes, no doubt; they were such old friends. Only that—only friends! Nothing else could ever be, for Nigel did not wish it.

Ethel's note to Mr. Carden-Cox, with its enclosure, left Newton Bury on Tuesday evening, just too late for the post Ethel had meant to catch; this fact not having been discovered by her. Consequently the note did not reach Burrside until the midday post, one half-hour after Mr. Carden-Cox had, under a sudden impulse, quitted his blissful solitude for the cares of Newton Bury.

Mrs. Simmons was out when the note arrived, and the little lodging-house maid put it thoughtlessly on a side-table, saying nothing to anybody. There it lay till late the same evening, when Mrs. Simmons came across it, at once instituting inquiries.

"And been there this whole day, and not a soul knowing!" exclaimed Mrs. Simmons. "And Mr. Carden-Cox that particular about his letters, as he'd be fit to cut your head off if the post was five minutes behindhand, and you knowing of it, Betsy Jane, and never paying no heed! You're the trouble of my life, and that's what you are, never thinking nor caring! And you'll put on your hat this minute, and go straight off to the post, you will, for all it's too late, for I wouldn't keep that there hemberlope in this house another hour, no, not if I was paid for it, and Mr. Carden-Cox so mortial particular!"

Betsy Jane was not likely to pay Mrs. Simmons out of her small earnings, neither did she attempt to defend herself. She only drooped her lower lip, half deplorably, half in sullenness, and endured the harangue; for after all, what could she have pleaded except forgetfulness? and everybody agrees with everybody that to forget is no excuse at all, because one never ought to forget. Betsy Jane put on her hat, of course, and went to the post; and the poor little note wandered off once more, missing again the evening post, and again arriving not far from midday.

The return of Mr. Carden-Cox had become known, and Nigel had speedily found his way to Mr. Carden-Cox' house. When Ethel's note, with half-a-dozen other epistles, was handed to Mr. Carden-Cox on a silver waiter, Nigel was seated opposite to him, speaking.

Mr. Carden-Cox took the letters, and turned them over dreamily, while he listened.

"Humph—ha—yes—just so," he assented. "Yes, I see—no doubt—sent them all wrong. Yes; not at all like me, eh? I am a most methodical individual generally."

So he was, perhaps, in certain lines and in certain moods; but, like most people who attempt to analyze themselves, he made no allowance for oppositions in his own nature.

"Methodical," repeated Mr. Carden-Cox, holding Ethel's note, and tapping it gently. "Yes, now I think of it, I had placed the four letters in a row upon my desk—in a row, as I always do, following the order in which I write. It seemed hardly needful to examine the addresses. I may have done so cursorily, but only cursorily—not with especial care. I was sure of the order in which the letters lay; yes, I can recall that now. Yours first, to the left; then Fulvia's. I noted that, coupling you and Fulvia together, you see—ha!— then Ethel's, and lastly Daisy's. No mistake about the matter; no mistake possible, in fact. Extraordinary that the postscripts should have become disarranged. I don't see for my part how they could have done so. Still—facts are stubborn. You are sure that it was as you state?"

"Perfectly."

"Well, I don't understand; I don't understand at all." Mr. Carden-Cox rubbed his hair till it stood on end. "Four envelopes, four letters, four postscripts— yours, Fulvia's, Ethel's, and Daisy's. That was the precise order. I could take my oath in a court of justice as to the way in which they were placed. Extraordinary! Did you say I wrote 'N.B.' instead of 'P.S.'? Comical, rather! Never did such a thing in my life before. Must have been thinking too much about you, my dear fellow—you and my dear Fulvia! Nothing unusual in that, perhaps. I suppose you and Fulvia— Well, well; yes, and then—to be sure! 'N.B.' on all four postscripts, you say?"

"I know nothing about the four. Fulvia's postscript came to me, and I sent it to her at once, unread. Ethel's came to Daisy, and was read by mistake."

"And the other two: Daisy's and yours?"

"There were no others."

"I beg your pardon. There were two others. Four altogether. One to each."

"Then the other two were not posted. You will most likely find them in your desk."

"I shall most likely do nothing of the sort. The other two were posted." Mr. Carden-Cox was growing irate. "My recollections are perfectly clear. I can distinctly recall putting the four postscripts into the four envelopes, one into each. I tell you I could declare this on oath, in a court of justice. It is a matter of absolute certainty. If the first two went wrong, the third and fourth went wrong also. But somebody has got them—somebody has. No possibility of a mistake there. Ethel and Fulvia have had a postscript each, and not their own postscripts, since you and Daisy received those."

"I saw Ethel within half-an-hour of getting your letter; and the post must have been in at the Rectory. She would surely have told me if there had been a postscript for anybody at home."

"Hallo! This is the girl's own handwriting!" Mr. Carden-Cox was gazing at the note he held.

"Ethel's!" and a slight flush rose.

"Ethel Elvey's, of course. Humph! Why, here it is!"

Mr. Carden-Cox held up the half-sheet with his own handwriting.

"Sent back to you, instead of sent on to Daisy," Nigel said quietly; but he had again the chilled sensation. Why had Ethel said nothing to him?—if, indeed, it had arrived when he called.

Mr. Carden-Cox was not commonly supposed to be wanting in reticence; on the contrary, some counted him "a great deal too reserved." But here again there were curious oppositions in his character; and like many reserved people he was capable of running to the other extreme. Being over-excited he ran now to the other extreme, and forthwith read aloud Ethel's note.

"I don't understand. Who is 'he'?" asked Nigel.

Mr. Carden-Cox glanced at the paragraph again, and burst into an uncomfortable laugh.

"He! ha, ha! The girl's a thorough woman, and no mistake! Uses adjectives—pronouns, I mean—without an antecedent. That's the way to express it, I believe. Rather long since I went through Lindley Murray; but antecedents are important things, very important. 'He!' ha, ha! as if there wasn't another 'he' in the world. But girls never think! I shall have a little fun with Miss Ethel about this! She'll appreciate the joke. Well, well, I'm glad she approves. You and she were always good friends, but—eh? what?"

Nigel was trying to edge in a question.

"Eh? Oh, only a little jest of mine in the post-script to herself, about a certain knight rescuing his faire ladye from fire and water. No, by the way, that wasn't to her; I'm forgetting—but something tantamount—you and Fulvia, you know."

"You seem rather fond of coupling my name with Fulvia's," Nigel could not resist saying.

"Old habit of mine, my dear boy. Always did couple you together, and probably always shall. Why, now, you know yourself that nobody can take precisely the place with you that Fulvia takes—eh?"

"Perhaps not precisely; but that does not mean—"

"No; just so; it doesn't mean more than it does mean. It only means that you are on the high-road to— No, you needn't deny it. You needn't attempt to deny anything. We are willing to wait; your father and I. Merely a matter of time, of course. But you see Ethel approves, quite approves—glad to think you are going to be so happy. Yes, certainly—in reference to that—to you and Fulvia. Good sensible girl, Ethel Elvey. Much too sensible to expect—well, of course, she expects nothing; never did expect. You and she are good friends, no doubt; always will be. But that would never have done; never! Serious reasons against it; and your father would not consent. Entirely out of the question. Fulvia 'very nice,' etc. Might have said a little more, when she was about it. Mind, you mustn't let out that you have heard this note. She doesn't wish it to be known—about her seeing the postscript. There!" and Mr. Carden-Cox chucked his now useless half-sheet into the fire. "Daisy must go without."

M

Nigel was silent.

"Three of the postscripts accounted for," said **Mr.** Carden-Cox. He began to reckon upon the ends of his fingers. "Fulvie's, Daisy's, Ethel's. Fulvia's sent to you; Daisy's to Ethel; Ethel's to Daisy. That's it, eh? Yes, I see; plain as a pikestaff. Ethel's and Daisy's were exchanged. Then yours and Fulvia's were exchanged too. Fulvia's to you; yours, of course, to Fulvia. What is the girl after not to give it up?"

"Fulvia has not received it."

"She has, I assure you. Must. Positively must." Mr. Carden-Cox was delighted at the flash of Nigel's eyes. "I put a postscript into each one of the four envelopes, and here is the only one not accounted for. Fulvia has yours to a dead certainty."

"It is the most extraordinary thing to accuse a lady of—" began Nigel. "Fulvia would have told at once. Why not?"

"That's right. I like to put you up in her defence. It positively does one good. My dear fellow, I don't accuse her of anything. I don't know why she has not passed the postscript on. Women's reasons are not easy to fathom. Fulvia trustworthy. Yes, no doubt. Like the rest of her sex. Acts upon impulse, and never thinks of consequences. Probably put it away in a drawer, and forgot all about it; as likely as not! Anything possible to a woman. I'll ask her when we meet; or you can put the question meantime. 'Rather not!' Too much of a coward, eh? But never mind; you just leave it to me. I'll bring her to book."

Nigel managed at last to get away. He was very sore at heart, longing for quiet, that he might think over Ethel's note, which had been a sharp blow.

He walked homeward swiftly, after his usual direct fashion, only not as usual taking in all about him with glances to right and left as he went. His eyes were steadily downcast, and certain friends found themselves unconsciously passed by. "Young Browning in a state of meditation!" one acquaintance remarked; and a lady of sensitive temper was offended to be overlooked; while another of more robust mental make had leisure from herself to wonder if that nice young fellow were in trouble. His arm was in a sling still; but "it wasn't that," she said, and she said rightly.

Nigel had long known the wish of Mr. Carden-Cox' heart about himself and Fulvia. He had hitherto ignored the idea, ridden over it, or laughed at it, as the case might be. Even the knowledge that his father was much bent upon the same could only cause regrets.

But Ethel—if Ethel approved and was glad, this, indeed, made all the difference. For if Ethel could wish him to marry Fulvia, then it must have been that she could not and would not marry him herself. Life would be changed for Nigel, if things were so.

No steel blade could have cut more deeply than the closing sentence of Ethel's little note to Mr. Carden-Cox. Glad to think he was going to be so happy!

Glad to believe that he would marry Fulvia! Nigel's heart sank as if weighted with lead.

The mere fact that she was able calmly to write such words to Mr. Carden-Cox seemed to him conclusive. He did not feel that he could have done it in her place, if he had cared one tithe as much as he cared now!

Of course not. But he was a man, and she was a woman. In his estimate of things he forgot to allow for· this fact.

Then her manner to him, when he had seen her last, the sudden coldness and indifference! Was it that she had just read by mistake the postscript meant for Daisy, whatever the postscript might have. contained? Something undoubtedly had aroused her, to the sense of a certain need to show Nigel that, he. must not think of her.

Tom Elvey!

Yes, that was it, no doubt. That was at the bottom of the tangle. Fulvia's words on the steam-yacht had been almost driven out of Nigel's mind by succeeding events, and by his first meeting afterward with Ethel; but now they returned in full strength.

Ethel had been so pleased and thankful, after the adventure, showing perhaps under excitement more warmth than she felt on consideration to be right. Probably she feared to mislead Nigel. As his friend and old playmate she would rejoice in his escape— perhaps also for Fulvia's sake, if she held the notion about him and Fulvia—but it was very evident that

she wished Nigel now to understand the moderate
nature of her feelings.

Tom Elvey, to wit!

Nigel sighed heavily as he entered the Grange gates.
Nobody was at hand to hear.

CHAPTER XIV.

SOMETHING WRONG—BUT WHAT?

"I do not greatly care to be deceived."—SHAKSPEARE.
"O mad mistake,
With repentance in its wake."—JEAN INGELOW.

"FULVIA!" Nigel said in surprise. She was creeping down-stairs, step by step, evidently uncertain as to the extent of her own powers. Nigel walked to the mat at the foot of the flight, and stood there looking up, while Fulvia came to a pause four steps above, resting and looking down. Her face broke into a smile, half mischievous, half apologetic; and then the smile vanished, for it gained no response. His features were set and pale, even stern, Fulvia thought.

"Don't be angry," she said. "I shall collapse, if you are. It's as much as I can do to manage the descent."

"What made you leave your room?"

"What made me? My own naughty will, I suppose. Nobody else's, certainly. Madre is out shopping with the girls, so I thought I would use my opportunity. I'm tired of seclusion."

"Have you your doctor's leave?"

" I didn't ask it. He has not been yet. Besides, if one is bent on one's own way, it's no use to court forbiddal."

" I don't think you are right."

" Perhaps not; but you needn't look so awfully solemn about it. What is the matter ? "

She came down the last steps in tremulous style, laughing at herself, and put a hand on his arm.

" Anything gone wrong ? Have you seen Mr. Carden-Cox ? "

" Yes. Where are you going ? "

" I'm bent on a talk with the padre; but I must rest for five minutes first. Yes, please help me."

Nigel responded without words, and she crossed the hall into the morning-room, dropping on the nearest chair with a vanquished look.

" I didn't know a few days in one's bedroom could make one so horribly weak. I feel just like a teetotum, ready to go down. What are you thinking about ? "

Weak as she felt, her eyes scanned him with their usual penetration, and Nigel could not stand it. He turned abruptly, and walked into the bow-window, taking a book from the table, and making believe to read it. Fulvia might think him ill-tempered if she liked. He was not able to endure being questioned.

Fulvia made no further attempt at the moment. " Poor boy !" she said to herself, and a softened look came into her face. She was accustomed of old to think of him as a boy, and to count herself a little

older in mind, a little better able to manage things for
him as well as for herself than he was; and she had
not yet shaken off the old habit of thought.

But when he came back from the bow-window, holding his open book in one hand, it was no boy's face that
met her glance. He was very pale; and the compres-
sion of the lips, the restrained lines of suffering, the
bent brows, were unmistakably those of a man.

"Have you a headache?" she asked.

"No, thanks."

"Has Mr. Carden-Cox been saying anything to worry
you?"

She had no business to ask the question, and she
knew it, even before saying the words; but at the
moment the temptation was too strong. And at once
Fulvia knew that she had lost ground with him. She
had done the very thing for which she lately had so
blamed Anice—catechizing where she held no right to
catechize. Nigel was silent, but his gravity had now a
tinge of displeasure. Fulvia had far too much tact to
persevere in a mistake.

"I beg your pardon," she said humbly. "It was
rude of me. Of course I ought not to expect an
answer." Yet she did expect, and was disappointed that
none came.

"Did you say you wished to speak to my father?"
inquired Nigel, after a pause.

"Yes. I'll go to the study. He is there, isn't he?
One can so seldom get hold of him alone—I mean,

without madre. I don't mean you." She paused and
looked at him earnestly. "Am I forgiven?"

"For what?"

"You know. Meddling in your concerns."

"Sisters are supposed to be at liberty to say what
they like," Nigel replied, smiling; but it was not his
usual smile.

"And brothers, too," Fulvia added, while the word
"sisters" fell upon her coldly. Did he mean it? or
was he speaking without thought?

She seemed so tottering that Nigel had no choice
but to offer her again the use of his left arm, when she
left the room.

"Absurd!" she said, with a laugh, as she accepted
it. "I, who am always strong! but I shall be all right
in a day or two."

"I doubt if you are so robust as you profess to be. I
told the girls so one day."

"O yes, Daisy informed me." Then the remainder
of Daisy's report rushed into Fulvia's mind, and Nigel
glanced in surprise at her flushed face. It was very
evident to Fulvia that his own recollections of what
he had said brought no self-conscious feelings. "Just
after you first came home," Fulvia added, with an effort,
trying to seem indifferent.

Nigel paused for a moment outside the study door.
"Yes; I thought the girls wanted a hint. You mustn't
let them put upon you too much. It is not right."

"What isn't?"

"Their making use of you upon all occasions to save themselves trouble. Anice is desperately lazy, and Daisy follows in her wake. You must not let them put upon you."

"I don't see why. I like doing things for people."

"Yes; that is your kindness. But it is not necessary or right. If you were their own sister—"

"I thought you called me so just now."

"That is just it. We call you so, but in reality you are Fulvia Rolfe, the heiress, not even a distant relative of ours."

"I don't see what difference the heiress-ship makes. I owe more to madre and padre and all of you, than the biggest fortune in England could ever repay. And nobody could call my few thousands a fortune. Just enough to be comfortable on. Yes; please open the door."

"Fulvia, my dear! This is unexpected," Mr. Browning said, rising with his melancholy air and habitual sigh. "I was told that you could not come downstairs for two or three days yet. I am glad to see you looking so well."

Mr. Browning was in the way of counting everybody well except himself. Like Anice, he desired always to have a monopoly of ill-health. Fulvia's colour might, however, have deceived keener eyes than his.

"Sit down, my dear, and tell me all about yourself. Yes, sit down there; that is a comfortable chair. I am only pretty well—only so-so—not at all up to the mark.

You wished to speak to me? Yes, certainly, anything except business. I am not equal to business yet; sometimes I doubt if I ever shall be again. Don't go, Nigel."

"I will come again presently," Nigel began, but Mr. Browning repeated, "No, don't go, pray don't go!" and Fulvia added, "Yes, please stay, I have nothing to say which you may not hear."

Rather reluctantly Nigel remained, leaning against the mantelpiece, not far from where Fulvia sat. She did not look her best this morning. Ill-health was unbecoming to Fulvia, as indeed it is to most people. Her hair was not so well dressed as usual, being a little awry; her eyes were heavy; her complexion was flushed in patches. Nigel compared her with a mental picture of Ethel—fresh, dainty, delicately pale, sunny-eyed—and he thought—but one hardly needs to say what he thought. Fulvia was dear to him as the adopted sister of his whole life; but she was not Ethel; she could not be Ethel.

"Your mother has gone out with the girls," Mr. Browning said in a pathetic and dejected tone. "I quite urged her doing so, though not equal to the exertion myself. She is the better, I feel sure, for an occasional turn in the open air. Well, Fulvia, what had you to say, my dear?—if it is not business. I am not in a condition for business just now."

"I am afraid it verges on business," said Fulvia. Mr. Browning put up one hand, as if to ward off an enemy; yet she continued, "About my money—"

Mr. Browning's face grew perceptibly paler, and the apprehensive look in his eyes increased. He was not commonly wanting in colour, though it could hardly be called a healthy tint. Now a wan hue crept over his features, and he held one hand to his side. "I cannot, indeed," he said; "I am not equal—"

"But this is not business to try you—not accounts or calculations. I don't want to bother you with anything disagreeable—lawyer's business, I mean. I only want to say a few words. You know I shall be twenty-one very soon—on the 21st of next month—and December is nearly here."

"So soon!" Those two words had the sound of a groan.

"Yes, very soon. But that need not be any worry to you—need it? If the thought of a fuss on the day is a trouble, we'll give it up, and have no fuss. I don't care in the least, and I will speak to uncle Arthur. What I wanted to say to you is about the money that will be mine then—forty thousand pounds or thereabouts, is it not? I think Nigel said forty thousand. I suppose I shall have full control of it, or at least of the interest. I have been reckoning up, and the interest would amount to something like fifteen hundred a year, would it not?—more, perhaps. I don't know much about such matters, practically. Fifteen hundred a year of my own would—"

Fulvia stopped short, staring; for an extraordinary pallor had crept over Mr. Browning's face, and the lips were blue. His hand was pressed to his side still, and he leant back with half-closed eyes, as if overcome. But overcome by what? Not, surely, by what Fulvia was saying.

"Padre, dear, am I really worrying you? I am so sorry. Indeed, I only want to say a few words, which I think may be a comfort. Won't you believe it, and listen for a moment?"

"Not quite equal—" Mr. Browning tried again to murmur. "Another—another time."

"Only, if you are bothered, would it not be best now?" She left her seat, and went to his side as she spoke. "It seems a pity to put off. I can't think why you should mind so much my speaking, for indeed I only wished to say that things must go on very much the same as before. Look at me, padre, and try to smile. Won't that be the pleasantest plan? You have always used a part of my income, ever since I came to live with you; and you must use it still. I wouldn't deprive you of a penny that you are accustomed to have. Why, it is your due! what else could you expect? I don't know how much it has been—do you, Nigel? About half, you think? But it ought to be more? If you had a thousand a year, padre, the five hundred remaining would be a great deal more than I should ever care to spend. So you see how easily everything can be arranged! Will not that make it all right?"

There was no answer except a groan. Fulvia knelt down by his side, looking into his face with a softer and sweeter expression than Nigel could recall having seen in her before—though she could be very sweet at times.

"Poor dear padre! I am so sorry. What wicked thing did you suppose I was going to say? But you understand now, don't you?—that my coming of age will make no manner of difference. Except, of course, that I shall have the control of perhaps four or five hundred a year, instead of my dress allowance, and that you will have more—not less—than before! We won't have fusses, or parties, or lawyers, or congratulations, until you are well again. And you will be good, and will see Dr. Duncan, so as to get well quickly. Will that .do? Do you mind my having said so much? For, after all, I am your child, am I not? and I couldn't possibly be so still on any other terms. Just think how much I owe to you and madre! Does this put things smooth and straight?"

Mr. Browning burst into tears.

Such a thing had not been known in the Grange annals! Some men, contrary to common theory, do cry very easily—as easily as some women; but Mr. Browning was not of their number. Even under the pressure of a great sorrow, he would not be known in public to shed a tear. He must have been thoroughly unnerved, before he could thus break down before his son and Fulvia.

Fulvia was so startled as to become white. It was like having the house come down, to see Mr.

Browning burst into womanly tears, his face hidden, his chest and shoulders heaving. She gave a glance of ghastly astonishment at Nigel, and had no glance in response, for Nigel was watching his father intently with a pair of pained and troubled eyes. What was to be done or said next? Fulvia, kneeling there, began to shake all over.

"Padre!" she said in a tone of expostulation; and then she did the worst thing possible, gave way to tears herself. Perhaps her own "rainy season" was hardly at an end yet. "Oh, what is the matter? What does it mean?" she cried.

"I think—I think, perhaps—I had better see—James Duncan," panted Mr. Browning.

He sat up, or rather leant forward, grasping an arm of the chair with either hand, and drawing difficult breaths, almost like sobs. The natural colour had not come back to his lips; and even Fulvia, inexperienced in illness, noted something strange in his look. "James Duncan!" he gasped once more.

At the same instant, opportunely, a man's step sounded on the gravel path outside, and Nigel saw Dr. Duncan pass the window. Come, of course, to visit his patient, Fulvia; supposed to be a prisoner in her own room all this while.

"He is here," Nigel said.

Fulvia stood up. "That had better be first," she said, aware that delay might cause a reversal of Mr. Browning's resolution, and not at all conscious how

great was the present need. " I will send Dr. Duncan
at once."

" Thanks," Nigel answered, again examining his
father with anxious eyes, perplexed what to think of
it all. The gasps of oppression grew worse, yet somehow neither Fulvia nor Nigel was alarmed. It was
not the fashion at the Grange to be alarmed on the
score of Mr. Browning's health; only to show a gentle
solicitude. He talked too much about himself to
induce anxiety. People grew used to it, and were
kindly pitying, but not afraid.

Nigel was far more troubled about the possible
reasons for Mr. Browning's agitation as to Fulvia's
money, and his dread of Fulvia's approaching birthday.
Nervousness alone might lie at the bottom, but nervousness seemed a hardly sufficient explanation. Fulvia
thought nothing further of the matter than that it
was "one of poor padre's fancies, which had to be
humoured;" while Nigel, man-like, weighed cause and
effect, finding the cause inadequate to the effect. He
did not know what else might lie behind; but from
the moment of his father's break-down into tears he
distinctly foresaw " something wrong."

Fulvia went out hastily, and met Dr. Duncan in the
hall, pulling off his great-coat. " Down-stairs!" he
said, with an accent of surprise, not of approval. " Is
that wise ? "

" I don't know."

" Who gave you leave ? "

" I took it."

Dr. Duncan laughed. "Fulvia Rolfe all over!" he said. He had known her from infancy. "I am not sure that the plan has answered;" and there was a critical look.

"I don't know; it doesn't matter. Please go to the study first; yes, padre! He will see you now, and— and if we put off—oh, you understand. Nigel is there; and he doesn't seem right."

" Nigel ? "

"No, padre, padre. I don't see why. I had to say something about my birthday, and he couldn't stand it. He seems—I don't know how—not like himself. He actually—cried." She brought out the word in shame-faced style. "Do go quickly."

"Somebody else needs attention," said Dr. Duncan, who never could be pressed into a hurry.

"I—O no—only I was silly, and it upset me too. But please afterwards tell me how padre really is, and if anything is wrong."

Dr. Duncan disappeared within the study door, and Nigel did not come out as she expected. Fulvia went across to the morning-room, and sat within the open door, keeping watch.

The watch lasted a good while. She could hear nothing at first. Hardly a sound came from the study —unless—was that Mr. Browning? Fulvia fancied she caught a slight moan. Then stillness again, except at intervals a word or so in Dr. Duncan's voice, suppressed,

and not as usual, cheerful. Fulvia did not know what
to make of it. She had expected a continuous murmur
of talk—Dr. Duncan asking questions, Mr. Browning
answering. Was that the key of the study door
turned? Then they were afraid that she or Mrs.
Browning might walk in, and interrupt the conference?
But what harm if either had?

Fulvia's solitude was invaded suddenly by the return
of Mrs. Browning and the girls, accompanied by Mr.
Carden-Cox, who had picked them up, or been picked
up by them, somewhere in the town. Fulvia wondered
what he had come for, since to her knowledge Nigel
had called on Mr. Carden-Cox since breakfast. But
when she saw him, nothing was farther from her
thoughts than that which occupied the whole foreground
of Mr. Carden-Cox' mind—the fourth postscript.

"Fulvia!" was the astonished cry, as she came
forward into the hall. Patchy flushes had faded during her vigil, and she looked haggard. "Fulvia down-
stairs! My dear, how wrong of you!" Mrs. Browning
added.

"It will not hurt me, madre; and one good has
come of it, dear," Fulvia said, kissing Mrs. Browning.
"Padre is seeing Dr. Duncan."

"My husband! Then he is—"

"Oh, it is nothing; really nothing," Fulvia could
reply honestly in her ignorance. "Only I stupidly
said something about my money—something I knew
he really would like, and he was a little fussed and

upset by it. And then he consented to see Dr. Duncan, and Dr. Duncan turned up in the very nick of time. So now they are having a proper consultation, and they ought not to be interrupted."

"You think not? But I—"

"No, indeed, madre; not even you. I would leave them to have it out, if I were you," pleaded Fulvia, taking Mrs. Browning's hands in a detaining grasp. "I would, indeed. If you go in, padre is morally certain to try to seem better or worse than he is; it doesn't matter which. I'm not speaking unkindly. You know what I mean. He won't be natural, because he will be imagining what you may think, and trying to meet it. Besides, they don't want anybody just now, for I heard the door locked. Do come into the morning-room and wait a little."

"How long has James been with my husband?"

Fulvia did not choose to know. She had a shrewd suspicion that the interview had already lasted nearly three-quarters of an hour; but she was not going to say as much to Mrs. Browning; and by resolutely refraining from a glance towards the hall clock, she was able to answer, "I don't exactly know. I should not think he could be much longer. Come, madre."

Mrs. Browning yielded, as every one in the house did more or less yield, to Fulvia's authority, when she chose to exert it; and they adjourned to the morning-room, leaving the door open by a kind of tacit agreement, in readiness to capture Dr. Duncan when he should appear. Fulvia said nothing as to Nigel's presence within the study.

Mr. Carden-Cox was "splitting" to introduce his own subject, finding each moment's delay insufferable, and Daisy, who had already heard the tale, came to his help.

"Fulvie, what do you think?" she cried, lounging against a sofa arm. "Fulvie! do you know, one of Mr. Carden-Cox' postscripts has actually vanished! Nobody knows what has become of it."

Had Fulvia guessed what might be coming, she would not have placed herself in her present position, facing the window, with the light falling full upon her, Mrs. Browning by her side, Mr. Carden-Cox and the two girls exactly in her front. But it would not do to make an instant move. Something would be suspected. She braced herself for the encounter with a strong effort, comforted by a certainty that Mr. Carden-Cox would be vague in his notions. His first words seemed to lend support to this theory.

"Stupid thing, wasn't it?—yes, I couldn't have believed it of myself. Eh, Fulvia! Fancy the old uncle mixing up a lot of postscripts, and sending them all wrong! Putting 'N.B.' in place of 'P.S.'! Fudge! Wouldn't have believed it of myself, if somebody else had told the tale! However—however—however—"

He paused, looking hard at Fulvia. She leant back in her chair, and returned the gaze with an air of indifference. Fulvia had considerable power of acting on occasions, when strung up to the mark.

"Doesn't look guilty," muttered Mr. Carden-Cox.

The words sent a light shock through every nerve, yet she did not visibly wince.

"I wonder if—" she began, looking towards the hall.

"No, no; no hurry—not yet; you said yourself, better wait. Interviews shouldn't be interrupted— important interviews. Duncan knows what he is about; doesn't want our advice. Eh? Sit still. What's the matter?" with a suspicious glance which brought her instantly to quiescence. She let one hand drop upon the other, and waited. "I say, Fulvie, do you know anything of these precious postscripts?"

"Anything!" Fulvia repeated calmly, with a lift of her eyebrows. "I know that you must have been in a very 'mixed' state of mind when you sent them off."

"Tut, tut! Do you know anything of the missing one?"

Fulvia could not, with all her will, prevent a fluttering blush. It deepened slowly. "I did not even know that one had been missed," she said, carefully truthful thus far.

"Of course it has. Now, you needn't keep staring towards the study. Time enough for that when Duncan comes out. Just listen to me. Daisy understands, and I want you to understand. I wrote four letters and put them out in order on my desk; and I wrote four postscripts, putting one inside each envelope. Mind, one into each! I'm as sure of that as I am of— well, of anything!" a particular simile failing him.

" One postscript into each envelope, taking them in a regular succession. By some extraordinary fatality I put the wrong postscripts into the wrong envelopes. Can't imagine how. Never was guilty of such an absurdity in my life before. However, there it is ! Each went to the wrong individual. Three have turned up, and the fourth hasn't ! "

" Very odd ! " said Fulvia.

" Odd ! It's inexplicable."

" Things do disappear unaccountably, sometimes."

" No doubt. But just listen. It's as plain as a pike-staff, if you'll give your mind to it for half a minute. The postscripts went two and two, so to speak, in a double exchange. Ethel's and Daisy's were exchanged. Daisy sent hers to Ethel, and Ethel returned the other to me. Either plan open, of course. That's Ethel and Daisy disposed of. You and Nigel remain. You see ! Now your postscript went to Nigel, and was returned to you. The fair inference is that Nigel's went to you, and that you ought to have returned it to him. Eh ? You see, eh ? "

Fulvia had not expected this. She had reckoned on a good deal of confusion. Mr. Carden-Cox was growing excited, but his recollections were clear. Fulvia kept perfectly still, conscious of an internal trembling, yet conscious that it did not show. One cheek burnt and the other was white, as she remarked—

" Inferences are often great nonsense."

" Tut, tut ! " once more. " I don't want any beating

about the bush. You girls are queer creatures; no knowing what you'll do next, or why you do it. Tell me plainly, did you have Nigel's postscript, or did you not? Eh?"

Fulvia had known that the question must come. She had seen it approaching, as an inevitable thing, even while trying to stave it off. Her mind was not so much in a state of turmoil as in a state of blank, unable to think. She did not reason upon the right and wrong of the question, did not pray to be helped. Wrongdoing had landed her in this difficulty; and the one way out of it seemed to her too hard to be taken. In that moment she had the choice. The straightforward and painful path lay one way; the crooked and seemingly easy path lay the other way.

If she had but taken the right path, regardless of consequences! At the worst, the consequences of welldoing, even when painful, can never be so hard to bear as the consequences of evil doing. But to Fulvia it almost appeared that she had no choice. The upward step was in her eyes so entirely impossible, that the other step became a necessity.

Perhaps in a certain sense it was almost impossible. Fulvia stood alone at the junction of these two paths, unaided, unadvised. She might have had Heavenly aid, Heavenly counsel, Heavenly strength; but she did not ask for them. What wonder that by herself she was weak—the weaker for having been already overcome?

All through the dialogue she had not made up her

mind what to do. She had only allowed herself to drift; and nothing is more certain to bring a vessel to disaster than leaving it to drift.

When Mr. Carden-Cox put the direct question, "Did you have Nigel's postscript?" a curious hardness came over her, the hardness of desperation. She looked straight at Mr. Carden-Cox, neither blushing nor trembling, and replied—

"No."

"Not any postscript?"

"No."

"Quite sure?"

"Yes."

"It couldn't have remained in the envelope unknown to you?"

Fulvia was tempted to catch at the suggestion, but Daisy spoke promptly—

"O no; it wasn't there, I'm sure. I found the envelope on the floor, when Fulvie was in bed; and I looked to see that it was empty."

Fulvia kept silence.

"Well, it's a very odd state of things, I must say —very odd indeed—very odd! That is all! Most extraordinary," said Mr. Carden-Cox.

To Fulvia's intense relief the study door opened. At first she only felt relief, to have the ordeal over. The sense of grief and humiliation at her own fall would come surely, but more slowly.

CHAPTER XV.

FULVIA'S EXPECTATIONS.

"About my monies."—SHAKSPEARE.

"Occasions make not a man frail, but show what he is."
THOMAS À KEMPIS.

"I SHOULD have no objection whatever to a second opinion. It would be as well—better, perhaps. But I am afraid there can be no doubt about the matter. It is pronounced heart-complaint," said Dr. Duncan.

He had broken his tidings as gently as possible. Mrs. Browning and Fulvia, Mr. Carden-Cox and Nigel, were all present. Dr. Duncan would have preferred to see Nigel alone, but he was allowed no choice. Mrs. Browning insisted on hearing the whole that he had to say; Fulvia remained as a matter of course; and everybody knew better than to speak of banishing Mr. Carden-Cox.

Mrs. Browning listened calmly to her cousin's statement; pale, but not overcome. Fanciful worries would bring tears quickly, while in a great trouble she could be brave. Perhaps things proved to be no worse than she had long suspected.

Fulvia was the more openly distressed. It came out gradually that Mr. Browning had been very ill after she had left the study. "A sharp attack," Dr. Duncan called it—sharp enough, they found, to mean actual peril to life. He might have passed away there and then, during his wife's absence, with no previous warning.

"I can never leave him again," Mrs. Browning said, her dark eyes full of meek resolution.

But the cause of the "attack?" It was Fulvia who pressed this question, and she insisted on being told. Could it have been simply the little agitation of being reminded about her birthday? of hearing what she had to say about her money? Impossible. Why he had no reason whatever to mind her speaking. Dr. Duncan evaded the question at first, and Fulvia would not permit the evasion. Was that, or was it not, the cause? She would have yea or nay from him; and Dr. Duncan was a thoroughly truthful man. He might try to avoid giving an answer; but if he gave one, it would be true. He said at length—

"There may have been more involved in the subject than you could know. Almost any agitation might be sufficient."

"Sufficient to bring on a really dangerous attack, do you mean?" persisted Fulvia.

"Yes," was the doctor's laconic rejoinder.

"But—do you mean—you don't mean that at *any* time he may have it?"

"Yes."

"From just a little mistake; letting him talk of what excites him ? "

" Yes ; or rather, forcing him to do so. He will keep clear of agitating subjects, if he is allowed. He will keep clear of them instinctively. Mind, you insist upon all this from me ;" and there was a touch of reproach. " I would rather have given a general warning only."

" But we would rather know the whole—every inch of it," cried Fulvia. She was for once the excited member. Mrs. Browning remained pale and still; Nigel as still, and even paler than his mother; Mr. Carden-Cox bewildered and fidgety, yet silent. " We would much rather be told everything," repeated Fulvia. " Not padre, of course, he is too nervous; and not the girls—but we four. It is only right. Now we shall know how to act."

" Yes, it is far better," Mrs. Browning murmured. Her cold hand crept into Nigel's, and received comforting pressure, though he said nothing. Nigel could not easily speak, under strong feeling. " But I think I am glad we did not know sooner," she went on, with almost a smile ; " until my boy came home."

Dr. Duncan glanced from her to Nigel, with a look which the latter was quick to interpret.

" You have heard what Jamie has to say, and now you will go to my father," Nigel said, rising. " Fulvia too. He is better, and will be looking out for you both."

Mrs. Browning obeyed his touch, as if grateful for

direction; and Fulvia did not resist, though she cast a reproachful glance at Nigel, which he disregarded.

"I was sorry to have to say so much before Mrs. Browning," Dr. Duncan was observing to Mr. Carden-Cox, when Nigel came back from the door; "but Fulvia allows one little choice."

"Fulvia is a woman of character," said Mr. Carden-Cox.

"Fulvia is a girl who likes to have her own way," responded Dr. Duncan. "That may or may not go with character."

"Fulvia was wrong," Nigel added. He stood facing Dr. Duncan, his hand on the back of a chair, and his brows drawn. "I suppose—" and there was a break; "I suppose it is—hopeless?"

"As to the final outcome of the illness? I am afraid so. Not hopeless as to prolongation of life. Absolute recovery may be impossible, but these cases often last on indefinitely."

"With care—"

"Yes; that is essential."

"What kind of care?"

"I have told you already, in a measure. A quiet life, free from exertion and anxiety; if he can have this—"

"One would say he had it already."

The negative movement of Dr. Duncan's head was decided.

"My father is naturally inclined to worry himself about unimportant things, perhaps; but—"

"He must not worry himself. Every kind of worry

must be kept at a distance. His own instinct will tell him often what to avoid; and that instinct must be obeyed. Fulvia did wrongly this morning, forcing upon him a subject from which he shrank. She might not know any reason for his shrinking; but he knew that he could not bear it, and we have seen the result."

"You can give us no hope that by-and-by he may be in a better state than now?"

"Yes, very possibly. He has been brought to his present state by long pressure of worry. No doubt about that," in reply to Nigel's surprised look. "Your father has gone about for months under a heavy burden."

"Since when?"

"Soon after you left England, if not before. I think I was particularly struck with it about last Christmas. He has had a look of trouble more or less for years; but not to the same extent. For months he has been like one under a heavy cloud, unable to rise above it."

"What cloud?" Nigel seemed bewildered.

"That is the question."

"One would say there was hardly a man in Newton Bury with less to worry him than Browning," remarked Mr. Carden-Cox. "But—"

The "but" was significant. Dr. Duncan cleared his throat, and looked at Nigel, who was studying them both.

"I am not sure that you don't know more about the matter than I do," said Nigel. "I have been away for a year, and before that—"

. " It did not exist to the same extent before that."

" If it had, I might not have seen."

" No; you had not reached an observant age. But since you returned—"

" I have noticed worry and uneasiness—a burden or cloud, as you say. My father never seems at rest. There is a kind of unhappy looking forward, expecting trouble to come." Nigel spoke slowly, weighing his words. " Now and then I have fancied it to be connected with money. Fulvia says he is always talking of expenses, and the fact that he objects to college for me—"

" Fudge!" said Mr. Carden-Cox.

" I should have thought my father's income equal to that strain, certainly. He made no difficulty about my trip."

" I took care that he should not."

Nigel failed to catch the muttered sentence.

" Of course he has had the use of Fulvia's money, to some extent; and he may have been looking forward to losing—"

Nigel stopped short. There was an odd click of Mr. Carden-Cox' tongue against the roof of his mouth.

" The fact is, nobody knows much about *that*," said Mr. Carden-Cox, as if addressing himself. " Browning has been entirely irresponsible to anybody all along—everything left in his hands—absurd arrangement; putting temptation in a man's path. May be all right, or may not be. Honourable of course; means to do his best;

but what about business qualities? Hey? Well, well; I've kept my own counsel hitherto, and I mean to keep it—till— Fact is, everybody must know everything soon. Twenty-first of next month! Why on earth has Browning a mortal horror of that day?"

Neither of the two spoke. Nigel's face had become rigid, and a steady defensive glow shone in his eyes.

"I don't wish to suspect—nobody has any business to suspect. Everything may be all right and above-board. But I confess there are signs which stagger one. Something queer about the way he won't have Fulvia's money alluded to in his hearing! Why shouldn't he? Mind you, I wouldn't say this to Clemence or the girls for anything you could mention. But Nigel and you—Nigel ought to be awake."

"He is my father!"

"That doesn't alter facts, my dear boy. Don't look angry, but just listen. Here is Browning, been sole trustee and guardian for nearly twenty years, with absolute control of the child's money, *and*—mark you, her father didn't know this, and I didn't till lately—*and*, with his own affairs in a state of embarrassment all along! There's the rub! If it wasn't for his present condition of mind, I wouldn't suspect him of impru-dence, even now. Imprudence, mind you, no deliberate wrong. He's not capable of that. He is capable of imprudence; and he is capable of speculation. Whether with his own or Fulvia's money I don't know. Nobody

knows, except Browning himself. Done everything
with the best intentions, no doubt; but if a man
dabbles in that sort of thing, why, he's apt to get his
fingers burnt."

"Why should you suppose him to have speculated?"

"I don't suppose—I know. He began it ten years
ago. Had success of course now and then, and was
flush of cash for awhile. So much the worse; just
tempting him on. Talk of economy began after that.
Haven't an idea how far things went, but so much I do
know. Then this last year, as Duncan says, life a
burden to him; something obviously wrong."

Dr. Duncan had not said so precisely, but he let the
inaccuracy pass, beginning to draw on his gloves.

"Fact is—" Mr. Carden-Cox wanted to say something more, and began to fall into a hurry. "Fact is,
that has been my theory for some time—as to Fulvia!
He thinks it would make up to her if— You believe
I'm talking nonsense," with a nervous laugh, meeting
Nigel's glance; "but I'm not. Tell you, I can see
through a stone wall quicker than some folks. Eh?
It's many a year since I first set my heart on something—Nigel knows what; but Browning and I don't
commonly hit upon the same object. Well, for once
we have. Don't believe he would, if it wasn't for
something he knew must come out. Can't say what,
of course. All guess-work. But, suppose now, suppose
Fulvia's £50,000 to have been clipped a little by
injudicious speculation, say, down to half the amount!

Wouldn't be a bad stroke, eh? to throw in a husband for the remainder."

"Said husband valued at £25,000!" remarked Dr. Duncan dryly; nevertheless he did not like this style of talk, and Nigel said coldly—

"I thought the amount was to be £40,000."

"Fifty, if a penny!" Mr. Carden-Cox was very positive. "Might have grown to sixty, under good management. Ought to have done so, too!"

Dr. Duncan shook hands with both, and the subject dropped.

As Fulvia's birthday drew near, an indescribable cloud lay upon the house; felt by all, owned by few. Every thought of merry-making had been given up. Mr. Browning was markedly worse; indeed, it seemed as if, from the hour of admitting himself to be ill enough for medical advice, he had gone steadily downhill.

Or it might be the approach of the birthday. Nobody dared mention the day to him. Nobody dared allude to the coming of age. "Fulvie's money" were words tabooed in his presence. All knew—even Daisy—that agitation might mean death. What could they do, but put possibilities of agitation far away? Fulvia was foremost in this aim, never forgiving herself the mistake which she had made, in forcing upon him the subject of her own affairs.

Despite all efforts to the contrary, the burden upon

Mr. Browning grew heavier, the dire apprehension in his eyes became more marked. Every day he noted the flight of time; often, on asking or hearing the day of the month, with an audible groan. It was "like somebody looking forward to his own execution—so odd!" Daisy said with girlish impatience.

There could not at this time be a doubt about his eager desire to throw Nigel and Fulvia together. Whether Mr. Carden-Cox had suggested the idea to Mr. Browning, or whether it, were his own thought, either way he began from the day of his severe attack to press things forward. "Fulvia and Nigel;" "That dear girl and my boy;" "That noble girl and you, Nigel," were phrases ever on his lips. The wish was an old wish; but it seemed to have suddenly sprung from a torpid to an active condition. Mr. Browning could not leave it alone. He was always harping on it, making nervous little allusions, talking about Nigel to Fulvia, discussing Fulvia with Nigel, weighing possibilities in the hearing of his wife. He watched the two whenever they were together, anxiously, pitifully, as if craving some sign of that which he wanted. Nobody who saw all this could doubt the private touch of Mr. Carden-Cox' finger.

Fulvia neither helped nor hindered. She was too proud to help, too deeply attached to Nigel to hinder. Her aim was to hold an even course, inclining to neither side; and she was well again in health, which perhaps made self-control easier.

Yet not all her self-control could prevent the quick blush, ready to spring on the least provocation. A meaning word or look from Mr. Browning was always enough to bring it. Nigel saw, of course; he could not help seeing; and he found himself in no easy position. Between gratitude to Fulvia for her generosity, and dread of injuring his father, he had sometimes a nightmare sense of being dragged into that from which he utterly shrank.

He was very careful, very watchful over himself, most desirous not to be betrayed into any rash word or act, equally anxious to avoid distressing his father and to avoid giving the least handle to the notion that he sought Fulvia; but he was young still, and naturally impulsive. With all his manliness, he had not learnt to veil passing moods, and his very simplicity made his course more difficult. It was the simplicity of a fine nature. He was not much given to putting his deeper feelings into words, but neither was he given to artificial concealment of them. Fulvia could be artificial at times, for a purpose; Nigel could not. Whatever else he might be, he was always natural.

It was natural to him to be kind and affectionate towards Fulvia. He and she were, and always had been, on such easy terms, that he continually found himself saying or doing something which made the tell-tale blood leap to her face. This might not have meant so much with some girls; but Fulvia was not addicted to blushing, commonly; and Nigel knew it.

When he caught himself in such a mistake, he pulled
up instantly.   But the mischief was usually done first;
though how much "done" he never guessed.   He was
far too transparent to allow for her non-transparency.
If she made him uneasy by a vivid flush one minute,
she made him easy by her careless indifference the
next; and he did not discriminate between that which
was real and that which was put on.

The question of college was still in abeyance, for
Mr. Browning could endure no discussion.   He alluded
once or twice, in his most nervous manner, to the
opening at the Bank, but shrank from any decision.
There was "no hurry; an answer was not required till
after Christmas; Mr. Bramble was quite willing to
wait," he said.   "By-and-by, when I am stronger—
perhaps—anyhow, we cannot spare you yet, my dear
boy!"

Nigel acquiesced with a resolute patience, which he
would not once have shown.   For he was not naturally
patient, being eager, and having a good deal of impetuosity.   The longing to enter upon a career was
strong.   Past ill-health had thrown him back; and the
year abroad had meant further delay.   Most young men
of his own age were already launched on some definite
line of life; and Nigel was keenly conscious of the difference.   He wanted to waste no more time; to be hard
at work as soon as possible, with a settled aim ahead.

Still he acquiesced; and with no mere show of
willingness.

Allusion has just been made to Nigel's "deeper feelings." That such "deeper feelings" did exist, not artificially hidden, but by no means always rising to the surface, none could fail to know who knew Nigel well. Through the pattern of his everyday-life ran golden threads, not earth-born, lending a brightness to the duller earthly warp and woof. He had learnt some things during his year of absence, not very real to him before. Honourable and high-principled he had always been. Even as a boy he had never counted it a sign of manliness to stay away from Church, to shirk family prayers, to neglect Bible reading. There was not, and there never had been, anything small or narrow about Nigel. But it was only during the last few months that he had been aroused to the living claims of the Crucified One upon himself and all that he had. Thenceforth he served in deed and truth the Divine Master, whom he had before only hazily acknowledged.

Though he patiently bore the continued uncertainty as to his future, he did not the less feel it; and but for the greater trouble about Ethel, he would have felt it much more.

In that direction, hopelessness increased. He could not get hold of her, could not bear down the barrier of her changed manner. Not that she was unkind or uninterested; not that he could exactly have defined what was wrong; only ever since the Postscript affair, she had been different; not fully her frank joyous self; never entirely at her ease. She seemed to be always slipping out of his reach; always too busy to give him any time; and when they were together there was an indescribable something which rose like a barrier and kept them apart.

Ethel did not mean it to be so. She had not the smallest intention of repelling Nigel. She was only startled by Mr. Carden-Cox' insinuations, dismayed at the idea that any one could suppose her capable of wishing to marry Nigel if he did not wish to marry her, bent upon setting things straight; and in her efforts she went farther than was needful. Where she meant to be only kind and pleasant, but not too warm, she was distinctly distant and cold. Nigel then was hurt and grave; and this told upon Ethel, adding to her constraint. It was very hard to give him pain; and she knew that her changed manner did pain him sorely; yet how could it be helped? She dared not allow herself to meet him in the old style, for fear of what others might think. The pain reacted sharply upon herself: and those were sorrowful weeks to Ethel. She had often a severe struggle to keep up some appearance of cheerfulness.

Part of life's discipline, all this; and Ethel would be none the worse for it in the end. Strength can only be won through fighting, and patience through endurance. Ethel hardly knew at the time how her trouble was driving her more and more to prayer. Later on she would look back and see more clearly.

Fulvia's watchful eyes noted the difference in Ethel's

bearing towards Nigel, and in Nigel's towards Ethel; and her heart beat fast often with a wild joy. For she thought she understood. She believed that Nigel was at last awake to the fact, that Ethel was not and could not be more to him than the sister of his friend. She believed that Nigel was willing to have things so; and that she—she herself—Fulvia would hide her face at this point, clasping her hands in an ecstasy of delight, so intense as to be almost unbearable. What would life be to her without Nigel? But these reasonings were never allowed to have sway except when Fulvia was alone; never, if any one were present to mark her look.

So a month went by, and the tangle grew, and Fulvia's birthday came near. There had been no more talk of the Continent for Mr. Browning. He was in no state for travelling. Neither had preparations been made for any merry-makings on the day itself; everybody seeming to be anxious only that it should be allowed to slip past as uneventfully as possible.

" But I'll have a lawyer to look into things for the girl, or my name's not Carden-Cox!" the owner of that name muttered from time to time, choosing Daisy for his confidante.

CHAPTER XVI.

ANTIQUITIES.

"A little learning is a dangerous thing :
Drink deep : or taste not the Pierian spring.
*   *   *   *   *   *
Words are like leaves ; and where they most abound,
Much fruit of sense beneath is rarely found."—POPE.

WITHIN two days of Fulvia's birthday, Daisy came
sliding down-stairs, leaning her whole weight upon the
balusters, and ending with a ponderous leap of five
steps at the bottom. She was addicted still to such
little amusements when nobody was at hand to cry,
"Oh !" Perhaps a certain sense of propriety, despite
her objection to young-ladyism, made her dislike wit-
nesses ; and it was particularly provoking, when she
rallied from her leap, to find Mr. Tom Elvey in the hall,
pensively regarding her. He had a way of putting his
head on one side when interested, and it was a good
deal tilted at this moment.

"O, it's Mr. Elvey !" said Daisy, recovering herself,
and assuming a wooden air. "Have you come to see
Nigel ?"

"I—yes—I certainly came—to call," announced Tom.

"Your brother was so good as to call upon me, I believe, the last time I was here."

"He left his card." Daisy objected to Tom Elvey; and she was a downright young woman, priding herself on showing what she felt; so she folded her arms footman fashion, and held her chin stiffly.

"True—yes—just so," assented Tom, studying Daisy with the mild wonder that he might have bestowed upon an infant kangaroo. She was quite a new "specimen" of humanity; rare in his experience. Tom thought her rather pretty, but her curt manner was perplexing. That it should spring from dislike to himself never entered into Tom's calculations. Tom had always been accustomed to appreciation; indeed, he always expected it.

"Yes," responded Daisy, more shortly still, wondering how he had found his way in. Possibly her glance from him to the door was readable, for Tom said apologetically—

"I am afraid it was a liberty—rather. I—in fact, I—I could not make anybody hear. The bell was not answered, so I thought I had better open for myself."

"What could the servants be about?" demanded Daisy. She marched before Tom into the morning-room, where Fulvia sat painting flowers upon a screen, and Nigel stood, gloves in hand, as if going out. Daisy had seen him enter a minute earlier, peeping over the balusters on her way down. She had no business to bring Mr. Elvey to this retreat, as she knew well enough; only she did not pause to think.

"Where is Daisy? I want her," Nigel was saying when Daisy flung the door open.

"Here's Mr. Elvey, come to call on Nigel," quoth Daisy, still with lifted chin and injured voice.

Fulvia did not get up. She shot one indignant glance at the culprit, then held out a hand streaked with paint.

"Daisy ought to have taken you to the drawing-room," she said. "We don't keep this in trim for callers."

Tom assured her that it was a charming room—delightful, natural, unsophisticated. He seemed bent upon using all the adjectives he could find. Nigel's greeting was polite, but not of the most cordial description; for it might be that this fellow was to carry off his dearest hope before his eyes. He could not be warm.

Tom seemed blissfully unconscious of any lack of welcome. He deposited his hat upon one chair, and sat down upon another, into an open box of paints. Fulvia uttered a warning word too late, and Daisy shrieked, then collapsed into a convulsion of laughter. Tom got up, looking mildly at the box, which had suffered dilapidation from his weight, and walked to the chimney-piece. He could not better have displayed the streaky state of his own coat, one glimpse of which in rear sent the younger girl into a fresh paroxysm.

"·Daisy !" Nigel said, under his breath, in displeasure;
" Daisy !! "

Daisy hid her face behind the nearest window-curtain,
and only an occasional choke was audible. Tom's smile
was benignity itself.

" I have a sister about her age, I should say," he
observed. " A very merry age ! "

Choke, again !

" This room seems to be a receptacle for curiosities,"
meditated Tom, poking at a little object on the mantelpiece with his awkward fingers. " I thought this was
—a—but I see you have an elephant's tooth there,
quite a good specimen; yes, killed no doubt in your
travels ? " He looked at Nigel.

" It has lain on that shelf for thirty years, I believe,"
Nigel answered.

" Not on that shelf ! In the house, if you like,"
murmured Fulvia.

Nigel laughed ; he had spoken absently.

" An Indian elephant, no doubt," Tom said, regarding
the specimen critically. " I believe the—a—the molar
tusks of the African elephant are—a—somewhat
differently formed." Tom was not sure of his ground,
but he had of course to keep up his character for learning.

" And the grinders ? " asked Fulvia.

Tom was alarmed. Here might be a modern blue-
stocking of great attainments, before whom he must be
cautious. He had not seen much of Fulvia hitherto,
for she was not what Daisy called " addicted to the

Elveys;" but he had heard her spoken of as "out of
the common," and her frizzly reddish-golden head
looked "clever" in Tom's estimation.

"Yes, just so—a—the grinders," hesitated Tom,
wondering whether "molar" had been the right word
to use. It had come to mind so pat for the occasion as
to be irresistible; but his specimen-hunting hitherto
had not included elephants' teeth, and Tom resolved to
adopt a safe vagueness before Fulvia. "The grinders
—just so," he repeated. "By the bye, you have some
curious weapons here. This odd attempt at a sword—
abortive, rather!—must belong to a—a—rather early
date."

"Pleistocene Period?" suggested Fulvia, playing
with her brush.

Daisy exploded anew, and was again called to order
by Nigel. Tom tried to recall the exact position of the
Pleistocene Period, and failed, not having read up his
geology of late. "I—a—I should say—not far removed
from the Stone Age," he said, pouncing on a happy
thought.

"Wouldn't it rather be the Tin Age?" asked Fulvia,
with lifted eyebrows, not yet looking towards him.

How like a girl! No lady of learning, evidently.
Tom hastened to explain, greatly relieved. There had
been a famous Stone Age, and a Bronze Age, and an
Iron Age, but no Tin Age. He enlarged upon the fact
geologically, if hazily, for Fulvia's information.

"I suppose every country has had its Stone Age

sooner or later," said Fulvia at length. "The Malay Stone Age must have been very recent, but not the British. Which weapon are you speaking of? *That* thing!"—as if she had not known it all the while— "why, Nigel made it for a charade ten years ago—King Hal's sword of State, was it not? Hardly so antique as the British Stone Age, I'm afraid. The fact is, it was buried underground in the tool-house for an indefinite time, and was found again by accident, which gave it a history, and explains its ancient appearance. One certainly might take it for an antediluvian implement of war," Fulvia added indulgently.

Tom was crestfallen. He did not so much mind making a mistake here or there; but he could not endure being found out in a mistake. Very human this; only it does not belong to a lofty type of humanity.

"I suppose you are antiquarian as well as scientific," said Fulvia. "Ethel could give you some help as to antiquarian spots in the neighbourhood. She has more of a leaning in that direction than towards science."

Tom was happily started anew. He forgot his discomfiture, took another seat, and expatiated upon Ethel's good points.

She was "a nice girl," he said—"a very nice sort of girl." Tom was too circumspect to call her "awfully nice," as Nigel would have done in his place; but he meant it plainly. "Really sensible, quite intelligent," continued Tom, with his superior air of approval. He enjoyed intercourse with a mind like hers; young, fresh, capable of assimilating others' knowledge, worth expending trouble upon. Tom spoke with an air of cousinly proprietorship, which might or might not be more than cousinly.

When at last the caller departed, Daisy burst out— "I can't bear that man! He isn't half good enough for Ethel!"

"Daisy, I want you for a walk," interposed Nigel, and she rushed away to dress, Fulvia saying at the same moment, with a smile—

"Poor fellow! he is hopelessly far gone!"

Nigel made no answer; and the silence lasted until Daisy pranced in, exclaiming, "The day after to-morrow is Fulvie's birthday."

"Be quiet, Daisy," ordered Fulvia. "Everybody knows that. It is not to be talked about."

"Mr. Carden-Cox talks," said Daisy. "He means to have a lawyer to look into your affairs. I know he does, because he told me so."

Daisy's voice was penetrating. She spoke in the open doorway of the morning-room, and the study door lay opposite. A faint groan came across after her speech.

"Daisy, *will* you hold your tongue?" cried Fulvia. "He shall do no such thing."

"But he will. He told me so. He says he's not going to have your interests sacrificed to everybody's nerves."

"Nigel!" Fulvia spoke in a tone of despairing appeal.

"I'll see to that. Mind, Daisy, it is not to go any

further. Do for once be discreet. Now are you ready? What's that?" touching her glove.

"O, only a hole. It split last time I went out."

"Couldn't you have mended it before now?"

"I—suppose so—if I hadn't forgotten."

"Have you no other pair?"

"Yes, one other. Won't these do? O, bother! must I go all the way up-stairs again?"

Nigel showed no signs of relenting, and Daisy's face certainly showed no annoyance. She went off at full speed, and reappeared with two gloved hands spread out for inspection.

"That's better," Nigel said, and they were off, Daisy asking in the garden—

"What did you want me to do?"

"Help me choose something for Fulvia's birthday."

"Ah, then I guessed! Father hasn't got anything this year."

"Never mind—my mother has. Fulvia will understand."

"O, Fulvia never gets vexed at that sort of thing. She's a dear. But it will be a horribly dull day. Such a pity! Mr. Carden-Cox is quite put out. He didn't mind so much a week or two ago, but now he says it is all nonsense, and he doesn't believe anything is the matter with father. Nigel, why does father mind so about the day? I wish you would tell me."

"Nobody knows." After a pause, Nigel said abruptly—

"What makes you think of Elvey marrying Ethel?"

" Everybody says it."

" Who ? "

" Mr. Carden-Cox, and Fulvia, and the Brambles, and—O, all sorts of people."

" Have you seen signs of it in Ethel herself ? "

Nigel spoke quietly, and it was growing dusk; but when Daisy looked up in answer, with a meditative, "I don't know," she thought her brother oddly pale. "Why, Nigel!" she said, staring.

" What is the matter ? "

" Why, you look—"

" Well ? "

" Seedy."

" I'm not—thanks."

" Well, you look so. Is anything wrong ? "

"Something is always wrong, when a lady can't answer a question."

" O, if you can make fun !" said Daisy, satisfied. " But I really thought for a moment that you minded something very much. What was it you wanted to know ? O yes, about Ethel. I'm sure I can't tell. What sort of ' signs ' do you mean ? I never do see when people are in love, except when they get to the stupid stage, and by that time it isn't a secret at all. Ethel says she likes Tom, and Tom says Ethel is nice. And Ethel laughs at Tom. And Tom bores Ethel. At least, I should be bored in her place. But they spend lots of time together, so I suppose they get on pretty smoothly. Mr. Carden-Cox declares they will marry, and he is very glad it is Mr. Tom Elvey and not you, because he says that would never do."

"What would never do?"

"Why, you and Ethel! When you first came home, you were always going after Ethel, and Mr. Carden-Cox didn't like it, any more than mother did. He wants you to marry Fulvia, and he says the other is out of the question. He says there are reasons against it, and father would never consent. And he says you care for Fulvia more than for anybody else in the world. Do you?" asked innocent Daisy. "More than mother?"

Nigel's temper was not very easily roused, but Daisy had said enough to rouse it now. The idea of Mr. Carden-Cox discussing him and his affairs in this cool fashion with his youngest sister was unbearable. Nigel could not trust himself to speak at once in answer. He was too angry to have control over his own voice. He only walked faster and faster, till Daisy could scarcely keep pace with him, and words on her part failed for lack of breath. Now and again she glanced up at his closed lips, first in wonder, then in fear.

"Are you vexed?" she panted at length. "I didn't mean— Nigel, I can't race so!"

Nigel slackened speed. "I did not know we were going so fast," he said. "Yes, of course I am vexed. Mr. Carden-Cox had no business to say anything of the sort to you. Remember, Daisy—not one word of this is to go a step farther—least of all to Fulvia. It is absurd rubbish, the whole of it—mere gossip."

P

"Mr. Carden-Cox!" exclaimed Daisy, aghast.

"Mr. Carden-Cox or anybody. It doesn't matter who talks so. The whole is mere gossip. You understand? If you repeat a word, you may make no end of mischief."

"No, I won't; indeed, I won't," said Daisy. "But, O! please don't tell Mr. Carden-Cox that I let out what he said."

CHAPTER XVII.

HE AND SHE.

"Such is the bliss of souls serene,
  When they have sworn, and steadfast mean,
  Counting the cost, in all to espy
  Their God, in all themselves deny.

"O could we learn that sacrifice,
  What lights would all around us rise !
  How would our hearts with wisdom talk
  Along life's dullest, dreariest walk !
  *   *   *   *   *
"Seek we no more ; content with these,
  Let present rapture, comfort, ease,
  As Heaven shall bid them, come and go—
  The secret this of rest below."—*Christian Year.*

THE afternoon before Fulvia's birthday !

All the morning snow fell; and when lunch was over, it grew into a storm—flakes whirling thickly, clouds low, ground white, wind gusty and strong. The girls congratulated themselves on having bought Fulvia's presents in good time.

Mr. Browning was in the lowest depths of depression and misery. It was hard to look upon him unmoved. Dr. Duncan had been to see how he was that morning, and had spoken of the need for mental repose. "If this went on—" he said significantly. But who was to give the mental repose? How were they to minister to this mind diseased? Mr. Browning was like a hunted creature, shrinking before some terrible shadow, from which he might not escape. He could not rest, could not read, could not stay in one place, could not bear the presence of others, could not endure to be alone. His face was shrunken, the lips were blue, the eyes were filled with a nameless apprehension; yet what he feared none knew, and none dared ask.

Not a word was spoken in his hearing of the morrow, and not a word spoke he. He knew the date, however; and they all knew that he knew it. "Fulvia's birthday" was written in each line of his haggard cheek and brow.

Fulvia sat with him for a while, trying to be cheery, but finding cheeriness no easy matter in the face of his persistent melancholy. If she laughed, he could only groan. Mrs. Browning had a brief respite while she was there, for which all were grateful. Soon, however, Mr. Browning demanded once more his patient wife, and would be content with no other companion.

Nigel alone went out. "It was no weather for girls," he said, when Daisy begged to accompany him. He plodded through the heavy snow, all the way to Mr. Carden-Cox' house, and there sat over the fire with the old bachelor, hearing much vague talk about nothing in particular, intermixed with dark and dim hints about the morrow.

At first Nigel hardly noticed these. He was unwontedly depressed, feeling the strain of the last few weeks, and little disposed to speak. Then a passing phrase recalled Daisy's warning as to the lawyer, and in a moment Nigel was himself. He had actually come to settle this matter, and had almost lost sight of it in anxious thought about Ethel.

" I say, Nigel, that's all very well, my dear fellow," remonstrated Mr. Carden-Cox, when a judicious question had drawn from him a statement of his intentions, and Nigel had represented the peril to Mr. Browning of the proposed action. " I say, that's all very well. I've a sincere regard for your father's health—indubitably— don't wish to do him any harm. Still, right's right and wrong's wrong, and the girl is my own flesh and blood. She must have her due."

" Of course—"

" And everything ought to be clear and ship-shape at once."

" As soon as possible."

" To-morrow, I say."

" That is the question. As soon as possible," repeated Nigel.

" If your father doesn't bring *his* lawyer forward, I shall bring *mine* forward—that's all."

" It would be a serious step, in his present state. Not that I see what you and your lawyer could do without Fulvia's consent—short of going to law."

" Stuff and nonsense! Going to law! I merely wish

to know how things stand. There's nobody else to see that the girl has her rights."

"Except—"

"Eh! what? yourself! Yes, yes, to be sure—if you'll assume the responsibility. But I'll not have the question shirked."

"It shall not be."

"Well, if you say so!" in a mollified tone. "I've no faith in your father's business capacities; but yours are different. Yes; I trust *you*—" pointedly. "Who are your father's lawyers just now? He has been given to changing."

"Brown & Berridge, I believe. He has not much to do with lawyers."

"Dare say not! That's the worst of leaving a man irresponsible. Nobody knows anything about it. Brown & Berridge! Where?"

"London."

"Humph!"

"Will you leave the responsibility of Fulvia's money to me?" asked Nigel, in a resolute abrupt tone.

"Yes; when you are settled to be her husband!"

Nigel's colour rose. "That is not likely," he said.

"But, I say—you like the girl?"

"Yes."

"What more is wanted?"

Nigel's laugh had no ring in it. "A good deal more," he said. "One ay 'like' a great many people."

"You know t e sort of liking I mean. And you

know that you *don't* like ' a great many people ' as you
like Fulvia."

"Perhaps not," Nigel answered carelessly.

"Then what on earth keeps you back? It's your
father's wish—it's my wish—and you care for her!
What more do you want, eh? That Fulvia should
'like' you, I suppose! No fear about her! Daisy
says—"

This was too much, and Nigel started up. "Another
word, and I'm off!"

"Come, come; don't be excited. Lover-like, but unnecessary," laughed Mr. Carden-Cox. " I'll not betray
confidences. Can't you see for yourself? Sit down."

Nigel remained standing.

"When I speak of undertaking responsibility for
Fulvia, I mean it simply as her brother. Nothing else
is possible."

"For you, or for her? Which? Ha, ha! Well, so
be it just now. I'll leave the matter in your hands,
for—let us say, for a few weeks. Concession enough,
that! Why, bless me, if Browning doesn't hand over
the money to the girl this week, he's defrauding her—
nothing short of defrauding her. And if he can't bear
to have the subject mentioned, how is anything to be
arranged, eh? Talk of health! It is a matter of
conscience, not of health. Well, well, sit down, my
dear fellow, and I'll not say anything more about it
just now."

Nigel obeyed; and Mr. Carden-Cox, to escape from

the engrossing subject of Fulvia's money, turned to the scarcely less engrossing subject of "the four N.B.'s."

He was always able to talk of this for any length of time. He could not get over the mystery, could not forgive himself the blunder, could not rest without solving the riddle of the lost half-sheet. Postscripts haunted him night and day. He was like an ardent devotee of conundrums—unable to enjoy life till he should find a clue to the puzzle. Nigel had to listen to a new and profuse statement of all the details, wound up by a graphic description of his questions put to Fulvia, and of her emphatic denial.

"Said plainly enough she hadn't received yours— hadn't received any postscript at all, in fact. What do you think?"

"It settles the matter, of course, once for all." Nigel spoke with a touch of impatience, for he was weary of the subject.

"Unsettles the matter, you mean. Why, now, I have told you a dozen times at least"—"Quite true!" thought Nigel, with an inward groan—"that there were four envelopes and four postscripts, and that I put one postscript into each envelope. Now, under those circumstances, how could Fulvia have failed to get one?"

"She evidently did fail."

"But I say, my dear fellow, she could not!"

"You meant to put in the four. Whether you did so is another question. I suppose we all make mistakes sometimes. And Fulvia's word—"

"A lady's word! Pshaw!"

Nigel was coldly silent.

"I don't suppose the girl means to deceive. She has blundered somehow. But as for my not putting in that postscript—! Of course it may have dropped out, —been stolen, or lost, or burnt, or—"

"It seems to me a very insignificant matter."

"Insignificant!" Mr. Carden-Cox was scandalized. *His* correspondence to be counted "insignificant!" He could scarcely believe his own ears.

"O, very well; if the thing isn't of sufficient importance to claim your attention, I have no more to say. I should have thought—but it doesn't signify. You young fellows think such an amount of yourselves; nothing else is worth a glance. I should have thought that the question of *my* truthfulness being impugned was of some weight even in your eyes; but no, that is quite insignificant. Fulvia is to be believed, of course; and I—I may look to myself." Then a twinkle broke into the anger. "Well, well—after all, any amount of infatuation is allowed to young lovers. I ought not to be surprised. All perfectly natural, just as it should be. Fulvia is a good girl—wonderfully good to everybody; wouldn't say what wasn't true. Dare say you are right enough there. Shouldn't wonder if she burnt the paper, unknowingly. Women are capable of anything. Most inscrutable creatures!"

Nigel would not risk further discussion by further opposition. He knew well that nothing he could say would alter Mr. Carden-Cox' determined linking of his name with Fulvia's ; and presently he managed to escape, feeling that the lawyer-peril was deferred for a time. Why peril should exist in connection with a lawyer, Nigel was only able to conjecture.

Once more he was buffeting the wind, which had risen much. No use to open an umbrella; he could not have held it up. He pulled his cap low, bent his head, and fought his way steadily through the gale. Yet he did not turn homeward. A thirst had come over him for another glimpse of Ethel. She would surely be at home after dark, this stormy afternoon, and he turned his steps towards Church Square.

When almost close to the Rectory gate, he saw in the lamplight a slight cloaked figure run out. " Ethel ! " passed his lips, but he was not heard. She crossed the road, battling her way with difficulty, and he followed, overtaking her at the vestry door, where three steps led upward. As she mounted them, a gust of snow-laden wind swirled round the corner, carrying her off her feet. She threw out both hands with a little cry, as if grasping for support ; and before she could go down Nigel had her.

" O, thanks ! " she gasped, conscious of the friendly clutch, not in the least recognizing her deliverer.

The short struggle had rendered her breathless, and he held her still while helping to open the door. So far he said nothing, and Ethel made no inquiry. It was pitch-dark. She could not see his outline, and she believed the helping hand, which had saved her from a fall, to be the sexton's. That the sexton should be just then on the spot was at least not more unlikely than that anybody else should.

Nigel went inside with her, and shut the door, while Ethel struck a light. In one corner of the vestry lay a heap of holly. "How kind of you to be so quick!" she said gratefully, turning to her companion. "I thought I was— O! Nigel!—"

Ethel was completely taken by surprise. Her face coloured up for once brilliantly, and a light shone in the blue eyes.

Nobody was at hand who could misconstrue her manner—nobody except Nigel himself. At the moment, somehow, she did not fear him. His appearance was so unexpected; she had not time to think of Mr. Carden-Cox or Fulvia, so had not leisure to shape her welcome. There was a ring of gladness in the utterance of his name, which brought to Nigel's mind their first meeting after his year of absence, and made his heart spring with hope.

"I thought I might find you in to-day," he said. "Such weather! And then I saw you coming here."

"So you came too?"

"Yes, I came too. It was *you* I wanted to see," pointedly. "Not—" and a pause.

"I only ran over just to do a little of this—" Ethel glanced at the holly. "We always start it rather early; and if the snow keeps on I can't depend upon all my helpers. So I thought I would begin a piece of

wreathing. But I am afraid it was not really that—
not only that, I mean," her eyes looking up at Nigel
with their old half-roguish frankness. "I was so tired
of poor old Tom."

"Were you?" Nigel's whole frame was in a
glow.

"Yes, only you must not tell anybody. I wouldn't
hurt his feelings for the world. But I really could not
stand it any longer. Always those dreadful herbariums
and specimens and Latin names. If he would call a
spade a spade, one wouldn't mind; but he is content
with nothing short of five syllables and what Lance
calls 'a Latin sneeze' at the end."

"A sneeze!"

"Papaver*aceæ*!" instanced Ethel, with a mischievous
transposition of the last syllable into an imitation of the
catarrhic "tshyee!" "But"—when they had had a
laugh—"it isn't as if Tom knew a great deal, and could
teach one what is worth knowing. That would be
different. Tom only looks upon the world as a great
museum of curiosities; and all he cares for is to get up
a little imitation museum of 'specimens,' pegged down
in rows. And surely God's beautiful world means a great
deal more than that—a great great deal more," Ethel
went on, warming with her subject. "Sometimes I
get so cross, I should like to peg down Tom himself
as a dried 'specimen of the modern scientific young
man.' But that wouldn't be fair; for a really scientific
man, who knows about things, not only about names, is

different from poor old Tom. And I suppose it is not
his fault that he can't see below the surface."

If "poor old Tom" had but heard ! At this very
moment he was seated beside Mrs. Elvey, complacently
and ponderously giving forth his views on the "intelli-
gence" of Ethel. "Such a nice unassuming girl, and
so ready to be taught!" quoth unsuspecting Tom.

"Of course I have the chief part of it all," pursued
Ethel, resting one hand upon the vestry table, and
smiling still. "My father and Malcolm are very busy just
now—extra busy; and I can't let them be teased. And
mother only cares to talk to Tom now and then; and
the boys detest him. It has been such a day, none of
us could get out much; and I thought at last I must
have half-an-hour's peace. So I slipped away without
telling Tom, and here I am. But I didn't come for
nonsense," she said, with dropped voice and sudden
soberness. "I almost forgot where we were—seeing
you, and— It was just that I wanted a little quiet, to
think about Christmas, and—and the kind of life one
ought to lead."

A look showed full appreciation of the last words.
"Couldn't I help you with the holly?"

"I don't know—thanks. I can hardly stay long
enough to make it worth while. I shall have helpers
to-morrow." Ethel was waking up to the fact that
it would not do for her to remain here, after dark, alone
with Nigel. It would not quite do, old friend and playfellow though he was. "There is poor Tom, you know,"

said Ethel, the light fading out of her eyes. She had so enjoyed this little bout of unrestrained talk, and now she began to wonder at her own unrestraint.

But Tom's sting was gone. "Poor fellow! Shall we go and have a lesson from him together in Latin terminations?" Nigel asked joyously.

"Is Mr. Browning better to-night?" inquired Ethel, struck with the light-hearted manner.

"No; I'm afraid not. I can never tell you about him now, you are always so busy. Couldn't you sit down for five minutes?"

"I don't think I ought."

Ethel leant against the table, grave again, and a little anxious. Had she gone too far, shown too much pleasure at seeing Nigel? Had she not broken through her own resolution? If Mr. Carden-Cox knew—Ethel's breath came quickly at the thought! Nigel seemed so pleased to see her again like herself; but, of course, that meant nothing—there was Fulvia in the background, and it would not do for her to study Nigel's feelings. He might wish her to be still on the old frank playmate terms, but it could not be; the time had come for a change, and he must grow used to it. Just for a few minutes everything had felt so natural, so like past days; and now she would have to be careful again, to rein herself in. It was hard, but it had to be done. Whether or no Nigel understood, she must be firm. Ethel did not hear her own sigh.

Nigel stood in front, upright and broad-shouldered,

streaked still with half-melted snow; and his dark eyes were bent upon Ethel with their most earnest look. She could not fathom the look, or know why it sent so strange a thrill through her. What did Nigel mean—gazing, and not speaking?

"I think we ought to go home," she said.

Then a question came, not in his usual voice. "Ethel, what is the matter?" he asked very low.

"Is—anything?" she asked, with an audacious attempt at a smile.

"Yes."

Ethel found her lips quivering, and she straightened herself, resolute not to give way. "O, just the common worries of life."

"I wish I could bear them for you."

"That wouldn't be fair. You have enough of your own," and she laughed huskily, biting those unruly lips.

Nigel was silent again, thinking. He could not yet make up his mind whether or no to say more. To detain her he drew from his pocket-book a little folded paper.

"I don't know whether you will care to have this. I promised to make a copy," he said.

"A copy of—"

"Don't you remember the extracts I carried off? I don't want to part with them—" a pause, followed by an emphatic "ever!" and another pause. "But I have had this copy by me to give to you; only there has been no chance."

Ethel said only "Thanks!" as she received it.

" You don't mind my keeping the other ? "

" O no—not if—I like you to have it."

" And I like you to have this. I read it through pretty nearly every day." Ethel mentally determined to do the same. " That fourth quotation always seems to me an exact description of—you."

She started. As he spoke her mind had leaped ahead of the words, putting " Fulvia " at the end.

" O no ! " she said again. " If you knew me—"

" I think I do ; better than I know any one else in the world. And, Ethel, I am trying to make it my rule of life, just as I know you do. Yes, I know, because I can see. But one doesn't find the rule easy to follow." He opened the folded page in Ethel's hand, not taking it from her, and read : " ' To sacrifice self as an habitual law in each sudden call to action ; to take more and more secretly the lowest place ; to move amid constant distractions and above them undisturbedly—' as you do, and as I don't."

" I am not like that, indeed, indeed," Ethel murmured, as if begging to be believed.

" I think you are. But never mind ; it is what we both want to be. I suppose one never would sacrifice oneself in a great matter, if it had not first become ' the law ' in small every-day things," said Nigel thoughtfully.

" My father says every small choice between right and wrong is a rehearsal for some greater choice to follow. One can understand that. But I ought to go home."

" Are you in such a hurry ? "

"No ; not a hurry, only—"

"Only you think you ought. I believe 'ought' governs every inch of your life."

"It ought," Ethel said involuntarily. She was moving towards the door, and with a sudden impulse she lifted her eyes again, smiling. "At all events, I have not come here for nothing. I'm afraid I talked nonsense at first ; but you have given me a thought for Christmas."

"What thought ?"—though he knew.

"Just that—self-sacrifice in little things. Great things don't come in my way ; but there is no end to the little opportunities. Now we have to turn out the gas and grope to the door."

"One word !" Nigel's voice was husky, and Ethel looked at him in wonder. "We don't often get a chance of a few minutes together, like this. Ethel, you won't mind if I ask a question. Has there been something wrong lately ? something I have done to—I won't say to vex you, but—don't you know what I mean ?"

"No ! nothing ! I mean—I was not vexed."

"But there has been something. I thought it was Tom Elvey."

"O no, indeed !" with energy.

"I have been afraid, till the last few minutes. Was it anything I said or did ?"

"No ! O no !"

"Or something somebody else said ? Mr. Carden-Cox !" with a sudden recollection of the postscripts.

"Please don't ask any more. It doesn't matter in

Q

the least. Nothing matters—now!" said Ethel. The colour rushed into her cheeks. "I only mean—please never think again that I could be vexed—"

"With me," Nigel concluded for her. Then in a quiet happy tone he added: "No, it doesn't matter. Nothing matters—now!"

Ethel turned off the gas in a great hurry, but not before he caught the flash of an answering glance, brighter than she knew it to be. Then they found their way to the door, and were out in the whirling gale. Ethel had to cling to his strong arm for support; and it came over her how easy life would be, thus clinging. She heard one question spoken by the way, spoken in the midst of their struggle, as the snow drifted in their faces—

"Ethel, can you trust me?"

"Yes!" she answered at once, not asking what he meant.

"Even if—" and the sentence was not finished. Perhaps he hardly knew what he wished to say.

"*Yes!*" came with stronger emphasis; and she never once thought of the postscript about Fulvia, till she was at home, and Nigel was gone.

But the recollection made no difference. She echoed her own "Yes!" joyously in the solitude of her own room. Trust him? Yes!!

CHAPTER XVIII.

AGED TWENTY-ONE.

"In that hour of deep contrition,
  He beheld, with clearer vision,
  Through all outward show and fashion,
    Justice, the Avenger, rise.

"All the pomp of earth had vanished,
  Falsehood and deceit were banished,
  Reason spake more loud than passion,
    And the truth wore no disguise."—LONGFELLOW.

HALF of Fulvia's twenty-first birthday was over, and she had not yet seen Mr. Browning.

It had been a most uneventful day thus far. Fulvia had presents from all in the house, except Mr. Browning. Nigel gave her a gold locket; Ethel sent a dainty basket arrangement of holly and ferns; old school friends wrote letters; but that was all. Nothing had yet occurred to mark the fact that on this day Fulvia Rolfe would, or should, come into possession of some forty or fifty thousand pounds.

She had not even donned a better dress for the occasion, which was a Grange fashion on birthdays. Mr. Browning would remark the change, Fulvia thought.

After all, the dress she wore daily could not have been improved upon. It was a fine navy-blue cloth, fitting, perfectly. She did add lace ruffles and the new locket, and she dressed her hair with extra particularity. Care bestowed upon that mass of reddish golden-brown was always repaid. Fulvia looked well, almost handsome. She was conscious of the fact, and conscious that Nigel noticed it with brotherly interest—only Fulvia unhappily did not count the interest to be brotherly. Nigel liked his sisters to look their best; and a little earlier he would have told Fulvia, without hesitation, as one of the three, that she had turned herself out successfully for the occasion. He was growing cautious now, however, and so he said nothing not guessing that she saw the thought in his face, and misconstrued the silence.

He was in high spirits, radiantly happy, as he had not been for weeks, nobody guessing why. Nobody knew of the interview in the vestry. Even the knowledge of his father's state could not depress him, this first morning after the lifting of his own heavy cloud, though it did keep down, to a moderate pitch, the spirits which would otherwise have been wild. He had his dreamy bouts, too; going over and over in mind the words which had passed between him and Ethel, wondering whether he had taken it too much for granted that she might care for him, and whether he had said enough to be understood, but always coming round to a glad remembrance of the last emphatic " Yes ! yes ! "

The sunshine in his eyes perplexed Fulvia; he had been so grave lately. Then she made up her mind that her birthday was the cause; he wanted to please her by making it a cheerful day. Fulvia responded to the supposed wish with all her heart. There had not been such an amount of fun in the breakfast-room for many a week, as on that morning of December 21st.

Snow had ceased falling, and a slow thaw had set in, rendering the streets slushy, while the air was full of cold moisture. Fulvia and Daisy braved the weather in a brisk morning walk; Anice remaining indoors as a matter of course. Fulvia had hoped for Nigel's company, and was disappointed, for he vanished. Where he went he did not say, and Fulvia had learnt not to question him; she was not one who needed the same lesson twice over. At luncheon he looked sunnier than ever; yet Mr. Browning was still in complete retirement. None but his wife had spoken to him.

More oddly, Mr. Carden-Cox had not appeared, and this perplexed everybody.

"Why, he always gives Fulvia something nice," protested the aggrieved Daisy, desiring excitement. "Surely he won't forget! And doesn't father mean to speak to Fulvia? So odd! on her birthday! As if she were in disgrace!"

"He will do as he chooses," Fulvia answered.

It was getting on for the time of afternoon tea; and the aspect of the Newton Bury atmosphere, through glass panes, was not inviting. Nigel had been up-stairs since lunch, supposed to be reading; and the three girls were spending their afternoon over the drawing-room fire, having indulged themselves into a state of easy-chair inertia. Even Fulvia was not proof against the lazy mood—until Nigel appeared. She brightened up then, and replied to Daisy's complaints with her usual elastic air.

"Of course he will. Everybody does," said Daisy. "But I don't see that people ought. I think he ought to come out of his den for just a little while. Nigel! what have you got? Chestnuts! How lovely! We'll have some fun now!"

Plainly this was Nigel's object. He was a very boy again in the next half-hour, helping Daisy to balance chestnuts on the hot bars, watching for the critical moment of "done enough and not too much," using Daisy's fingers in pretence, and scorching his own in reality. He and Daisy were down on the rug to-gether, and shouts of laughter sounded, when Mrs. Browning came with her soft lagging step and sweet graciousness.

"I have persuaded your father to take a cup of tea with us here," she said to the group. "He is very sadly to-day, but he liked to hear your merry voices, and indeed he proposed to come. It is such weather, we shall have no callers."

"Don't stop laughing, pray, when he appears," whispered Fulvia; and they did not, but the real ring *of mirth* was gone. Mr. Browning's heavy steps and

down-drawn mouth-corners were not provocative of fun.
He looked both ill and wretched.

Fulvia was the first to spring up in welcome. She
gave him a daughterly kiss, made him sit in the chair
she had occupied, chatted about weather and chestnuts,
tried to make it seem that nothing was farther from her
thoughts than the remembrance of her own age. Mr.
Browning seemed relieved, and he even smiled dimly at
one or two of Nigel's sallies.

"Hallo, Daisy! That fellow's rolling! He'll be gone!"

"Oh! oh! I'm burning my fingers. What shall I
do? He's done for—black as a coal."

"Never mind; we've plenty more! You are getting
your face a most awful colour, my dear. Look at Anice."

"Anice has a complexion, and I've none. Can't take
care of what I haven't got. I say—what are you after?
Is that for me? Thanks. And Fulvie would like
another. Don't you care for chestnuts, father?"

"No, dear," mournfully.

Tea came in, and was dispensed by Fulvia; in the
midst of which operation a fly drove up to the front
door. Daisy capered to the window, and peeped out.

"O, it is Mr. Carden-Cox! With a huge parcel!
Here he comes! Fulvie's birthday, of course," cried
thoughtless Daisy. "How jolly! I said he was sure
to come."

"You little goose!" breathed Nigel; and "Daisy!"
Fulvia uttered impatiently; but the culprit heard
neither.

"He's coming!" she exclaimed again, and Mr. Browning put his hand to his side, as the door opened to a rustle of brown paper.

Mr. Carden-Cox carried the parcel—a big one, as Daisy had said. He was in one of his excited states—that could be seen at once. Fulvia rose to greet and silence him, but found herself powerless. She might as well have tried to stem a rivulet with her hand. By going forward she only absorbed the whole of his attention, and rendered him unconscious of Mr. Browning's presence.

"How d'you do, Fulvia? How d'you do, my dear? Many happy returns of the day! I wish you all manner of good things through life : health to enjoy your money, and wisdom to use it. I've brought you a little remembrance—sort of thing a lady of property ought to have, hey! A dressing-case, nothing more; don't expect too much. But it's a tidy concern, I flatter myself—tidy little concern, good of its kind. Here, have off the wrappings. What's the matter? You look as if it would bite you. Eh? what do you say? Couldn't get what I wanted in Newton Bury, so sent to London for this, and it has only just arrived. Shameful delay! Couldn't think what to do this morning, when it hadn't come. Telegraphed to London, and found it had gone off all right, so went to the station, and there it was. Abominable carelessness! I'll write a complaint to headquarters. However, here it is at last, just in time; birthday not over yet, eh? Got one of a good solid kind—see—silver fittings and the rest—here—"

Fulvia was trying to thank and to check him, in vain.

"Yes, yes, yes, I understand—pretty, of course. Had a nice day—plenty of presents, eh? Don't at all like nothing more to be done to mark your coming of age. Don't at all like it, my dear! Can't be helped, but—Well!" in a loud whisper—"had any business talk yet —statements as to your finances? You've got a right to that. Necessary, you know. Don't you let him put things off! I meant to call a lawyer, but Nigel wouldn't let me—said he'd take the responsibility. Ha! makes you blush, that, doesn't it, child? But of course you've had a statement—know how things stand—fifty thousand, eh! Ought not to be less by now, properly handled. How's Browning to-day? Oh! ah!" as a faint groan reached his hearing. "Oh! ah! I didn't see! How d'you do? Quite well? Come to congratulate my niece on attaining her majority—lady of fortune, hey?"

No efforts could stop him thus far. When Mr. Carden-Cox was resolved to have his say, he commonly did have it. Fulvia clutched in vain with two eager hands, thanking, entreating, doing her best to entice him from the room; Nigel in vain drew near, signing caution; and the younger girls looked aghast, in vain. Mr. Carden-Cox saw nothing, heard nothing, knew nothing, except that he had certain utterances to make, and that he chose to make them.

Albert Browning offered no response to the greeting

of Mr. Carden-Cox. He stood up slowly, breathing
hard, and leaning on his wife's shoulder,—a frail support, yet firm through force of will,—and Nigel went
quickly to give more efficient help. Mr. Carden-Cox
spoke again to Mr. Browning, but again had no answer.
Albert Browning's head was resolutely turned away ;
and the three went out of a farther door.

"Offended ! eh ? But I say, Fulvie, my dear, you
have a right to know—a right to ask ! Your money—"

"O, how could you!" cried Fulvia, in distress. "We
were so happy all together, and you have quite spoilt
the day. How could you come and say such things ? "

Mr. Browning was not taken ill there and then, as
everybody feared—everybody except Mr. Carden-Cox,
who showed dire offence at Fulvia's remonstrance, and
required a large amount of polite attention to win his
pardon. Being a man who never avowed himself in the
wrong, he naturally could not stand blame.

No particular ill effects were apparent that evening,
from the unwished-for agitation. Mr. Browning even
came to the drawing-room after dinner, and exerted
himself to a certain degree of melancholy cheerfulness.
He was particularly affectionate to Fulvia, calling her
"my dearest child" repeatedly. Still no allusion was
made to Fulvia's affairs.

"He is better than I expected," Nigel remarked late
in the evening to Fulvia, others having disappeared.
Fulvia usually remained five minutes later than the

rest of the party, clearing away odds and ends. "Seems none the worse for Mr. Carden-Cox."

" I was afraid he would be."

" At the moment—yes."

" I am glad the day is over," Fulvia said, with an accent of relief.

" Not very satisfactorily over, for you."

" Why ? "

" You ought, at least, to have had what Mr. Carden-Cox calls ' a statement.' "

" Time enough. I am in no hurry. The money is there all right; and when padre is up to business, he will make as many statements as you like."

Was the money "there all right ? " Mr. Carden-Cox' suspicions had infected Nigel; yet Nigel would not let himself doubt. Mr. Browning's nerves might account for anything.

" I really believe padre is stronger already, in fact. He would not have borne this so well a month ago. But I am glad, very glad, that the day is over. It has been a strain upon us all, looking forward. Now things can go on just as they always do."

" You are the most unselfish of beings ! " Nigel said involuntarily. Then, when he saw her look—the heightening colour and dropped eyelids—he was vexed with himself for the unguarded remark.

" I don't know about unselfishness; I seem to be so completely one of you all, that what affects you affects me," she said, almost shyly.

Nigel could have replied, "Is not that the very essence of unselfishness?"—but he would not risk it. He saw that she was disappointed at his silence, and the light in her face faded.

"At all events, I know somebody else is relieved too," she said in her usual tone. "Confess! you have been dreadfully worried lately; and to-day—well, you are not depressed."

"Chestnuts and nonsense! That doesn't mean much. One gets a fit of high spirits sometimes unreasonably."

"I must be off to bed. Good-night," she said, and the tone was flat. Nigel never offered to kiss her now, of course. He had not since the first day of his return. She moved away, and he sat long, thinking—dreaming rather—not of Fulvia, but of Ethel.

In the early morning there came a sudden alarm. Mr. Browning was ill. A severe attack of pain and breathlessness came on, like in kind to the short attack he had had before, when only Nigel and Dr. Duncan were present, but worse in degree. He had been in danger then, and had rallied quickly. Now there was no real rally; only a slight occasional improvement, followed by a worse relapse. Dr. Duncan, summoned hastily, stayed long, but could do little, for remedies failed to touch the evil.

"He will not stand this long," Dr. Duncan said in a low voice to Nigel. "Yes—great danger. I doubt if he will last through the day."

The suffering and oppression increased, till it was

hard to look on unmoved. Mr. Browning could not lie down, could not endure to be in bed. He sat up in his easy-chair, leaning forward, his face livid, his eyes full of helpless affectionate appeal, which went to their very hearts.

Mrs. Browning, worn out by long previous strain, broke down under the distress of seeing him thus. She had to be taken to another room, and was there tended by Daisy, who at such a time could rise out of her childishness, and be useful. Anice was absent from the sick-room, of course; poor weak-natured Anice, always fleeing, unwomanlike, from aught that aroused a feeling of discomfort.

But Fulvia never left Mr. Browning, and he could scarcely endure to have Nigel out of his sight. It fell to those two to watch side by side through many long hours of that trying day—trying to both, but most so to Nigel. For Fulvia was in her element, and Nigel's presence meant rest to her; while the sight of what Mr. Browning had to bear, racked Nigel's powers of endurance to the utmost. He did not give in; and Fulvia, herself absolutely unwearied in the necessities of her position and in the comfort of having him there, did not realize the severity of the tax upon one unused to sick-rooms.

About three o'clock in the afternoon, Dr. Duncan came in. He said little, beyond giving needful directions, and promising to return soon—"in a couple of hours or so." Fulvia thought his look not hopeful.

"Have you seen madre?" she asked.

"Yes; she tried to get up and fainted. I have ordered her to bed. She can do no more."

Soon after, unexpectedly, Mr. Browning dropped asleep, leaning forward on a pillow, his forehead against a chair-back. Fulvia had knelt at his right hand a few minutes earlier, and she remained fixed in that position, not daring to stir. Nigel had taken a seat not a yard distant, where he had been off and on through the day. A glance of hope was exchanged between the two, and Fulvia, noting Nigel's wearied look, signed to him to leave the room, but the sign was disregarded. Neither of them stirred.

Twenty minutes of repose : surely this meant recovery. Fulvia's face grew bright, Nigel's less harassed. The sufferer seemed peaceful, and breathed more easily, not struggling.

Then he woke, and the first words were, "Nigel! Call Nigel."

"I am here, father." Nigel rose and came nearer, glad to have stayed.

"My dear dear boy!" Mr. Browning said feebly.

"A little better?" Nigel asked.

"I don't know. Just at this moment—perhaps—"

He looked from one to the other, in a wistful troubled fashion, strangely too, as if gazing from a distance.

"Something I had to say," he murmured. "If I were not so—so weak—"

"You must not talk, padre," said Fulvia.

A great agony came into his face, changing its very form.

"Fulvie, forgive—forgive," he groaned.

"Don't, padre—O, don't," she cried. "Don't think —don't worry yourself; only get well, for madre's sake."

But his shaking fingers clasped hers.

"No, no; you do not know," he panted. "It was not—was not—intention."

"What was not intention?" Nigel asked, before Fulvia could speak; and a moan was the answer.

"This must not go on." Fulvia spoke in a clear voice. "Padre, listen—don't be distressed. I forgive anything—everything—no matter what—if there is anything to forgive. And you are to feel happy— you understand? Not to worry yourself. Things will be all right."

"No, no. Wronged! Wronged!"

They could hardly catch what he said. Then, with more distinct utterance—

"My dear child! My own dear child! No—not intention—folly and weakness—not wilful. HE will for- give—I think—I trust—but—the misery and loss—"

"Nigel, stop him! He must not," whispered Fulvia. "Padre dear, don't! don't!" she went on aloud. "You will be worse. Can't you rest now?"

"Forgiveness," he panted.

"Yes, O yes—don't ask again!"

But a solemn sound came into Mr. Browning's voice,

as he went on,—"Forgiveness with Thee—Thee!—that
Thou mayest be feared! My God, Thou knowest I have
repented—bitterly—most bitterly!"

A sob interrupted the words. With a sudden effort,
he took Fulvia's left hand and placed it in Nigel's right
hand.

"We owe her much," he said.

Then the troubled eyes turned to Fulvia.

"He will make up to you—my child—for everything!
You will be his own—his own! But for that, how—
how could I bear it? Nigel, I charge you—never—"

Utterance failed. It was an embarrassing moment
for both; worse for Nigel, however, than for Fulvia,
since she believed Mr. Browning to have only given
expression to Nigel's desire.

. During two seconds her hand lay where it had been
put, and she did not look at Nigel. A flush rose to her
very brow; the downcast eyes brightened; the lips
parted with joy. Nigel saw, and his heart died within
him. What was he to do? How could he explain?—
yet how could he not explain?

Strange to say, she did not miss the response which
she might have expected. At the first instant, when
her hand touched his, and he little dreamt what was
coming, Nigel's fingers had closed with a slight kind
grasp, merely as an expression of gratitude. Then, as he
heard, he saw his mistake; and he grew cold, knowing
his own position.

Something had to be said, but what? That was the

question. Nigel could not answer it. He was almost stunned. Yet he would have said something—anything—the first words which should spring—but there came an ominous sound, hardly a groan, hardly a gasp. Fulvia's glad colour faded, and she snatched her hand away to give the needed support, thereby releasing Nigel.

For Mr. Browning was dropping forward, lower and lower, breathless, voiceless, changed in look.

Nothing could be done. There was no time to summon Dr. Duncan, no time to warn his wife. Even as Fulvia started to Mr. Browning's help, all was over.

R

CHAPTER XIX.

THE MONEY!

> "I do not ask, O Lord, that life may be
> A pleasant road;
> I do not ask that Thou would'st take from me
> Aught of its load;
> I do not ask that flowers should always spring
> Beneath my feet;
> I know too well the poison and the sting
> Of things too sweet;
> For one thing only, Lord, dear Lord, I plead—
> Lead me aright;
> Though strength should falter, and though heart should
> bleed,
> Through Peace to Light."—A. A. PROCTER.

STRANGE to say—or others thought it strange—Nigel was more knocked down by the blow than almost any one.

This did not show itself at first. He was the mainstay of them all during the first hours of that grievous day—resolutely calm, undertaking to break the news to his mother, to comfort his sisters, to make needful arrangements. He went to and fro, pale and serious, even severe in his self-repression; and every one said how much he felt his father's death, and how good he was; but no one guessed the racking misery of doubt below, as to Fulvia and that father's dying words.

The position in which Nigel found himself was indeed almost intolerable. Whether justly or no, he felt that he was in some measure to blame for it. True, he had been debarred from open speech to Mr. Browning; but, knowing whereto things tended, why had he not at least spoken out to Fulvia about Ethel? He hated himself now for what might have been a cruel silence to Fulvia. When he thought of Fulvia's face, at the moment that her hand was placed in his by Mr. Browning, his heart sank as if leaden-weighted; and he felt like a bird caught in the toils.

All through the hours of that endless morning the struggle went on. What Mr. Browning had meant or had not meant?—what he was to do, or not to do?—what he could say, or could not say?—how he might free himself, and yet spare Fulvia?—these questions racked his brain incessantly, while he sat with his mother or saw to things that had to be done, never thinking of rest for himself, only longing unbearably to find out the worst as to his father's affairs—and Fulvia's! This last became in time the leading desire, so engrossing his attention that everything else was done as a stepping-stone to that end, and he did not even know how bodily overwrought he was.

Mrs. Browning bore the shock wonderfully, so others said. She wept indeed much, showing all due natural grief, and clinging to Nigel for support; still she could find comfort in talking to Nigel about her husband. Not to anybody else, only to Nigel; and she never guessed how he shrank from it, craving to escape. The more keenly he felt, the less he could speak; also it was difficult to satisfy her with sufficient details of that last hour, while ignoring what had passed about Fulvia and himself. There seemed so little to tell, and she longed for more.

It was not till mid-day that he had a chance of a quiet time in the study.

All the long morning since Mr. Browning's death he had not once seen Fulvia. Half shyly, half unconsciously, she had kept out of his way, longing for yet dreading the moment when they should come together; and by no means unconsciously Nigel had seconded these efforts. He did not come to breakfast, only having a cup of tea in his mother's room; and when breakfast was over, Fulvia went out with Daisy, about mourning, which could not be put off. She would not trouble Mrs. Browning, but ordered everything that might be required, not sparing expense. Why should she? If Mrs. Browning should be short of money, there was Fulvia's money! She could always fall back upon that.

Coming in from the shops, Fulvia found herself overpoweringly tired and sleepy. Nigel was still with Mrs. Browning, and no one seemed to need her. Anice noted her condition—it was a rare event for Anice to notice anybody's condition except her own—and advised repose. Fulvia meekly followed the counsel, and went to bed.

She did not expect to sleep, of course; but sleep she did, peacefully as an infant, never waking till nearly four o'clock in the afternoon of that strange sad day— most strange indeed, but not altogether sad, to Fulvia. Yet she grieved sincerely over her "padre's" death.

How vexed she felt when she awoke—vexed to have slept so long, and vexed yet more to feel refreshed and buoyant; absolutely hungry too! So heartless under the circumstances!

Going down into the darkened drawing-room, she found Anice crying over the fire; and the tea-tray just brought in.

"O Fulvie!" Anice started up to cling to the elder girl. "I have wanted you so, but Nigel said you were not to be disturbed. He said you must sleep as long as you could."

"I had no idea of forgetting myself so long. Stupid of me!" and there was a tingling blush at the mention of Nigel's name. "How is madre? Has Nigel had any rest himself?"

"No, he wouldn't. Mother is in her arm-chair just now, and Daisy with her. Nigel was there ever so long, all the morning off and on, till twelve o'clock; and then his head was aching, and mother wanted him to go into the garden for a turn, but he went to the study instead. He has been there ever since, except just a few minutes at lunch; and then he couldn't eat, and hardly said a word. He only said he had papers to look through, and he told us you were not to be called. Mother wants him, I believe. But Daisy doesn't mind being with mother, and I *can't*, you know—"pitifully. "I think Daisy and Nigel are so wonderful, keeping up, and— Won't you have some tea?"

Fulvia was ashamed of her own hunger. "Yes," she said, and helped herself, hoping Anice would not see how much she could eat. Anice dallied with a cup of tea, sobbing and talking by turns.

"Daisy is so strong," she said self-excusingly, "and I am not. I never could do things like other people. If I could I would stay with mother, but—when she cries so and says— Oh, I don't know how to bear it."

"My dear, it is not a question of strength, but of will," said Fulvia. "People can do a good deal more, commonly, than they think they can, if only they would make up their minds to it, and manage to forget themselves."

Anice was hurt, of course, by the home-truth, and wept anew.

Then Daisy entered, with red eyes and broken breath. "Mother sent me," she said. "Is Fulvie up? Mother wants Nigel so, and I promised to tell him."

"Anice can tell him. Sit down, Daisy, and have some tea. You have done your share."

Anice complied reluctantly. She did not like being sent on errands.

"He is coming," she said, on her return. "But I

don't think he is pleased. He had a lot of papers out, and he stopped to put them away."

"Did you tell him I was here?" Fulvia could not resist putting the question.

" No, he didn't ask."

The study-door was heard to open and shut. Fulvia wished she could have controlled the rush of blood to her face. An impulse came over her to escape, yet she sat still; and when Nigel entered, there were no signs of a corresponding agitation on his part. He looked paler, sterner, older, than she could have imagined possible. His eyes seemed scarcely able to lift themselves under their heavy lids to see her or any one, and the purple hollows below rendered superfluous Daisy's pitying remark, " He has *such* a headache."

" I don't wonder," Fulvia forced herself to say; and a distinct start made it manifest that he had not before been aware of her presence. He said nothing, however, but sat down, resting his elbow on a small table, and his forehead on one hand.

There was complete silence for two or three minutes. Then Fulvia asked timidly, " Will you have some tea?"

" Thanks."

Fulvia brought it herself. "I am afraid your head is very bad."

" Yes; " and no more. The tea remained untouched.

Glances were exchanged by the three girls; and Daisy spoke in response to a sign from Fulvia—" Nigel, the tea is getting cold. Won't you take some now?"

Nigel roused himself to comply; but after a few sips the cup was pushed aside, and he went back to his former position, as if overpowered by grief and weariness. Fulvia told herself that she ought not to wonder; and yet she did wonder. She had expected a word from him, or a look—and she had neither. But perhaps such expectations were unreasonable. It was very, very soon—only a few hours since his father's death; and Nigel had always been an affectionate son. She signed to the girls to say no more; and for ten minutes the clock ticked in unbroken silence. Nigel spoke at last without stirring;—

"Did you say my mother wanted me?"

Daisy's "Yes" and Fulvia's "No" came together. Daisy showed surprise.

"No," repeated Fulvia; "not when she knows how you are."

"I don't wish her to know."

Fulvia could not take upon herself to answer. She could only look again towards Daisy, and Daisy made response—

"Nigel was up all night, and he has had no rest. Everybody has rested except Nigel."

Nigel paid no heed, and another five minutes passed. Then he stood up, and without a word moved towards the door.

"Fulvie, do go too," begged Daisy. "Nobody can manage so well as you; and I'm sure he isn't fit."

Fulvia obeyed the suggestion, thrusting her own

reluctance into the background. She counted Nigel too worn out to care what she or anybody might do; and certainly it was desirable that the interview should not be prolonged.

But how to shorten it was the question. Mrs. Browning, absorbed in her own grief, did not notice anything unusual in his look. He sat down close beside her, leaning his head against the back of her chair out of sight; so, after the first minute she had no chance to observe. Mrs. Browning welcomed him tenderly, bidding Fulvia also remain, which settled the perplexity of the latter how to act.

Then came a long low monotone, broken by sobs, all about Albert Browning, her husband—his character, his goodness, his devotion to wife and children, together with details of his suffering state during weeks past, and conjectures as to the cause of his long depression, varied by soft reverent utterances regarding his present rest, the contrast of his present peace, and how they must not grieve for him too much.

It was all very sweet; just like gentle Mrs. Browning. She was a very embodiment of sweet gentleness, sitting there, with her little nervous snowflakes of hands clasped together, and her lovely eyes wide open, sometimes filling with great tears; but also it was very trying to other people. Those who are in trouble do not always think of this.

Fulvia began to wonder how much longer it was to go on. She grew impatient, even while most stirred by those reverent and resigned utterances in the madre's dear tones. Any amount for herself would have been endurable; but she was enduring for Nigel also. He was quiet enough, even impassive, only saying a word now and then when needful; still, Fulvia had a very good notion what the interview was to him. In a general way she would not have allowed it to last five minutes. Now, however, she was under constraint; afraid of taking a wrong step. If Nigel should not like her to interfere !

There came a movement at length, as if he could bear no more. Mrs. Browning was saying something in her sorrowful voice about — " Your dear father's money anxieties. Always so scrupulously exact and honourable —so distressed if—"

Nigel's sudden movement stopped her. It was a start forward to an upright position, as if from some intolerable sting of pain, and he pushed the hair from his forehead twice, with a restless gesture. Fulvia could restrain herself no longer.

" Madre, dear, I think one of us had better be with you now—Daisy or I. Nigel is so tired."

" Nigel tired ! Are you, my dear ? Yes, of course— why did I not see sooner ? You had a headache, Daisy said. Is it no better ? "

" About as bad as can be, I suspect," Fulvia said, coming forward. " I think the kindest thing we can do at present is not to let him talk any more. He must go to his room, and be quiet."

"Yes; do make him; and I don't want anybody here. Never mind about me. I am of no consequence. How could I be so thoughtless?"

"Not thoughtless, indeed," Nigel said, as she broke into a flood of tears. "Fulvia did not mean—"

"Oh, I know—I understand. Everybody is kind. But now he is gone, I am so desolate. I have nobody but you —nobody to lean upon. Nigel, my own boy, say you will not leave me! Say you will never, never leave me."

She clung to him, pleading; and Fulvia felt that in the abstract nothing could be more touching than the poor widow's turning to her boy for comfort. In the particular it was— No, Fulvia would not let herself look on another side of the question.

"Mother, you are my charge now," Nigel said, with a manly self-control. He would not bind himself with rash promises; but he would assume to the full the responsibility which had fallen upon him.

Mrs. Browning wept on, and clung to him faster; and Nigel waited with dull patience. He might have waited thus another half-hour, but for Fulvia. She hardly knew how she managed to end the scene; yet she did manage it. Nigel followed her out of the room in a mechanical fashion, and stood outside in the gas-lit passage, leaning against an old carved press, as if energy for another step had failed him.

Fulvia struck a match, and lighted a candle.

"Nigel, you are perfectly dead-beat. You will go to bed now."

There was no immediate answer. Fulvia cast one or two wistful glances at his face, which might have gained years in age during the last few hours.

" No," he said. " I must speak to you first."

A swift electric shock darted through Fulvia's frame. Speak to her! Speak about what? She could put only one interpretation on the words.

The girls' boudoir was close at hand, just across the passage. Nigel had always been free of entrance there, and he turned to go in. Fulvia followed with the candle, which she placed upon the mantel-piece, and Nigel stood facing her, his hands laid upon the back of a chair as if for support. Fulvia trembled, and her colour went and came in rushes, while Nigel was pale as death.

" I have something to tell you," he said. " It has only come to my knowledge to-day. About your money—"

" My money! Oh!" Fulvia came a step nearer, both relieved and disappointed. " I can wait about that!"

" I cannot!" The words were stern.

" There is no hurry—no need yet! As if I cared!"

" You will care. It is no good news."

" The more need to put off. We have had trouble enough to-day. Must we think of money so soon—when we have only just lost him? I would rather wait, far rather. And you are not well—you are ill!"

" I cannot rest till I have told you."

" Well—" she answered reluctantly, " if it is a relief

to you, of course—only please get it over as fast as you can."

Fulvia paused; and she could see that he was striving to speak; striving and unable. The lips parted, and drew together again; and he put his hand to his forehead, pressing hard, as if for the endurance of acute pain. "O, don't! pray don't!" she begged piteously. "If you would but wait!"

"I have found out—" he tried to say, and the voice was so husky as to be inarticulate. A resolute effort conquered this. He grasped the chair again with both hands, and spoke in a distinct tone: "I have found out what my father meant."

"Meant!—when?"

"When he begged your pardon."

"I don't care what you have found out. I don't care what he meant. I will *not* hear it now," cried Fulvia passionately. "What do you think I am made of?—talking of money, money, to me to-day! To-day of all days! I can't bear it, and you can't either! Please, please leave off!"

"No use. You must hear soon; and the sooner the better. I can't stand not telling you." There was a touch of appeal in the words, almost as if he craved her help. At the moment she hardly noticed it. "I have been looking at papers," he went on.

"Then you ought not! It was wrong, so soon! I don't care what you have found. The money isn't so much as uncle Arthur fancies, I suppose. What if it is not? What do I care? He has done harm enough with his meddling. He shall have no voice in my affairs now. I shall never be able to forgive him for —yesterday!" She had to pause and think before saying "yesterday." Her twenty-first birthday seemed so long ago.

"He was not to blame—wilfully."

"He *was* to blame! He knew better, or he ought to have known. But never mind that now. I only want you to say what must be said, and have done with it."

Only to say what had to be said! That meant more than Fulvia guessed!

"I cannot give full particulars yet. There has been —no time. My father's affairs are—have been for years —in a state of complication—embarrassment. How much so I have never guessed. The crash must have come in—in any case. It has been staved off by—by means of—" Then a break. "Ruin to us all!" followed abruptly.

"To—us all!" She laid a slight stress on the pronoun.

"Yes."

"I don't think I understand."

Nigel was again hardly able to speak, and drops stood thickly like beads over his forehead. Fulvia felt bewildered! Ruin to them all! Did that mean—to her? Was she included? In her wildest dreams this had somehow never come up as a possibility. Her money had always in imagination remained secure, only perhaps a little diminished from the Carden-Cox estimate. Her money had always been waiting to supply deficiencies for other people.

She said again, "I don't understand." It was not in human nature at that moment to insist on hearing no more. "Ruin to whom?" she asked.

"Absolute ruin to us! Hardly less to you."

"And—my forty thousand pounds—are—"

"Gone!"

He said the one word clearly as before; then a change of mood overmastered him; he sat down, and covered his face with both hands.

What wonder? His father, not ten hours dead!—and already to have found out that father in a course of action which must cover his name with dishonour. Trust betrayed! trust-money appropriated! A heavier blow could scarcely have fallen upon the children of Albert Browning, brought up to regard him with loving reverence.

Fulvia could not look on unmoved. Tears rushed to her eyes. She forgot the uncertainty of her own position, forgot how words and acts might be misconstrued. They were boy and girl again—brother and sister—he as he used to be, a little the younger in character, turning to her for guidance, and she—"Nigel, I can't bear you to feel it so!" she cried, with a sob, coming to his side, and then she sat down, leaning towards him. ".What does the money matter to me, except that I wanted to help you all? It is worse for you, of course—worse to know— But he did not mean it! He never meant it! It has been some accident—something he could not help. We will never think a hard thought of him, or hear a hard word said. Somebody else was to blame; not dear padre—always so good and kind to me. Only don't mind—don't distress yourself—please don't think anything of it."

The nobility of the girl—and Fulvia's was a noble nature, despite one sad fall of late—could not but strike home to Nigel, not only with a sense of admiration, but with a rush of new pain. For it made his position with respect to her only the more difficult. Yet, trying to rally, he said—

"All that we can do—" and there was a break. "Everything we have is yours, until—"

"Nonsense! How can you talk such nonsense?" cried Fulvia. "Everything *I* ever had is *yours*—madre's, I mean!" and she blushed vividly; but the blush passed, and with it thoughts of self, as she went on—"After all, how can we know? How can we be sure? It is so soon. Things may not be so bad. You cannot have looked into matters fully yet. Don't you think there may be some mistake?"

He lifted his face, and looked straight at Fulvia. "No; there was a letter for me."

"A letter—from—"

"My father."

"Where?"

" In his desk."

" Addressed to you ? "

" Yes—to be opened—after—"

" And—telling you about—"

" About—what I have told you."

" Not saying how it happened ? "

" Yes. It has been the work of years. Embarrass-ments always increasing. Borrowing from—yours—to stave off this and that—meaning to repay, and never able. Speculating, failing, getting deeper and deeper into trouble ; always hoping things would right them-selves somehow, until—until—"

" Yes, until—"

" A very heavy loss, just after I left home—failure of a speculation, from which he had hoped everything. I think that was his death-blow. He faced the truth then ; realized for the first time how things were, and how near your coming of age was. It has been one long misery since. He could never make up his mind to speak."

" Poor padre ! Better if he had. But madre must not know it now."

" She must. We have no choice."

" Why ? "

" Life will be changed to us all. Everything will have to be given up."

" Not the Grange ! Not college for you ! "

" Everything."

" O, I am so sorry. I do mind that."

S

Fulvia sat looking at him, tears in her eyes.

"But madre need not know," she repeated. "Madre must not know—all. Not that *he* was to blame, I mean—if he was to blame. Only that there have been losses, and that we shall all be poor together. You must not let her think anybody can find fault with him. It would almost kill her."

Nigel's face was hidden again. How could he say that other thing which had to be said? how put matters right between this noble-hearted girl and himself? Tell her first that her guardian—his father! —had recklessly made away with her money, committed to his trust!—then tell her that the dying words of Albert Browning were false, that he loved another and could not make up to her for the loss, could not offer himself in place of her wealth—even though he had too good reason to fear that she cared for him as for no other human being!

All the day through Nigel had been struggling, fighting, praying for strength—had been striving to bring himself to the pitch requisite for those words, so hard to be spoken. At the beginning of this interview he had believed himself to be capable of them. But now—!

Something about his "brotherly" feeling for Fulvia; something about his sense of responsibility in having to provide for her, as for his other sisters; something about what might have been soon between him and Ethel, if this crash had not come, altering his whole outlook; something which should kindly, gently, let her·

see the truth. Yes, he had thought all this beforehand, had shaped the very phrases. But now that the
moment had arrived for saying the words, he could not
say them.

Things were changed indeed for him during the last
twelve hours. How could he ask Ethel to wait during
interminable years, while he set himself to the task
of supporting his widowed mother and sisters, and of
paying back at least a portion of Fulvia's lost money?
Whether he could ever repay the whole might be
doubted; but Nigel felt that it would be his aim.

Unless he married Fulvia! There would be no
question of repayment then! Whatever he possessed,
she would possess.

If he did not marry her, then he would have to toil
the more to place her in a position of comfort. If she
were doubly wronged, he would have doubly to make
up to her.

Either way, he saw himself hopelessly cut off from
Ethel!

Was it his bounden duty to marry Fulvia as things
stood? A father's dying wish has power; and Fulvia
had too clearly shown her heart's desire. Could he,
and might he, escape from the tangle? One moment
he felt that he had no choice: another moment,
that to become Fulvia's husband was an utter
impossibility.

If the latter—if he could not and would not ask her
to be his wife—then she ought in justice to learn

quickly how matters stood. Delay would be cruel to her, and would, in fact, bind him.

But—to tell her at this moment!—how could he? To inflict another blow close upon the first—and Nigel knew that it would be a blow! To reveal the bitter truth—and Nigel was aware that it must be an unspeakably bitter truth! How could he so meet her noble self-forgetfulness in ignoring her own loss, thinking only of his grief? Theoretically, immediate speech might be best. Practically it was impossible. Nigel *could not* say the words he had purposed. His parched lips refused to utter them.

At another time he might have felt and acted differently. He was suffering now severely from the strain of twenty-four hours past. Vigour of mind and vigour of body were at a low ebb, and the power of decision was almost gone. He could only let things drift. He was turning faint with the inward struggle, and his head throbbed beyond endurance. The moment for speaking went by. Fulvia, watching him with her kind troubled eyes, saw the physical pain and read little beyond, for she had not the clue.

"Poor Nigel!" she said compassionately, and the next thing he knew was of something wet and cool upon his brow.

Nigel could not protest or refuse. He could only give himself over into her capable care-taking hands; too ill for more speech, yet all the while dimly conscious of a certain sense of possession in the touch of those same hands. Was it consciousness or fancy? Nigel did not know. It might have been either. He was in no condition for weighing of evidence.

One thought only was clear, twining itself in and out of the fierce aching which at last mastered him—one little sentence from Ethel's paper—

"To sacrifice self, as an habitual law, in each sudden call to action."

It haunted him for hours, together with Ethel's face.

CHAPTER XX.

AN UTTER TANGLE.

"O life, O death, O world, O time,
  O grave, where all things flow,
'Tis yours to make our lot sublime,
  With your great weight of woe.

"Though sharpest anguish hearts may wring,
  Though bosoms torn may be,
Yet suffering is a holy thing,
  Without it, what were we?"—TRENCH.

DAYS passed, and nobody yet knew the state of
family affairs.

Nigel was confined to his room by a "severe feverish
attack"—not surprising under the circumstances. Business talk in his presence was tabooed; and Fulvia said
not a word elsewhere. Not a soul, beyond herself and
Nigel, knew aught of the dying man's utterances, aught
of the letter he had left, aught of the vanished wealth.
Newton Bury never doubted that the Brownings would
still be extremely well off.

In a general way Mr. Carden-Cox would very early
have set himself to ferret out something, more especially when goaded on by previous suspicion. Mr. Carden-

Cox, however, had not been to the Grange since the afternoon of Fulvia's birthday. He knew that others must blame him for Albert Browning's fatal attack of illness, and he could not endure to be blamed. Inwardly he suffered sore remorse ; outwardly he would have defended his own conduct through thick and thin.

There was nothing for it but flight, and he did flee. Thirty-six hours after Albert Browning's death saw him in his old Burrside lodgings, in glum and miserable, enjoyment of solitude. At the Grange his absence was scarcely regretted, for interviews must needs have been painful.

Mr. Carden-Cox did not return for the funeral, and Nigel could not be present—no small grief to Nigel's mother. He was unable to lift his head from the pillow when that day came. Mrs. Browning stayed with him, and the three girls went, as did many Newton Bury friends. Much sympathy had been shown to the Brownings in their trouble. The very idea of any possible slur upon the honoured name of Albert Browning had not so much as occurred to any one, outside their immediate circle—if one includes in that circle Mr. Carden-Cox and Dr. James Duncan.

Albert Browning had left no will, had appointed no executors. All arrangements, therefore, devolved upon his son, to whom it was known he had left written directions or advice in the form of a letter. Mrs. Browning had not been told even so much as this.

Arrangements had to wait until Nigel could give his mind to them.

So nearly another week passed after the funeral; and then Nigel came again into the stream of every-day life.

It was a changed life for him; and he was changed, —thinner, older, with a careworn expression. The eyes had ceased to sparkle, a weight lay on the brow, and the lips had a sad resolute set, unlike their old quick curving into smiles.

Mrs. Browning and Daisy had been his nurses; not that much actual nursing was needed. The occupation was good for Mrs. Browning, Fulvia said. Fulvia had not seen him for ten days; and when he reappeared, she noted sorrowfully the alteration.

Sometimes she wondered, would he soon allude to those dying words of his father? She could not under-stand his manner. It was kind, grave, brotherly perhaps, certainly restrained. Yet at first Fulvia was not anxious.

He had so much on his mind; and it was natural that he should wait awhile. Decorum almost demanded delay, just for a time after the padre's death. So Fulvia told herself, and thought or tried to think. Moreover, though Nigel had not been seriously ill, not ill enough, that is to say, to cause real anxiety, he had suffered a good deal, and had distinctly lost flesh and vigour. He was hardly up to anything exciting yet. "Poor Nigel!" she breathed pityingly.

The three girls in their deep mourning were gathered round the drawing-room fire, early one afternoon,— the second day since Nigel had come among them again. Fulvia's mourning matched that of the other two. She would not make a grain of difference, for she was one with them in their loss, though united by no tie of blood. The profound black set off well her ruddy hair and clear skin. She looked sad, trying to realize what was hard to believe—that not one fortnight had passed since the padre's death. To the imagination it was more like two months than two weeks. On the other hand, it seemed strange that so many days could have elapsed, while no one beyond herself and Nigel had an inkling of the true state of affairs; yet Fulvia herself had insisted on delay. Nigel would have spoken to his sisters two days earlier, but for her entreaties.

"Mother was asleep when I went in just now," Daisy said.

"My dear, let her sleep. It is the best thing she can do. And if she wakes, keep her away from here."

"Why?"

"I think—I am not sure—but I shrewdly suspect Mr. Carden-Cox may come in for a talk. He is at home again. Madre could not stand that."

"*I* couldn't," sighed Anice.

"You will have to stand it, and a good deal besides. We must all three be brave, and keep up for madre's sake—and—"

"And for Nigel's," added Daisy unsuspectingly.

Fulvia flushed.

"Yes. He has a great deal resting on him, and he will have hard work. Anice—Daisy—I want you both to promise me to be good and thoughtful—not to seem vexed and unhappy, whatever happens. Above all, don't let yourselves blame padre."

"Why should we blame him?" asked Daisy.

"Never mind. You will know everything soon enough—too soon for my wishes. Promise me not to think about yourselves, but only about madre, and how you can best help Nigel. We have to bear what comes; but the way of bearing makes all the difference in the world."

"I'll try, of course."

"And Anice?"

"Yes"—faintly; "but what shall we have to bear?"

Fulvia was silent.

"Will Mr. Carden-Cox come exactly at tea-time, like last time?" asked Daisy, with a choke in her voice. "I hope he won't; but he is so odd, one never can tell. Shall I take mother's tea to her? And Nigel's? He has been hours and hours over those papers."

"What papers?" inquired Anice.

"I don't know; father's, I think"—in a lower tone. "All the morning, and now ever since lunch. He ought not, ought he, Fulvia? I should think he would be ill again, if he does so much. Why, he has only been down-stairs twice before to-day, and only for a little while."

"Has anybody been to him?"

"Yes; I went—when was it? nearly an hour ago. I asked if he wouldn't come for a walk with me. But he seemed vexed, and said he was too busy, and couldn't be disturbed. So of course I can't try a second time."

"Anice could."

"I'd rather not. You can, if you like. You are always trying to put things off upon me," said injured Anice.

Fulvia hesitated; then she went, tapping lightly at the study door. There was no answer, and she opened it.

Papers lay over the table, letters and account-books mingled with other documents. Fulvia bestowed upon them only a cursory glance. Nigel sat as if reading, the fingers of his right hand pushed up into his hair; but Fulvia knew that at the moment of her entrance he was thinking, not reading. The eyes slowly lifted had a far-away look. She closed the door, coming to the other side of the table.

"This is too soon—not right," she said. "You are not well yet, and you ought to wait a few days."

"Time to speak out," was his reply.

"O, not yet. Think of poor madre!" Two bright drops fell from Fulvia's eyes. "It will break her heart. If only we could keep the worst from her!"

"Impossible!" Nigel spoke firmly, yet with a sound of weariness.

" At least she need not be told now ? "

" I don't know. I must have things in train."

" And get yourself into bad health again, like old days. Is that wise ? "

" No fear ! "

" Must you begin so soon ? I can't see the need."

" We have no means of paying our way. Everything has to be given up."

" How have we paid our way hitherto ? "

" *We ?* "—bitterly. " With your money."

" But if that is all gone—"

" Nearly."

" Nigel, I am very stupid ; I can't quite grasp things. If poor padre had not been taken, how should we have paid our way then ? "

" As we were doing, I suppose, till the whole was gone, and a crash became inevitable. The only difference would have been a little longer delay, and nothing left to anybody, instead of the pittance left now. I don't believe he fully realized how things were. There was always a vague hope that difficulties would right themselves."

" No reason for the hope ? "

" None that I can see."

" Do you mind telling me how much the 'pittance' really will be ? I don't want to tease you "—wistfully —" but if I could be any help—"

" You have every right to know."

"I don't ask it as a right; but are things so desperate?"

"So far as I can make out, when all claims have been met, there may be some three hundred a year left."

"Of madre's ?"

"Yours."

"And how much of yours—hers and yours ?"

"There can be nothing of ours, in strict justice, till your claims are satisfied."

"Nigel!" she exclaimed indignantly. "What do you take me for?"

"I am talking of justice, not of your wishes."

"I don't care what you mean; it is cruel to speak so. As if I—and it is untrue. The three hundred a year will be *ours* if you like—not mine, but all of ours together."

"Half of it is yours exclusively. The other half is my mother's marriage settlement; but she will feel as I do, that you have a right to—"

"Will you stop? I won't hear it! How can you say such things?" cried Fulvia. "Do you want to put separation between us? Am I to be cut off from you all by this trouble? May I not even live with madre still?"

For it came across her, as she stood there, that no allusion had yet been made to those dying words, to the clasped hands by Albert Browning's side. If Nigel had felt as she felt, he would surely, before this, have made some sign—have broken into some speech. She had been silent perforce; he was not bound. Her whole being was wrapped up in Nigel; while he—if she should find that he did not care for her, how could she endure it? Did he care? Sudden dread crept over Fulvia. Would it be anything to him if she went away from the home, and was one of them no longer? A chill came with the dread, and she sat down, because she could not stand. A changed sound found its way into her voice, as she repeated, "May I not even live with madre still?"

Nigel looked up with a momentary expression of surprise.

"Yes, certainly. What could make you think—" he began, and then broke off, to add simply, "Why not?"

"You are the master of the house! It is for *you* to decide—for *you* to decide now." Fulvia did not know that she had said the words twice, or that a wail of pain crept into them. She only meant to speak coldly. "That might be one of the 'changes' necessary;" and there was a hard little laugh.

"For *you* to decide!" struck home. It brought to Nigel's mind vividly, as was already present in hers, the scene by the side of Albert Browning, just before he died. Nigel heard again the laboured breath, the faltering accents—"He will make up to you, my child, for everything! You will be his own! Nigel, I charge you, never—" and then the hand put into his, and the glow on Fulvia's face! All this came back to Nigel in an instant, not quickening his pulses as it quickened Fulvia's. One glimpse of Ethel would have set them beating fast, but not these recollections. They only brought a sense of weight and strain, of weariness and perplexity, and he leant his brow on his hand again, to control the aching. One thing alone was distinct— that he could and would take no hasty steps. Till he had seen Ethel, he must leave all else in suspense. Seen Ethel! The very thought brought relief. She would help him! She, with her clear sense of duty, her practised spirit of self-denial, would guide him to the knowledge of what he ought to do.

Fulvia spoke in a tone of compunction, which yet was not soft—

"I don't want to worry you; I forgot your head was bad still. After all, we can settle nothing yet. Sometimes I think I will go out as governess."

"Never!" Nigel started as if a wasp had stung him.

"Why not? I have some capabilities. What do you propose to do?"

"Let or sell the Grange as soon as possible. Go into a small house, and get rid of all superfluous furniture. Dismiss most of the servants. Retrench in every possible way."

"And land yourself in a brain fever, by way of saving expense."

Nigel was in no mood for light words.

"What will you do yourself?" asked Fulvia, having no response.

"The Bank."

"So I feared. But I thought you were expected to

—what was it?—take shares, or invest money in the
Bank, or some such thing, in order that you might in
time become partner?"

"I can't do it now."

"They will have you—without?"

"Yes.   It will make a difference in my standing, of
course."

"Are you going to see Mr. Bramble?"

"I have written to him, and have had an answer."

"Already?"   She was struck with his independence
and resolution.   "Nigel, will you grant me one favour?
Let me tell the girls and madre as much as is necessary,
—and uncle Arthur too.   Let *me* do it."

Nigel would not accept the generous offer.   He was
bent upon not sparing himself.   Fulvia had suffered
enough already through him and his; he would not lay
upon her a feather's weight in addition.   When she
pleaded he said "No" again, and followed her to the
drawing-room, with an evident intention to speak
without further delay.   There were the two girls still,
and there was Mr. Carden-Cox, who had not waited for
the tea-hour, but had come, as Fulvia foretold.

CHAPTER XXI.

COMPOUND UMBELS AND BLUE EYES.

" A man must serve his time to every trade
Save censure—critics all are ready-made.
Take hackneyed jokes from Miller, got by rote,
With just enough of learning to misquote ;
A mind well-skilled to find or forge a fault :
A turn for punning—call it Attic salt."

" ONE of the Umbelliferæ," said Tom.

He stood watching Ethel, as she painted a flower upon a wooden panel, his head being inclined to one side. It was not long before Mr. Carden-Cox' call at the Grange that same afternoon.

Ethel had a gift in the flower-painting line; but this was not done so well as usual. Ethel's fingers were nervous, not quite obedient. She had taken to her paints as a refuge from Tom, and there was no getting away from him. He followed her even into her pet sanctum, the little lumber-room, where, as she would have said, she "did her messes." It was no use to suggest his being elsewhere. Tom's mild good-humour was impervious to the broadest hints. Ethel felt for

once uncontrollably cross in her satiety of Tom's talk;
yet she tried to be patient. In a few days he would be
gone.

" One of the Umbelliferæ," repeated Tom, finding his
information disregarded. "Umbel-bearing. Umbel—
from the same source, so to speak, as 'umbrella'—
spreading outward from the centre. This little flower
is a simple umbel; but there are compound umbels
also—umbels of umbels,—you understand ? "

" O yes. Like a lot of sunshades branching out of
one umbrella."

The illustration was so new, that Tom had to give it
serious consideration.

" Yes "—came slowly, at length. " I do not know
that your idea is—altogether inappropriate. No, perhaps not—on the whole. As an instance of compound
umbels, we have—a——"

" An umbrella-shop."

"I am afraid that you would be pushing the—the simile
—too far." Tom was perfectly serious. " As a matter
of fact, an umbrella can never be other than a simple
umbel—ha, ha !" Tom could always laugh at his own
jokes, though never at those of other people. " Ha, ha !
Yes, an umbrella is undoubtedly a simple umbel. But
in nature we have compound umbels, as for instance,
the hemlock, the parsley, the—"

Tom paused, and Ethel was silent.

" You are making too much of a curve. That stalk
does not bend in reality," said Tom, who looked upon

the said stalk from a different standpoint, and failed to allow for the fact. He knew about as much in respect of painting as the Rectory cat. A row of "flower-heads," with stalks as stiff as pokers in parallel lines below, would have seemed to him the correct thing.

"Nature deals in curves. When she doesn't it is a mistake, and art has to put her right," declared Ethel sententiously, for when dealing with a sententious man, one has sometimes to pay him in his own coin.

Tom undertook to prove her mistaken, and Ethel listened with wandering thoughts to his laboured disquisition. It was hard to attend enough to prevent his discovering her absence. Her heart was at the Grange, for the last fortnight had been a severe trial of her fortitude, and each day added to the trial.

She had not seen or spoken with Nigel since his father's death; and one or two brief interviews with Daisy had been unsatisfactory. Ethel was not intimate with the Browning family as a whole, only with Nigel as Malcolm's friend—not to speak of his being her own friend!—and in a less degree with Daisy. She had always a distinct consciousness of being avoided by Fulvia. Her own feelings would have carried her daily to the Grange, if only as an expression of her intense sympathy with them all, if only to learn how Nigel was : but this could not be ; and certainly neither Mrs. Browning nor Fulvia would have welcomed any such expression of solicitude from a member of the Elvey family, albeit they were most polite to Mr. Elvey, who had paid more than one visit to the widow. Ethel had to stay at home, and to wait for such information as came by her father and Malcolm, or filtered through less direct channels. She seized any scrap of news with avidity, yet her hunger was not satisfied.

All these days of waiting saw her the same good home-daughter and sister as usual; busy as always; unselfish as always; giving the best of her time and thoughts to others; only reserving little odd corners of leisure here and there for her private anxieties and interests.

"Now, these are instances of straight lines in nature, which I venture to think you will hardly disparage," said Tom.

Ethel woke up to the fact that "these instances" had been thrown away upon her. She had travelled to the Grange while he discoursed, forgetting even to paint, and sitting, with suspended brush, in an attitude of absorption, which Tom took for devoted attention to himself. He was much gratified, naturally!

"O yes,—O no, I mean," she said hastily. Alarmed lest he should catechise her on what he had said, she began to paint again in vehement style, and Tom's attention strayed back to the "flower-head" expanding under her touch.

"I have not yet introduced you to the Umbelliferous Family," he observed, by way of a ponderous joke. "This is not a bad opportunity, while you are actually engaged in taking the likeness of a member of that family—ha! ha!" Tom stopped to laugh complacently, and Ethel felt like throwing her brush at him. "You are fairly acquainted already with the family characteristics of the Ranunculaceæ, the Papaveraceæ, the Onagraceæ, the Myrtaceæ, the Violaceæ, the Cucurbitaceæ, the Malvaceæ—"

"Seven sneezes," murmured Ethel. It really did seem as if Tom were laboriously selecting all those tribes which rejoiced in this particular sound at the end of their names.

"I beg your pardon. Did you speak?" asked unsuspecting Tom.

"O, nothing. Please go on."

"I was about to say, you are already acquainted fairly well with the characteristics of these and other tribes. But the Umbelliferæ are, I believe, new to you. Umbelliferæ — umbel-bearing. One principal characteristic—the ovary inferior. You should remember this. Fruit dry and hard—not juicy. I think you comprehend now what the ovary is."

"The ovary?" Ethel was away at the Grange once more.

"The ovary. I believe you understand what is signified by the ovary of a flower," repeated indulgent Tom.

Ethel looked up vacantly, then sighed.

"Tom, I am busy. I can't be bothered with ovaries and things to-day," she said. "I have so much to do, and those long names are detestable."

Tom's face fell. He was thunderstruck. Never till this moment had Ethel allowed such a remark to escape. "I thought—I hoped—you had learnt to appreciate—" he faltered.

"I have tried—really I have—and I can't. I shall never appreciate putting beautiful things into stiff rows, and giving them long names. It isn't in me," said Ethel, her tone half petulant, half apologetic. "You must try your hand on somebody else."

"But"—protested dismayed Tom. "But"—and he could say no more. After all these weeks of careful instruction, it was too much. Tom's whole course of thought was turned upside down by it. He found himself saying, with displeasure, "I imagined that you were a girl of sense."

"O no! Not botanical sense, Tom." Then she was afraid she had hurt his feelings, and she looked up penitently with her blue eyes. "Tom, you mustn't mind me. I'm worried, and it's of no consequence. Another day I'll try to listen. If only you will leave me in peace this afternoon, I'll be good afterwards, and I'll learn all about those horrid umbels. I will, really."

Tom did not know what to make of her. He was more won than ever—fascinated, in fact, though Ethel had not the smallest wish to fascinate him. At the same time he was desperately disappointed to find that her "listening" was a matter of "trying." He had flattered himself that she listened because she could not help it; because his speech was of such engrossing interest that she could not turn away.

He objected very much to the girlish expression, "those horrid umbels;" but the girlish blue eyes were too much for him. In the general *bouleversement* of Tom's ideas, one alone kept its equilibrium, and grew more definite. Umbels or no umbels, science or no science, Tom liked Ethel, and he wanted her for his own. She had grown necessary to him these weeks. Existence could not be the same to Tom, if he were bereft of the occupation of watching Ethel. Those deft little fingers enchained his masculine intellect. It came over him now, almost as a new idea, that in a few days this occupation would cease.

Not that he wished to go. He could have remained at the Rectory for an indefinite period, so far as his own wishes were concerned. A gentle intimation had been made to him, however, that the spare room would be required for another visitor after a certain date; so Tom had no choice.

By-and-by he would be returning to Australia, hopelessly out of reach of Ethel, and far beyond the touch of those little fingers, which had somehow become inextricably entwined in Tom's mind with the dried herbarium specimens, for the gumming in of which they were so admirably adapted. What success might not Tom achieve, with Ethel as his coadjutor?

Ethel little dreamt that her momentary tartness was bringing him to a most undesirable point.

Tom to yield to sudden impulse! Tom to be betrayed into ill-considered action! The thing was incredible. Tom had had floating ideas of how he would one day address himself to Mr. and Mrs. Elvey on the subject of marriage. He had planned a careful exposition of his prospects and intentions, such as might win the consent of Ethel's parents. He had pictured the circumspect choice of a suitable time and place in which to open his heart to Ethel, the clothing of his ideas in well-selected language, perhaps even the making of one or two apt quotations, conned beforehand for the occasion, for Ethel loved poetry.

All this Tom had proposed to himself. And that all this should go to the winds, that Tom should precipitately have the matter out with Ethel herself, saying no word to father or mother—who could have thought it? Not Tom, certainly, and not Ethel! Never in Ethel's life had she been more astonished than she was by Tom's next utterance, after her pettish remark about "those horrid umbels." The pause following was long enough for Ethel to lose herself anew in thought, to forget Tom and painting, umbels and botany. Suddenly her attention was arrested by a shaky voice of genuine emotion—

"It's no good, you know, Ethel! I can't help it. I can't go off, and—and leave things like this. I'm going back to Australia, you know, before long, and you'll—you'll—you'll come with me, won't you? Say you will, Ethel! I can't get along without you, and that's the truth."

Was there ever a more unscientific " specimen " of a proposal ?

Tom seized Ethel's hand, and held it as in a vice. Ethel's eyes opened widely, and stared at him in blank bewilderment.

" Tom ! "

" Just say you will, and it'll be all right," pleaded Tom, discarding long words and Latin terminations with shameless promptitude. Somehow, neither long words nor Latin terminations lend themselves to love-making, or to the expression of strong feeling; and Tom's feeling for Ethel was strong of its kind. " Just say you will," reiterated Tom. " I'll do my very best to make you happy, I will indeed ! " and his grasp tightened.

Ethel could not have released herself by struggling, and she did not try. She looked straight at Tom, and said, " Please let go ! "

Tom dropped the hand as if it had been a hot potato, and Ethel rubbed it.

" You hurt me ! " she said. " But it doesn't matter; only you must not do that again. And please understand that I don't want any more nonsense. We are cousins and friends, that is all. We never can be anything else—never ! "

Tom began to beg. Tom began to implore. It was not nonsense, but sense. He meant fully all that he had said. If Ethel would only consent, he would be the happiest man living.

"O no, you would not. We should both be wretched. I could not make you happy, and you could not make me happy."

"Why not?" Tom demanded fiercely. He was unhappy, and therefore fierce. At this moment he felt that Ethel was worth more than all the world could offer beside. He would have sacrificed even his herbaria to win her! Who then might say that he could not make Ethel happy?

"We are not made for one another," Ethel asserted. "Our tastes are different, and our ways. It would be a perpetual rub and fret."

"Why should it?" insisted Tom. "Husbands and wives don't always like the same things." He was right enough there, no doubt.

"No, I suppose not. But they ought to be able to agree to differ, able to go their own separate paths in peace. It doesn't sound like a cheerful arrangement exactly, but it is what has to be in a great many cases." She spoke soberly, out of her girlish experience, as if familiar with various phases of matrimonial life. "And you know that is what you and I never could do. You would never leave me in peace."

Tom broke in to assure her that he would. He would do anything, everything. There was nothing under the sun that Tom would not do to please Ethel.

"Yes, that is all very kind," said Ethel, smiling. "But one has to look forward, and when a lover becomes a husband, things are not exactly the same.

Everybody says so, and I have seen it. You might mean to leave me in peace, but you wouldn't be able. It is not your way. You would never be happy unless I could like what you liked, and then I should be cross, and you would be vexed."

Tom was indignant. As if Ethel ever was cross! As if he ever could be vexed—with her!

"O, I can be desperately cross; and I assure you, Tom, you would very soon be vexed with me. Scientific specimens are all very well for a month, but you don't know how I should detest them if it were always!"

"I believe you have other reasons," declared Tom, with no small annoyance. "It's inconceivable that you should refuse me for nothing but this."

"I don't say I have no other reasons. Of course I have. But isn't one enough?" asked Ethel cheerfully.

"No; one isn't enough!" said wrathful Tom. "One isn't enough, especially when that one's not the true one! I believe you care a great deal too much for that fellow at the Grange."

Ethel's gentle face flamed into anger, and she stood up to leave the room.

"Tom, if you are going to be rude, I have done with you. I didn't wish to hurt your feelings more than was needed, but as you are determined to have another reason, it's easy enough to give. I don't care an atom for you, and I never shall care! I don't want ever to see anything more of you at all."

Tom was crushed. He had done the business now,

and no mistake. The proverbial dove flying in his face would not have amazed him more than this indignant outburst. He did not dare to follow Ethel; but presently he heard a step running down-stairs, and when he looked out of the window, there was Ethel in the garden, dressed as for a walk.

Where could she be going? Darkness fell early these wintry afternoons. It would soon be dusk.

Tom saw nothing of Ethel for hours afterward. Nobody seemed to know where she had betaken herself. "In the parish, of course," everybody said, when Tom went about asking questions. At five o'clock tea she did not become visible. Tom felt sufficiently punished; yet he began to count Ethel's absence almost a compliment. It seemed to clothe him with a certain fictitious importance.

CHAPTER XXII.

THE BREAKING STORM.

"For life is one long sleep,
  O'er which in gusts do sweep
    Visions of heaven ;
  The body but a closèd lid,
  By which the real world is hid
  From the spirit slumbering dark below ;
  And all our earthly strife and woe,
  Tossings in slumber to and fro ;
  And all we know of heaven and light
  In visions of the day or night
    To us is given."
        Author of "Schönberg-Cotta Family."

FOR Mr. Carden-Cox to have a disturbed equanimity
meant talk. Whatever he felt flowed outward in the
natural vent of talk. This is usually supposed to be a
feminine characteristic, but some men inherit it largely
from their mothers, and Mr. Carden-Cox possessed it
in perfection. The more his feelings were stirred, the
more he had to say.

This was the style of thing :—

"Your mother resting—asleep! Best for her, much
best. Well, girls, how are you? Pretty well, eh?

Poor things—sad, very—most trying time. Everybody feels for you all—nice feeling expressed—and— Well, my dear boy, how are you? Not very robust yet? Grown thinner, I declare. O, it won't do for you to fret; no use at all. Nothing gained by fretting. What has to be, has to be. I tell everybody it is wrong to fret—tempting Providence!"

It was true that Mr. Carden-Cox did tell everybody this, and some people were apt to ask responsively behind his back whether it were right to "sulk," which was the Newton Bury term for Mr. Carden-Cox' occasional retreats from society.

"Quite wrong," repeated Mr. Carden-Cox. "Trouble has to be borne. 'Man is born to trouble.' Poor Browning—poor fellow—your poor father, I mean," stumbling awkwardly over the different modes of expression. "Yes, it's most unfortunate—sad, I mean. But you've got to think, all of you, that he is no doubt spared something worse—heart-disease—might have suffered severely if he had lived. I'm sure nobody could have thought—but one ought to think! Wonder we don't understand more the uncertainties of life. Seems always to take us by surprise. 'In midst of life we are in death;' but it is very astonishing."

Anice cried quietly, with subdued sniffles, as he talked, and Daisy looked indignant, while Fulvia's eyes wore a combative expression. Nigel appeared not to be listening.

"You've all got to buckle to now, and get things

arranged for your poor mother, eh, girls? Must think of her comfort. Nigel will be going to college by-and-by, so you'll have to be her dependence. What of your poor father's affairs, Nigel? Looked into things yet? Some little embarrassments, I suppose. Nothing serious, or we should have heard. Everybody would have heard."

" Nobody has heard anything yet."

Mr. Carden-Cox peered at him inquisitively. " Then there is something, hey?"

" We must give up the Grange."

Daisy burst into a round-mouthed " Oh!" Anice uttered a little shriek.

"Give up—the Grange!"

" Let or sell, whichever we can. There will not be enough money to keep the place going. We must find a small low-rented house somewhere, and do our best to live economically."

Mr. Carden-Cox screwed up his lips, emitting a tiny whistle.

" And—college—"

" Is out of the question. I shall be at the Bank."

" In what capacity?"

" Clerk."

" You—a clerk!"

" On £200 a year. But for friendship and kindness, I should have had to begin with less than half as much."

There was no falter in Nigel's voice thus far.

"But, I say!" broke from Mr. Carden-Cox. "I say! What about Fulvia?"

"If I don't go out as governess, I shall be useful at home," said Fulvia. A touch of hardness was visible in her manner.

"You—go—out—as—governess!" Mr. Carden-Cox could hardly give utterance to the words.

"Fulvia is talking nonsense. That will not be." Nigel spoke resolutely, but Fulvia could see what the interview was to him. The colour had left his lips, and a band of dead whiteness grew round them.

"I don't know who is to prevent, if I choose."

"I do. It will not be permitted," said Nigel.

"Permitted! I should just—think—not!" gasped Mr. Carden-Cox. "Fulvia Rolfe to go—out—as—governess! And pray, what of Fulvia Rolfe's fifty thousand pounds? Eh? What of my niece's fifty thousand pounds? I am her uncle, remember! her only near relative, remember! I have a right to know, to demand! What of Fulvia's money, intrusted to—to—to—your father?"

Mr. Carden-Cox was in a towering passion, too much of a passion for lucid speech. He already saw what he had to expect, and he nearly foamed at the mouth.

"Fulvia's money!" he reiterated. "Fulvia's fifty—thousand—pounds! Eh? eh? eh? What of that? eh? Where is it?"

One word would have been sufficient answer, just the little word "Gone!" Nigel could not say it. His self-command was not equal to the strain. To have to confess this of his dead father before Mr. Carden-Cox, before the wronged Fulvia, before Albert Browning's own daughters, was too much. There was a parting of the lips, and an effort to speak, but no sound came, and the lips closed again with rigid pressure, as if he were hardly able to endure himself. Fulvia had meant to remain in the background, but the sight of Nigel's distress overpowered her, and she started forward impulsively.

"Nigel, don't! I wish you would not! Do leave me to tell. Uncle, you are *not* to worry Nigel and all the rest of us about that wretched money. I will not have you do it. I am of age now. It is in my hands, not yours. And I choose to have nothing separate. I am madre's child, just like Anice or Daisy. Madre has had terrible losses, and I am ready to work for her as I would for my own mother. I will not have them all bothered and plagued, just when they have so much to bear."

"And your fifty thousand pounds, child! Fifty thousand, mind you! not a penny less!"

"You don't know anything about it. How should you? It is not fifty thousand, and I don't believe there ever was half that. Some of it is gone—I don't care how much—and it is nobody's concern except mine. If padre used some, he had a right, and I won't hear anybody say he had not. He was my father," cried the generous girl, ready to say anything in her hot

U

defence. "And he meant to repay; of course he meant to repay; he would have repaid if he had lived."

"Father use Fulvia's money!" uttered Daisy.

"Daisy, will you hold your tongue? Have you no eyes? Can't you see? Nigel can't bear it—nobody can bear it! Why must you all try to make the worst of everything? Things can't be helped now—now he is gone! He never meant it—he told me so when he was dying. I will not hear hard words said of him. I tell you, we will all have everything together, and I don't mean to allow a single word more about my money."

"Community of goods, in fact!" growled Mr. Carden-Cox. "That's all very fine, but—you mean"—he looked from her to Nigel, and back again—"you mean, in fact—as I might have guessed!—that your money is lost—flung away—squandered—stolen! Ay, stolen! Nothing more nor less than stolen! And that man—Browning!—Let me alone, girl!" as Fulvia distractedly clutched his wrist—"let me alone! I'll have my say! That man, Albert Browning, trusted by your poor father as the very soul of honour—he was a scoundrel! A mean pitiful *scoundrel!* A miserable base SCOUNDREL!"

Mr. Carden-Cox was beside himself with wrath, or he would hardly have gone so far. Fulvia turned to Nigel in an agony.

"Nigel! stop him!" she implored.

Nigel himself could not endure this. He had already started up, ashen white.

" Retract your words or leave the house ! " he said hoarsely ; and before Mr. Carden-Cox could reply, Daisy burst into a terrified exclamation—

" Mother ! Look at mother ! "

Mrs. Browning was in the room. How long she had been there no one could tell. When Daisy first saw her, she stood near the door, perfectly still, like a living image of wax in her deep mourning, one hand hanging carelessly over the other on a background of crape, the dark eyes wide open and fixed. But Daisy's words aroused her, and she came forward.

" Clemence ! If I'd guessed—" groaned Mr. Carden-Cox.

He advanced, holding out his hand in a half-apologetic manner, muttering something like " regret." Mrs. Browning gazed beyond and through him. She swept past slowly, and came among her children, laying a hand on Nigel's arm.

" What is it all about ? " she asked in her sweet low voice. " I do not understand. Some one can open the door for Mr. Carden-Cox."

Mr. Carden-Cox absolutely went, there and then, without a word of self-excuse, opening the door for himself, bowing to the decision of that fair woman as he would have bowed to the decision of no other human being. Fulvia gathered her wits together, and rushed after him to the front door.

" One word—one word ! " she said. " Hear me, uncle —I will be heard ! " as he was turning away. " You must listen. This is not to be known—not to be spread abroad. No one is to know it except ourselves."

Mr. Carden-Cox' face was dark with wrath. He had obeyed Clemence Browning, but he would not easily forgive either her dismissal or his own submission.

"Atrocious!" was the one word he uttered. Then he shook off Fulvia's hand. "Let me go, girl! I've done with you all! An ungrateful crew! After all these years—to be turned away like a tramp!—ordered off by her!"

"It is not ingratitude! You *know* it is not! You *know* you were wrong! You *know* a wife could not hear such words of her husband! And whatever you think, the matter is not to go any farther. It must not —shall not! What is the good? What could be the use—now?"

"That may be as I choose," said Mr. Carden-Cox. A sudden consciousness of power brought coolness to him. He held the family secret, and he was not bound.

"If you do—if you tell—" cried Fulvia. "Uncle, you must understand! If you make this known, I will never speak to you again. I declare I will not. And what is the use?" she went on passionately. "The money is gone, and talking will not bring it back. Have you no pity for those who are left? He is dead, and you cannot touch him—only his name! That will hurt them, not him! If he was wrong—ever so wrong —what then? I don't believe he understood, but if he did, why are they to suffer? Do you want to kill madre? I could not have thought you so hard, so cruel! I thought you cared for us all."

Mr. Carden-Cox stood still, looking at her.

"Child, you don't understand," he said at length. "Women never do! You think fifty thousand pounds a toy, to be tossed from hand to hand." He was composed now, not less angry, but able to feel a certain admiration for Fulvia's generosity. "Not one woman in a thousand knows the meaning of a 'trust.' You don't!"

Another pause. Was he relenting?

"I shall not set foot in this house again. That is, not until Clemence requests it. She will not; and I shall not come. Best settle the matter now. Send Nigel here at once. I will wait for him. Yes, you may go."

"You will keep our secret?"

"Send Nigel, and be quick," was the answer.

Fulvia obeyed; what else could she do? Nigel came, stern and silent. The two men stood together in the open doorway; no one else within hearing.

"Fulvia wishes this matter hushed up. It rests with me, of course, whether or no. If I choose, I can drag the whole matter to light of day."

Nigel merely said, "Yes."

"You acknowledge my right—"

"Your power."

"Well, well, let it be so. My power, if you choose. As Fulvia's uncle, I have the right, unquestionably.

I have asked to speak with you, as I am not likely to call again in a hurry."

"Without an apology, you hardly could."

"Pshaw! As if I had not known you all long enough! But as for this—Fulvia says that to spread the thing abroad would punish the living, not the dead."

"Yes."

"You think the same? Don't know that I see it so. A man's good name is not supposed to lose its value, even after his death. However, my chief care is for Fulvia's interests. Are you willing to make up to her what she has lost?"

"If repayment is ever in my power—"

"Repayment! Pshaw! Fifty thousand pounds are not made in a day. By the time Fulvia is an old woman, perhaps—and what good would the money be to her then? No, no; you have it in your power to recoup her now—now! Will you do it, or no? That is the question."

Nigel was silent; understanding only too well.

"Mind, my line of action depends on your decision. If you are to be Fulvia's husband, I may safely leave her interests in your hands. If not, I shall see to them myself."

"In what way?"

"Whichever way I choose. I shall have the matter openly looked into."

"You have no thought for my mother in that case."

Nigel spoke in a measured icy voice.

Mr. Carden-Cox could verily have answered "No." He was only angry with Clemence Browning just then.

"I have thought for my niece," he said. "That is more to the purpose."

Another break took place; Nigel looking on the ground, Mr. Carden-Cox looking at Nigel. At any other time he would have felt for Nigel, but now he felt only for himself. His self-love had been deeply wounded, and all other sensations were lost in this.

"Well?"

"You do not expect an instant decision, I suppose."

"Instant! After these weeks! Then you had not made up your mind yet?"

"To do what?"

"Marry Fulvia."

"I have not made up my mind to propose to her. A lady is usually supposed to have a voice in the matter," Nigel said satirically. He was not given to satire, but at the moment it was a relief.

"Of course, of course. If Fulvia said no, that would not be your fault. She won't though," muttered Mr. Carden-Cox. Aloud he went on—"You understand the alternative. Fulvia, as your *fiancée*, may demand what amount of secrecy she pleases, for the family of her future husband. I shall not, in that case, oppose her. Fulvia standing alone will be a different matter. I shall feel it my duty to take action on her behalf."

"To blazon our private affairs abroad!" Nigel spoke bitterly. It was not wise, neither was it surprising.

Mr. Carden-Cox shrugged his shoulders.

"Fulvia's private affairs, made known, may unquestionably drag yours to the forefront. It is only under one condition that I promise to shelter your father's name. People will begin to talk—have begun already. You can take—say, to the end of the week for consideration. Then, if I do not hear—"

"I understand."

"You can send me a line; or come and see me. Whichever you choose. But remember, my mind is made up. Nothing can alter it."

Mr. Carden-Cox was gone, and Nigel went back to the drawing-room.

The past scene appeared to have had a curiously bracing effect on Mrs. Browning. The languor and sadness of the last fortnight were thrown off. Her children had never seen her look so young and fair, so lovely and dignified, as she did, standing in their midst, when Nigel returned from the front door. Nothing, or next to nothing, had been yet said; they had waited for him.

Mrs. Browning laid one hand again on his arm, as if for support, though she had not the look of one needing support. A soft rose had flushed her cheek, lending a light to the eyes.

"Has he apologized? Will he be silent?" asked Fulvia.

Nigel answered only the first question. "Mr. Carden-Cox is not given to apologies."

"But—this time—surely—"

"What does it all mean?" Mrs. Browning inquired.

"It means—oh, it means that uncle Arthur has behaved shamefully, madre. I used to think him a good man, and I'll never call him so again. But you must not mind—you must never remember what he said. He was in a passion; and words spoken in a passion are worth nothing. Promise me to forget—promise me not to believe—"

"My dear Fulvia! *I* believe anything against my dear husband!"

"No, no! I might have known you would not—could not!"

"But I should like to know what led Mr. Carden-Cox to behave in such an extraordinary way. If you would all leave me with—"

"He magnifies and distorts everything!" Fulvia broke in. "Madre, dear, we need not mind him. We will never listen to a single word breathed against the dear kind padre. Oh, never!"

Fulvia was over-doing her part. She glanced in vain towards Nigel, hoping to be seconded; but his face was rigidly irresponsive.

"Mr. Carden-Cox said—" began Daisy.

"Uncle Arthur knows nothing about things—nothing more than we have told him. Daisy, do be sensible; do be kind; don't rake up worries," whispered Fulvia energetically. "It is of no use—none whatever. Nothing can be altered now by any amount of talk."

"But your money?"

"Hsh—sh!"

"I wish to know what it all means," said Mrs. Browning in her calm voice. "There is no need to whisper. I must, of course, be told everything. Anice and Daisy can leave us for a little while." As the door closed behind them, she continued: "Fulvia knows more than the girls."

"A little more, perhaps. We will talk over everything some day soon—you and I, madre. Only not to-day!—it is too soon. Nigel ought not to have all this thrust upon him till he is stronger."

"No?" The word was not acquiescent. In her own fashion Mrs. Browning could be graciously wilful. She moved in front of her son, looking up at him. "Yes—tired, I am afraid;—but a few minutes will be enough. I must understand how things really are. It is not possible that any one could seriously accuse my dear husband of—of carelessness in—"

"Mr. Carden-Cox always speaks before he thinks."

"Yes, he does that! But what did he mean by saying that all your money had been—stolen? Is it really lost? Has somebody run away?—in a bank or an office?"—with truly feminine vagueness.

"I don't know that anybody has—exactly," faltered Fulvia.

"Then it was not true about your money being—stolen, my dear?"

"No; not true. It is a wicked falsehood, madre. There has been no such thing as stealing. You are never to think of that word again. It has been just a question of mistakes. Nobody could help things being as they are, and no one is to blame. There have been losses, of course. Money *will* go, sometimes; everybody knows that it will. A great deal of yours and of mine, too, is gone. Poor padre's health, you know—how could he keep accounts or attend to business?—and so things have got wrong. It wouldn't matter so much, only we have to leave the Grange, and live in a small house; and that will grieve you. It does seem hard for you; but nothing else signifies. I can't think why troubles should come as they do, on the very people who deserve them least."

"They come as God wills, Fulvie. I would not choose to be without them. But there are different kinds of trouble. I think I could bear anything, as long as—" and a quiver. "It would kill me to hear things said—said against him! Anything but that."

"But you will not—you shall not! Nobody shall dare!" cried Fulvia. "If only Mr. Carden-Cox will hold his tongue, nobody else will speak. Nobody has known how much I was to have. Nigel, why don't you help me to comfort madre?" Then she regretted her words.

Mrs. Browning's eyes again searched wistfully her son's face—a set face, strong and pale, the lips stern, and quick beating visible in the temples. A strange look crept into her eyes as she gazed—a look of hidden affright. Yet she turned with a faint smile to Fulvia.

"My dear, will you go to the girls—for a little while? If you do not mind! I wish to speak to Nigel alone."

Fulvia could not but obey; and when she was gone, the look of affright came back, hidden no longer. It blanched Mrs. Browning's cheeks, and widened the mournful eyes.

"I must know—now!" she said, in an undertone. "Not when others were here, but now we are alone. What does it all mean?"

He did not speak, and the look of terror increased.

"It cannot be Albert—my husband!" she said. "He could not have called him *that*—with reason! But what did he mean? Not blame to my dear Albert?"

"If only you would not ask, mother!"

"I must ask; I must know. Only you can tell me. Yes, sit down, if you like. I am so sorry. This worry is bad for you, and makes your head ache, does it not? But how can I wait? I have only you now—no one else!" She took a seat beside him, and put back the hair from his brow, with her cold fingers, and her sweet motherly air. "It is hard, I know—everything coming upon you; and you are so good to me. Only—think!

—he is my husband!" She did not say "was." "He is my husband, and I have the first right to know all. Tell me plainly, is he—was he—has he been in any way to blame?"

"He will be blamed," Nigel said hoarsely.

"Why should he?"

"Fulvia's money—"

"Yes,—Fulvia's money—?"

"It has been—used."

"How?"

"Different ways."

"You don't know how?"

"He always hoped to repay; he did not intend—"

"You mean—he had not enough of his own, and he used— But—but—that—surely—!" She thrilled with horror, like a wounded creature. "That! my husband! But, Nigel! it was not—honourable—honest!"

Nigel's lips hardly formed the word "No!" He forced himself to add: "My father did not intend—"

"How do you know he did not intend? What do you mean by 'intending'? He knew what he did; he must have known."

"I don't think he realized—fully."

"Do people ever?" she asked, with positive scorn. "Isn't that always the way—borrowing, and meaning to repay?" Then she dropped her head, and broke into a low wail: "Albert—my husband!"

Nigel had no comfort to offer. He could only wait in silence; and soon the question came again—

" How do you know what he intended and did not intend ? "

"He said it to Fulvia—dying; and asked her pardon."

" And I not told ! I ought to have been told. Did he say any more that I have not heard ? "

" He asked me to repay Fulvia—to—"

" Yes ; tell me his words—every word."

Nigel could not; she was expecting too much. He made an effort, and failed; then drew an envelope from his pocket, and gave it to her. " From my father to me," he said huskily. " I found it—afterwards." He did not watch his mother while she read, but sat with his right hand pressed across brow and eyes.

" Yes," she said, in a slow quiet voice, when she reached the end; and a long breath of sorrow was woven into the word.

Then a pause.

" Has Fulvia seen this ? "

" No."

" Or—any one ? "

" No."

" He never told me—never let me suspect— But Fulvia knows ? "

" Yes."

"We must shelter his name—his dear name !—at any cost."

" Fulvia does not wish it to be known." Nigel spoke without stirring. " But—"

" It must not be known; his name must be guarded. It would break my heart! If this becomes known, I shall—die!" she whispered. "I could never look any one in the face again. It would be—fearful!"

She laid her hand on his—ice-cold, both hers and his. "Nigel, help me; tell me what can be done. It will kill me if this becomes known. Think of all New- ton Bury talking —talking of—*him !* I could not bear it!" and there was a terrible sob. "What can we do? Fulvia does not wish—but will—will Mr. Carden-Cox keep silence ? "

" Yes, if—"

Nigel caught himself up; he had not meant to say so much.

"If? Has he made a condition ? "

"He will do nothing till I write or see him again."

" No; but ' if '—you said ' if.' Did you mean nothing ? You must tell me all. I cannot bear the thought of its being known. It would be too—too—fearful—now he is gone! He cannot defend himself. And people are so hard; they would judge him cruelly. I wish you would look at me—not hide your eyes. Why do you ? I feel so—alone;" with another deep sob. "And no one but you can help me. If you would only speak out —only hide nothing! I think I have a right to be told —I, your mother!"

His chivalry could not disregard the appeal of her bitter distress, and of her lonely widowhood. He was all that she had left—all she could lean upon. Wisely or unwisely, he came to the resolution to speak out. Perhaps he was in despair of escape; perhaps—though he did not guess this till later—he had a faint hope of finding her on his side. He knew the jealousy of her love for him; and he did not allow for concomitant circumstances.

"Mr. Carden-Cox will not speak—if I should marry Fulvia," he said.

"Fulvia!" Mrs. Browning looked wonderingly at the set joyless face, with black shades of pain under the heavy eyes; not the face of an expectant lover speaking of his love. "If you marry—Fulvia."

"That is his wish."

"Fulvia! And it was my dear husband's wish! He spoke so often; but I thought—I was afraid—"

"Mother, I said 'if'! It is not to be spoken about. If I ask her—"

"And you will! O, you will! He wished it so much —so intensely."

Nigel made no reply. She gazed with anxious questioning.

"And if you do not—if you do not—will Mr. Carden-Cox keep our secret?"

"He says—not."

"Nigel! and you can hesitate!"

No answer again.

"Hesitate! when it means that. No, no—impossible! You are only playing with my fears. And caring for Fulvia as you do! It is not as if she were nothing to you; she—the most unselfish, the noblest— Yes, I know you had another fancy once; but what of that? Everybody has a boyish fancy first, which has to be given up. And that could not be; it could never have been! *He* would not have consented; and now he is gone, how could I? O no! I have always had objections—strong objections. But we need not talk of that now. We have only to think of our dear Fulvia—my child already! I don't know if you will like me to say it, but there cannot be much doubt, if you speak, what Fulvia's answer will be. She has shown at times so plainly—not meaning it, of course—has shown what she feels. If you could have seen her, as I have, always on the watch for you, always thinking of your comfort, —her happiness depending on your very look. It is not a thing that one can be mistaken about!"

"Mother, you are saying all this to me!—and if I should not ask her?" Nigel said, in a low tone. It was his nearest approach to a rebuke with Mrs. Browning. He would not have heard the words from any one else.

"You will ask her! I know you will. I have not a doubt. Think, if you did not; think of the misery, the terrible misery to us all—your father's dear name dragged in the mire—trampled upon. The very thought half kills me!" and indeed a ghastly look came into her face. "I could not bear it! I could never endure it! Promise, O, promise me, for his sake, my Nigel—promise to shelter him—all of us! Only promise!" she implored.

x

CHAPTER XXIII.

A STRANGE INTERVIEW.

"When we two parted
 In silence and tears."—BYRON.

" Had we never loved sae kindly,
 Had we never loved sae blindly,
 Never met or never parted,
 We had ne'er been broken-hearted."—BURNS

WHEN Ethel left Tom, she really was angry with him. Such rudeness to speak of her "caring too much" for anybody ! What business was it of Tom's whom she liked or did not like? And to call Nigel "that fellow !" I am not sure that this little insult to Nigel did not rankle the most. Ethel cared little for Tom's opinion of herself, but she could not stand a slight to Nigel.

Ethel's anger was never bitter in kind, or long lasting, and annoyance soon gave way to a pitying amusement. Poor old Tom ! After all, he had not meant any harm ; and he did not know Nigel : but how Tom could ever have thought such a thing possible was the marvel. Leave all she loved in England, and go to Australia with only Tom and Tom's herbaria ! " O, never !" said Ethel. " Never !" She repeated the word energetically, half aloud, as she passed through the square—"Never!" and a passer-by turned to look at her, smiling. Ethel did not see; she went quickly, without any particular aim, towards the river.

It was a tempting afternoon for a stroll, balmy and soft—one of those mild gray days, with occasional gleams of sunshine, which do sometimes intrude themselves into an English winter. They are not exactly invigorating days, and enthusiastic skaters are wont to abuse them; but to haters of cold they come as a cheery foretaste of spring.

Gleams of sunshine were at an end when Ethel started; still, she had a spell of daylight and twilight ahead, long enough for a brisk little walk, by way of shaking off recollections of Tom. When dusk shoul. fall, she would look in at a friend's house for a cup of tea—one of the numerous single ladies "of the usual age" abundant in Newton Bury. It would never do to go home till after five. Mrs. Elvey was up-stairs with neuralgia; and a fresh *tête-à-tête* with Tom so soon was not to be thought of. "If mother doesn't come down, he must manage for himself for once," thought Ethel.

Along the river-bank was the one "country walk" within easy distance of the Rectory. Some ten or fifteen minutes at a brisk pace, going down stream, brought one to a region where buildings were scarce. Newton Bury ended abruptly in this direction. The other way, up stream, there were gentlemen's houses and gardens, reaching far; for that was the "west-end" of the town. Towards the south, working-men's quarters

predominated; but the old Parish Church of St.
Stephen's, in its venerable square, lay towards the
north-east, very near country lanes and fields, in a poor
but quiet part—the oldest part of Newton Bury.

Ethel did not keep long to the river-side. An
impulse seized her to visit the cemetery—a natural
impulse under the circumstances, her thoughts being
constantly bent upon the Brownings and their trouble.
She had not been to the cemetery since the day of the
funeral. There would be just time enough for her to
get there and back before dark. The idea no sooner
occurred to Ethel than she acted upon it, quitting the
towing-path, and making a short cut straight to her
destination.

The cemetery, though outside the town, was not far
off. It was a singularly pretty place, more like a large
garden or a small park than a burial-ground, with soft
grassy slopes, abundance of trees, and masses of ever-
greens. In fine weather the cemetery was a favourite
resort of people living at this end of Newton Bury.

Ethel reached the large gates, and went through,
passing at a rapid pace towards the quiet corner which
the Brownings would now hold dear—which would also
be dear to Ethel, for Nigel's sake. She found the place
somewhat lonely, and darker than she had expected,
under the shadows of the great yew-trees. The black
branches had an eerie look. Once Ethel almost turned
back, thinking it had grown too late for her to be there
alone; but she changed her mind, and went on. She

had a dislike to giving up a definite intention; and, after all, nobody was here except herself—nobody was likely to be here.

The low mound loomed suddenly upon her gaze, almost solitary upon a triangular patch of grass, which on one side was bounded by a fringe of trees, their bare boughs making a lace-like pattern against the sky. Ethel saw so much, then she slackened her pace, and faltered; for she was not alone.

Though she did not at once tell herself whose solitude she had invaded, she knew well—knew instantly. The position might be unwonted, but the outline of the broad shoulders was unmistakable. He was a little way off from the new mound, seated on the only other tombstone near—a flat stone with a recumbent cross upon it—and his head was bent forward, resting on his hands. The attitude was one of intense trouble; but he remained perfectly still. Ethel had never seen Nigel thus before; yet she recognized him, despite the gloom.

She did not know whether perhaps she ought to go away; only it seemed impossible to leave him thus. So she went forward gently, and stood beside the mound, her heart very full for his sake. Two or three minutes passed; and she stirred, touching a loose stone with her foot. It rolled over, and the slight rattle caused him to lift his head.

"Ethel!" he said.

They had not met since Fulvia's birthday—since the

morning after their interview in the vestry. Life had
seemed then very fair, and full of promise for them
both. Now all was changed; but how much changed,
how dark the sky had grown, Ethel did not yet
know. She came forward when he stood up, and put
her hand into his, only intent on showing her sympathy.

"Thanks; I knew you would feel for us," he said.

The dazed white misery of his face was almost too
much for Ethel; she had great difficulty in controlling
herself. "I didn't know you were so ill still," she
faltered.

"Ill! no, I don't think so." He spoke as if hardly
knowing what he said, and motioned Ethel to the seat he
had quitted. She took it obediently, without question;
and he sat down beside her. "I have been wishing for
a few words with you," he went on.

"If I could be a comfort—any comfort!" murmured
Ethel. "I know how much you must feel his death;
the loss of—"

"If that were all!" Nigel spoke with despairing
calmness, and Ethel looked at him in amazement.

"That—all!" she repeated. "Did you mean—"

Nigel made no answer. He seemed to be gazing
at the faint light visible still through bare trees.
For more than half-an-hour he had sat here alone,
trying to unravel the perplexities of his position, striving
in vain after definite thought. He had come to the
cemetery from the Grange drawing-room, straight and
fast as walking could bring him, not so much to be

near his father's grave as to be away from people, beyond reach of human eyes.   One thing alone was clear,
—that speak with Ethel he *must*, this very day if
possible, and before he could or would give any decisive
answer to his mother and to Mr. Carden-Cox.   He did
not count himself free, for he had distinctly sought
Ethel hitherto.

Now, indeed, he could not ask her to be his.   Apart
from all questions of marrying Fulvia, he could not
rightly ask Ethel to wait for him, under the circumstances.   So he told himself; and yet he felt that, but
for this terrible complication, he would have hoped—she
might have waited.

Still, she had a right to know how things were.   He
could not simply draw back, holding his peace, and
seeking her no longer.   She must understand; and he
would explain—nay, more, he would ask her advice.
She had so clear a sense of right and wrong, so candid
and calm a judgment, so firm a habit of self-denial, that
she would be able to see clearly what he had lost the
power to distinguish, from physical and mental strain.

All this he had resolved to put before Ethel, picturing
even the words to be used.   But now that she had
suddenly appeared, now that she was seated by his side,
he found his lips sealed; for it came over him with a
rush of new realization what he was purposing to do.

Give her up—and for ever !   Give her up—for the
sake of Fulvia !   Could he ?   The old sense arose vividly,
which he always had with Ethel, that nothing in life

was worth consideration apart from her! Give her up! Place a barrier between himself and her for ever! Had it been a question of waiting, he would have resolved to wait in hope—to wait for years, if that needed to be!— but to cut himself off from her hopelessly was another matter. Yet, if he did not—and the reverse side of the picture arose, a picture of his father's name publicly dishonoured, of his mother broken-hearted, of the wronged Fulvia wronged anew!

"I don't know how to bear to see you like this!" Ethel said sorrowfully; and her voice unsealed his lips. He knew that he must not let the opportunity pass of speaking openly. Such another might not occur.

"What did I say just now?" he asked. "Something, was it not, that surprised you?"

"I thought you did not quite mean what you said. About your trouble; and—'if that were all!'"

"Yes, I meant it. There is worse than you know."

"Will you tell me what? You always do tell—us things," she said, in a gentle voice. The "us" came after a pause. She had almost said "me;" and it would have been true.

Ethel wondered if he were going to speak, he waited so long; but she too waited, and presently he began.

"We have lost almost everything. The Grange cannot be our home any longer. A small house—somewhere; and I—my mother and sisters will be dependent on me."

"Yes." It was a quiet grave monosyllable. As if

on second thoughts, she added, "That will be a great trouble to you all."

"Not the worst yet! Fulvia's money is gone!"

"Gone! Where?"

Nigel made a movement of his hand towards the new mound. "He is—there! One cannot speak against him—now! It is a miserable tale. This is only for yourself—not to go further. He did not intend, of course, to injure any one—Fulvia least of all—if that is any excuse. I can't see that it is. As my mother says, no one ever does intend. But—we can't judge. I don't feel as if I could face his side of the matter; only to think of what has to be done. There will be something left—not much. I shall be a clerk at the Bank, on £200 a year."

"I see," said Ethel gently. She grew more pale than usual, and there was a curious sense of constriction at her heart, as if a tight band impeded its beating; for she knew what all this meant. "Yes, I see; but you will make your way. Perhaps even— Does Fulvia mind very much?"

Nigel could speak more freely now. Once started, he had power to continue, and he even found speech a relief. He never felt it so with any one else, but with Ethel he did. Her silent sympathy drew him on. He told her of his father's death; of the dying words spoken to Fulvia and himself; of the hand placed in his; giving details that he had not given even to his mother, only omitting the look of joy on Fulvia's face,

which had haunted him ever since. Nigel went through
all this in a low monotonous voice, as to a well-tried
friend, and Ethel read it so. When he spoke of
Fulvia's disinterestedness, she detected a weariness of
tone, a want of enthusiasm. He praised her, and was
grateful; but the words of praise were measured.   ⁕ ⸴

Ethel listened patiently, shivering a little. It was
dusk by this time, and the grass under their feet was
wet. A cemetery is not a warm or cheerful place late
on a January afternoon; and Ethel might well be excused
for shivering, with the gravestones lying coldly around,
while a little tomb of buried girlish hopes was being
made in her own girlish heart. It was no wonder that
she shivered and looked white. For she understood well
whereto all this tended; even before Nigel went on to
speak of Mr. Carden-Cox' condition of silence, and of his
mother's distress. She understood—first, that he would
not be free to marry her; secondly, that he would be
called upon to marry some one else.

These details took time in the telling, however briefly
expressed. No needless words were used; but they did
not come fast. While Nigel talked, it never occurred
to Ethel that the afternoon was passing fast, that daylight was waning.

He came at length to a pause. Now she understood
the position of affairs. He had not mentioned, had not
directly alluded to, his love for her; but Ethel knew it,
—had never known it more surely than in this hour.
He had left nothing else out, except the one item of

Fulvia's too evident feeling for him; and Ethel could supply this item from her own knowledge. She, too, had noted with observant eyes, since a certain clue had been supplied by a certain mis-sent postscript.

As she listened to Nigel, one sentence of that post-script flashed up, with all the force of a prophecy coming true: "Nigel will never marry *her!*"

"Never! never!" echoed the silent graves and the silent trees. "Never! never!" The words repeated themselves in Ethel's brain, and twined in and out of the straggling yew branches. "Nigel will never marry *her!*" Mr. Carden-Cox was taking care to bring his own prophecy to pass.

The story was ended, and Nigel's monotonous voice changed. It grew hoarse and troubled as he said—

"Ethel, tell me what I ought to do."

Ethel woke up from a maze; and as she woke, a dream of long years died a quiet death. She saw it die while she sat there, saw it fade away, and another dream arise, gray-toned, of a long lonely life, apart from one whom she loved best. Yet no tears threatened, no agitation came. She was so full of thought for Nigel, so grieved for him, that self-pity had as yet no place. Perhaps she was a little stunned by the unexpected blow—as one is apt to be, at first.

"Tell me," he repeated; "I want your advice. Ethel, —*must* I do this thing?"

"Must you marry Fulvia?"

"Yes." Unconsciously he caught in his the hand lying on his knee. "Tell me what you think I ought to do!" he pleaded. "No one else can help me."

Ethel drew her hand away, but so gently that he could not be pained.

"I think you feel sure yourself already," she said, in a soft still voice. "It is hard for one to see clearly for another. If I were in your place—"

"Yes, that is what I want. If you were in my place, how should you feel?"

Another break. Ethel noted the growing darkness. She was so composed as even to draw out her watch.

"No, I cannot see the time;" and she put it away again. "But it must be getting late. I think we ought to go home."

Did she wish to avoid giving an opinion? She stood up, and Nigel did the same. They had to go cautiously over the uneven grass, and along the narrow path bordered by yew-trees; but the broader path beyond was straight and level, with more light. Nigel said then again—

"Yes? If you were in my place—"

"It is so difficult to be sure. I am trying to see things rightly for you—from your standpoint. But one little touch either way might make all the difference; and I cannot know the whole as you do."

"Tell me, so far as you can, at least. If you were in my place—"

"I think I might perhaps feel, as you do, that I

ought—perhaps even that I must!" There was again the sense of constriction at Ethel's heart, though no sign of it appeared in her voice. "I mean, I might feel that I must do all I could to repay Fulvia, and to spare my—to spare Mrs. Browning. That would be your side of the matter—to feel bound—perhaps—to try— if—" Nigel could not see the two little gloved hands wrung together, and she went on, scarcely faltering, only hesitating for words; yet somehow he understood. "To feel bound—" she repeated, "to try if—to offer to Fulvia— But if I were in Fulvia's place, there would be a difference. Nothing could seem to me more dreadful than—to—"

"Than to—marry me!" He said it seriously.

"No—no—than to marry anybody who did not really mean it—wish it; to be asked out of duty by one who—" and a pause—"one who did not care for me—as I cared."

"If you were Fulvia, you would think I ought to hold back—not to offer?" Ethel's calmness was calming him; her apparent strength was strengthening him. "You would think me wrong to speak, unless—"

"I should think you ought to be quite open, quite plain with me. Not pretend to care more than you did—if—but I don't think you could pretend; you could only keep from saying much. And that might deceive her. I could not bear to be deceived, if I were Fulvia. I would like to know how you really felt. I should wish you to speak out."

"Even, supposing—supposing you cared a little for me ? "

"Yes; even supposing that !" Ethel knew that Fulvia did care, more than a little, and she was sure from Nigel's tone that he knew it too. She believed that Mr. Carden-Cox' anxiety to bring about the engagement lay also in a knowledge of this fact.

"Yes," Ethel repeated firmly. "I think it would be worse, if one cared for somebody very much, to marry him, and then to find out that he had only proposed because he thought it right! Much worse than if one did not care for him at all. I don't think I could ever bear it—ever forgive him ! It would be wronging Fulvia—cruelly. O, it is always, always, best to be quite true, quite outspoken. I am sure it is. If you feel that you ought to propose, then you are right to propose. But you would not be right, if you allowed Fulvia to think that you cared for her more than you do care. If it is only—only duty—she ought to understand."

How strange it seemed to Ethel that he should come and ask her this—ask her, as it were, to sign away her own happiness ! Ethel's was an intensely conscientious nature. She would never turn aside from what was right, merely because it gave her pain. Nigel had put this question before her, as a question of right and wrong, and she could do what not one woman in a thousand is capable of, she could view it dispassionately, weighing the absolute right and absolute wrong, without reference to her own desires. If Nigel had not known her to be capable of so much, he could not have come to her for help. He came, not because he loved, though he did love, but because he entirely trusted her.

Fulvia's was a fine nature, yet Fulvia could not have emulated Ethel here. Self would have swayed her decision; but it did not sway Ethel's. At the moment she did not even see a certain hope involved in her advice, a hope which flashed quickly upon Nigel. Although she felt in the abstract that she could not herself marry a man who should propose to her from motives of duty, she had not the smallest doubt that Fulvia would accept.

"That might be a way out of the difficulty," Nigel said, speaking as if involuntarily. Ethel did not at once understand. "But would it be—honest—right? Would it not be a mere farce? To ask her, and tell her I do not wish it! Would it not be adding insult to injury—almost cruel?"

"No, I think not. I mean, I think the other might be more cruel. Of course it depends, everything depends, on how you do it. But you would not be cruel; you would not say an unkind word. I suppose you would not need to say much? only just to let her know that it is not *all* wish—that it is partly duty— that you will learn to feel as you ought even if—if you don't quite yet."

There was a sound like a little gasp at the end of these words.

" I suppose one may conquer, always, in such a case, if one ought," continued Ethel, with a dim smile, and the tightness at her heart again. " Only I do think Fulvia ought to know just so much. Sooner or later she must, and it would be worse after—after—marriage. If she goes into it, she should go with her eyes open; not wait to find out later—too late."

They were leaving the cemetery now, passing out into the broad road. It was too dark for the narrow path by the river, and they had to keep to the road, which was much deserted at so late an hour. They walked on quietly, slowly; for Nigel seemed as if he could hardly drag himself along. During some minutes neither spoke, and then his excessive weariness dawned upon Ethel. She said—

" You must go home the shortest way."

" When I have seen you home—perhaps."

" I would rather you should not. I am all right when we get to the houses."

Nigel made no answer, and she knew he did not mean to yield. She knew it more certainly when they reached a little gate leading to a field, for he paused and held it open.

" This way ? " Ethel asked, knowing that it would lead them to the kitchen garden behind the Rectory.

Nigel said " Yes," and she could not remonstrate. She could only let him have his will, this once. They would have to speak that mournful word, " good-bye," very soon—such a good-bye as they had never yet said one to the other.

It was damp, slushy and dark, going through the meadow. Ethel's foot slipped, and Nigel drew her hand within his arm.

"I can get on—I am all right," she said, not so steadily as hitherto, for something in his touch unnerved her. He made no reply; and she would not draw her hand away—would not risk adding to his pain.

Something told her that he had reached almost the outer limit of endurance; and the consciousness of this, with the continued silence, had a curious effect upon her. She began to tremble—to wish she might escape. She thought of many things to say, one after another—things to comfort him. For somehow Ethel knew, and could not help knowing, that this death of her hopes was the death of his also. But one thing would not do, and another she could not trust her voice to utter; and so they went on in silence.

The silence grew at last too oppressive, and Ethel tried to break it.

"Must things be settled soon about your leaving the Grange?"

But she had no answer whatever; and then she knew that Nigel did not speak because he could not.

Three of these small dark fields had to be crossed, surrounded by houses and gardens, but in themselves lonely and deserted. They reached the gate of the

kitchen garden, still in silence. The Rectory windows
shone with varied lights. Nigel paused beside the
gate, and Ethel forced herself to say steadily—

"Thank you for coming so far. I shall be all right
now. Good-bye."

She put out her hand, and he held it in a passionate
clasp. There was a struggle, but no words would come.
Ethel stood still, tears running down her cheeks. What
could she do or say to comfort him?

"Ethel!—Ethel! my love!" broke out at length, in
a momentary abandonment of such agony as only a
strong man can show.

"No—no—you must not say that! Don't say any
more!" she implored.

"Ethel—!" came hoarsely again, despite her entreaty;
and she could feel the shaking of the gate against which
he leant.

"No—no—" she repeated. "Not now—not any
more. I must not let you say what you will be sorry
for by-and-by. Don't—please! I think I am glad we
have had this talk, because—because I shall understand. We will never speak of it again. By-and-by
we shall be—friends—like other people."

There was a negative movement on his part.

"Yes—I think so. You have to do what is right—
about——and we will be brave—we shall be helped.
Doesn't God always help, if—if one wills to do right?
Perhaps a little hard for you—for us—at first, but that
won't last. It will be all right."

Ethel could not bear much more. She had kept up well so far; but reaction was at hand. The interview had to be ended; good-bye had to be said; and the sooner the better.

"I must not stay!" she said, and then, without warning, unexpectedly, she broke down. "Nigel—let me go!" she sobbed.

Nigel mastered himself for her sake. "I have been wrong—unkind!" he said. "It has been too much for you."

"O no; only I can't bear to see you so unhappy. Please—please let me go."

"I shall see you again soon. This isn't really—" and a falter. "Yes, we will be—friends."

Then he wrung her hand once more, and was lost in the darkness,—not to return to the Grange till late at night. He had to fight his battle out alone.

But Ethel could have no such relief. Ten minutes of bitter weeping she did allow herself in the lonely garden. Then she was obliged to hasten home, to wash away traces of tears, to evade family inquiries, to elude Tom's troublesome solicitude, to spend a cheerful evening,—no easy task, under the circumstances.

CHAPTER XXIV.

WOULD SHE? COULD SHE?

"It may be hard to gain, and still
    To keep a lowly steadfast heart;
Yet he who loses has to fill
    A harder and a truer part."—A. A. PROCTER.

"FULVIA!"

"Yes."

"There is a house in Bourne Street—"

"Yes." Fulvia spoke curtly, looking up from her work with hard gray eyes. She was alone in the morning-room, and it was Saturday.

"I want you to come and see. It might do."

"Bourne Street!"

"Not a bad part."

"Highly respectable, and the quintessence of dulness! Well, your miseries won't last long there, which is one comfort. You will all die of *ennui* before six months are over."

"We!" Nigel tried to laugh. "Are you to be the sole survivor? Superior to such influences, I suppose."

"I shall be superior through absence. There are a

whole lot of advertisements for governesses to-day. I
shall answer three of them."

"You will not!"

"That depends——I am of age."

"You do not think what it would be to us—to me—
knowing what had driven you to it."

Even this did not touch Fulvia. She gave a dry
little laugh. "I am very much disposed to please
myself in the matter—irrespective of other people.
Why should I not?—if I choose. Poky houses are not
to my taste; and I am sick of Newton Bury."

"And of everybody in Newton Bury?"

"If you like—yes. Are we to start on the expedition
now?"

Nigel stood thinking, his brows drawn together.
Fulvia studied him in a succession of slight glances.

This was Saturday—the last day allowed by Mr.
Carden-Cox for Nigel's decision, the third since his
parting interview with Ethel. No one knew of that
interview. He had said nothing about it. Why, indeed,
should he? His late return at night, after prayers,
had given umbrage to his home-folks; the more since
he offered no explanation, and permitted no questioning.
Even his mother ventured to say little, save in manner;
and an attempt on the part of Daisy was quashed at once.

They knew he had not been to the Rectory, had not,
in fact, dined anywhere; and that was all. It was all,
at least, until this morning, when a report reached
Fulvia of somebody having seen him walking with

Ethel Elvey, after dusk, on the road near the river. She said not a word of the report; but it stung her sharply.

None of them knew or guessed of the interview in the cemetery, the parting with Ethel, the long hours after of wrestling and bitter battling. He had walked far under a starlit sky, forgetting physical weariness, braving out his conflict with no human help. There is better than human help for such times, and Nigel knew whither to turn.

He had come off conqueror. The path he had to tread was plainly marked, and he would tread it manfully. Self had to be sacrificed, and he would sacrifice it resolutely. Ethel had to be given up, and he would give her up completely. He was no longer in doubt as to his rightful course.

But he could not act at once—could not turn without a break from Ethel to Fulvia. He had put off speaking until this last day allowed by Mr. Carden-Cox, being meantime very busy with money matters, lawyers, arrangements,—so busy that his home-people saw little of him. Better this, than too much leisure for thought.

Occupied as he was, others noted a difference in him, a something unusual, not to be defined. Daisy questioned Fulvia, "What was the matter with Nigel?" and received a sharp reply. Yet Fulvia asked the same of herself.

This morning she asked a further question. What could it all mean? Had Ethel refused him? Refused

—because of his lost wealth! Fulvia's heart bounded at the thought. She would not have done so in Ethel's place. Certainly he had not the look of one who has gained his heart's desire. Rather, it was the look of one bracing himself to the endurance of trouble and difficulty. If he had asked Ethel, and she had accepted him, would he wear such a look? Yet they had been out together after dark—walking a lonely road. What could it mean but a proposal on his part, and acceptance or refusal on hers?

"Have I been mad not to see?" she thought, seated alone in the morning-room, work in hand. "Why have I not understood? But Ethel will have him sooner or later. She will not hold out long. And I—I cannot stay to see! I am glad my money is gone. That will be my excuse to run away. I could not live here, looking on. I shall be a governess."

Then she heard Nigel saying "Fulvia," and looked up, to answer, "Yes."

"Are we to start on the expedition now?" she said at length, rising. "I am ready, if you wish it. Daisy had better come as well."

Nigel assented absently, and Fulvia left the room. Coming back, she wore a look of vexation.

"Daisy has gone out, no one knows where, and Anice declines. She says she can't."

"Anice's 'can't' is equivalent to 'won't.' I don't think it matters. The decision will rest with you."

"Why should it?"

"You are the eldest daughter, are you not?"

Fulvia shrugged her shoulders slightly, but in words she raised no objection. Fifteen minutes' quick walk brought them to No. 9, Bourne Street, hardly a word being uttered by the way.

As Fulvia had said, it was a respectable locality. The houses were of white stucco, with neat porches and balconies, and tidy oblong gardens behind. A narrow strip of enclosed grass, with small trees, occupied the centre of the street from one end to the other. Beside the porch was one window; and two windows above were capped by yet two others.

A cosy little house, no doubt, containing possibilities of comfort. But after the Grange—ah, there was the rub! Everything in this world is comparative! What one man counts to be luxury, because of what went before, another counts to be beggarliness, from the same cause.

Nigel had the key, and he let Fulvia in, following her. They tramped steadily over the interior, from bottom to top, hearing the echo of their own feet on the bare boards. Reaching again the front ground-floor room, when all had been inspected, Nigel said—

"Well?"

"Is this the best we can afford?"

"Forty pounds a year, not counting taxes. I dare not go beyond that. If things did not promise to be a degree better than we thought at first, we could not venture on so much."

"Madre will not like an up-stairs drawing-room."

" I am afraid there are a great many things that she
will not like."

" There will be a study for you." .

" Behind this ?   Why not make it a morning-room
for everybody ? "

" No ; a study, of course.   You will be the bread-
winner, and your needs must be considered first.   A
study for you is a necessity.   Madre must have the bedroom on the next floor,—behind the drawing-room.   She
will have Daisy to sleep with her permanently, I hope ;
and there is the dressing-room for Daisy to use.   Anice
can have the little half-way room jutting out at the
back ; and you—if you don't mind—the one over it.
Then there will be the top front bedroom for friends.
We can make it look very pretty."

" I thought of that room for you."

" There are two behind.   One will be for the maids,
—we are not to keep more than two maids, are we ?—
and the smaller can be mine."

" That corner-room, with no fire-place ?   Nonsense ! "

" It will do well enough, when I am at home.   If
you like, you can treat me as a visitor, and put me in
the spare-room.   Governesses don't get a superabund-
ance of holidays, so there will be no real difficulty."

Fulvia seated herself on an empty chest, left in the
middle of the room, with the air of having settled everything.   Nigel stood gravely in front.

" You do not really suppose I shall consent to that
scheme ? "

Her eyes sparkled.

" I may choose to act with nobody's consent except my own."

" It would not be right."

" People differ in their views of 'right!' "

" Fulvia—" he said, in a different tone.

" Yes."

He had gone over the possible scene fifty times in imagination. He had pictured himself as saying that or this in careful kind words, hinting, indeed, at the true state of his own feelings, yet so as not to shock or grieve her. But he had not once pictured himself as coming out suddenly, in desperation, with the bald request—

" Fulvia, will you be my wife ? "

It was not a well-selected place for an offer of marriage. The room was absolutely empty, with the exception of their two selves and the box on which Fulvia sat. Everybody knows how dreary is the impression made by an absolutely empty room. Streaks of paint disfigured the blindless and curtainless window, which glared dismally on the pair. Fulvia had torn her dress walking down-stairs, and her crape had gathered dust by the way. Nigel's own shoulders were whitened by contact with the pantry wall. No whit of what Mrs. Duncan called " poetical glamour " existed to enhance the occasion. All was bare and cold.

A pause followed, Fulvia gazing fixedly down. She did not flush now, but grew pale.

"Is it because Ethel has refused him, and he turns to me as a *pis-aller?*" she asked herself.

As she made no answer, he spoke again, not without agitation—

"I have not much to give you. It is not as things have been—but I would do my utmost—would strive to repay something of what you have lost. I would devote my life to that. I will, if you will let me."

Still no reply.

"It seems early to speak—in the midst of all our trouble, I mean. I should have waited a little longer. But if you are bent on this governess plan—and—" with a break—"I am not allowed to put off. Mr. Carden-Cox has made my speaking at once the condition of his silence."

"I see!"—calmly. "And that is your reason!" Tears gathered on the downcast lashes, yet she forced a laugh. "Yes, I understand. It is most praiseworthy! For the madre's sake, no doubt!" Then she looked up, straight and hard, into his face. "A convenient arrangement for managing uncle Arthur!"

Nigel was stung deeply by her tone, and Fulvia saw it.

"If I say 'No'—what then?" she asked mockingly "Will you have done your duty in uncle Arthur's eyes?"

He turned away, and went to the window, while Fulvia sat still, thinking. She did not know what

to say next. Dismiss him !—no, that she could no
Recall him !—no, that she would not.

Nigel came back presently, unrecalled. He look
depressed and spiritless.

"I do not wish you to misunderstand me, Fulvia.
have no wish to profess more than I feel. It is best t
be open in such cases. You have always been a grea
deal to me—more, perhaps, than you yourself knew
But—there *has* been another hope. I have had
give that up. It is at an end now."

He spoke without a falter, without any of the usua
signs of strong feeling, and Fulvia was deceived by hi
calmness, at the very moment when he was endeavour
ing to undeceive her.

"That is over ; and I am ready to pledge myself t
you for life—to endeavour to repay all ! And if—i
anything is wanting in my love for you, I will do m
utmost to learn—to conquer——I think you understand
Will you have me ? "

Fulvia gave him one more glance, and dropped he
eyes. She understood plainly enough that he allude
to Ethel—to Ethel and no other.

Could she accept him, knowing herself to have bee
only second ? For a moment there came an impulse
fling aside the offered devotion, which fell so far shor
of the love she gave to him. But this impulse ben
before a stronger impulse in the other direction
Whatever he had once felt for Ethel, the composur
with which he spoke of giving her up seemed to tell o

no absorbing affection now. If she said "No," he might turn again to Ethel. Could Fulvia endure that? Once his, might she not hope in time to win his whole heart?

Besides, there was the question of Mr. Browning's name—of the secret to be kept on the madre's account. She tried to believe that this pressed her on; that for the sake of others she ought not to refuse Nigel. Silence lasted long; then slowly, silently, with a strange rush of warmth and chill, of joy and sorrow, of hope and dread, Fulvia placed her hand in his.

CHAPTER XXV.

SWEET MAY-TIDE.

" I come, I come ! ye have called me long,
  I come o'er the mountains with light and song ;
  Ye may trace my step o'er the wakening earth,
  By the winds which tell of the violet's birth,
  By the primrose stars in the shadowy grass,
  By the green leaves opening as I pass."—F. HEMANS.

THE month of May had come—a bright typical May ;
not one of our modern snarling specimens, which
perhaps our forefathers knew as well as ourselves, but
which of course no poet or historian ever wrote down
on the "deathless page" of literature. A dazzling blaze
of spring sunshine streamed upon the stiff row of trees
in the green enclosure of Bourne Street, and made its
way through the draped lace curtains of No. 9, where
ingenuity had been hard at work, to transform a most
ordinary little drawing-room into a finished and æsthetic
gem. It had to be done cheaply ; but that matters
less where clever fingers and cultivated taste have
sway. Grange furniture was present—not Grange
drawing-room furniture, which would have been far
too large : but dainty small tables and pretty chairs,

selected from all parts of the big house. Fulvia had combined tints gracefully, had put up brackets, had spent hours over finishing touches, had acted throughout as guiding spirit. If she could win a smile from Nigel for his mother's sake, she was content. She would have slaved herself to death for that reward.

A worn outline of cheek was visible now, as if the last few weeks had left their mark. The sunshine which lit up her ruddy head showed this plainly. She was on the music-stool, sewing hard at an antimacassar. They had not long been in the house, and nobody had yet grown used to its smallness. Anice fretted, and Daisy talked viciously of "kicking down those dreadful walls," and Mrs. Browning was sweetly resigned and sad. Fulvia alone did not care. She was sorry for others, not for herself. The one thing in life she cared for was pleasing Nigel; and having him, she had all she wanted.

Fulvia could not entirely make him out. She was always trying to do so, yet always feeling that something lay below, which she could not reach. He was in many respects an altered being; himself, yet different. The light-heartedness, the sparkle, the fun, were gone. A "grave young man" strangers now called him; old-looking for his years, quiet, handsome, manly; one to be liked and esteemed; but to his own people, changed. Friends said how acutely he had felt his father's death, and how creditable the feeling was to him; also many supposed the lost wealth and lowered prospects to weigh upon him a good deal. Fulvia ascribed his seriousness to the unhappy secret about his father and her money. She made it her aim to cause him to forget, and yet she knew he never could forget. She would not let herself think of Ethel. He had enough pressing on him to render that additional cause needless.

Ethel had not come in Fulvia's way since the latter was engaged. There had been a singular break in the intercourse between Ethel Elvey and the Brownings, coming about naturally. Ethel caught a bad cold the evening in the cemetery, and was a prisoner for many days after. She could not shake off the cold, and seemed unaccountably poorly, her parents thought. Then the younger boys had slight scarlatina, which made quarantine needful. Ethel nursed the boys, and ended by having it herself, not severely, though she was much pulled down. Dr. Duncan talked of a want of rallying power, and sent her to the sea for a month with the convalescent boys. When she came back, pale and weak still, an opportune invitation arrived from a kind old friend living under the shadow of Snowdon.

Certain difficulties existed; but Ethel showed an unwonted eagerness to be absent, and Dr. Duncan was strongly in favour of it. Mr. Elvey took the matter in hand, over-rode all objections, told Ethel to go, and desired her to stay as long as she could. Perhaps he suspected her trouble in some degree. He had surprised her once shedding very bitter tears, after Nigel's en-

gagement had become known, and Ethel had clung to
him for comfort, secure of no worrying questions being
asked. Mr. Elvey was not far-sighted about such matters,
but he had keenness enough to put two and two together
when the twos were very plainly written.

So Ethel went to Wales, and stayed long away, and
Nigel had never once seen or spoken with her since
their sorrowful farewell. Better so for them both!

Mrs. Browning watched him anxiously these weeks.
Somehow she was more strongly alive to the change in
him than was Fulvia, perhaps because Fulvia would
not let herself see. Mrs. Browning did see. She had
a constant feeling that this Nigel was not altogether her
Nigel, her boy! A grave of buried hopes lay between
her and the Nigel of old.

She had nothing to complain of definitely. He was
very good to her, as to Fulvia; carefully attentive to
them both; but the old sunshine was wanting. Life
seemed with him to have grown into an embodiment
of severe duty, unrelieved by pleasure. There was no
relaxing. He worked hard, read hard, walked a certain
amount daily, went through a steady routine; but
nothing was done lightly. He had never shown so
little inclination for talk. Except in the evenings, he
was chiefly away, and in the evenings he always had a
book. If Mrs. Browning or Fulvia showed a wish for
conversation, he responded kindly, but with a manifest
effort, and it never lasted long.

Mrs. Browning craved for his old look, his old smile,

—craved at times with a passionate longing. She did not know how to give up her former Nigel.

There is no love on earth like a mother's love; no love so pure, so lasting, so unselfish; no love which comes so near the love of God Himself,—though infinitely distant from it. As everything human varies, so in different natures the quality of even this varies; and Mrs. Browning's was not, perhaps, of the very highest type of mother-love. She did love her children intensely, but in some measure it was for and in herself. Yet when a test time came, the reality of her love would lift her superior to her ordinary self; and such a test time had come now. She knew that Nigel was not happy, and she was far too true a mother to rest in that knowledge. Worse still, she knew that she had had a hand in bringing on the present condition of things, and that she might not lift a finger to undo what she had wrought. This knowledge weighed upon her heavily.

Thus, when the sunny month of May came, there were clouds as well as sunshine in the sky of No. 9, Bourne Street.

Fulvia was alone, but Daisy presently came in with a whisk and a rush, upsetting two small chairs.

"Daisy!" remonstrated Fulvia.

"There's no room for anything here."

"The more need to carry one's limbs discreetly! I wish you would help me with these antimacassars. I want to get them done before lunch."

"Why? There must be lots of old ones good enough."

"I want to put out these. It will be a change. Nigel admired the muslin."

"Well, I hope I shall never be engaged!" declared Daisy. "Since you went and got engaged to Nigel, you haven't had one single idea apart from him."

Fulvia did not take the trouble to contradict her.

"And there's that story I'm reading! O, bother! If I'm to sew, I must wash my hands."

"You need not be an hour over the washhand-stand. Do be quick."

Daisy stood still. "Ethel has come home," she said.

"Ethel Elvey?"

"Yes. I met her just now."

"Is she all right again?"

"I don't know. I didn't ask. She looks—as if—" and a pause.

"As if—?"

"I don't know. I shouldn't think she was well."

Fulvia had ceased to sew, and was gently pricking her finger with the needle.

"She has been a long time away."

"Heaps of time. I never knew her do such a thing before. And staying with one old maiden lady all the while. It must have been awfully slow. She says she's going to be awfully busy at home now——lots of Parish work. I shall go and see her. I like Ethel."

"She is nice enough," said Fulvia carelessly.

"Nigel used to be awfully fond of Ethel. He never speaks of her now."

"Are you going to help me with this work, Daisy?"

Daisy sauntered away, and Fulvia sat idly, with bent head, thinking. A sound made her glance up, and Nigel stood in front.

Fulvia sprang to meet him, with exclamation and glow of delight, her whole face changing. "But what has brought you home now? Is anything wrong?"

"Nothing much. I have a stupid headache"— running his fingers through his hair,—"and Mr. Bramble has let me off. The figures were all turning into live creatures. Will you come for a walk with me?"

"O yes!" Fulvia was ready to leave anything. She could never hesitate about a request of Nigel's. "You are sure you are not ill?"—for he looked unusually pale. Then a jealous fear darted into her mind: had he seen Ethel? She could not put the question, but Daisy ran in and asked it for her.

"Going out, Fulvia? And you in such a hurry to have things done! But I sha'n't work at them if you are out. And Nigel home so early! O, I say, Nigel, only think! Ethel has come home at last. They couldn't do without her any longer. I met her just now, and I dare say you did too."

"No; I met Malcolm on my way to the Bank, and he told me."

Nigel said no more. Fulvia could only wonder

silently—was that the cause of his sudden indisposition ? He had been well enough in the morning.

They had their walk, and Nigel talked more than usual, exerting himself to be agreeable ; but Fulvia was conscious of effort, even of strain, on his part. She scolded herself for fancies, yet the impression remained.

Ethel did not come quickly to call, as Fulvia expected ; neither did Nigel seem in haste to go to the Rectory. Daisy went, and found Ethel out. Days passed, and, beyond the one encounter, none of the Brownings had seen her. Bourne Street was a good way off from Church Square.

Nothing had been seen or heard of Mr. Carden-Cox for weeks. Except that he sat in his usual seat at Church, and was occasionally to be perceived walking or driving along a busy street, he might, so far as the Brownings were concerned, have dropped out of existence altogether.

"I detest family quarrels," Nigel said, more than once. "But what is to be done ? It is his place to take the first step."

"He will never do that," Fulvia answered decisively each time. "He will never forgive the madre for ordering him off."

Fulvia was wrong. People are perpetually doing just the things that their friends do not expect of them, and it was so in this case.

On Saturdays Nigel always came home early. Lunch was deferred till a little after two o'clock, that he might be present; and in the afternoon it was the regular thing for him and Fulvia to take a country walk together. Sometimes he would relax from his gravity, and be more like the Nigel of old days, not indeed so sunny as then, yet more easy and natural than at other times. Fulvia was very happy on these occasions. She would cast care to the winds, feeling that she had all she could wish.

No, not quite all. For, during these early weeks of her engagement, there came to Fulvia a growing sense of a want in her life, a want which did not exist in Nigel's life. She had not so definitely felt the lack before. A consciousness crept slowly over her of being at a lower level, possessing lower aims, acting from lower principles, than Nigel. Sometimes she could almost rejoice in this, could revel in looking up to him as to an utterly superior being. That was only woman-like. But on the other hand, a woman does wish to be a true companion to the man who chooses her, a help fitted for him; and sometimes her heart sank with the knowledge that she was not so fitted, that there were matters upon which she could offer him no true response.

Now and then he would say a few words which gave her a sudden glimpse of depths beyond her ken. She could not follow him into them, and she could not *there* act what she did not feel. In slighter everyday affairs, Fulvia might disguise her feelings, might wear an occasional mask, but in religious matters she was strictly honest.

She always knew on these occasions that her answers
repelled him, threw him back into himself. She always
felt, with a jealous pang, " Ethel would have gone with
him where I cannot." And though she dreaded such
embarrassing moments, yet she was grieved to the heart
when they came more seldom ; for she knew that Nigel
was learning not to turn to her for sympathy in his
deepest interests. Reserved they both were, and he
actually had not known before that such turning would
be vain. Fulvia's very grief and jealousy drove her to
more thought about religion, though as yet it was only
for Nigel's sake. Other teaching than this was needed
for Fulvia.

A succession of fine Saturdays had meant a succession
of long rambles for the two, when at length one came
which could be described only as consisting of one
continuous pelt. Rain began early, and went on all
the morning in a dogged and resolute fashion, with
good promise of doing the same during many hours
to come. At luncheon a note arrived for Fulvia, which
she read and gave to Nigel, with an involuntary " O,
I can't !" It was as follows :—

" DEAR FULVIA,—

" Will you spend the afternoon of to-day with a lonely
old man ? I have been thoroughly out of sorts lately,
and I want a few words with you.

" This nonsense has gone on long enough. You ought
to know, all of you, by this time, that my bark is worse

than my bite. Manufacture any sort of pretty message
that you like from me to the madre, and pray get
things right somehow. I can't manage without you
and Nigel. Besides, I am going to make a fresh will,
and you may help me.

"A fly shall call for you at a quarter to three precisely. Mind you come.—Your affectionate uncle,

"A. C.-C."

"What am I to do? To-day! I can't go," said
Fulvia, dismayed.

"You cannot set this aside," Nigel replied at once.

"But to-day—your one afternoon at home?"

"I don't think that matters. We could not walk in
such rain. And even if we could, to make peace with
Mr. Carden-Cox ought to come first."

Did he care? Not, certainly, as she did. Fulvia
saw this with a sharp pang, yet Nigel's manner was not
cold or careless. He only spoke with quiet resolution,
as of an unquestionable duty.

"If uncle Arthur had but chosen some other day!"

"He has not. I think you must not refuse."

Fulvia yielded to his decision.

At "a quarter to three precisely" a closed fly appeared,
and she was ready. She looked wistfully at Nigel as
he held open the front door, then stood under the porch
putting up an umbrella. "It doesn't matter so much to
you, of course," she murmured, "but I *am* disappointed!
I shall feel cross with uncle all the afternoon."

"No, you will not. It would make mischief. A good deal may depend upon you to-day."

"Why? How?"

"His will, if you must have it put in plain terms."

"O, money! I hate money!"

Nigel's expression was curious. He sheltered her across the pavement, and handed her into the fly, wearing that look still. Fulvia wondered what it meant. She said penitently, "I'll be good. It won't do to think only of myself!"—and was rewarded by a smile. Then Nigel stepped into the house, and as the fly was about to start, Daisy rushed out bareheaded into the rain.

"Fulvie!"

"Daisy, come back! You will be soaked," said Nigel.

Daisy disregarded him. "Fulvie," she cried, "may I arrange your new jewel-case for you? It's such a beauty, and you have never begun to use it."

Fulvia heard with pre-occupied ears, hardly taking in the sense of Daisy's request. "If you like. Anything! I don't care."

"And your keys?"

"Keys?"

"Your own bunch?"

"Oh, I left them——somewhere. In my dressing-table drawer, I think."

Nigel pulled Daisy into the shelter of the porch, and Fulvia was gone. Daisy danced from one foot to the other. "What fun!" she said, chuckling. "Fulvia looks as dismal as if she never would see you again. Just for one afternoon! Well, I don't mind now about the rain. I've something nice to do."

Daisy had noted that morning the handsome silver-mounted dressing-box, Mr. Carden-Cox' birthday gift, standing on a side-table in Fulvia's room—not the little back room, but the pleasant front one, for Nigel had settled that point. Beside the new box was the shabby old dressing-case, and Daisy, having used curious fingers and eyes, discovered that the latter was locked, the former unlocked and empty. Thereupon she conceived the idea of emptying the old box into the new, as a pleasant rainy-day occupation. Daisy was not sensitive as to associations, or she might have shrunk, as Fulvia had shrunk, from bringing forward the gift connected with so sorrowful a day as Fulvia's twenty-first birthday.

And Fulvia at the moment of being asked, did not recall associations past, did not realize what Daisy meant, or to what "jewel-case" she alluded. If Daisy had called it a "dressing-case," she might have listened with quicker perception; but "jewel-case" was not one of Fulvia's words. She heard a request vaguely and granted it, never thinking what the request meant. Her mind was wrapped up in the thought of having to leave Nigel for hours on his only free afternoon.

More than this, she had no vivid recollection of the crumpled half-sheet hidden away in the old dressing-case. The matter of the four postscripts had sunk of

late into a background. Since all cessation of intercourse with Mr. Carden-Cox, nothing had occurred to
call it up. Fulvia had reached a standpoint far removed
from the hopes and fears of those days. The lost half-
sheet was nothing to her now. She could not have told
why it remained still in her box, except that the all-
absorbing events of the last few months had almost
driven it out of her mind. Perhaps a dim expectation
existed below, of some day making confession, and
restoring the paper to its rightful owner. But not
yet,—oh, not yet !

Yes, she had reached a stand beyond those hopes and
fears. Nigel was hers, and she was his. She had
indeed her anxieties and dreads, but they were different
in kind, and as yet the joy of devoting herself to him out-
weighed all troubles. In the main she did not, would not,
doubt his love, though at times she was nervously disposed to weigh the amount of it against her own for him.

Every one, who has watched with care, can tell how
strangely things which were once of vivid importance
may slip into the background of memory, unaccountably
failing to spring up just when one would most expect
that they should. Daisy's sudden question, called out
in haste through the pouring rain, brought no recollections to Fulvia of the crumpled half-sheet hidden
away. She was entirely absorbed with Mr. Carden-Cox'
provoking unreasonableness, in taking her from Nigel
on this particular day. And oh, if Nigel had but cared
more ! That, after all, was the real pain !

CHAPTER XXVI.

" A pen—to register : a key—
That winds through secret wards:
Are well assigned to memory
By allegoric bards."—WORDSWORTH.

" WHERE are you going to sit ? " demanded Daisy of Nigel.

" In the study for the present. Why ? "

" May I come too ? I won't disturb you, or be a bother. Do let me."

Nigel would have preferred an hour or two alone, but he hesitated to refuse, looking in Daisy's beseeching eyes. She was a very devoted younger sister, and had not had much of his company of late.

" If you like," he replied. " But why ? "

" I'm going to do something that madre ought not to see ; and anywhere else, she might pounce down upon me."

" Pounce " was not precisely the correct word for Mrs. Browning's slow and graceful movements ; but girls of Daisy's age are not critically exact in their use of language.

"I want to clear out Fulvia's old jewel-case, and put all her things into the new one—the one Mr. Carden-Cox gave her, you know. I don't see why that nice box shouldn't be used. It wasn't *its* fault that Mr. Carden-Cox behaved as he did. And I dare say he would be awfully vexed, if he knew she had not begun to use it. And he is sure to ask, now that we are to see him again. Besides, Fulvia once said she would give her old one to me when she had another, and I want to have it. But it might upset mother to see Fulvia's birthday present, so I thought I would bring it to the study."

"Why not manage affairs in Fulvia's room?"

"O, I'd rather be with you?" coaxed Daisy. "Madre won't come. She'll think you are busy."

"So I mean to be. Well,—if you like."

Daisy established herself with much satisfaction at one end of the table, placing side by side the handsome empty box and the shabby full one. She had found the keys without difficulty. Nigel made himself comfortable in the arm-chair with a book. He had letters to write, but "they could wait," he said. Daisy did not strictly keep to her promise of "not disturbing" Nigel, if that meant not speaking; but perhaps Nigel was not disturbed. He listened to her remarks, and answered, laying down his book; and this naturally encouraged chatter on her part.

"Fulvia has such a lot of nice rings. I wish I had a quarter as many. But she says she doesn't care for any of them, except her engagement ring, and the locket you gave last birthday. I do like this sapphire. It's grand. And her diamond brooch; doesn't it flash? I should like to have a diamond pin to wear in my hair, —just one huge blazing diamond that would flash all across the room. What are you thinking about?"

"Wondering if you will ever be anything but a child."

"Not till I'm an old maid," promptly responded Daisy. "But is it childish to like diamonds?"

"That depends on the mode of liking——and the manner of expression."

"O well, I can't help it. People must take me as I am. There, now things begin to look jolly. I hope Fulvia will keep to my arrangement. The pink cotton wool is pretty, isn't it?—under silver and pearl. See, I've made quite a bed of it in one place for the silver Maltese brooches, and the gold filagree things are opposite. You won't need to buy lots of jewellery when you are married, because your wife will have enough."

"That's fortunate, since I shall not have lots of spare money."

"Yes; isn't it a pity Fulvia won't be rich? Now, I'll put the chains into this tray. Nigel"—with one of her sudden flights into a new region—"have you seen Ethel Elvey yet?"

"No."

"I thought you might. You did call one day, didn't you? Anice said you had, and she said you found everybody out. But Ethel does look so altered, you can't think !"

" How ? "

" I don't know. You'll see. Her face seems to have shrunk, and her eyes have grown so big. She laughed and talked just as she always does, but somehow—I thought—I don't exactly know what, only she didn't seem like herself. Malcolm told me yesterday that she has not been well for ever so long. She has never quite got over that bad cold, and the fever coming after it. At least Malcolm seemed to think it was that. Poor Ethel ! I am so sorry."

Nigel pushed his chair farther back, thereby putting his face into shade. Daisy was too intent upon her occupation to notice him.

" I thought you'd like to know, because you and Ethel always were such friends. It seemed funny that she had not been to see us; but Malcolm says she gets so easily tired, she really can't walk far, most days. That's not like Ethel. Now I have done both trays. The old box is quite empty, so Fulvia may as well let me have it. There's only the place in the lid for the looking-glass; nothing else, of course. Just a piece of crumpled paper, written all over ! Why, it must be part of a letter, and in Mr. Carden-Cox' handwriting. How comical of Fulvia to keep it here ! I dare say she tucked it away in a hurry, and then forgot all about what she had done."

" Did what ? " Nigel asked dreamily.

"This! Look; it is part of a letter. Funny of Fulvia! I think I'll see what it is about? 'N.B.—One line more. My dear fellow, you do not really mean—' Oh! O, I say! O Nigel! Oh!"

"What's the matter now?"

Daisy's eyes were round; her mouth was open. She could only articulate, "O, I say!"

"Daisy, pray explain yourself. Don't be idiotic!" said Nigel, with unwonted sharpness.

"It's the lost postscript."

"Nonsense!"

"But it is! It must be! Look; it is, really! Half a sheet, and Mr. Carden-Cox' handwriting, and it begins, 'N.B.,' and it says, 'My dear fellow.' Look! That can't be Fulvia. And none of the other three was to a 'fellow.' Ethel's and Fulvia's and mine were found. I know mine was, because Mr. Carden-Cox let it out, though he made a secret of it at first—I wonder why! But yours was never found, and Mr. Carden-Cox has always declared it must have gone to Fulvia. He said she had put it away somewhere and forgotten. But I don't see how she could forget——do you? Fulvia *said* she had never had it, you know."

Daisy held the half-sheet before Nigel's eyes.

"It's yours. I shall tell Fulvia. How could she be so stupid?"

A red flush rose to Nigel's brow, and his eyes darkened. He received the paper from Daisy's hand, but looked at her instead of it.

" Where did you find this ? "

" In Fulvia's old dressing-box, hidden away behind the glass. Didn't you hear me say so ? "

" No. What business had you to examine it ? "

Daisy was disconcerted.

" I—don't know. I thought I would read a word or two. I didn't think it was anything really, till I saw ' N.B.' and ' fellow.' "

" Another time you will act more honourably, if you don't look at all."

" But Fulvia gave me leave to turn out her box. She did really, Nigel, and she didn't say there were secrets."

Nigel was silent. He folded the half-sheet, unread, and put it into his pocket. The next remark was—

" Daisy, you are not to say a word about this."

" Not tell Fulvia ? "

" No. You are not to tell any one."

" Not even Mr. Carden-Cox ? "

" Certainly not."

" But won't you tell him ? "

" No."

" Won't you speak to Fulvia ? "

" That is for me to decide, not you. I forbid you to say one word ! Mind !—I mean it ! "

" Of course I'll do what you wish," said Daisy reluctantly. " Only Mr. Carden-Cox would have liked to know."

" It doesn't matter what Mr. Carden-Cox would

A A

or would not like. You are to keep the thing to yourself."

Daisy gazed at him dubiously.

"Do you think—are you—?" she faltered. "Are you angry with Fulvia? Poor Fulvie! I do wish I hadn't fished that stupid postscript out! After all this time! I do wish I had not said a word to you."

"Nothing is gained in the end by concealment," Nigel made answer.

"No—poor Fulvia!"—applying the axiom to another, instead of herself. "I wish she had spoken out. But perhaps she was afraid. She gets so frightened now of doing anything you may not like. I never knew Fulvia could be a coward till lately. Are you very angry?"

"I am"—and a pause—"disappointed in Fulvia. I could not have thought it possible."

"But I don't believe she meant to do wrong. Perhaps she forgot. O don't be vexed; because it is my fault."

"What! the finding of this?"

"Yes. If only I had not told!"

Daisy actually burst into tears.

"There is no fault, so far as you are concerned," Nigel said quietly. "The finding was accidental. The hiding could not have been. But I don't wish to discuss Fulvia's conduct with you, Daisy. I trust you not to let it go any farther. Now you can take these boxes away, and leave me alone."

"But—if Fulvie asks—?"

"She will not. If she should, you may refer her to me."

Daisy gave him a frightened look of acquiescence, and caught up the empty box. Nigel carried the heavy full one up-stairs for her, and then he disappeared into the study.

"If only I had not found it! I wish I hadn't!" sighed Daisy.

Mr. Carden-Cox did not look particularly ill, but he proclaimed himself so, and required much pity. Fulvia gave him some expression of it, to the best of her power, while her thoughts wandered constantly to Nigel. The first hour of talk was aimless. Then Mr. Carden-Cox arrived at the point, with a jerk.

"So your madre allowed you to come! Didn't forbid it!"

"No."

"You made up a decent message from me, I hope."

"I told her you wanted me to do so."

"Humph! And she said——"

"Madre supposed that to be meant for an apology."

"Humph!" again. "Well, when she wants me she can send word."

"She is willing to see you now. You cannot expect more," Fulvia retorted with spirit.

"That's your opinion! A chit of a girl like you! But you were brought up among them. However,—enough about that. I'm going to have my will made."

"Yes."

" Leaving all I have to you."

Fulvia was silent.

" May be more, may be less, than folks expect. That's neither here nor there. Not much use to expect gratitude in this world," pursued Mr. Carden-Cox, with a moralizing air. " If I did—but I don't! Do your duty, and never mind what is said. That's my axiom!" It might be his axiom, but it was not his rule of action, as Fulvia could have told him. " My duty is plain now. If your fortune had come to you intact, you wouldn't have needed my pittance. Ha! Things are different, and I mean to make a difference."

" Where would your pittance have gone then ? "

" Half to you—half to Nigel."

" Pray let it stand so, uncle Arthur. If you change at all, leave all to Nigel."

Mr. Carden-Cox laughed.

" Why not ? It comes to the same thing."

" Would, if you were married. Ceremony hasn't taken place yet ! "

A chill shot through Fulvia at the implied suggestion.

" I would much rather there should be no alteration," she repeated.

" And I would rather there should be. *I* know what young men are—and girls too! No, no! you've lost enough already through the Brownings—through that scoun— Well, well, no need to say more. But I'll secure this to you, hard and fast. Don't mean to lose another day. Why, who knows?" demanded Mr.

Carden-Cox, with a lively air. "Not one of us may be alive a week hence!" .

"Your money will not do me much good in that case."

He laughed again, and asked—

"When is the wedding to take place?"

"I don't know. Nobody knows. How can you ask —now? Our trouble so new, still! And people cannot marry upon nothing."

"I'll have a talk with Nigel. Don't like affairs dragging on interminably. Sure to end by getting tired of one another."

Fulvia could have burst into tears; for there was an underlying consciousness which gave a keen edge to his words, but she only said—

"A happy look-out for married life!"

"O, after you're married, it's different. Comes as a matter of course, then, to put up with what can't be helped. Tied together, and no escape, so no use to struggle. Well, I'll have a talk with Nigel, now we're in smooth waters again. See if I can't bring it about. Wouldn't need much additional, to set a young couple going."

"Uncle, please leave things alone; please do not interfere. Nigel will not like it."

"Not like it! Fudge! He may do without liking. Not like it, indeed! As if he didn't know me by this time! Don't be so squeamish, child; and don't take to looking cross. It doesn't suit you. I didn't ask your advice; don't need anybody's advice. We'll let that matter drop. I say—nothing ever come to light all these weeks about the lost postscript?"

"The lost postscript!" She spoke bewilderedly. The abrupt change of ideas brought a moment's confusion.

"Nigel's postscript—the fourth 'N.B.,' you know— ha, ha!—sent to you and never found! Nothing heard of it all these weeks, hey?"

A vision of the past flashed up. Instantly Fulvia saw the crumpled slip of paper, hidden away in her dressing-box. Daisy's parting request was clear, with all that it involved.

Fulvia actually sprang to her feet, aghast. By this time, four o'clock, Daisy might have found the concealed paper; and outspoken childish Daisy would of a certainty proclaim her "find" to the household. Nigel would hear of it! Already he might have heard; already the thing might be done, past recall. And if not yet, could Fulvia reach home in time to stop its being done? She stood with dilated eyes, terror-struck. Mr. Carden-Cox put up his eye-glass, and examined her curiously.

"Eh! what now? Sit down. Postscript found? Come, confess!"

Fulvia controlled herself to meet his gaze; but she could not control the startled hurry of her voice.

"Something—something I have remembered," she said rapidly. "Something I ought to have done before leaving home; it has just come to me. I must go at once."

Fulvia did not mean to make any untrue statement. She scarcely knew what she said; and that which she wished she had done was, definitely, to have forbidden Daisy's meddling with her box.

"Nonsense, child. Sit down and be quiet. Something you ought to have done! What do you mean? What ought you to have done?"

His black eyes examined her, with a look of suspicion.

"It doesn't matter what. I must go home. I am going home."

"The fly will be here at half-past five. You will have tea with me first, of course. This 'something' must be of mighty importance. Fulvia Rolfe is not a girl to be disturbed about nothing! Has it to do with the lost postscript, hey?"

A natural question, since his mention of the postscript had been the seeming cause of her sudden fright. She was so unnerved by the shock she had received, that his suggestion renewed her trembling. She was obliged to sit down, even while she reiterated, "I must go! I can't stay! I must get home at once!" For she might still be in time.

"Stuff and nonsense!" Mr. Carden-Cox spoke angrily. "The girl is demented. Fact is, it's one of two things. Either you are tired of being here, and you want to get off the rest of the time; or, you are deceiving me about

the postscript, and can't stand being questioned. I
believe it's that."

Fulvia seized on the first suggestion.

"I am not tired of being with you, but I can't endure
to be away from Nigel all Saturday afternoon," she said.
The assertion was true enough, though this had now
ceased to be her prominent feeling. "Any other day
I should not mind, but Saturday—Saturday is his only
free afternoon. Uncle, do let me go. I will come
another time, and stay as long as you like. Monday,
Tuesday, any day. Only not Saturday. I always have
him then."

Mr. Carden-Cox grunted out a laugh, not ill-pleased.

"You're a pair of model lovers!" he growled. "Well
—have things your own way. But the fly is not ordered
till 5.30."

"O, I don't mind rain. I never catch cold. It will
not take me long to get home. And any other day—"

She did not finish her sentence, and could hardly
wait to say good-bye. Mr. Carden-Cox seemed in doubt
whether to be amused or vexed by her precipitate flight.
He lent her an umbrella, and apologized for the lack
of a lady's waterproof. Fulvia had come in her best
black walking-dress, which would suffer from pelting
rain; but what did she care? What did anything
matter, in comparison with getting home?

The distance had never seemed so great, and Fulvia
had never traversed it at such speed. She would not
let herself think by the way. Distracting possibilities

presented themselves, and Fulvia refused to look at them. Her arrival at home, dripping and forlorn, with flushed face and bespattered skirt, was greeted by a triple exclamation from Mrs. Browning and the girls—

"Fulvia!—already!"

"Yes; I didn't want to stay any longer. Uncle let me off. Where is Nigel?"

Fulvia dropped into the nearest chair, and Anice cried out at the contact of her wet clothes with the furniture. Fulvia did not care for that; but she did care for the curious questioning look in Daisy's eyes, fixed upon herself.

"Why didn't he send you home in a fly?" asked Anice.

"I did not want to wait. Where is Nigel?"

"Down-stairs."

"Not in the study. I have been there."

"Then he must have gone out. I heard the front door open and shut."

Fulvia rose, and dragged herself up-stairs without another word. There, on the chest of drawers, stood, as before, her two boxes. She tried both with trembling fingers.

Too late! The new box was locked; the old one unlocked and empty! Daisy had done her work.

Hoping still against hope, Fulvia loosened the looking-glass in the lid, and peeped behind it. No crumpled paper was there. She snatched her keys from the table-drawer, and opened the other box, to see if perchance Daisy had passed on the postscript with the trinkets. Daisy's neat arrangements were tossed into reckless disorder in the search; but Fulvia looked in vain. The half-sheet had vanished.

Too late! All her hurry and toil for nothing. And Nigel gone out! Was it on account of this? Had Daisy given him the paper?

Sick with fear, Fulvia removed her wet things, dressed herself in dry clothes, and smoothed her ruffled hair. Then on shaking limbs she crept down to the study, to await Nigel's return, like a culprit awaiting judgment.

Daisy did not come to her. Anice found out where Fulvia was, and wanted Daisy to bring her thence, but Daisy flatly refused to act messenger. She did not wish to be questioned by Fulvia.

She needed not to fear. Fulvia was in too abject a state of misery to question anybody. The long-buried wrong-doing, almost forgotten by herself, had found her out sharply. She saw her own action once again, as at first, with Nigel's eyes, and she was overwhelmed with shame. Would Nigel cast her off for this? Would he be glad to avail himself of the excuse? Nay—more than excuse—would he not have reason?

Anice before long brought a summons to afternoon tea, and Fulvia refused to go.

"I want to wait for Nigel here. I am tired," she said. "Somebody can bring me a cup, or I can go without. I don't want to be bothered."

The maid brought a cup, since Daisy would not. The laziness of the latter was unaccountable in the eyes of Mrs. Browning and Anice, for Daisy did not usually shirk trouble, like indolent Anice; but she offered no explanation, only she would not go.

Fulvia stayed on in the study alone, leaning back in Nigel's easy-chair, with his open book beside her, the picture of mingled misery, fear, and self-condemnation.

From a quarter to five till a quarter to seven, she waited; the longest, most unhappy two hours Fulvia had ever known. She lived through a lifetime of misery, compressed into so short a space. Nobody came near her for awhile. Then Mrs. Browning appeared, and wanted to know what was wrong. Fulvia evaded her inquiries with a forced smile; she could see that Mrs. Browning knew nothing of the postscript. But Daisy—why did not Daisy appear, as on any other occasion? Daisy's resolute avoidance of Fulvia spoke plainly.

The front door opened at length; and Fulvia again grew sick. She stood up slowly as Nigel came in. He too was pale; his hair wet and plastered; his coat damp. Even a great-coat had not served to shelter him from the driving rain. For a moment he did not see Fulvia; then their eyes met.

Fulvia knew at once that he knew all; and he saw that she was aware of what he knew. Fulvia had never seen him graver, sterner, colder; nor had he ever seen her so bowed with misery and shame. She gave him only one look, and hid her face.

No sound broke the silence. Was Nigel gone? Fulvia could not endure his absence. A tremor ran through her, as from a shock of cold water. She looked up in an agony; and he was there still, not gazing towards her, but lost in his own thoughts. Fulvia held out both hands, and said wildly, "Nigel! speak!"

"I did not expect you would be home so soon."

"No—I—I could not bear it. I wanted to come back—to you. Nigel, say something!"

"What do you wish me to say?"

She shook to such a degree that she was obliged to resume her seat. He had not responded to the offered hands, and she clenched them together.

"Will you forgive?" she gasped. "Will you—— can you forgive? I don't know how I could! It was cowardice. I never thought at first—but—and after— how could I speak? O, will you forgive?"

Nigel placed the folded paper in her hand.

"It is yours, not mine," she said faintly.

"Daisy told me so. I have not read it. Daisy had no business to make the discovery. But since she did——"

Fulvia gave the half-sheet back to him, not lifting her eyes. She knew then that he was reading; and presently she heard him tear it across, more than once.

"Will you forgive?" she whispered once more.

"Yes. There is nothing else to be done."

"You mean— I don't understand," she said, with dazed streaming eyes.

"I mean that there is nothing for it but to take things in that way," he said gravely, after slight hesitation. "I do not think excuses or explanations could touch the question. I could not have thought it possible of you; but——"

"But you will not feel differently about me. You will trust—still! I don't know how I could ever do it! I don't know how I could!" she moaned. "I cannot —could not—ever again! Say you will forget—you will trust me still."

"That must depend," he said, in the same restrained tone. "I will not speak of it. One can hardly promise to forget. It is not feeling angry; don't misunderstand. But this sort of thing gives a rude shake to one's confidence. How am I to know in the future—?"

"But, O, Nigel! think what a lesson to me it has been!"

"Yes, I hope so."

"If you mean——if you wish to give me up——"

"No! That is not possible. I have devoted my life to you."

"But—" she sobbed aloud, with the longing for something more. "O, say one kind word! I shall die if you don't."

She knew then that he had come nearer, though he did not touch her.

"I think you are hardly reasonable," he said seriously.

" It is not really a question of forgiveness, Fulvia. What I mind is not the thing itself—but that you could do such a thing, that you are capable of it! That is what I could not have believed. I have always felt, whatever else might be wanting, *that* was not wanting. I could trust you, anywhere and everywhere. And now—"

Fulvia could not speak. Nigel's words crushed her. He saw that he had said enough, and no more came. Fulvia waited in voiceless despair, but the sentence was not finished.

"We need never speak of this again," he said at length; and he went away, leaving her alone. Fulvia dragged herself once more to her own room, locked the door, and crouched upon the ground in a paroxysm of weeping. She could not appear at dinner; could not show herself again that night.

CHAPTER XXVII.

IN SUDDEN PERIL.

"When the dimpled water slippeth,
    Full of laughter, on its way,
And her wing the wagtail dippeth,
    Running by the brink at play ;
When the poplar leaves atremble
    Turn their edges to the light,
And the far-up clouds resemble
    Veils of gauze most clear and white.
     *   *   * · *   *
"Though the heart be not attending,
    Having sorrows of her own,
Through the fields and fallows winding,
    It is sad to walk alone."—JEAN INGELOW.

FULVIA'S storm was over, but gray weather remained. No further words passed about the discovered postscript. Mr. Carden-Cox was not told. Daisy never referred to the subject.

Fulvia longed to explain more fully to Nigel, yet she had not courage to begin, and after all, if she did, what could she say? As Nigel had told her, excuses meant little; the dishonourableness of her conduct would remain the same. To read that which was not meant for her eyes ought to have been impossible to her; and to keep it back after reading, ought to have been no less impossible.

There was a difference in Nigel's manner from that day; not visible to lookers-on, and not intentional, but very patent to Fulvia. She could not help knowing that she had sunk many degrees in his estimation: that the position she held with respect to him was altered. Things could not be otherwise, and Fulvia knew it. Nigel was rigorously truthful, intensely honourable. And she—not only had she yielded to the first sharp temptation, which ought not even to have been a temptation; but there had been long-persistent secrecy, deliberate deceit, untruth upon untruth.

Nigel knew the whole now; and Fulvia's strong spirit quailed before what she felt to be his view of the matter. His very silence was eloquent. He asked no explanations, because no explanations could touch the main fact. Nothing that Fulvia could say might raise her to her old position. He did not mean to show any change of manner towards her; yet a change existed. During the days following, though kind and courteous, he undoubtedly held a little aloof, and was more wrapped up in his own concerns, not appealing often to Fulvia's sympathy.

Fulvia was at times oppressed by a terrible belief that he would have been willing to break off the engagement, had he not felt bound by his own promise, by the family wronging of Fulvia, by his father's dying words. She felt that this was the rift which might widen into parting, this the beginning of real unhappiness to her. Hitherto she had had doubts and questionings, but in the main she had been content. Now she felt—she knew—that duty was the bond which held him to her. In truth, the shock of this discovery about Fulvia had sent Nigel back with a strong rebound to his old exclusive trust in Ethel; for Ethel could never have acted thus.

He had been growing more used to his shackles, more able to think calmly of life with Fulvia, more ready to depend upon Fulvia for companionship and interest. Now all was altered. Fulvia knew it, and she knew that she had only herself to blame.

But she could not resolve to give him up; even though she had come to the belief that Nigel himself was willing to part. That which would have been the more dignified step was to her impossible. Fulvia did not know how to live without Nigel. If he gave her up, pride might step in to her aid. To take the initiative herself required a different kind of resolution; and Fulvia had it not.

Through the week following that unhappy day she was perpetually looking forward to the next Saturday afternoon. She built her hopes on the quiet *tête-à-tête* walk, wherein she might be able to break through this barrier, to win her way back to him again. She did not know exactly what to say or how to say it; but she was resolved to lead him to the subject of the postscript,

B B

to explain how, after the first wrong step, she had been
entangled by her fears in a crooked path, to appeal to
his pity, to make out somehow a better case for
herself.

Saturday came, and at breakfast Nigel said, "I am
afraid I shall not be much in to-day."

Fulvia gave him a startled look.

"Where are you going?" asked Daisy.

"Malcolm and I talk of a row on the river."

"That will be jolly! You have not been on the
river for ever so long. Only you two? Will Ethel
go?"

"No."

"When do you start?" Fulvia inquired, trying to
speak indifferently.

"Half-past two or three."

"And you will be home—?"

"I don't know when. Not till late in the afternoon."

He did not seem to think she could object, and
Fulvia would show no annoyance. Indeed, her feeling
was far deeper than annoyance. Daisy offered herself
as a companion to Fulvia in Nigel's absence; but Fulvia
could stand no companionship. She wanted to be alone;
and to sit still indoors was impossible. Daisy's offer
was evaded; and somewhat later Fulvia slipped out of
the house, unseen, for a solitary ramble.

Nigel had spoken of going down the river, and Fulvia
made her way to the towing-path, following the same

direction, not with any expectation of seeing him. She meant to be at home in time for his return.

It was a beautiful afternoon, very different from the preceding Saturday. A blaze of sunshine lit up all around, but could not chase away the shadows in Fulvia's heart.

"Will he ever get over this? Will he ever feel the same for me again?" she asked herself drearily. "How could Daisy be so cruel as to tell him? But she did not mean to be cruel. She does not understand." Fulvia would not be unjust, even in her pain; and she had noticed Daisy's air of anxious kindness this week, a manner as of one trying to make up for some wrong done to another.

Fulvia walked slowly, for there was no need to hasten. She could be as long as she liked.

The towing-path which she had chosen was the same which Ethel had chosen one wintry afternoon, some months before. Only the surroundings now were of green trees and golden sunshine, and of water reflecting the blue of a summer sky.

Somebody was walking in front of Fulvia when she passed round the next river-bend—a slight girl, in a gray dress, with a shady black hat, and movements so languid that they seemed to speak of ill-health. Fulvia did not pay any particular regard to her, being pre-occupied. They were nearing a lock, and the girl paused to lean against one of the great gate-handles, as if for rest, turning towards Fulvia with the action.

Fulvia saw her plainly then; saw a fragile-looking creature, with a delicate colourless face, and large blue eyes, dreamy and sad. She noticed the brown hair straying over the white brow, and noted even the thinness of the little ungloved right hand, yet all without recognition, partly no doubt because she was herself so absorbed in thought.

But a flash of recognition came to the other face, and the blue eyes smiled brightly.

"How do you do, Fulvia?"

"Ethel!" Fulvia could hardly believe her own senses. At the first moment an impatient jealous throb shook her frame; for Ethel was Fulvia's dread. Thought for the altered girl before her followed quickly. "Ethel! I did not know you! Have you been ill?"

"Not ill lately. Not very well, I suppose. I don't get up much strength somehow. Is it not a perfect day?"

Fulvia stood still. She did not want a companion— Ethel Elvey least of all!—still she could not at once pass on. She was not personally fond of Ethel, and never had been; but their acquaintance dated from infant days, and Fulvia was kind-hearted. It was impossible not to pause, in view of Ethel's changed look.

"Daisy said something—" she began, and broke off. "I know you had scarlatina; but that is so long ago."

"Ages—isn't it?" Ethel said, smiling again. "And I have been an immense time in the country since, doing nothing. Yes, in North Wales. Snowdon is so beautiful. There is nothing in the world like mountains. They seem to bring one nearer heaven."

" Are you talking poetically ? " asked Fulvia.

" Am I ? No; I don't think so."

" Did you go up Snowdon ? "

" Once, on pony back. I did not try it a second time."

" Has looking on a mountain from below the same effect ? "

" What effect ? "

" Bringing you—what you said just now."

" Yes." Ethel did not explain her meaning. She went on in a quiet and natural tone—" How is Nigel ? I have not seen him yet."

" He is all right. He has gone boating with Malcolm."

" Yes, up the river."

" No, down—"

" I was not sure. Malcolm did not say, but I fancied they would go up."

" No; Nigel told me. Are you going home now ? "

" Not yet, perhaps; but I must rest for a few minutes, and I am in a mood for loitering to-day. Don't wait, if you would rather go fast," said Ethel, with a recollection of Fulvia's energetic ways. She smiled again that curious sweet smile, sunny, yet sad.

Fulvia had not walked fast, but she at once decided to do so. Rather bluntly and awkwardly, though seldom disposed to awkwardness, she said good-bye, and went on.

She kept up a quick walk till well out of sight. "Has Ethel cared too much?" she asked, thinking over the brief interview. "Bright enough; but is it natural brightness? Nigel and she have always been friends. Could Nigel have made her hope, and then have left her? No, that would not be like Nigel." Fulvia felt sure of this; still Ethel might have hoped, without reason. Fulvia pitied Ethel, thinking what might have been Ethel's happiness, but for certain circumstances; and then she pitied herself, recurring to the present trouble. Her step soon slackened under its weight.

Presently she reached a bridge. The towing-path thereafter continued on the other side of the river, but Fulvia did not cross. She made her way along the broken bank, where no path existed, wishing to get out of sight, if Ethel should follow so far.

A snug spot near the water on a steep slope presented itself. There were shrubs and trees on either side, enough to shelter from observation, or so Fulvia thought. She edged herself downward cautiously, not wishing to slip into the stream; though Fulvia was not given to slipping. When comfortably placed, with one aged piece of jutting tree-root for her seat, and another for her footstool, she found that the retreat she had chosen was not invisible either from the bridge or the opposite bank; but after all it did not matter! Ethel would not invade her solitude.

Time passed, Fulvia did not know how. She had not

looked at her watch since leaving home. It was a relief to be alone, beyond reach of questioning eyes, and she could safely allow herself here to sink into a mood of melancholy, for nobody was at hand to note how she looked. Once in such a mood it was hard to rouse herself out of it. She felt like sitting on indefinitely, letting her mind drift as leaves drifted past in the stream below.

Would Nigel ever get over this miserable affair of the postscript? She recurred to the question which had tortured her through the walk. He forgave, no doubt, but Fulvia could not be content with mere forgiveness; she wanted to be reinstated in his good opinion. That good opinion had always been hers, and she could not endure to lose it. Would he ever again have his old confidence in her?

"Whatever else might be wanting, *that* was not wanting." So Nigel had said, "Whatever else—" then he too had been conscious of a want, either in himself or in Fulvia. Only it had not been want of trust. He had trusted her entirely, and now his trust was shaken.

Whatever else is lacking between brother and sister, between friend and friend, between husband and wife, if there is perfect trust there cannot be misery. It is hardly possible that perfect trust should exist without growing love; but trust must stand upon a firm foundation; it can only exist where such a foundation is found. He who trusts must know from practical experience that the one whom he trusts is trustworthy. And whatever else is present, if trust fails everything fails; there is then no firm ground to stand upon; love sinks at once to a lower level.

Fulvia's own hand—Fulvia's own folly—had cut away this firm ground from beneath her feet. In the main she was, as Nigel had always counted her, truthful and honourable; but one grievous failure, persisted in, had undone all that went before. She might indeed never so fail again; but how could Nigel know? How could he be sure what course she would follow in the future? Where one cannot trust there can be no security of happiness. He might forgive and be kind to any extent; but how could he rest upon her, how depend upon her word?

"If only I had not done it! If only I had not!" moaned Fulvia, dropping bitter tears. "If one could but undo the past! O if I had not given way that moment! if I had prayed for help! Would Ethel have been tempted? But she would have prayed, and I—I never thought of that! . . . To think that *I* could stoop to anything base! And it did me no good. Things would have come about just the same! . . . If I had destroyed the paper! But would that have been enough? Things do come out so strangely! It might have been known some day; or I might have felt that I must tell! If only I had not done it!"

Round and round the sorrowful circle of regrets she travelled; and when at length some sound aroused her, she was startled to find how quickly the afternoon was passing.

Unless she made haste, Nigel might reach home before her. That would never do! And what if he and Malcolm should at any moment row by, detecting her on the bank? Fulvia had liked to follow in his steps; but she did not wish to meet him, since he had not asked her to do so.

There was indeed no time to lose, if she would avoid the possibility, still more if she would insure being the first to arrive at home. Fulvia sprang up, somewhat carelessly in her haste, and found the ground giving way beneath.

Late spring frosts had loosened the soil, heavy rains since had carried on the work of disintegration, and Fulvia's weight bestowed the finishing touch. A complete landslip on a tiny scale seemed to be taking place. She struggled round to a kneeling position, and strove to find her feet; but in vain. The earth was sliding, and she was sliding with it.

Fulvia resisted fiercely, clutching at grass, weeds, rotten roots, anything within reach; but everything in turn failed. Screaming was not her natural mode of expression, unless under a very severe shock, and she kept her self-command, making no outcry, though keenly aware of her predicament. The steep bank ended abruptly in a natural upright wall of clay, the stiff clay being surmounted by a layer of more friable earth—that which was now yielding. Close underneath flowed the stream, shelving at once into deep water, deeper now than usual from spring rains.

"How stupid!" gasped Fulvia, and in another moment she found herself on the verge, kneeling, with her back to the river, her feet actually hanging over the bank, soft soil threatening each instant to slip anew with her weight, both hands clutching at an infant shrub growing near, and the gentle "swish" of the water close below.

"Hold on! I'm coming!" a clear girlish voice rang out from the bridge.

CHAPTER XXVIII.

THOU OR I!

" What's brave, what's noble,
Let's do it, after the high Roman fashion."
SHAKSPEARE.

ETHEL ELVEY had been standing on the bridge, unconscious of any human creature's presence, when Fulvia's movement drew her attention.

"I shall be in! Make haste!" cried Fulvia. The baby shrub might at any moment prove false to her trust, and nothing then could hold her back from the threatened bath. Fulvia had no idea how deep the water might be. She had never learnt to swim. Still she did not lose her collectedness; and with a vivid sense of alarm was mingled a sense of her absurd position. "I am glad Nigel is not here to see!" flashed through her mind, and then, "But he would have me up directly! What can Ethel do?"

She dared not attempt to climb alone—dared not stir. The slightest movement might precipitate her downwards.

Not many yards lower one big bough of a large tree

curved over the stream, actually dipping its leaves and twigs into the running water. Fulvia cast a longing side-glance at this bough. If it had but been nearer! The thought occurred to her that, should she fall in before Ethel could arrive, she might reach and cling to the said bough. It looked strong, extending so far out that the current would probably carry her within grasp of its extremity. Fulvia was able to consider so much while waiting. She resolved to keep cool, not to be flurried.

Ethel uttered the one encouraging cry, and then rushed round at her utmost speed to the bank above Fulvia. The question was, how to proceed when there? She heard Fulvia calling, "Take care! the ground will give way!" and she knew that it would not do to follow in Fulvia's steps.

After one moment for observation, Ethel fixed her hopes upon a slender ash, growing slightly to one side of the position which Fulvia had occupied. She had been unused to exertion lately, and already she found herself panting for breath, with beating pulses and a sense of failing power. But there could be no delay, no thought of self. At any instant Fulvia's support might fail.

"O make haste!" implored Fulvia, as Ethel sprang downwards quickly, yet with caution. "Make haste!" It seemed impossible to hold on longer; and surely the little shrub on which she depended was coming up by the roots.

The branch on which Ethel had fixed her hopes proved to be out of reach—almost, perhaps not quite, if she had breath and strength to spring. She made a hurried attempt, once, twice, in vain; and then her heart was throbbing so furiously that everything around grew hazy, and she was compelled to pause, leaning against the tree.

"Ethel! Ethel!" cried Fulvia.

Ethel collected her energies, and made one supreme effort, throwing all the strength she had into it, and very nearly losing her own balance. This time she did not fail; the bough was in her clasp. If only she had not felt so weak and dizzy——but there was no time to think of her own sensations.

"Ethel!" shrieked Fulvia hoarsely; for again the earth seemed to be sinking under her.

She held on desperately—how she did not know; and she grew terrified, losing her collectedness.

Ethel, clinging to the tough ash-branch, sprang fearlessly down the bank, bending forward with outstretched right hand. Fulvia's came to meet it, and the two met in a firm grip.

Success so far; but in the same moment the ground beneath Fulvia broke away, and Fulvia hung over the brink, depending alone on Ethel. The sudden pull drew Ethel from where she had stood, and she slid down the yielding bank towards the verge.

Perhaps the ash-branch might have borne them both, had Ethel's strength been equal to her share of the task; which it was not. The weight of both girls rested now mainly upon Ethel's slender left hand, and the strain was terrible.

For two or three seconds she set her teeth, and held on desperately; but that could not last. She was turning faint; specks danced before her eyes, and Fulvia's voice was unheard. The drag upon that poor little wrist tore the muscles, and the agony became unbearable. Another moment, and the released branch sprang back to its old position, while the two girls rolled helplessly over into deep water, each clinging to the other with unconscious force.

This was Fulvia's second involuntary bath in the river! Last time the water had been her friend, saving her from a deadlier peril; now it was her foe, endangering life.

*   *   *   *   *   -

Fulvia's presence of mind forsook her at the moment of the plunge into cold water, and she forgot the low-hanging bough; but happily the stream fulfilled her hope. As the two girls rose, still together, Fulvia flung out her arm against something firm, and in a moment she had fast hold.

"Cling! cling!" she gasped, so soon as speech became possible. She dashed the water out of her eyes, and cast a look round. "Ethel, Ethel, cling; we are safe now!"

Ethel had uttered no sound. She was deathly pale; her eyes were half shut; her lips had grown blue. It

was not easy to make her transfer her grasp of Fulvia
to the friendly bough. They were so near its extremity
that the wonder was they had not been swept past it
by the current. Ethel inevitably would have been,
since she was outermost, but for her instinctive grip of
Fulvia.

Fulvia, as she seized the bough, drew Ethel nearer;
and the gentle force of the stream rather tended now
to wash them against it than to carry them away. But
they could feel no ground for their feet; and though
the water buoyed them up, it was very cold—far colder
than Fulvia would have expected.

She gazed about in eager quest for help, and could
see no one. While they could cling, they were, as she
had said, safe. The question was, how long the power
of each would last.

To get to shore unaided was not possible. Even if
they could have attempted to work themselves along
by the side of the bough, passing hand over hand—an
easy matter to a boy, though by no means easy to a
girl—it would have been useless. The branch soon
curved upwards out of reach, and unless they could
climb into the tree, which was out of the question, they
would have to cross unaided a space of deep water,
which was equally out of the question.

Moreover, Fulvia had serious doubts as to the
strength of their support. She did not think it would
stand any severe strain. The branch, as a whole, was
less stout than it had appeared at a little distance;

there were signs about it of age, and of something approaching to rottenness, and higher up, half-way to the bank, she could actually see a slight split, as if the part on which they depended had begun to break off. It might only have begun with the pull of their sudden weight, as Fulvia was swept against it.

She found herself watching that visible split in the wood with fascinated eyes, composed enough to speculate how soon it would widen, yet with dire terror below.

They could do nothing except cling and call for help. Fulvia called and called again, without result. Ethel made no such attempt. She seemed just conscious, just able to clutch the bough with one hand, the other being under water out of sight; but no words had yet passed her white lips, and her look of increasing exhaustion alarmed Fulvia.

"I don't see or hear anybody. Some one must surely pass soon. Ethel, are you faint? You look so pale," Fulvia said uneasily. "Don't let go!" This companionship in misfortune drew them together, and she felt that Ethel was in peril for her sake. "Don't let anything make you! Can't you hold with both hands?"

"I can't—"

"Why not? Have you hurt yourself?"

"I think—my wrist—"

"Yes; what is it?"

"Only—twisted—"

"Was that why you had to give way? Is the pain very bad?"

"Yes." The monosyllable did for both questions.

Fulvia had one arm over the bough by this time. She quitted her grip of it with the other, and grasped Ethel's dress instead.

"That will help you, will it not?" she said. "Now you cannot go. Ethel, do be brave; do try to hope. Somebody is sure to come soon. You must not let yourself faint. This can't last long."

It could not indeed, in another sense, as Fulvia well knew. Their position was rapidly becoming most serious. Her own powers lessened fast, and Ethel drooped more each minute. Now and again it seemed to Fulvia that the clasp of those little thin fingers was loosening. She held Ethel tightly, alternately imploring her to keep up, and shouting for aid; but still no one came, and it was impossible that Fulvia should long support Ethel as well as herself.

A new terror arose. Ominous creaks sounded, slight at first, then more distinct; and Fulvia, watching with wide-open eyes, felt certain that the crack above had begun to widen. In a few minutes the whole bough would split off. This was the finishing touch to her misery. Once more Fulvia's composure failed her as terror rose high, and she screamed again for help, in a voice sharpened by fear.

Either the creaks or that new sound in Fulvia's voice aroused Ethel from her semi-trance of exhaustion. The eyes, so dim and unseeing a minute earlier, grew clear, and she said distinctly—

"It is giving way."

Fulvia broke into despairing sobs. "Ethel, Ethel, what shall we do? Why does no one come? It is cruel —cruel. Must we be drowned? I can't die! I cannot —cannot—leave Nigel!"

"Poor Fulvia!" Ethel's faint tones were full of pity. "But if God calls?" she murmured.

"No, no, no! I cannot die! Not yet! I am not ready. I can't, I can't!" Fulvia cried bitterly. "And if I were sure of heaven—what would heaven be to me—without——?"

"Fulvia!" There was a touch of reproach in the soft utterance. Fulvia could not hear Ethel's thought of joy—"But Christ would be there!" She only heard an urgent, "Fulvia, pray! There may not be much time."

Fulvia shut her eyes, and tried to obey, tried to cry for help, for pardon, before it should be too late; but she could not think, could not fix her mind. In days of safety she had not drawn near to God, and now, in the hour of danger, she felt Him far away. The dazzle of the water was all around, even when her eyes were shut; and the stream gently swayed her; and the creaks grew louder, more frequent. She heard Ethel speaking again—

"Don't hold me! Let go!"

"Why?" Fulvia involuntarily loosened her hold on Ethel as she spoke.

"It will not bear us both."

"The bough! Breaking!" gasped Fulvia, too much agitated to understand fully.

"Yes. Don't be startled. I think you will be all right. I think I ought!"—and there was a quiet smile. "Tell Nigel why. And—O Fulvie!" with a passion of longing in the blue eyes—"be very very good to him!"

Then she calmly unclasped the clinging fingers, which held her to the bough, and fell off. The strained support ceased to creak with the lessened weight, and Ethel's slight form was borne away, carried round the next bend in the river.

A piercing scream burst from Fulvia. She had cried for help before with all her force, but this cry rang far and wide, with a shrill intensity unequalled hitherto. No second cry followed it; voice failed in a convulsion of sobs. Fulvia had not dreamt what Ethel's words meant.

The Bramble family had organized a small expedition that afternoon to a certain Roman encampment some miles down the river. The encampment consisted only of a few stony heaps, well grown over; but a charming wood stood hard by, and Newton Bury people made the most of their one little lion.

Mr. Bramble was there, middle-aged, good-humoured, a degree pompous, and willing to be amused; Mrs. Bramble, plump and complacent; Rose Bramble, and two young lady-cousins of Rose. Only the Duncans went, beside themselves, and for a wonder Dr. Duncan, in addition to his wife and daughter, was of the party. He could seldom find leisure for any such relaxation. Two open carriages bore the eight, and Baldwin Bramble accompanied, or rather preceded, them on his bicycle.

Having enjoyed afternoon tea in the wood, the merry party drove homewards. Dr. Duncan's presence had been secured only through a promise of early return; consequently they stayed a shorter time than was usual with excursion parties. Baldwin, on his bicycle, speedily shot ahead of the more lumbering vehicles. He reached the neighbourhood of the spot where was Fulvia, a short time before she thought of moving. The carriage-road lay not far from the river, though not within sight.

Baldwin had begun to find solitude uninteresting. He resolved to wait for the carriages, and to restrain his ardour for awhile to match their pace. Leaning his bicycle against a grassy bank by the road-side, he passed through a gate and sat down under a hedge, intent upon his favourite solace—"a smoke." To his disgust he found that he had mislaid his match-box. Cigars being useless, only one recourse remained to the dis-appointed young man. He fell sound asleep.

Ethel's voice and Fulvia's cries, in the succession of events which followed, failed to disturb Baldwin's peace-ful slumbers. He had an uncomfortable dream or two but he slept on. Then Fulvia's wild shriek, when Ethel left the bough, effected that which all previous cries had failed to effect. Baldwin awoke, with the echo of her scream still ringing in his ears.

He was not a rapid young man at any time, either in understanding or in doing; but as he sat up, it dawned upon him that somebody was in distress somewhere.

" What's the matter now ? Bother !" he said aloud.

Had anybody else been at hand to take the initiative, Baldwin would doubtless have remained quiescent, since he never troubled himself to act unnecessarily. No one except himself appearing to be within call, he made his way towards the river. Where water is at hand, and an appeal for help is heard, one naturally connects the two together.

Baldwin had not far to go. Sobbing wails in a woman's voice guided and quickened his steps. He was soon looking downward upon the low bough, to which a girl clung, her hat off, her face and hands above water, her tones and gestures expressive of urgent appeal for help.

" Hallo !" exclaimed Baldwin.

The question was, how to get at her? Nigel, in Baldwin's place, would probably have taken a header straight into the river, without a moment's hesitation; but Baldwin was not so impulsive. He was a tolerably capable young man when moved by a sufficient motive, and the dire need of the lady below was evident; still he had on a brand-new bicycling costume, never worn till that day; and not everybody is willing, without consideration, to sacrifice a brand-new suit of clothes.

It was plain that the lady saw him, and was calling out eager entreaties, broken by sobs. Baldwin paid small regard to what she said. Rescue was of course what she wanted; and the difficulty was how to rescue her without getting wet himself. He reluctantly came to the conclusion that the knickerbockers at least must submit to a ducking.

The road was entirely out of sight; but Baldwin was not afraid of the two carriages going by. He knew that the sight of his bicycle would bring them to a halt.

For two seconds Baldwin debated with himself whether to climb down the bough to Fulvia. He decided against that mode, doubting whether the bough would bear his additional weight, and feeling sure that he could not get the young lady to land by any such means.

"Yes, yes; I'm coming," he called, with cheerful. deliberation, as he pulled off his coat. The girl seemed in a desperate hurry, he thought. She was urging something passionately, with hysterical vehemence, but he could not distinguish a word.

Where Fulvia and Ethel had fallen in, the bank was steep. Here, below the tree, it sloped gradually into the river, and Baldwin waded several steps with caution.

"Hallo!" he exclaimed, stopping short, when the stream rose above his waist. "I say! If it isn't—! Why, it is—Miss Rolfe!"

"Ethel! Save Ethel!" sobbed Fulvia incoherently.

"I wouldn't be so frightened—I really wouldn't, Miss Rolfe," expostulated Baldwin, in a tone of concern.

" See, now, couldn't you manage to pull yourself along the bough towards me, just a yard or two ? It's no earthly use speaking to her ; she won't hear a word," muttered the young man. " Nothing for it but to swim. I say," raising his voice, " don't you grab me, Miss Rolfe. We don't want to go under together." He had vivid recollections of her conduct on a former occasion, when he had not been the rescuing party.

A few strokes carried him across the intervening space, and he laid one hand upon the low-lying branch. It snapped away like tinder, and he made a vehement snatch at Fulvia, just in time, as she was going with it.

" Hallo ! " he once more ejaculated.

Fulvia gasped, and struggled. Baldwin held her dexterously at arm's length, and struck out for the bank, which he reached somewhat lower down. He sprang out, helped her up, and gave himself a disgusted shake. The knickerbockers were done for.

Streaming with water, breathless and stupefied, Fulvia sank to the ground; but as her gasps lessened, sense and speech returned.

" Don't mind me !—O don't mind me ! " she implored. " Ethel has gone down—drowning—the river—O go and save her ! "

" Hallo ! you don't say there's another ? "

Fulvia almost shrieked in answer, " Yes !—yes !— Ethel—Ethel Elvey ! " Would he never understand ?

" Bramble, what's all this ? Fulvia ! " exclaimed Dr. Duncan, arriving on the scene.

"She'd better drive home. Just got her out of the river. Yes—nice, isn't it?" with a rueful glance at his boots. "I don't think she knows what she's saying—" in an undertone, confidentially. "That's rubbish, you know, about Miss Elvey."

"No! no! no! He will not understand," cried Fulvia. "We fell in together—Ethel and I—and she has gone down—down the river! The branch was breaking, and she let go! O save her! She'll be drowned!"

Dr. Duncan turned sharply to Baldwin. "Send her home in one carriage at once," he said. "Keep the other, and come after me."

Then he was off at full speed, losing not a moment, active as a boy in his movements, quickly out of sight.

"O go—go too!—never mind me!" urged Fulvia.

"I've got to see you off first. Dr. Duncan will do all that can be done," said Baldwin, feeling little doubt that the rescue of Ethel, if not already accomplished, must come too late. "You'll catch your death of cold, if you don't hurry."

"No, no! you must leave me and go!" implored Fulvia; but she implored in vain—Baldwin would not so much as listen. He half led, half dragged her over the rough ground, till the road was reached, where the two open carriages waited.

A chorus of exclamations greeted Baldwin and his dripping companion. He singled out Mrs. Duncan, and explained tersely how things stood. "Miss Rolfe was to drive home at once," he said; "Dr. Duncan ordered it.

The other carriage had better wait." In an undertone
Baldwin added, "Don't you let her put off. She's half
frantic already, and if Miss Elvey——you know what
I mean."

Mrs. Duncan did know too well, a shudder passing
through her with the unexpressed fear. She wrapped
·warm shawls round the shivering girl, and despatched
her without delay, under charge of Mrs. Bramble and
the two cousins, Rose Bramble taking to the coach-
box. Better all of them out of the way, thought
Mrs. Duncan, regretting only that Annabel could not
go also.· Fulvia hysterically begged to be allowed to
wait, but, like Baldwin, Mrs. Duncan would not listen.

"My dear, it is as much as your life is worth," she
said; and she gave parting directions to the others.
"Tell Mrs. Browning and Daisy that Fulvia must take
off all her wet things, and get into bed as fast as possible,
and have something hot to drink."

"Farewell, oh dream of mine !
 I dare not stay ;
The hour is come, and time
 Will not delay :
Pleasant and dear to me
 Wilt thou remain ;
No future hour
 Brings thee again."—A. A. PROCTER.

"HASN'T been a bad day for a row," observed Malcolm.

" No."

" Well, now we have tried it once, we'll try it again. You used to be such a one for boating. Grown tired of it lately ? "

" No."

" You've not gone in for it ! "

" No."

" I would sometimes, if I were you. 'All work and no play,' you know—"

" Yes."

" What's the matter to-day ? "

This question came abruptly. The friends had been

to;ether since half-past two, and the above is a fair sample of the conversation which had taken place.

"Nothing," Nigel said, adding—"at least nothing in particular."

"Only everything in general. That's as bad."

"No. It's all right."

"Sure? You seem out of sorts somehow."

Nigel rowed on in silence. The lithe muscular figure found evident pleasure in the exertion, moving with careless ease. There was no lack of good health apparent in the bronzed face; but the immovable gravity differed much from Nigel's old light-heartedness. Malcolm noticed it more than usually this day. He had started in high spirits himself, ready for any amount of gaiety, and he found scant response. No answering fun was to be got out of his serious companion.

"What's the matter, old fellow?" he inquired again. "I don't want to be a bother, but really one can't help knowing there's something. What are you thinking about?"

"Varieties," was the answer.

"When are you coming to see us again?"

"I don't know. Some day perhaps."

"You are busy now, of course. Still, if Ethel didn't know you so well she might be affronted." Malcolm spoke thoughtlessly, and the next moment was vexed with himself. He did not understand the exact position of affairs. Nigel's engagement to Fulvia, after years of apparent devotion to Ethel, had been a sore perplexity

to him; but he did know that there were reasons for
Nigel's action which had not been told to him, yet
which Ethel counted to have weight; and he had
strong trust in his friend. Moreover he could see,
as every one could see, that Nigel was not happy.
Malcolm's private belief was that Nigel cared too little
for Fulvia, too much for Ethel; therefore he regretted
his own hasty words.

"How is Ethel?" asked Nigel, speaking with a
manifest effort.

"Not so strong as she ought to be. We hoped more
from Wales."

The two rowed on again, more slowly than before; or
rather Nigel rowed, Malcolm having taken to steering.
Nigel was buried in thought.

"We shall have to think of a change to some more
bracing place, if she doesn't look up soon," observed
Malcolm. "I don't like to see her as she is now."

A shill scream rang out suddenly.

"What's that?" burst from both.

"Where from?" exclaimed Malcolm.

"Ahead!" and Nigel worked at the oars with vigour.

"Sure? I thought——"

"Yes! Listen!" But no second cry followed the
first.

"Nigel, you didn't know that voice? I had a fancy——"

Nigel uttered one word, "Fulvia." He had lost
colour, but he spoke calmly, redoubling his exertions.
The boat shot swiftly up stream.

"Let me take an oar." Malcolm started half up, but Nigel's answer was imperative—

"No; keep still. Can't wait for that."

Malcolm submitted. He knew that he could not rival these strokes, and he could better be on the look-out where he was. They swept round a slight bend, and then a cry escaped Malcolm.

"Ha! See there!"

"Where? What?"

"Some one in the water! A woman!"

"Make for her—straight."

Nigel did not even glance round. "Fulvia!" was in the minds of both, and Nigel was deeply moved; for whatever she might or might not be to him, his love for her was of its kind thoroughly genuine.

"It may not be—her," Malcolm uttered. "Take care; not so fast. Now—slacken! Now—here."

Nigel looked, drew in his oars, and sprang up, always the first to act. Malcolm kept his seat, balancing the boat, as Nigel leant over and caught something, drawing it nearer—caught a girlish dress.

Then they both saw——

A still face, pure as alabaster, the eyes closed, the brown hair matted and streaming, the lips peacefully parted!

"Ethel! O my God!" broke from Nigel. No careless or irreverent utterance this, but a very heart-cry of intolerable pain—the appeal of despair to One who alone could help.

"Ethel!" Malcolm echoed hoarsely.

No other sound passed Nigel's lips. He grew fearfully pale, but there was no loss of control over himself. With steady balancing, aided by Malcolm, he drew up the slight heavy figure, held it one half-instant in his arms, gazing, then laid it gently down.

"Nigel, she can't—can't have been in long. She must have fallen just now. That scream," Malcolm said with difficulty.

Nigel made no repiy in words. He gave Malcolm one glance, caught up the oars, pointed to the bank, and rowed with fierce energy.

A possible landing-place was near, and in less than two minutes they were there. The boat's keel no sooner grounded, than Nigel dropped his oars, lifted Ethel once more in his arms, and sprang ashore. He seemed to have unnatural strength. Every movement was rapid and light, as if he did not feel her weight.

"The Parsonage?" Malcolm said, and Nigel made a gesture of assent. He had at once remembered the little hamlet Church of Buryfield, not ten minutes distant, with its liliputian Parsonage and gentle elderly Incumbent. "Let me help. You can't carry her all the way."

"No;" and Nigel strode on at a frantic pace, his face ghastly. Malcolm kept pace by his side.

"She can't be gone. It can't be too late. She was in so short a time," urged Malcolm. "Don't give up hope." He almost lost sight of his own fear and grief in view of his friend's distress, which yet he could not understand. Nigel had not worn that look when they believed the scream to be Fulvia's,—as indeed it was. The idea that Fulvia, not Ethel, had screamed, and that Fulvia too was in danger, did not occur to either of them.

Mr. Dacres was at home. He knew the young men slightly, and had seen Ethel before. This sudden incursion must have been a trial to an unmarried man, advanced in years, but he met it bravely, summoning at once his capable housekeeper to see what could be done. Hot water, hot flannels, anything they might need, were at their service. The gardener was sent, rushing at his utmost speed, to summon Dr. Duncan, or any doctor who could be found, from Newton Bury, for this hamlet did not own a medical man. Little dreamt any of them that Dr. Duncan was even then within a few minutes' walk, hurrying along the bank in search of Ethel.

Malcolm knew something, at least in theory, of what had to be done in such an emergency. The housekeeper and a girl who worked under her were willing enough to follow his directions. They removed Ethel's wet clothes, wrapping her in warm blankets before the kitchen fire, with vigorous rubbing. Nigel and Malcolm waited in the passage while these things were done; and then as all efforts failed, they stole back into the kitchen, Malcolm to assist in rubbing, Nigel to watch the still face with despairing eyes.

Dr. Duncan could not come yet. Half-an-hour more was the shortest time possible. But as they said and thought this, the door opened, and James Duncan walked in.

No needless words were spoken. Dr. Duncan was quiet, as always. He bent over Ethel, listening to the heart, feeling the pulse, lifting the eyelids to look into the eyes. Then his glance fell upon Nigel's face, and a slight change crept into his calmness, as if he had seen something unexpected.

" No ; not dead," he pronounced.

" Thank God !" Malcolm said fervently.

No answering sound came from Nigel, and the doctor's glance fell on him again.

" We are too many here. The less the better. Yes, go for a little while "—to Malcolm. Then in a lower voice, " Take that poor fellow into another room."

" But there is hope ? "

" I trust so. We have no time to lose. Now, Mrs. Willis—"

Malcolm did not wait for more. He had complete faith in Duncan's skill and kindness. Mr. Dacres lingered, while Malcolm slipped an arm through Nigel's, and drew him from the kitchen regions, into the clergyman's little study.

" Come, cheer up," he said gravely. " It will not be so bad, Nigel,—thank God. Dr. Duncan does not fear the worst. Cheer up, my dear fellow ; we may hope now."

Nigel had never broken quite down through all the pain and grief of past months; but he broke down now. His face was hidden, bowed low on his crossed arms, and the whole strong frame shook with passionate agony. No sobs were audible, yet Malcolm knew what it meant. He drew the bolt softly, for none but himself might see this; and he could only look on in silence, with eyes full of tears, till the worst was over.

Mrs. Browning and Daisy were inadequate to the management of Fulvia, when Fulvia chose to take the bit between her teeth. It was all very well for Mrs. Duncan to send directions that Fulvia ought to go to bed. Mrs. Bramble delivered the message faithfully, but Fulvia refused to obey.

"How can I, till I know about Ethel?" she asked wildly. "Take care of myself, when Ethel is perhaps— O if they had only let me stay to hear. It was cruel to hurry me away. But Nigel will soon be at home, and he can find out. I must stay down-stairs till Nigel comes. Not good for me! What does that matter? What do I care? I only want to know if Ethel is safe."

She built her hopes upon Nigel's return, which seemed to be unaccountably delayed. Meantime she had consented to change her soaked clothing, and to dispose of what Daisy called "a hot drink." Then, as she shivered incessantly, despite her warm shawl, a fire was lighted in the study, and Fulvia cowered over it.

D D

Daisy offered to go to the Rectory for news, but Fulvia would not consent. "They may not have heard," she said shuddering. "If Ethel is safe, it would be brutal to frighten Mrs. Elvey without need. And if——if the worst has happened, they will hear soon enough——too soon. Why should one be in a hurry to bring misery to people? It is hard enough to bear one's own wretchedness."

Suspense in her present mood found relief in speech. Fulvia talked incessantly, going over every detail of the day's adventures, enlarging with feverish admiration on Ethel's self-devotion. She did not shed tears, but she could not be silent or turn to another subject. Her limbs were aching, her face and head burning. Mrs. Browning listened uneasily, trying in vain to soothe her. Agreement or opposition alike made her worse. Anice was up-stairs, keeping aloof, as usual, from uncomfortableness, and Daisy watched at the dining-room window, coming from time to time with the report, "No news and nobody,"—always to be ordered back by Fulvia to her post of observation.

"Nigel will be here directly. He must," Fulvia said, on one of these occasions. "Let me know the moment you see him. No, I won't have you do anything. Only wait." Then she recurred to the grievous refrain: "If Ethel is drowned I shall never forgive myself. It will have been all through me. I shall never look any one in the face again."

At last!—the sound of wheels! Daisy flew in.

"Some one has come," she cried. "Cousin Jamie, and—I'm not sure, but I think I had a glimpse of Nigel."

Fulvia kept her seat, trembling violently. She did not grow pale, but the flush deepened, spreading to her brow. "Call them here—quick," she said. "If not, I will go out. Quick!"

Daisy obeyed to the best of her power. Dr. Duncan came in first, looking as if the events of the last two hours had told upon him. Nigel followed,——not the Nigel who had left home after lunch, but white, worn, heavy-eyed, as he had been after his father's death. Fulvia's wandering gaze concentrated itself on him, while he stood, resting one arm on the back of a chair, apparently not even seeing her.

"Then—Ethel is gone!" she said, gasping. "It was too late? And I—I—the cause!"

She turned her burning face away, and wrung her hands together, breaking into a wail of distress, like a child, and then she found Dr. Duncan's hand upon her arm.

"Hush! you are over-excited. Ethel is better."

"Not dead! But Nigel looks—" Fulvia broke off. "He looks—! Was Ethel saved? She—went down the river,"——with a bewildered glance round. "I can't explain. I feel so strange! Is this the way people go out of their minds?"——and there was a short laugh. "Feel my hand; I am all on fire. But think—think of Ethel! The branch was breaking, and she let go

—for my sake! O it was noble! And she is not drowned? I thought she must be drowned. Not drowned, you say? You are sure—quite sure?"

"Yes." Until then Fulvia's rapid utterances allowed no space for reply. "Perfectly sure."

"How do you know? Have you seen her? Has Nigel?"

"Malcolm and Nigel were coming up the river in their boat—just in time."

"And she is—not the worse?"

"She will suffer, of course; but we were able—mercifully—to bring her round."

"She will get over it—will get well? Promise me!"

"I trust so, in time. We have taken her home, and my wife will stay there all night. I have come now to see you."

"I! O that does not matter," said Fulvia bitterly. "What does anything signify about me? If you will save Ethel——people love Ethel, you know. And for Nigel's sake! It doesn't matter about me! Why don't you go back to Ethel? She ought not to be left. She might die; and if she did, Nigel would die too. Look! can't you see?"

"Fulvia, you are wrong! You must not give way like this," said Dr. Duncan, in a low voice.

"Why not? I may do as I like. Who cares?"

She turned petulantly from him, and with uneven steps walked across to Nigel. Dr. Duncan would not follow her. He sent Daisy from the room, on some slight pretext, and at once set himself to engross Mrs. Browning's attention.

Fulvia cared little, in her then mood, whether or no she were observed. She stood in front of Nigel, who had remained passive and silent since his first entrance, and her intent gaze caused a slight movement, as if he shrank from it—or from her.

"Have you been so frightened about Ethel?" she asked.

"Yes."

"Not about—— ?"

Nigel understood. "I did not know of your danger too, Fulvia, till——" he said, in a low voice, and then he faltered, as if scarcely knowing how to continue.

"Yes—till when?"

"Jamie told me—half-an-hour ago, I believe—I am not sure."

"No; that was a secondary matter," said Fulvia. Her face hardened, and her tone grew harsh. "If you had known us both to be drowning, would you have left Ethel to come to me?"

Nigel attempted no answer.

"Nigel—look at me!" she said sharply—even imperiously, as she had before spoken to Daisy. "Look at me, and answer. Why should you be afraid? Would you have left Ethel to come to me?"

Even these words did not rouse him. He made an effort to respond, but the heavy dark eyes seemed almost unable to lift themselves under their weighted lids to meet hers. Fulvia had seen him like this once before. Her mood changed with curious suddenness, as Fulvia's moods were wont to change. The hardness vanished, and pity took its place.

"You have a fearfully bad headache," she said, in her gentlest voice.

"Yes."

"I am sorry. When did it come on?"

"I don't know. Not long——"

"You are in such pain, you can't think. What made it so bad? Was it the thought that Ethel was drowned?"

Nigel was silent.

"And I—you did not think of me——"

"I did not know——"

"Was I cruel to ask that question just now?" Fulvia inquired, almost whispering the words. Dr. Duncan and Mrs. Browning passed out of the room, leaving them alone.

"Yes, I was cruel," she went on. "You cannot help it. You have tried so hard. I know that well. But till to-day I have not known Ethel——the noble girl that she is! I have dared to think her ordinary. Have you heard how things happened? You ought to hear?"

"Not all——"

"No,—I might guess Ethel would not tell. I slipped first, and she came to my help, and we fell in together.

She could not hold me up, though she tried. Then we clung to the bough, and it was giving way. I was frightened, but Ethel did not seem afraid. She and I are so different. We could not be sure if the bough would last, and Ethel let go to save me, and went down the river. If I had guessed in time, I would have held her fast; but how could I guess? That was the last I saw of Ethel. It was grand of her——more than I could have done in her place. I shall never forget her face, the moment that she let go——never! I shall always know what Ethel is."

Nigel said nothing, and not a feature of his face changed. Fulvia watched him closely, knowing that he would not show what he might have shown.

"Is Ethel always like that?"

"Yes—always."

"And you have known it?"

"Yes—" still lower.

"I think you ought to lie down," said Fulvia abruptly "I have not seen you so for a long while—not since padre's death." Then she looked round, to find Dr. Duncan by her side. "Nigel is ill," she said, with a shudder.

"Not ill, only overstrained. I am more afraid for you," said Dr. Duncan. "Why did you not go to bed at once?"

"O I could not—how could I? But I will now. Everything feels so strange!" and she laughed drearily. "I can't get clear in my head. You are sure that Ethel is not drowned? Nigel could not seem more unhappy if she were. You are not deceiving me?"

"Have I ever deceived you yet?"

"No!" Fulvia said at once. A look came into her eyes which Dr. Duncan could not fathom. "If you had, I should never trust you again, should I?"

"Never, certainly, to the same extent."

"I should always feel doubtful. Should I not?"

"Yes. You need not feel doubtful now."

"No. But if you had once deceived me, I could not help it. Whatever you said or did, I should always—always—always—feel that you might be deceiving me again."

Nigel glanced at her, and Fulvia met his eyes, breaking into a wild laugh.

"O I feel so strange," she said.

Dr. Duncan shook her band gently, as if to rouse her.

"Don't talk so, Fulvia. This has all been too much for you. The sooner you are in bed the better."

"Yes. I have nothing to stay up for now. But Ethel will get well. You arc sure—sure?"

"I trust so."

"She must! She must! For Nigel's sake! It will kill him if she dies! Yes, I am going! Make Nigel rest, please. Will you see Ethel again to-night?"

"Yes; and I shall look in again to see how you are, afterwards. Go straight to bed now. Daisy is waiting for you."

"Thanks. Good-bye," said Fulvia. She passed out of the room, without even a glance towards Nigel. His eyes and Dr. Duncan's met, each questioning the other; while Fulvia dragged herself up-stairs. "It is all over—all over!" she moaned.

CHAPTER XXX.

NOT I BUT THOU!

"Be satisfied that, in order to accomplish all that God would have done, there is in one sense but very little to do. . . . It is simply a question of yielding up our will; of going cheerfully from day to day whithersoever God may lead us."—FÉNÉLON.

"Thou who canst love us, though Thou read us true."
Christian Year.

SEVEN long weeks had run their course since the day when Fulvia and Ethel fell into the river. Much may happen in seven weeks! and it seemed to Fulvia that much had happened, all within the four walls of her own room, which for six weeks she never left. But more had taken place than she yet knew.

She had been very ill—so ill as to lie at death's door. The shock, the fright, the chill, the exposure in wet clothes, these, preceded and accompanied by great agitation, would have been enough to break anybody down. Even Fulvia's vigorous constitution was not proof against so severe a strain.

That constitution stood her in good stead, however, when the tide turned and she began to recover. Her improvement was steady, with few drawbacks.

Ethel had been ill too, and Fulvia knew it. Not desperately ill, like herself, but laid low with a bad feverish cold, and kept low indefinitely by weakness from which she could not rally. Fulvia asked after her daily, and could find out no more.

Fulvia was intensely desirous for Ethel's recovery. She could never forget the moment when Ethel had slipped away from the bough, as it seemed to certain death, that Fulvia might be saved. Nothing in Fulvia's life had made a stronger impression on her mind. She was penetrated through and through with a sense of Ethel's nobility of character. She thought of it awake, talked of it asleep, raved of it in delirium; and if Fulvia had not often prayed before, she prayed now—constantly, passionately—that Ethel might become well—not for her own sake, but for Nigel's sake! For side by side with Ethel's white face, floating away on the river, as Fulvia saw it perpetually, was Nigel's face, worn and hollow-eyed, as he had come back from the rescue of Ethel.

During seven weeks she had not seen Nigel. Once, when she was at her worst, he had nearly been called into the sick-room, in the hope that his face might soothe her restless excitement; but Fulvia, overhearing, had cried out against the suggestion. She was so much worse for the bare idea, that no one thought of proposing it again.

Mrs. Browning learnt some sharp lessons watching by the sick girl. It was difficult to fathom the meaning of her rapid unconscious utterances; but one thing at least was plain—that Fulvia had been, and was, terribly unhappy. The engagement which Mrs. Browning and her husband, as well as Mr. Carden-Cox, had been so anxious to bring about, was not a success. Nigel's spiritless gravity had long been in itself a silent rebuke; and Fulvia's broken mournful complaints struck even more keenly home; since their wish to press matters forward had been, at least in a measure, for Fulvia's sake.

Better far for all concerned, if they had been content to leave uncertainties in the hands of One who sees the end from the beginning. We are all too apt to think that *we* can arrange the lives of those around us: and our meddling often only mars what we would fain set right. Mrs. Browning knew this at last; and the gentle woman grieved sorely, though in silence, over her past mistakes. But at least she did not make the fresh mistake of interfering anew.

Fulvia had now been allowed for several days to go down-stairs, and had even had a short drive or two; nevertheless, she had not yet seen Nigel. He had left home a fortnight earlier, a holiday being kindly arranged for him by Mr. Bramble, that he might try to shake off the unconquerable lassitude which for weeks had weighed him down. Every one thought him looking ill, and this had come to Fulvia's ears, though she asked few questions, and, indeed, seldom spoke of him voluntarily.

The fortnight of absence being over on this day, exactly seven weeks after the accident, Nigel was expected home. Fulvia sat alone in the study, awaiting his arrival.

She looked better in health than might have been expected; which is often the case after a severe illness, with its necessary rest, and petting, and feeding up. Friends are always surprised; but it constantly so happens. Fulvia's complexion was clearer, her eyes were brighter, her cheeks were even a little plumper, than two months ago.

Yet she had gone through much suffering, mental as well as physical, and she had come out changed. The gold had been purified in the furnace. Life itself was altered for Fulvia thenceforward.

Self's happiness had been her chief aim through past years, side by side, indeed, with kindly thought for others, yet always holding its position. It had seemed to her impossible to live without the thing she craved, —without Nigel.

Now a higher and nobler view of life had dawned. The thought of self-sacrifice, as a great joy in life, had come.

Once before she had had a glimpse: once, many months earlier, when she had resolved to cast aside thoughts of self, and to help forward the happiness of one whom she loved, irrespective of her own desires. That feeble resolution had gone down like a reed before the hurricane rush of strong temptation. She had seen the possible nobleness, but she had not lived it.

Now matters were altogether different. Ethel's act of self-devotion had led her upwards to something far above—infinitely beyond. Fulvia gained in this illness new knowledge of ONE whose life and death were pure self-sacrifice, who had not lived to Himself, but to God and for men. That which had been a story to her before became at last reality. She saw the unutterable self-abnegation of the Son of God, and beheld the mighty Example from which all lesser human sacrifice of self has sprung. A fresh and wonderful light was shed upon everything.

Slowly, dawning like daylight, the teaching came. Fulvia was in no haste. She waited to see more, submitting like a little child. To such an attitude of waiting, the needed lessons are always sent.

Two clear thoughts gradually rose into prominence, the first embracing the second, the second springing from the first.

Christ had given His life for her! Could she do less than devote her life unto Him?

That was the first and greater thought.

Ethel had been willing to die for Fulvia! Could not Fulvia voluntarily give up her heart's desire for Ethel?

That was the second and lesser thought.

The first was the easier of acceptance. The second, which of necessity followed, caused hard battling. But gradually yet firmly Fulvia's resolution was taken.

She was thinking over this resolution as she sat in

the study, facing her lonely future, trying, not without success, to be glad in Nigel's coming happiness.

"For he will be happy!" she murmured. "And I may love him still——as his sister. We were brother and sister so many years. Just going back to the old order of things. It will not be so hard now—perhaps —now I can love and admire Ethel too."

There was a stir of arrival at the front door. Fulvia sat still, trembling. She was not strong yet, though she looked well. She had said that she would see Nigel alone, and the others had acquiesced; only Daisy asked her mother curiously: "I wonder why?"

"My dear, don't ask. Say nothing," Mrs. Browning answered sadly.

Some little delay took place. Fulvia could hear voices—Nigel's sounding cheerful. She locked her hands together, resolute to be calm. Then Nigel came into the room.

"They told me I should find you here," he said.

Fulvia had not resolved how to act, had not been able to decide; she had only been able to pray. Now a sudden impulse came; and when he entered, she rose slowly, holding out her hand.

"Am I not to have a kiss, Fulvie?" he asked, in his kindest tone.

He looked much better for the change, brighter than she had seen him for some time.

"If you like—as my brother!" she said distinctly, though her heart beat almost to suffocation.

His glance was of utter perplexity—more perplexity than distress, Fulvia knew, though the brightness at once died away. Fulvia withdrew her hand, and sat down, and Nigel did not give the kiss permitted on those terms. He stood gazing at her, intensely serious.

"Has your holiday done you good?" asked Fulvia, after a pause.

"Yes. Fulvia, I do not understand. Has anything happened to annoy you? What can you mean?"

"What I said—simply."

"I don't understand."

She held the arm of her chair fast, white enough now.

"Only—that we are brother and sister again. Reversion to the old order of things."

Dead silence followed. Nigel was motionless, leaning against the mantelpiece, his lips compressed, his whole face so grieved that she could not help the spring of a faint hope. What if, after all, she were mistaken?

"I do not understand," he said, for the third time. "There must be a cause. Either you have grown tired of me, or something has vexed you. Not—surely!—poor Mr. Carden-Cox' will? That would not be like you. Of course my share is entirely yours——would be, I mean, if——" and he hesitated. "Until this moment I have supposed that money coming to you and to me meant the same thing."

It was Fulvia's turn to look bewildered.

"Uncle Arthur's will!" she said. "Has he made a

new one ? He did talk of it, and I begged him not ;
but why should I mind ? "

"Then they have not told you ? "

"No one has told me anything about uncle Arthur.
I have scarcely heard his name mentioned. It has
seemed strange—sometimes."

Nigel was silent, and she cast an anxious glance.

"Is something wrong ? Has anything happened ? I
have a right to know, surely. It will not hurt me
now."

"You were not told before I left; but I fancied that
by this time——I ought to have asked first——"

"Tell me now. What is it ? "

"He was taken suddenly."

"Uncle Arthur dead ? "

Nigel made a sound of assent, and Fulvia's eyes filled
with tears. She was almost glad to have something
about which she might lawfully show sorrow.

"Poor uncle ! How sad ! And not long ill, you
say ? "

"No; it was an acute attack. I saw him the evening before, seemingly well, but distressed about you.
The next day he was gone."

"Poor uncle ! " sighed Fulvia.

Yet her mind at once reverted to the present question,
the present pain, which dwarfed all lesser troubles.
Nigel thought that her pensive look meant grief for
Mr. Carden-Cox. His own attention was very much
divided. He could not for a moment forget Fulvia's

E E

words of greeting; and after all, however kind to them, Mr. Carden-Cox was not a man to win generally any great love.

"Strange,—the last time he saw me he talked of making a new will," Fulvia remarked dreamily, forgetting that she had said the same before. "And I never went to see him again. I wish I had been."

"The new will was not finished."

"So much the better."

"It will come to the same thing."

"No; the old will left half to you. I am glad it is so."

"Half the income—not half the personal effects. The house and all it contains will be yours."

"Was his income—? How much was it?"

"Over a thousand a year. No one supposed him to have that amount. Of course you have—would have—a right to the whole."

"Certainly not. You will keep your five hundred a year, and I shall keep mine: enough, and more than enough, for me."

A rap sounded at the door, and Daisy's voice cried: "Aren't you both coming? We want you."

Nigel went to the door, and opened it.

"No, not yet," he said. "Pray leave us quiet."

Daisy fled; and Nigel came back, to ask once more—

"Fulvia, what did you mean just now?"

"I meant what I said," Fulvia answered low; "that

it will be better for us to be brother and sister again, as we used to be."

"But—why?"

"Must I say why?"

She was the more composed of the two. She had had her struggle beforehand, and was mistress of herself, while Nigel, taken by surprise, was visibly agitated. He sat down in front of her, leaning forward; and as he faced Fulvia, she noted a strange gleam in his eyes, together with rapid beating in the temples, which had grown thinner of late. A wonder crossed her mind: did this mean distress, or was it a sense of possible relief, even of joy?

"Yes; I have had no idea all these weeks——But you are changed! What has happened?"

"Not the will," she said. "You could not really suppose it to be that. I am only glad he did not make a new one."

"Then—what?"

Fulvia answered by a single word, soft and clear— "Ethel!"

Nigel did not move, and his eyes were on Fulvia still.

"What does this mean? Have I given you cause—?"

"No," she interrupted; "you have fought hard. I know it, and I don't blame you——I don't indeed. You have been open and true. And I accepted you, knowing ——if not, I ought to have known——for you were true! But——"

"You cannot trust me?"

"If either of us says that, I am the one to say it to you!"

"No; you do not trust me," he said, with marked displeasure. Yet, under the displeasure, under the gravity, the trouble, the suppressed emotion, Fulvia knew that there lay the dawn of a new hope, of an old dead hope revived, so radiant that he dared not look at it. She knew this as distinctly as if she could have seen into his heart.

"I think," she said firmly, though with unsteady lips, "that you and I are better as brother and sister. It is wiser for both of us. I do trust you. I know that you are true; and you would be true to me. You would give me all that is in your power to give. But I should expect more than you are able to give; and if I never had it, I should be miserable——we should both be miserable. You have tried hard, and you would try——to the end. You see I do not doubt you. But think how far off that end might lie! And your heart's love is for Ethel, not for me."

No direct answer came to this. Nigel sprang up, and paced the room with restless steps. Fulvia knew that he was troubled, but not sorrow-stricken, not in the least danger of being heart-broken. She could watch his face safely as he walked, for he did not look once towards her. It was worried and grieved, nothing more.

"I have seen—I could not help seeing——" she went on, after he returned to his seat. "That last day especially, before my illness, when you came back from thinking Ethel drowned! I am not fancying—one does not fancy such things! You love Ethel, and Ethel loves you, and I have kept you apart! Padre did not mean to be cruel when he was dying, but he was cruel. He had better have left us alone. People do such foolish things sometimes, don't they? I did not know till lately how Ethel has cared; at least, I was not sure. But that day——when she thought herself near to death——one could not mistake her look when she spoke of you! I have thought a great deal in my illness. And I know that I must do this. I know that I cannot keep you two apart, just for my own sake."

Nigel spoke at last in a resolute voice, breathing hard: "This does not touch the real question. I have devoted my life to you."

"In payment of my £40,000!" she said, with an odd sorrowful smile. "No; that would be over-payment ——or worse than no payment, if we were not happy. And it does touch the real question; for if I will not have you——"

"But if you are promised to me, Fulvia?"

Fulvia lifted her eyes, which had drooped. A light shone in them.

"If you wished it——wished to hold me to my word,——" she said. "Promised; yes! But you cannot claim my promise, if you cannot give the love I have a right to ask! Yes, you love me as a brother. Is that enough? Nigel, you are very true, and I may

trust you.   I do trust you—utterly!   Tell me in plain
words——don't be afraid to speak out, only tell
me——do you love me or Ethel best?"

Nigel's lips whitened.   He made no response.

"Tell me!   I will know!   One word only!   Ethel—
or Fulvia!   Which is it?   Which is dearest to you?"

Still Nigel did not speak.   Fulvia leant forward,
searching his face.

"Ethel—or me!   Which?"

"Is there need for this?   Is it right?" asked Nigel
slowly.   "Can you not trust me, when I say that my
life shall be yours?"

"I would trust you for the life, but not for the love,"
she said.   "You can promise the one; you cannot
promise the other.   Only love of a kind, at least, a
poorer sort.   Think—have pity!—could *you* marry one
who. loved another more?   Can you ask it of me?
Yes, I was willing once—madly willing; but I have
learnt better.   Now my eyes are opened, would you
force it upon me still? and all from a mistaken notion
of honour?   You see, I understand.   Would you have
me sacrifice your happiness and Ethel's, for the sake
of a happiness which would not be mine?   How could it
be?   If you can say that you love me most—first—
best of all—then I will still be yours!   If not——!   Tell
me—truly—do you love Ethel or me?   Which most?"

Nigel spoke the one word at last, as if it were dragged
from him, his voice husky, and even faint,—

"Ethel!"

Fulvia said nothing. She could not have been taken by surprise, yet the shock overcame her. Perhaps she had never entirely given up hope till now. Tears fell fast, and she was unable to control herself. Nigel was the first to speak.

"Fulvie, dear, you would have it!" he said gently. "You would have it; and I cannot say what is not true. But you were wrong to ask. It was not needed. The love for Ethel is such an old love, it cannot die in a day——cannot change, I mean, into——But indeed I have not thought of Ethel in that light lately, only as——We should have become friends—no more! I believe that one can conquer—may conquer! I would have fought it out, God helping me."

Fulvia held out her hand, and Nigel grasped it, repeating, "Why did you insist? It was cruel to yourself and me. I think you ought to know how dear you are to——even though——Why could you not let things alone? I would have conquered!"

"And all the time you and Ethel breaking your hearts for one another," Fulvia struggled to say.

"No—if it was right——and indeed I would have given you no cause——"

"O no! You have been so good to me always!"

"I will be again. Cannot we forget all this?"

Fulvia mastered her voice, and even forced a smile· "Yes," she said; "we will forget it all——the whole, from first to last. You shall be good to me still, only not *so!* We are brother and sister again, and you are

free. I know I am right. It will be right for us both,
——for all of us. By-and-by we shall all be thankful
things did not go too far. I shall find some work in
life worth doing. It is best so——indeed it is. Why
must you look so unhappy? I will try to be a good
sister to you——both."

"You make me feel how grievously I have failed."

"No; it is not failure. It is only——I think we can
say more another day. I am not—so very strong yet."
Fulvia knew that she could bear no more. "Will you
please tell madre and the girls——tell them it is my
doing? I am going up-stairs now, for a little—rest.
Nobody need come."

She gave him a soft farewell glance, and passed
quickly away, before he could detain her. Once locked
in her own room, the knowledge of what she had done
overcame her utterly. Calmness had to yield before a
sharp short agony of weeping. But by the time Mrs.
Browning begged for entrance, she was herself again.

"Fulvie, my dear, what is this? What does this
mean?" Mrs. Browning asked, in great distress.

Fulvia threw her arms round the gentle woman,
hiding her flushed and blistered face.

"It only means, dear madre, that I am your own
child again—Nigel's sister! We needn't talk much
about it, need we? Only please help me to be good
and brave. I know I am right, and you know it too!
We must think of—Nigel's happiness—must we not?
O mother, help me to be brave!" sobbed Fulvia.

CHAPTER XXXI.

NIGEL'S LOVE.

"Then He gave her peace,—
Because her heart had learned to rest on Him—
His perfect peace. . . . .
. . . . And so it was that she
Who looked on life and death with hate and fear,
Saw in her life a happy pilgrimage
On toward a better country, which she sought
With longing."—S. J. STONE.

ETHEL was lying on the couch in the Rectory dining-room. She could not sit up for any length of time. There was nothing radically wrong, Dr. Duncan said; but he did not like this persistent weakness. She seemed to have no rallying power. "Nothing radically wrong—yet," he said; "but if any mischief should set in, things would go hardly with her." Sometimes he added—"If one could find a new interest—anything to rouse her!" The question was, what interest? Change of scene had already been tried, and the slender Elvey purse would not submit to unlimited drains. "I don't want to go away again. I only want to be quiet," Ethel had said, smiling, that very morning.

But she looked very thin, and the white lids drooped wearily over the tired blue eyes, though it was yet early in the day. Her slender hands, after a vain attempt at work, were resting languidly one over the other.

"Ethel, my dear, here is somebody come to see you," Mr. Elvey's cheery voice said at the door.

"Come in, please," Ethel answered, not moving. She had often received callers, lying down, of late.

Mr. Elvey vanished, and Ethel could hear him speaking: "Yes, yes; she'll be delighted. Does her good to see fresh faces. She looks sadly to-day, poor child! I'm afraid I must be off, but do stay with her as long as you can."

Then to Ethel's astonishment, Fulvia Rolfe walked in—Fulvia Rolfe, cheerful and composed, apparently well in health, and handsomely dressed. She had taken particular pains with herself that morning. Fulvia had no notion of acting the "love-lorn damsel," with careless attire and dishevelled locks, for people to gossip about. Even before Anice and Daisy, the previous evening, she had carried matters with a high hand, resolutely making it appear that she and Nigel separated with equal willingness. It was "much better so," she answered lightly to any manner of condolence. She would release Nigel, but she would not submit to be pitied. If her eyes were a little heavy with midnight tears, who could wonder, after so severe an illness?

"Fulvia!" Ethel said, flushing faintly.

"Don't move"—and Fulvia bent for a kiss. "I have come to thank you."

"There is nothing to thank for!"

"One does not generally count it 'nothing' to have one's life saved——especially at the risk of——"

"Please don't say any more!"

"Well, if it distresses you; but I shall never forget! How is the wrist?"

"O, nearly well."

"And you are so poorly still." Fulvia took a seat as she spoke.

"I don't know——only tired."

"Always tired?"

"Yes. It doesn't matter. I can't get strong, somehow."

"So they tell me. You want change."

"I would rather stay at home."

"You want change," repeated Fulvia. "Ethel, will you say 'yes' to a plan I have in my head?"

"I—don't know."

"I have Nigel's consent."

The flush returned.

"Well, you shall hear. To-morrow I am leaving home with Daisy. We go first to the seaside for a week— to poor uncle Arthur's favourite lodgings. After that we hope to spend some time in an old Scotch farm. The farmer's wife was once a maid in our house. She is an excellent creature, and will take good care of us; and she has three or four comfortable rooms, which will be at our service. Dr. Duncan wants me to have change, and our going there has been planned for some days. Starting to-morrow for a week at Burrside first is a new notion. And I want you to come with us."

Ethel was silent, her eyes open and sad.

"It will not be any expense to you—if you don't mind my saying so. Perhaps you know that I have come into a little money lately, since my uncle's death. He left what he had between Nigel and me—part to each, I mean,"—rather hurriedly; "so you need not scruple."

"You are very good," faltered Ethel. "But I don't think I can go."

"Why?"

"I don't know. I think not."

"Why?"

Ethel made no answer. Her colour fluttered.

"I have something else to tell you. Ethel—it is all over between Nigel and me."

Fulvia spoke steadily. Ethel gave her one dazzled glance.

"We decided yesterday that it would be right. Things are best so," said Fulvia, with resolute self-repression. She shook out her handsome mantle carelessly.

"Not—really!"

"Yes. I have felt for some time that it must be. Especially since——" Fulvia paused. She could not trust herself to say anything, but only some things, and she would not venture where she was not sure.

"It is not a quarrel. It is simply that we both know this to be best. We shall always be a very affectionate brother and sister, no doubt,"—with a forced laugh—"but that is all! If other people had not had their fingers in the pie, things would never have gone so far."

Fulvia's manner altered. She leant over the couch, laying her gloved hand on Ethel's.

"It has been a mistake," she said very low; "and we have found out our mistake. I know now how Nigel loves you——and I know that you are worthy of his love. Don't answer me—only listen! Nigel has tried hard to conquer, because——well, because he thought it right. He fancied that it was his duty to repay what I had lost—to repay it in that way. And for a little while I——thought the plan would do. I thought we might rub on together comfortably!"—with another faint laugh. "But it will not answer. I am glad we have found out our mistake in time."

There was a pause. Ethel did not speak, and Fulvia's arm crept round her.

"He will not come to you directly. He thinks it would seem like a slight to me. That might not matter; but perhaps people would count him fickle, not understanding. So there has to be a gap——between the two. But I told him I should come and tell you how things are; and I think he was glad, though he would not consent. I did not ask his consent, for I had made up my mind. Ethel——do you at all know what you are to him?"

Ethel's fingers pressed Fulvia's. That was her only answer.

"Yes—I was sure you must. And—am I wrong in thinking that he is as much to you? You need not say a word——only you can tell me if I am mistaken. I should like to be able to say to him—no, not from you—only from what I know. Am I taking it all too much for granted?"

Another little break.

"Nigel must ask for himself, of course; I have no right. But—I am not afraid for him. I understand. And now—meantime—till he can——will you come away with me for a few weeks? I want you to be strong again; and I want to stop some of the Newton Bury gossip. And I want—I want you to learn to love me. For by-and-by—"

Fulvia's voice failed.

"I will do anything you wish," whispered Ethel.

Neither girl could see the other's face. Perhaps it was well,——so full was the one of trembling joy, so gray the other with pain.

* . * * * *

During full three months the girls were absent, spending their time in the old farm, under the shadow of Scotch mountains.

Ethel and Daisy had never known a happier three months. If Fulvia suffered much, as suffer she undoubtedly did, she was outwardly only cheerful. Ethel became convinced, as Fulvia wished her to be, that

Fulvia did not really care—never had really cared for Nigel, further than with a sisterly affection. Fulvia knew that Nigel would never undeceive Ethel in this particular, even when he should be her husband.

They were not engaged yet. They did not even correspond yet. But in a manner each was sure of the other.

Ethel at least could have no doubts, and the sunshine of her face was a sight to do others good. Nigel's spirits might be more variable; but Fulvia gathered from his letters to Daisy, and from those of Anice to herself, that he by no means showed habitual depression.

" I was right—quite right !" she repeated often to herself.

Sometimes she could hardly bear to look forward,—the prospect ahead seemed so empty, so wrapped in gloom. She could only go on, step by step, praying for strength.

On other days she could bear to plan for the future, to picture herself with Mrs. Browning and the girls living in Mr. Carden-Cox' pretty house, which was now her own.

At first she tried to grow used to the idea of Nigel and Ethel at No. 9, Bourne Street, but this dream gave way to another. Why should not Nigel go to College, fulfilling at last his old desire, and study for the bar ?

One day Nigel wrote to her about Mr. Carden-Cox' money; a frank brotherly note. He wished her to possess the whole.

Fulvia's answer was decisive. " Never speak of such a thing to me again," she wrote. " I will *not* consent. I will *not* have it so. If you say any more, you will insult and grieve me more than I can tell. I shall have nearly seven hundred a year of my own, and a house rent free; and if that is not enough, I don't deserve to have any at all.

" Besides, I have set my heart upon a different life for you than that of a clerk in Newton Bury Bank.

" Why should not you go to the University, and carry out the old programme ? You are so fitted for the bar. Uncle Arthur always said so. Even if you should marry soon, that would be no real hindrance ; only it would have to be Cambridge—not Oxford.

" I have set my heart upon this, and I think you will not disappoint me. Madre and the girls are to come and live with me; and Daisy and I will make ourselves useful to Mr. Elvey in the Parish. Then, if you like to let No. 9, furnished, that would be a little addition to your income.

" Write just one line to say that you will not disappoint

" Your affectionate sister,

" FULVIA."

The " one line " came by return of post.

" MY DEAR FULVIA—

" Words can never say what I owe to you. It seems that you are determined to heap coals of fire upon our heads,——upon mine especially.

"You shall have your will. I can only submit to your generosity. I would say much more if I knew how to say it; but perhaps you will understand.

"Ever your affectionate and grateful

"N. B."

*   *   *   *   *

Three months ended, the travellers returned.

It was a drizzling autumn afternoon, much like that on which Nigel had come home from his year of travel.

As the train stopped, Nigel's face appeared. Fulvia had known that it must be so, and she had schooled herself to meet him composedly. One throb her heart gave, but she smiled a quiet greeting. Ethel was very still. Nigel's eyes went to her face in a swift flash.

"How many trunks?" he asked.

"Pollard is there. Daisy and I will see that he has them all right," said Fulvia, turning away.

Nigel was left by Ethel's side, for the moment practically alone with her. Nobody else was near, for few people had come by this train. It was growing very dusk. He took her hand into his warm clasp.

"Ethel, are you well again?"

"O quite. And Fulvie has been so good to me,— so very good and loving."

"I don't wonder," he said involuntarily, yet the next moment he did wonder, knowing all. But he could hardly think of even Fulvia yet, standing by Ethel, knowing that at last she might be his own. "Just one look!" he pleaded.

F F

The blue eyes glanced up, arch and sweet.

"It is your own self," he said. He had waited patiently all these weeks, but now he felt that he could wait no longer. Another hour of uncertainty would be unbearable. Confident as he might feel at times, he had never really put the question to her; and it broke from him in this moment of meeting. "Ethel, tell me!" he said huskily. "There is nothing now to keep us apart. Tell me—my darling—will you have me?"

"Yes!" she whispered. It was the same answer which she had given once before, on a certain wintry afternoon, to a somewhat different question of his; and it meant a very plenitude of trust and joy.

Then Mr. Elvey hurried up, just too late for the train's arrival; and Daisy sauntered back from the luggage. Fulvia, following, gave one glance at the two faces, and lifted quizzical eyebrows.

"Already!" she murmured. "You are a prompt man! But of course——it is a mere matter of form!"

"Fulvie, I can never thank you enough," Nigel said earnestly, the same evening. "Never!"

"For what?" she asked.

"For—everything!"

"Don't try! I hate thanks! All I want is to hear of your first brief! How do you think Ethel looking?"

"Not the same girl that went away. How much I owe to you!"

"Not the same? But she is the girl you wanted," said Fulvia lightly.

Nigel broke into his old laugh. He could not help it; and even he was beginning to think, despite the past, that Fulvia did not greatly care. She had been so cheery and full of fun, all the hours since reaching home.

A smile came in response; then Fulvia went to her own room, to stand long at the window, star-gazing. Drizzle and fog had vanished, leaving a clear sky; and she had much to think about.

"Better so!" she said aloud. "How happy they are! After all, one's own happiness is not the chief thing! I shall be helped—and by-and-by it will grow easier. I *will* be brave; I *will* be glad for them!"

THE END.

Richard Clay & Sons, Limited, London & Bungay.

Lightning Source UK Ltd.
Milton Keynes UK
UKHW022222291218
334664UK00008B/898/P